Richard Barnes

DEATH AT THE OMMEGANG

AUSTIN MACAULEY PUBLISHERS
LONDON * CAMBRIDGE * NEW YORK * SHARJAH

Copyright © Richard Barnes 2024

The right of Richard Barnes to be identified as author of this work has been asserted by the author in accordance with sections 77 and 78 of the Copyright, Designs and Patents Act 1988.

All rights reserved. No part of this publication may be reproduced, stored in a retrieval system, or transmitted in any form or by any means, electronic, mechanical, photocopying, recording, or otherwise, without the prior permission of the publishers.

Any person who commits any unauthorised act in relation to this publication may be liable to criminal prosecution and civil claims for damages.

This is a work of fiction. Names, characters, businesses, places, events, locales, and incidents are either the products of the author's imagination or used in a fictitious manner. Any resemblance to actual persons, living or dead, or actual events is purely coincidental.

A CIP catalogue record for this title is available from the British Library.

ISBN 9781035860760 (Paperback)
ISBN 9781035860777 (Hardback)
ISBN 9781035860784 (ePub e-book)

www.austinmacauley.com

First Published 2024
Austin Macauley Publishers Ltd®
1 Canada Square
Canary Wharf
London
E14 5AA

Chapter 1

Jerry Gregory and Adrian Armstrong sat together at a table outside Savino's coffee shop, near the bus station, talking about anything and everything. From where they sat, they could see the St Joseph's College conference building, and it triggered the same memories every time.

"We were bloody lucky, weren't we?" Adrian would say.

"Too right," Jerry would say.

Then, sometimes, they might go over the details. They would be talking about the campaign conducted by Robert Jackson, a rapist from California, who had, after his release from San Quentin, followed his victim to Cambridge and conducted a vendetta against her and the gynaecologist who had treated her following the rape.

On this occasion, the details were left unspoken. Instead, Adrian let his friend know just how glad he was that Jerry was sticking around.

"I'm glad you're still going to be here," said Adrian. "I thought you'd got that Superintendent's job in Peterborough lined up and you were leaving."

"Well," said Jerry, "I was, but someone higher up pulled some strings and blocked it. I don't really know why but they want me to stay around here. I think it might have something to do with MI5, as well as Special Branch, but I guess I shouldn't be telling you that and I'd appreciate it if you forgot what I just said."

"Don't worry," said Adrian, "I signed the Official Secrets Act too, as you well know, or we couldn't be having any of these conversations."

Then he added: "I'm glad you're staying. I would have missed your wife's cooking, when she does come up and spend the odd day with you. And at least there's one person I can talk to when I'm bursting to talk over the assignments I get, alongside the academic stuff," said Adrian.

"We never managed to get those Rubinsky gang thugs who supplied Jackson with the explosives," said Jerry. "And when we reviewed the various explosions, plus the Semtex we found in the conference building at the college, we reckon there's still a hell of a lot of Semtex out there."

"But you got some more at the farm, didn't you?" asked Adrian.

"No. We found quite a few guns and several grenades. They appear to be mainly Russian weapons with a few American items, probably recovered from the gulf wars and sold on. I doubt we got all the munitions. We think that there's a lot more out there and that the gang managed to escape with, or hide, the rest of the Semtex, and a lot of other weaponry."

"So, do I need to be worried?" asked Adrian. "Stanislowsky's son, went to Berkeley, and he married his American girlfriend, but he's come back here now to do a PhD in Translational Research in one of the biology departments. He's got one of our research studentships, he changed colleges from St Alfred's to us. Do you think the gang is still after him as a way of getting at his father?"

"Maybe. It pays to be careful. I think most of the thugs managed to get away to Europe. My guess is that they're hiding out in one of the nearby capitals, Brussels, Paris, Amsterdam, perhaps? We're keeping a close eye on the incoming passenger traffic from those capitals but there are never any guarantees."

Jerry paused, then he added: "Another cappuccino and a couple of those amoretti?"

There was a longer pause in the conversation while Jerry fetched the coffees and homemade biscuits from the counter.

"We've a couple of the children of high-profile politicians here," said Jerry. "What with Lord Fairfield and his crowd inviting speakers every week, and the precious children running around without official protection, Special Branch has its work cut out."

Jerry and Adrian had become firm friends over the past few years, as Jerry protected the college and the university from the complications of having several very politically active masters, mistresses, presidents, provosts, principals and wardens. They finished their coffees in more social and personal chatter. They arranged to meet the following Thursday, with Marianne, Jerry's wife, to go and see the student production of "Into the Woods," the Sondheim musical based on some of the traditional fairy tales of the brothers Grimm and others. Jerry liked Sondheim musicals and Adrian was involved as a senior treasurer for some of the student theatre groups.

Adrian crossed the road back to the college. He opened the metal gate to the back of the conference building, partly hidden by overgrown hedge, and, as he had done every time he came in that way, looked slightly ruefully at the underground car park area and the bicycle storage racks and cage.

We could all have been killed, he thought to himself. It had indeed been a lucky escape.[1]

He went to his room and sat down at his desk and opened some envelopes which were clearly personal correspondence. They were mostly birthday cards. Several former students still sent him old-fashioned snail mail cards rather than just acknowledging his presence on Facebook. Adrian very much liked the old-fashioned courtesy of that. It felt, somehow, more genuine, and less of a token of acknowledgement. There was one from Rowan Pike, Dr Rowan it was now, and the surname had changed, no longer Rowan Pike but Rowan Stroud. A lot of the surnames of these former students, the medical students that Adrian had taught, changed not long after they had completed the round of training posts and either went into general practice or obtained more permanent hospital placements. There was one with an American postage stamp. Adrian tried to guess from whom it might have come. Then he noticed a few more with American stamps and he stopped speculating and just opened them all.

Martha McArthy and Cecilia Tan had both written. Now into their studies as medical students at University of California, San Francisco, Medical School, they were hoping he was well and reporting on how much they were enjoying their courses. He missed them; he always missed the good ones. The third envelope he opened came as a big surprise. It was from Charles Hoi.

Adrian had first met Charles Hoi when he interviewed Charles in a small room in Hwa Chong Institution, the high-powered education establishment in Singapore. Charles had applied to Cambridge to study law, he was, at the time, attending the American School in Singapore. He was an American Citizen, since his father, a medical doctor, had been in California, as a visiting professor, when Charles had been born. The family origins were from a mixture of the People's Republic of China, Hong Kong, and Singapore itself. Charles's great-grandfather had emigrated from China before the civil war that brought the communists to power but had somehow managed to maintain good relationships with the communist party and had been a conduit for trade and financial exchange

---

[1] *Karma*, 2023 Richard Barnes.

between the PRC and Hong Kong during the second half of the twentieth century. He had become very wealthy by dealing in property in the fast-expanding crown colony.

At the time of the interview, Adrian had little idea of the extent or direction of Charles's ambition. He took at face value the assertion that Charles, Charley as he was known to his friends and family, intended to become a lawyer. During the interview, Charles expressed an interest in human rights and in international justice. It became clear to Adrian that Charles had a good depth of knowledge of British law but an even greater understanding of the American justice system. Charles waxed lyrical about Ruth Bader Ginsburg and talked sensibly about the problems with the political bias of the appointments to the Supreme Court. Coupled with his deft handling of some tricky legal questions concerning the convention against torture, Charles's knowledge of legal systems and understanding of political governance made him a shoo-in for Cambridge.

Charles had followed law for one year and then decided it was not for him, despite doing well in the subject. He had changed to Politics in his second year and had gone on to do very well in that field too. He had done all the usual things that very fit and healthy young male undergraduates might do; rowing for the first boat, playing football and tennis, socialising, and enjoying his time at Cambridge.

When Charles left Cambridge, Adrian had no idea what Charles was going to do, but a few weeks into the following Michaelmas Term, Adrian had received a Christmas card from Charles explaining how he was now working for the US government. Charles explained that his knowledge of Mandarin and Cantonese was likely to prove useful during his career. Adrian's light bulb moment came immediately. Perhaps he, Adrian, had been watching too many Netflix second-rate movies.

Adrian, despite being quintessentially British, always thought Netflix had movies rather than films, but the idea that Charles was now CIA became a firm thought in Adrian's mind. Having been involved for many years in helping to recruit for MI6, Adrian was able to recognise a pure gold prospect when it presented itself. Mandarin, Cantonese, UK, Far East contacts, American-born, first-class degree—what could be better for the CIA?

Charles had sent a Christmas card every year since graduation and this time there was a little more written than usual. Adrian was immediately clear that Charles was trying to find out some things that related to his present work in the

CIA. Charles was back in Washington, having had several interesting postings in Hong Kong, Vietnam, and China itself. From the general chit-chat, Adrian realised that Charles had largely been following the president around for the past couple of years, including a visit to London. The fact that Charles had not come to visit college on his last London trip led Adrian to believe that Charles was now part of the elite group that formed the personal bodyguard of the president himself.

This sort of information and suspicion was something that Adrian would always keep to himself. It was too dangerous to mention these thoughts to anyone, dangerous for Adrian as well as the student. Adrian knew that his former students trusted him totally to maintain their confidences. In his letter Charles asked Adrian specifically about the Jackson bombing campaign, especially the bomb at St Joe's. It was all done in a gossipy sort of a way, but Adrian knew that he was being asked for more than what appeared at face value. He decided to answer in a minimalist way, nothing more than had appeared in the press, but he decided to bait a hook. Adrian himself had been more involved in MI5 and MI6 than most people knew, not all his trips to Singapore, Hong Kong, and Shanghai on "university business" had been genuine.

There had been other things he had been tasked to do. A little older now, he was missing the thrill associated with the danger of clandestine activity. The nearest he got to it these days was working out how to spend the undeclared income from seemingly legitimate trips to some of those places. He decided to invite Charles to come and see him—*anytime you are in the UK, do pop in, young man, and I can take you to dinner on high table.*

Adrian had lost count of the number of times he had written a note like that to a former pupil; sometimes they responded, and sometimes they did not. What surprised Adrian this time was that a reply came almost by return, suggesting that as Charles was going to be in the United Kingdom in a week's time it should be possible for the two of them to meet up that week. Adrian pointed out that Wednesday was out of the question because there was a formal college occasion, but that any of the other days that week would be possible. They settled on the Friday and agreed to meet for drinks beforehand in Adrian's office. Adrian wondered exactly what was making this meeting urgent, but he knew that he was going to find out.

Meanwhile Jerry Gregory was seeking further information about Viktor Rubinsky's gang and whether they had gone back to their home country. The security forces had found the vehicles in which the gang had fled the farm, abandoned and burnt-out, near Ely Station, but the CCTV, showing eight men boarding the Stansted train, had not given any clues about what might have happened to the missing munitions. Jerry decided that it was so important to try to recover as much as they could that he needed to put a team on tracking the route taken from the farm to the place where the burnt-out vehicles had been found. It was a bit like looking for a needle in a haystack, but it was about the only thing they could try, and it might just come up with something. He had a word with Jenny Taylor, who was now Detective Inspector Taylor, and was working with Jerry in Special Branch.

Jenny was working undercover. She had taken up a graduate course at St Joe's and was preparing a thesis on student unrest in the 1980s. It gave her a lot of cover to work with all the dissident groups attached to the university, and the proximity to London let her gather snippets of information from activities in the capital, as well as locally. There is also a direct trainline from Cambridge to Birmingham and Manchester. The trains are not frequent, but the communication lines mean that midlands and northwest information often filtered down through Cambridge. Close liaison with the Peterborough police, Peterborough being on the direct line from Newcastle, Edinburgh, and Aberdeen, let her gather information from almost all parts of the country quickly and efficiently.

They were still desperate to find the missing weaponry and much of Jenny's gentle probing was in the direction of the more terrorist related groups. She was also given the specific task of keeping an eye on Alexis Stanislowsky. As Adrian had mentioned to Jerry, Alexis had been taken on by the department to study for a PhD in Translational Research. The security measures put in place previously, when Alexis had been a visiting scholar at St Alfred's, had been increased by the appointment of a carefully vetted bodyguard and Jenny had the task of overseeing all the security arrangements as they related to the young man.

The Secret Service knew each of the members of Viktor Rubinsky's gang, and had put out a request, throughout Europe and to America, for information about them. There had been a bit of a delay between uncovering the hideaway near Ely and getting the names, photographs, and other information out to the various police forces, but retrospective analysis of surveillance tapes at airports had shown most of the gang members leaving on a flight to Brussels, from whence the trail had gone completely cold.

There was nothing to do now but wait and hope that the existing agents in the field might come up with some new information. The other thing, which Special Branch was already doing, was to increase vigilance at every major event where there might be a controversial speaker, or a contentious issue being discussed. It was exhausting, it was time-consuming, but it was necessary.

Chapter 2

The Michaelmas Term was well under way when Charles arrived from London on the "Fen Flyer" to keep his assignation with Adrian. Charles was bigger and beefier than Adrian had remembered him, but he still had the warm and ready smile that had endeared him to all the members of the college. Adrian always used to think that the students that got on well with the bedmakers, the gardeners, the maintenance staff, the secretaries, the porters, and the catering staff, were the ones who were going to do well in life. If the porters liked them, they were usually very decent people, Charles had been well liked.

"Hello Professor Armstrong," said Charles, holding out his hand in a gesture of friendship. Adrian took the offered hand, greeted Charles warmly, and noted the very strong grip with which his hand was clasped.

Adrian poured them both a sherry and they sat down in the comfortable armchairs in the study. They exchanged pleasantries about the weather, Charles was very familiar with English traditions, and then Adrian asked after Charles's parents.

"Dad's not entirely well," said Charles. "He's had a few problems with his health over the past few months but with a bit of a change of diet and some treatment, Dad got much better. I think he's now just a little older rather than a little less healthy; in fact, with his dietary change, he's probably healthier!"

"Glad to hear that," said Adrian. "Your dad was particularly kind to me on many of my trips to Singapore and Hong Kong and he was also charming when he visited us here. And how's your mother?"

"Ming Xi is as full of life as ever," said Charles. "She flies over to the States to see me whenever she can. She's coming to Cambridge later this month. Shall I ask her to let you know when she's coming?"

"Please do," said Adrian. "You know how generous your parents were to the college, and still are when our oriental studies students find their way to Singapore or Hong Kong during their time abroad. It would be great if your dad could come too but I suppose he might still be a little cautious about travel after his scare."

The pair of them kept the conversation very general, far more general than they had for many years. Ever since Charles had sent Adrian "that letter," Adrian had known that he was talking to a CIA officer; Charles, briefed by his superiors, knew that Adrian "did things" for MI6. They had often discussed world affairs without transgressing the boundaries of confidentiality. This time, Adrian sensed it was all a bit different. He knew Charles had something to say but he also knew that Charles would not be hurried. The matter on Charles's mind would have to wait for the right moment, and this was not yet that moment.

The pair of them sipped their San Patricio Fino sherry and waited companionably for the clock in the tower of the Wren Chapel to sound the quarter hour. When it struck Adrian fished out a guest gown for Charles, an M.A. gown, since Charles had accepted his M.A. by proxy at the earliest opportunity; Adrian put on his own doctorate gown, and the pair of them strolled over to the combination room, the lower parlour, where they topped up on sherry and sat by the fire waiting for the other fellows and guests to arrive.

Adrian noted with satisfaction that there was quite a good turnout of fellows. The junior research fellows were there *en masse*; to be expected since most of them were resident, relatively low paid, and dinner was free. However, on this occasion the Master was dining, and would preside, and there were several other more senior fellows and their guests, including Charles's old tutor, Geraldine Carter, an expert on Central African politics, and Gerard Baker, a political historian with a special interest in American social and political history since the 1900s.

The meal was excellent. A starter of scallop in hazelnut butter on a bed of beautifully dressed mixed leaf and herb salad; a main course of lamb, cooked three ways, with young carrots, baby beet, potato gratin and Salsa Verde; and a pudding of apple mousse in a gel casing, dressed up to look like a genuine dessert apple, with a dark chocolate stalk to complete the deception. The accompanying wines were good quality but, in keeping with the college's puritan tradition, not overly expensive; just good value and well worth drinking.

During the dinner Adrian lost his guest to the Master, who took his duty of entertaining the alumni very seriously. Charles carefully deflected any attempts to find out what he was really doing, being content only to offer the information that he was working mainly in Washington for the US government. Lord

Fairfield was a thoughtful and generous host, generous with his time and attention, but when they went through to the parlour after dinner, for dessert and coffee, Fairfield allowed Charles to be scooped up by Geraldine Carter and Gerard Baker, both of whom had taught Charles, and Charles was ushered over to the fireplace where the most Senior Fellow, Geraldine, sat in a large and comfortable armchair next to a small round antique table with three place settings. Charles sat next to Geraldine comfortably sandwiched between her and Gerard. They talked a lot about America and her foreign policy and, inevitably, the conversation turned towards the reasons why so many different groups throughout the world were either covertly, or overtly, anti-American.

They did not go too deeply into it, and Charles was sure that both his former teachers knew that his role in the government was more than just paper filing. At one point Geraldine asked him point blank if he were some sort of homeland security analyst. Charles smiled and deflected the question: "Everyone who works in and around our government is a sort of analyst, you can't have a conversation in Washington without talking about foreign policy and trying to guess where the next threat is coming from."

"So unfair," said Gerard, "America stands up for the whole western world and yet so many nations either hate her or are jealous of her. As for the Middle East…"

He let the thought fade away and they changed the subject to easier topics. Charles asked about the current crop of students, Professor Carter talked about the Faculty of Politics, and Professor Baker updated Charles on what he knew about the whereabouts of Charles's friends and contemporaries from the undergraduate years. They talked about Lord Fairfield and how he had raised the profile of the college on the national political and educational scene. Gerard was a little cynical about the Fairfield Mastership, but he kept his more cutting comments to himself and merely remarked that the new Conference Centre had cost an arm and a leg.

At around 9:30 pm, Lord Fairfield took his leave and, over the next half hour or so, everyone else began to drift away until only Charles and Adrian were left enjoying the warmth of the fire and the freely flowing port and claret. Adrian had moved to the large central chair opposite the fireplace, taking over the role of presiding when Fairfield had gone back to the lodge. Once Charles's two mentors had left, Charles came over to sit in the chair beside Adrian.

"OK, young Charley," said Adrian, "you aren't here for the catering, no matter how good it is. I expect it's a lot better than most of the food you get to eat at Langley. I'm right, aren't I, it's Langley and the CIA and not just Washington in a general wishy-washy sense?"

"Yessir," said Charles, sounding the most American he had sounded all evening. "I have permission from my controllers to talk to you about certain important matters. They've told me that you're constrained by the Official Secrets Act in the United Kingdom and that you're, what, in slang terms, might be described as a spook. They tell me that you've done some useful things for both the UK and the US Governments on your 'Academic' visits to China, Israel, India, and several other countries, including some in Europe. They say I can trust you completely."

"How *very* kind of them," said Adrian, somewhat sarcastically. "Perhaps I was a spook at one stage but when you get older your usefulness as a spook declines, and I think I may be known to several intelligence agencies, including Mossad and the Chinese. But you needn't worry. I'll keep your secret, along with the secrets of so many others who I wouldn't like to see compromised."

Adrian paused, took a further sip of claret, then he said: "So, what's this all about? When you accepted my invitation to dinner so quickly after I sent it, I knew there must be something more than just a social reunion on your mind, pleasant as it is to meet up on these occasions."

"OK," said Charles. "Where shall I start?"

It wasn't a real question, it was a rhetorical device to give him time to collect his thoughts, but Adrian could not resist saying it anyway: "Try the beginning. I find that usually works."

Adrian pulled one of his faces and Charles grinned. Charles knew the senior tutor too well to take offence and he was also aware that this comment was a device to lower the tension and allow him to come to the point in his own good time.

"Sir. Do you know who Martha Howland is?" asked Charles.

"I think so," said Adrian. "I think she's the woman who ran Governor Selwyn's Democratic nomination campaign a few years ago. Is that who you're talking about? I think I met her at a Meeting of the American Physiological Society in Durham, North Carolina. I believe she was there with her rather clever young son who was presenting a short paper on micro-RNA. I think she had two other children with her, both younger than the son. There was a daughter, about

14 years old, with blonde curly hair. and deep green eyes, very striking, and another son, also with those deep green eyes and curly hair, probably about 16 I would have said."

"Yep," said Charles. "That's the lady, and you're right that she has three children. The eldest child, Thomas, is now an assistant professor at Yale, and doing well with the RNA stuff. Stephen, the next child, is now about 20 years old and is a pre-med student at Stanford."

Charles paused, took another sip of his claret, leant forward in a very conspiratorial sort of way, and said quietly: "I've been sent here to talk to you about the daughter. Not so little anymore."

Another pause, another sip of claret.

"The daughter, the non-scientist among them, is Patricia; she's known as Patti. She's a potential linguist and she's about to apply to all the usual top US universities but really wants to come to the UK. Martha Howland's husband, Edward, is a former Rhodes Scholar at Oxford and he wants Patti to go to Oxford, if she insists on coming to the UK for her undergraduate education. But Patti has a mind of her own and doesn't intend to be bullied into doing what her dad wants; nor does she want any element of following in his footsteps."

"The other thing is, she's done her research and she wants to study Spanish and French, and she's found out that one of St Joseph's professors, Simon Barnsley, is an expert on South American literature, including Borges and Fuentes, and she just loves magic realism, and she simply must come to St Joseph's College for her undergraduate study. Couple that with the Fellow in French, Professor Nigel Black, being an expert on Flaubert and Guy de Maupassant, and she's resolutely set on applying here."

Adrian listened without interruption while Charles's tale unfolded. Then he said: "How clever is she? You know admission here is entirely on merit, and she would have to apply with no hint of bias and no knowledge to Barnsley or Black about who she is."

"She's more than bright enough, I think," said Charles. "Already done her SATs and all that other US stuff and has 100% in every single thing she's touched. She's doing the IB at an international school and she's predicted 45."

"OK," said Adrian, looking seriously interested. "Sounds like she's in the frame. It would all depend on what Barnsley and Black make of her. You're giving me a headache, Charley boy. Couldn't you simply have gone back to the family bank in Hong Kong?"

"You realise she could be a security nightmare?" said Charles, grinning.

"What do you think?" said Adrian. "At least she isn't the president's daughter. Wouldn't want all that fuss that Chelsea Clinton had. Probably wouldn't work here anyway. Daddy may be a prominent Democrat, and Mummy may be a daughter of the revolution, and both Mummy and Daddy are probably descendants of the Mayflower families, but that doesn't usually make waves here. The Howlands aren't that much spoken of in this country, I doubt that half the population knows who any American politicians are, except maybe the president. I guess she should be ok."

"That may be true," said Charles. "But the dissident groups do know their politicians and so if Patti came here, there could be a security risk. It would have to be discretely handled and I think she would also have to come under a false name. From what I understand, that's her wish, to be just Patti something and not the daughter of a prominent politician."

"It's getting late now but could we possibly meet up tomorrow morning to think about what accommodation arrangements might be made for her, if she were to get in on merit? I'd need to see any suggestions that you might have."

"I guess you know Patti quite well," said Adrian.

"I do," said Charles. "She *is* very clever. She has a stellar academic record, and she's a very good runner, she's a National Age group cross-country champion. But that's not the best thing about her. She's just a delight to be with. I reckon, if she wants it, and carries on developing the way she currently is, she could be president one day."

Adrian took in a deep breath and let it out very slowly. Then he breathed deeply again and was silent for a very long time. He was looking at Charles and he was not entirely satisfied that he had the full story.

Do we need this? he was thinking. *We've had Fairfield stirring things up with his political guests, and look where that nearly got us, blasted out of creation; and now there's this potential American challenge. And I don't think Charles is giving me the full story here. It's all a bit over the top for the daughter of a couple of New England professionals, even if they are prominent Democrats. A highflying CIA officer wouldn't normally come for a chat about a potential student, even one with a strong political background. What else is going on?*

"What are you keeping from me, Charles?" asked Adrian.

Charles knew the game was up, but he still wriggled.

"Nothing definite," said Charles. "Can we see whether this is even feasible, whether the security looks even remotely right, and if it does then maybe there are a few further things I need to say."

"I'm not happy," said Adrian, with a hint of annoyance in his voice. "But I'm tired, and I'm getting a bit irritated, so let's leave it for now. We need to lock up the silver and put the claret and port away in the store cupboard. Where are you staying tonight?"

The two of them collected up the silver candlesticks, the claret jugs and decanters, the silver trays, and the solid silver biscuit box, in which the charcoal biscuits were kept, and locked them away in the cupboard next to the fireplace. While they did it, Charles chattered on about staying at the University Arms and probably being able to come to St Joseph's around 11am to collect Adrian to go out for coffee.

"I know I'm an American," said Charles, "but I know good coffee when I meet it and I've missed my morning coffees at Savino's. No disrespect to college coffee but it's not in the same league."

"Look," said Adrian, "come for breakfast at about 9 and we can go over to Savino's afterwards. Nobody can ever have too much coffee."

They left the lower parlour and Adrian locked up. Charles headed off down the street to the University Arms Hotel and Adrian collected his bicycle from the racks and cycled off home to Chesterton. His mind was racing. What was Charles holding back, did he really want another such high-profile student? Stanislowsky was surely enough for one college? Would it even be possible to guarantee security?

Ah well, he would find out soon enough in the morning.

The following morning, Charles skipped breakfast at the hotel to join Adrian in college for a continental style breakfast. The Fellow's Breakfast Room was a quiet room just off the first-floor landing of the staircase leading to the upper hall where undergraduates regularly took their lunches. It was pleasantly decorated with a large picture of one of the notable alumni of the college almost covering the wall farthest from the entrance. There was an understanding that, when others were present, there would be no talking in the breakfast room. There was a "sulking room" just off the breakfast room, long, narrow, and sparsely furnished, with a chaise longue and a couple of small armchairs down one side of the room, where fellows could take a cup of coffee and talk if they wished. However, on this occasion the only two people taking breakfast were Adrian and his guest, Charles, and so they were able to talk throughout their meal.

"Now, young Charley," said Adrian, "what's the real reason behind your coming to talk to me this week?"

Charles paused, took another sip of coffee and a bite of one of the excellent Danish pastries, and then, having wiped his lips on his napkin, began to talk.

"Coffee's pretty good," he said. "Better than the stuff we got as undergraduates."

"Get on with it," said Adrian.

"What I've told you so far is absolutely true," said Charles. "Patti Howland is who I said she is, and she's bright, and I'm sure you will like her, and I'm pretty sure she'll get a place at Cambridge if she wants it. But you are right, that's not the full story. The thing is that it's odds on that Patti will become the First Daughter at the next presidential election."

Adrian nearly choked on his coffee.

"Aren't you going to say anything?" asked Charles.

"No," Adrian snapped back. "I might have something to say when you've finished."

"Now you know why I'm so concerned about security and why they sent me to talk to you," said Charles. "The smart money's on one of Patti's parents running for president next year. If they do run there's a better than even chance of them getting the Democrat nomination and there is, with the way that politics is tilting in the States now, a much better than even chance that they would then become our next president. We can't afford to wait until that happens before making sure that Patti is going to be safe wherever she goes to college. Our best guess is that she has about twelve months from now before her profile is raised out of all proportion. We're trying to work out how we handle this."

Charles paused for a moment to let the news sink in, and to finish his Danish pastry and pour himself another cup of coffee.

Adrian just grunted and stared at Charles.

Charles grinned. *Such a smart cookie*, he thought, *He knows I have more to say yet.*

There was a long silence. Adrian used the silent technique in his supervisions. If you waited long enough sooner or later one of the undergraduates would say something, quite often it was something worth waiting for, sometimes it was not. This time the silence did indeed lead to something worth listening to.

"Patti's been very low-profile," said Charles. "She's not had many public photographs taken and those that were taken are mostly from when she was very much younger, and her features have changed quite appreciably since then. The family have been very careful to keep Patti out of the public eye. Thomas and Stephen have been quite high-profile, Yale professor and pre-med at Stanford go quite well with the Democrat image and, so far, the family has been able to do the motherhood and apple pie bit without involving Patti very much. The family all have one of those 'almost English' New England accents and Patti could easily pass for English in many, if not most, settings. There's a feeling among her family that she would possibly be safer being educated at a school in Britain, she's considered Edinburgh University too, than in America. People would be far more likely to recognise her in America and the strong preference for Edward and Martha Howland is for Patti to enrol in a British university under an assumed name and remain incognito for the duration of her study. My question to you is basically about whether that's possible here at St Joseph's."

Adrian sat back and rubbed his hand over the back of his head, round the side of his face, over his chin, and then dropped his hand to the table. He took a deep breath and then let it out slowly. He thought for a moment.

"This needs to go to Pro-Vice Chancellor level," he said. "We use the personal details in a very formal way to keep track of student progress and manage almost all the administrative arrangements for our students. There are things we can do to keep students relatively safe, but we'd need to find out from the university how far they are prepared to go with allowing a false name to be used for things like exams and course enrolment. This is above my paygrade, I'm sorry to say. There would also be issues around visas for study, but I guess your government could take care of that with our Home Office."

Charles paused for a moment and then asked: "Can we see the accommodation where you might be able to put someone like Patti?"

"Sure. Let's finish our coffee and I can take you to the safest block of accommodation that we have for first years. I showed a prominent young actress the accommodation once, but she decided to go to America, ironically! I think you said Patti wants to study languages, so she would probably have to spend the third year abroad somewhere; I guess your people would want to talk to her about that. We dish out rooms with a ballot, but I reserve the right to retain some rooms for special purposes, so we could rig the ballot so that she had a safe room in the second year, and we could fix the fourth-year ballot too. I know you said you thought we didn't manage to protect Martha McArthy too well, but that was not strictly true; and we've improved security on the Cumberland Building a lot since then. But no point in talking about it. I expect you want to see for yourself."

They finished their coffee just as one of the late risers among the fellows came in for her breakfast. There was a brief word of acknowledgement and then a rapid departure by Charles and Adrian.

"See you at the tutors' meeting on Monday," said Helena.

"Can't wait," said Adrian, with a grin.

The newest block of rooms in the college had been built to complete the fourth side of the West Court. It consisted of a fifteen-foot-high ground floor, in which the maintenance department and one or two college offices were located, and a first and second floor, accessed via a spiral staircase at each end of the building, which had a number of moderate sized *en suite* bed-sitting rooms. There were eighteen rooms on each of the floors and each block of six rooms had a small gyp room, with cooking facilities and a table and chairs where students could sit and eat together in an informal way. Access to the block, and to each of the floors separately, was by a key card system. Charles noted that there were plentiful CCTV cameras in the building monitoring the main doors and each of the corridors. It would be easy to add a few more if necessary.

"If Patti were to come," said Adrian, "I would put her in one of these rooms for both the first and second years."

Charles looked out of the windows from the first-floor rooms, and from the corridor landing on that floor. The rooms had a pleasant enough view of the main West Court, with its chimera trees in the sunken garden in the centre of the Court. The corridor had small windows, high up near the ceiling, and the view was quite uninspiring, almost non-existent. The building backed onto the service alley and back yards of a row of commercial premises, owned by the college, on the main shopping street.

From the spiral staircase at the end of the corridor, Charles could see that there was a sheer thirty-foot drop from the corridor window level to the service alley. He also noted that the service alley was well protected by cameras. It seemed about as safe as any building might be in the centre of a city.

"This is pretty good," said Charles. "We'd probably be able to provide a few more safety measures for Patti's room. Chelsea Clinton had bullet proof glass fitted and we could do that, at State Department expense. I see that each of these rooms has an internet phone?"

"Yes," said Adrian, "and we also have panic buttons for some of the rooms, for diabetics and other students at risk. Obviously, Patti could have one of those."

"Can we go and look at Cumberland now please?" asked Charles.

They went back through the tunnel that connected West Court, under one of the main thoroughfares in the city centre, to the rest of the college.

The Cumberland Building was about three hundred years old but had been modernised, with bathroom pods, subtle double glazing, and insulation. It was the most popular choice for final year undergraduates because it was at the very centre of the college; it had 'character' and it had shared sets with separate bedrooms, but large communal sitting rooms. The Cumberland was the beating heart of the social life in St Joseph's.

The two men walked up one of the staircases to the third floor and, as they reached the landing at the top a deafening alarm started to sound.

Adrian rang the Porters' Lodge.

"Hi Paul. You can turn it off now," said Adrian.

"Intruder alarm?" asked Charles.

"Yep," said Adrian. "Smart alarm too. It's a bit like the smart cat flaps. I won't go into details, but the occupants can set the alarm and then take steps to prevent themselves from triggering it. Bloody noisy, isn't it. And it triggers an alarm in the Porters' Lodge."

The two men walked back to Adrian's office and Adrian, a bit of a caffeine addict, made them both a cup of coffee with his bean-to-cup machine, using specially sourced Costa Rican coffee beans. They took the coffees and sat in the comfortable armchairs in Adrian's inner sanctum.

Charles looked at Adrian.

"I'm sorry to have put you through this," he said. "But I have my orders and, having been on special protection duties with the Howlands, I wanted to be sure that Patti would be safe if she did come here. I like her. She didn't choose to have such a high-profile family and she's done very well to stay grounded despite it. Of course, if a parent doesn't get elected then it will all be a bit easier."

There was a pause for the sipping of coffee.

"This is pretty good coffee," said Charles.

"I expect you want to think about all this. Can I meet you Monday for lunch? I have a few things to do tomorrow, and I expect you want your Sunday for other things?"

"We could do a college lunch," said Adrian.

"I would like to buy you lunch," said Charles. "If that's ok."

Charles was grinning internally like a Cheshire cat. He knew his old senior tutor well enough to be confident that he had hooked him.

Adrian was indeed thinking, *What the heck are we doing? This could be a darn nightmare.* But then, as Charles knew he would, he thought, *But it might just be very interesting.*

At 12:30 on the Monday, Adrian was sitting at a table outside Savino's, stoutly fending off everyone who wanted to just move the other chairs from the table. He had a double espresso and a glass of water in front of him and was reading the morning edition of the *Times*, in between defending his territory. Charles appeared very promptly at 12.30 am. He asked Adrian what he would like for lunch and Adrian chose the Greek salad, with some bread.

"It's on the CIA," said Charles, very quietly.

Charles went up to the counter to order and while he was at the counter a slim, blonde, curly haired young woman, about 173cm tall, with startling green eyes, sat down opposite Adrian. She was wearing a black Ralph Lauren coat and an equally expensive looking beanie.

Adrian looked at her and was about to say that the seat was taken when he saw Charles, grinning from ear to ear, walking back with a tray of three coffees and a table number on one of those spikes that cafes use to reunite food with the customer who ordered it.

"Hello Professor Armstrong," said the young lady. "I'm Patti Howland."

The voice was warm and clear, with rounded tones, as Charles had said on the Saturday morning, it sounded more English than American.

Adrian's face was a picture. *Game set and match to you, Charley boy,* he thought.

Patti held out her hand and Adrian took it. It was warm, and the handshake was firm, just right.

"I'm delighted to meet you, Miss Howland," said Adrian.

Charles started to put the tray on the table.

"You didn't recognise her, did you?" he said.

Patti smiled, it was infectious, they were all smiling, even before the tray was at rest.

"You've been here all the time, haven't you?" asked Adrian.

"Yessir," said Patti. "Charles and I have done some of the sights. We did the bus tour of the city, including the American Cemetery, and then I made him walk to Ely with me yesterday, along the river bank. He wanted to go by train, but I told him not to be lazy. I loved the Cathedral. My guidebook called it 'the ship of the Fens'. This afternoon, Charles has promised we can go to the Fitzwilliam Museum."

"I don't suppose he ever went there as an undergraduate, so a bit of culture might do him some good," said Adrian.

Patti laughed.

At that moment their food arrived. Antonio brought it himself. He recognised Charles, they exchanged a few words, Antonio went back and brought them all another coffee and a glass of water each.

They started to eat.

"This chicken salad is good, Charley," said Patti.

While they ate, Adrian was able to look at Patti more carefully. She had brilliant green eyes, large and round, and quite stunning. Like all wealthy Americans she had perfect teeth and a smile to show them off. There was something about her. She had poise and confidence without a suggestion of arrogance.

They exchanged pleasantries. How long had Patti been in the country, when did she plan to go back to America, what was she hoping for from a degree, had she brothers and sisters, how many times had she been to England previously. The interesting answer to the last question was that she had regularly visited continental Europe but had spent very little time in England, only really a few days in London.

"So why Britain for a degree course?" Adrian asked the obvious question.

"At undergraduate level," said Patti, "I'm convinced that England, and especially Cambridge, gives the best education in the world."

Then she grinned at Adrian and spoke: "I know Charley has filled you in a bit about me, but I bet he left a lot out."

She looked at Charles who was squirming a bit in his seat.

"If I were in your position, I would probably hope that this was a nightmare I was going to wake up from. You don't really want all the hassle of having me at your college, not really."

Adrian noticed that Patti was almost on the verge of tearing up. It made him realise that, for all her sophistication and charm, she was still very young, and this situation, here in Cambridge, where she so hoped to study, was almost overwhelming her; but she blinked her eyes and continued.

"I'm so worried that nowhere would want to take on the security risk that I'm probably going to become. I suppose you could say that in some ways it's unfair on me, but I've led such a privileged life that I don't feel I have the right to complain." She took a shuddering breath in, and, as she paused, Adrian interrupted and, in a very gentle voice, said: "Patti, may I call you Patti? I've done as much homework on you as I could. I spent ages on the internet finding out about you and your siblings. Your mum and dad seem to have done a great job with all three of you. This place, Cambridge, and St Joe's, we even admit people as privileged as you, sometimes, if they have a brain."

The tears were blinked back again.

"Thank you," said Patti. "But whatever Charley told you, my past isn't the problem. What's likely to happen in the future is. I think there's a really good chance that my mother's going to be president; I truly believe that, and I hope that it happens. It matters to me that my mother and father have no strings to pull over here. If I get in, it will be because I deserve to. I'm very privileged, but that's a fact, and I can't do anything about it, but I can make my own way, within the boundaries that having wealth and privilege set. If I go to an American university, everyone will know what I am, but Charles tells me he thinks we can make it so that over here I'm just Patti, who happens to be American, and people might get to take me for *who* I am and not *what* I am."

There was a pause.

"I'm sorry. That was a bit heavy. But I guess you did ask me why I wanted to come here!"

Patti reached for a tissue and blew her nose.

"I did," said Adrian. "And a bit of passion never hurt anyone. But why Spanish and French?"

"It's the literature," said Patti. "I thought about Italian for a similar reason, but I think I prefer Spanish because of the wealth of modern Latin-American writers. That's why I'd like to apply to St Joseph's."

"I had lunch with Borges once," said Adrian, unable to resist the chance to name drop. Looking at Patti's face it had the desired effect.

"He was getting an honorary degree from the university and our Master was asked to look after him. I must confess that I was a bit ignorant about him, being a simple medic. I look back on it now with some regret that I didn't realise at the time how honoured I was. I've read him in translation a bit since then."

Patti smiled: "You're going to tell me next that you met Allende and Vargas Llosa and Fuentes?"

"I did. With Barnsley in the place, what do you expect?" said Adrian. "There were others too, most of the top Latin-American writers came here to talk to Barnsley."

They finished their lunch and took a takeaway coffee with them back over to the college. Adrian was about to give Patti the standard pre-application tour when he noticed a couple of the undergraduates reading languages walking down the other side of Main Court.

"Himi, Izzy," he called to them. "Can I borrow you for a few minutes?"

The two women walked round the central beautifully manicured lawn and came over to Adrian and his group. Adrian introduced them to Patti and Charles.

"Would you very much mind showing this young lady around?" asked Adrian. "You can talk to her about studying languages here too if you have the time. Can you make sure you show her the accommodation in the New Block in West Court and, also, the Cumberland? You can get keys from the porters but knock before you enter any rooms."

"My room is in New Block," said Himi. "And Isabella lives in Cumberland, so we won't need room keys. I think everything else we can get into with our university cards."

The two linguists promised to bring Patti back to Adrian's office when they had completed the tour.

Adrian and Charles watched as the three young women moved off in the direction, first, of the library, and then the Junior Common Room. They turned on their heels and went to Adrian's study to wait for Patti to return.

Chapter 3

It was the following October when an application from a Patricia Jones, an American youngster wishing to study French and Spanish at Cambridge, arrived in the in-tray of the admissions officer at St Joseph's. By that time the process of thinking about the next presidential election in America was well underway and, as Charles had predicted, Martha Howland had become the frontrunner for the Democratic nomination for president. Patti Howland had continued to have a very low profile, and her parents had kept her out of the media as far as they could, but the very astute admissions officer, Sarah Leslie, noted a remarkable likeness between the applicant for Modern and Medieval Languages and the daughter of the Democratic Party frontrunner. Sarah and Adrian had a conversation and Sarah, as always, kept her suspicions, which she now knew to be accurate, to herself.

Professors Barnsley and Black selected Patti Jones as their top offer for admission, and Patti Jones accepted her offer as a firm offer as soon as the offer was made. Several American institutions were very disappointed.

The next summer Charles Hoi found another excuse to visit Adrian at St Joseph's. Adrian was hardly surprised. The elections for the United States Presidency were due on the first Tuesday after the first Monday in November and, by that time Patti Jones would be in residence and her mother was almost certain, if the polls were to be trusted, to be the president of the United States. Adrian was confident that Charles was not the only CIA man to be visiting. He was also fairly certain that one or more of the new graduate intake at St Joseph's would be academically capable CIA agents on secondment for the four years of Patti's time at St Joe's. Some would have been recruited before they applied to St Joe's, and told to apply there; others may have been recruited after acceptance. At least one of the Stanford Scholars was perhaps a little older than the usual students arriving by that route. It might have been no coincidence that this particular student was planning to take an M.Phil. in Contemporary European

Theatre and Film Studies, with the possibility of conversion to a PhD if the year went well.

For both Adrian and Charles, while it was nice to catch up and chat, there was very little new to add to what had been said nearly two years earlier about security and safety. By far the most important thing was that Patti Howland would be at St Joe's under her assumed name and nobody other than Adrian was to know her true identity. Charley told Adrian that there were five very brave girls who had been recruited, straight from school, to act as doubles for Patti. They were already in character at their high schools and had gained admission to Brown, Stanford, Berkeley, Edinburgh, and Oxford. They, like Ms Howland, were being admitted under assumed names. They had the same blonde curly hair, green eyes, were all tall and slim, and excellent athletes.

The American Ministry of Disinformation had a busy and creative time spreading rumours about where the 12th grade student was going to go to college. It also ran articles about how Edward Howland had studied as a Rhodes Scholar at Oxford, and how keen he was to have one of his children attend his alma mater. Nobody was sure exactly where Patricia Howland was at high school. There were several reports from good schools, mainly on the east coast, of girls who looked like Miss Howland, and who ran, and played field hockey, and lacrosse, but the reports were more on the lines of *Is this where the elusive soon to be first daughter is at school?*—rather than definitive statements that it was the first daughter in waiting. In short, a very good misdirection of attention was taking place.

Charles left well satisfied with the arrangements that St Joe's was making. Adrian told him that Sarah had spotted the resemblance between Patricia Jones and Patricia Howland, so Charles went along and had a word. Sarah tolerated his slightly clumsy approach, she remarked on it with amusement afterwards to Adrian, but Charles was absolutely reassured by his conversation with her. Sarah was reminded that she would now be covered under the terms of the Official Secrets Act, and Charles said he would arrange an extra step pay rise at US expense. Sarah was clearly the soul of discretion and Charles, like Adrian, knew that Patricia's identity would not be disclosed by her.

About the only public appearance of the Howland family all together during the summer of that year was at the democratic convention where Martha was chosen as the presidential candidate. This took place, as was usual, in about the fourth week of August. There was plenty of time for Patti to disappear again from the public gaze before she departed for England.

****

That October began with the sort of weather that makes you believe that Cambridge is the only worthwhile place in the world in which to spend the autumn. Glorious and still warm sunshine appeared every day for three weeks. There was no sign of the harsh easterly winds that could sometimes wreck the temperatures, nor was there the slightest hint of the grey and gloomy low clouds which could invade the Fens at the slightest excuse. The freshers, arriving from all over the country, and from many warmer parts of the world, entered what must have seemed like a fairy tale kingdom. Even those who were a little shy and apprehensive, for many this would be their first time away from home, were comforted by the warmth, and the mellow colours of the autumn plants, and the rich sandstone and red brick buildings, glowing in the 'Indian summer' sun.

There was the usual fresher's week activity. Lord Fairfield gave his welcoming address, something about taking full advantage of the privileges that came from being at St Joe's, and the responsibility that came with that privilege. There was his exhortation not to waste time but to enjoy the freedoms and the challenges to the full. Adrian, in his address to the freshers, gave gentle warnings not to be deceived by the beauty of Cambridge but to realise that there was still potential danger in this small but very diverse city. He urged respect of the views and opinions of others. He talked of the college's abhorrence of all forms of prejudice and explained how the reputation of the college as a place of fairness and acceptance of all was based upon a zero-tolerance policy towards bigotry in all its forms. Then the great and the good handed over to the people that really matter in a college; the porters, the housekeeper, the gardeners, the catering staff, the computer officers, the tutorial support teams and, first among equals, the president of the student union.

Adrian noted Patti Howland, now Jones, sitting quietly with a group of fellow students in one of the balcony seats around the lecture theatre. Apart from the observation that her hair was beautifully cut, her clothes were beautifully tailored and she had a suntan to die for, there was nothing, if you did not already know, to indicate that she was the daughter of the presidential frontrunner. Only time would tell whether the secret would survive the attempts by undesirables to find her, or the possibility of an inadvertent slip by Patti herself, in response to questions about her family and her past life. Adrian, and Charles for that matter, knew that Patti had done so much in her still young life that simple conversations with others might lead to extensive speculation. Before she left America there had been some shopping trips to some of the less expensive stores, her security team had taken her on a shopping trip to Macy's and JCPenney, but she had still chosen her clothes with excellent taste. Just because Bloomingdales and Harrods and the like were out of bounds for the next four years it did not, to Patti, mean that she had to dress like a tramp. Although she was one of those lucky young women who would look good in a hessian sack, she had no intention of trying to prove it.

Two of the security detail were also sitting on the balcony of the lecture theatre, one on each side of the entrance from the foyer. They had been given access to all the fresher photos and, so Charles assured Adrian, would have learnt by sight every one of the freshers and, having gone through the tutorial files of all of the other members of the college, they would recognise them too. Adrian was aware that every member of the college staff would have been vetted by the Americans. He, himself, had already undergone positive vetting by the UK spooks but he expected that the Americans would have investigated him further, just in case.

It was not totally comfortable, this level of intrusive surveillance of college life and people, but it was probably necessary for Patti's safety and, from all that he had been able to discover, this was quite a special young lady who deserved every opportunity to follow, untroubled, the path she had chosen. It was likely that, if Martha Howland did become president, Patti and her two brothers would receive Secret Service protection for eight years, assuming that Martha was re-elected, but after that she would be on her own. Adrian comforted himself with the thought that the extra vetting and surveillance would also add to the security of young Alexis Stanislowsky.

Adrian had a conversation with Jerry Gregory as soon as Patti Jones came into residence. Jerry remarked that the Rubinsky gang appeared to have given up bombing as a tactic, for the time being at least, and was now more into assassinations and kidnapping. It was small comfort to Adrian to hear that and he was glad that the bullet proof glass had been fitted to all the rooms in the New Block.

"You just keep on top of the intelligence young Gregory," ordered Adrian.

"It's quite helpful to have the full attention of the Americans," said Jerry. "So far nothing but false alarms. We did have an issue when Fairfield invited that Turkish diplomat to speak at the Union. We intercepted what we thought was a would-be assassin on the Fen Flyer and ended up having to apologise profusely to some poor Greek Orthodox priest who had come to hear the rehearsal for the nine lessons and carols at King's."

For the new intake of undergraduates and graduates the routine meetings to sign the matriculation book and the university matriculation sheets duly took place. The matriculation photograph was taken, all the freshers lined up in tiered rows in alphabetical order, those at the back standing on precarious wooden trestles at varying, but significant, heights above the cobbles. Then there were the individual photographs that would be part of the student record for the duration of their course. Directors of studies and tutors received these photographs and marvelled at how little resemblance they bore to the photographs submitted on the application forms a little over a year ago. Hair lengths, hair colours, beards, moustaches, and facial jewellery had all miraculously appeared or changed in that intervening twelve months or so of the final year at school. In some cases, gender had changed too. It was all 'par for the course'.

Patti signed up for all her supervisions and classes, obtained her library card and her college and university key card, met her directors of studies and supervisors and her tutor. Patti's Director of Studies was a very lively young don called Elspeth Gray, an expert on Spanish theatre. They talked a little about Patti's interest in magic realism and Elspeth pointed out that Spanish theatre was interesting too. It was a fun conversation, full of promise for the future. The Spanish supervisions would initially be with Elspeth but Professor Barnsley would be involved as the course became more specialised and Professor Black would also be involved in the second and further years of Patti's course.

You cannot win them all, and Patti's tutor was a rather miserable human being, resentful at having been passed over for promotion in the faculty, who went through the motions of being a tutor, took home the money that it paid, and spent most of it on wine and cigarettes. Patti's college parents told her not to expect much from old Cranfield; if she had any sort of problem Elspeth Gray would be her best port of call. Since Patti was not particularly planning to have problems, this arrangement seemed fine.

Patti signed up for a lot of activities. There was college hockey, soccer, which she was not quite sure she completely understood, but rather fancied trying, tennis, and athletics. She also went along to the ADC theatre and signed up for some of the technical workshops with a view to becoming a 'techie' in due course, and she joined the choir. At university level she signed up for lacrosse, and for Hare and Hounds, the University Cross-Country Club. All this might seem a bit like overkill, but the signing up was more on a try it and see basis; she would quickly drop some of these activities if she neither enjoyed nor had the time for them. Patti was quite competitive, and she was not sure whether soccer, lacrosse, hockey or running would prove her most enjoyable and successful physical activity. Then too there was rowing. Her college mum had taken her for a run to Baits Bite Lock, along the tow path by the Cam. She had seen the rowers, with varying degrees of skill, from none to just a little, trying rowing for the first time, and it had appealed to her as something that everyone ought to try at least once in their lives. On this morning run Ellie, the college mum, had warned Patti against running alone at any time of day on the towpath, or on alternative routes out towards Grantchester or Coton.

"You won't always have two big chaps running behind you," said Ellie, looking back at these two rather large students somehow keeping pace at a discrete distance. "They're rather good looking. I reckon they're American, like you. I think they're a couple of those fresher graduates that started at St Joe's this year."

"I think you have it," said Patti, who knew that they were, indeed, American.

Before the end of October life had settled down. Patti had also decided, much as rowing was interesting, it started a little too early in the morning for her, and was cold, and wet, and sometimes a bit miserable; besides which she really enjoyed the team sports and her running much more, and the academic study was capturing her interest. The one new thing that she really enjoyed was the 'techie' activity at the ADC. She would have liked to be a 'techie' as part of the freshers play but there were one or two things stopping her, the most significant of which was the upcoming presidential election. Patti knew that she would be needed on the day of the election in early November; despite everything, she would have to stand on the platform with her mother, win or lose in the presidential race. A win would also require her to be on the platform one more time, at the end of January, for the inauguration. Then she should be free for the next two and a half years, until the next running of the campaign, either for election, should Martha be chosen as candidate again, or for re-election if President Howland had already served a term in office. Patti would be free to 'tech' a show in the Lent Term.

On the first Monday in November an armoured black Chevy Suburban SUV arrived at St Joseph's to whisk Patti away to one of the nearby USAF bases in Suffolk. A special presidential jet with a fighter escort flew her back to Washington and, in due course, she was paraded before the masses on that Monday, and for the next three days, which is what it took for a concession to be made. Martha Howland became the president of the United States of America.

It was, perhaps, fortunate that it was Martha and not Edward who was elected. There was so much media interest in Martha, women presidents are not the norm in America, that it quite distracted attention away from the other members of the family, especially the children. Patti enjoyed meeting her brothers; they always did enjoy meeting. They had kept in touch by calls and chats on special phones provided by the Secret Service, relying on the level of encryption to keep the conversation private. It would have been impossible for Patti to talk about Cambridge in a way that left it seeming little different from any American campus, so the rule was that the two boys talked only in the most general terms to their colleagues about their sister, but were able to ask, on the special phone lines, much more detailed and interesting questions.

Back in Cambridge, Patti's absence had been explained as a brief period of leave to attend a family wedding in New York, Patti let her imagination run riot on the details of the happy event. Someone in the know would have recognised the dress from the film version of 'Emma', the bridesmaids from 'Sex and the City', the catering from the 'Wedding Planner', and the guest list from 'Four Weddings and a Funeral', suitably Americanised. But all events in student life are nine days' wonders, or even nine hours' wonders, so the absence was soon forgotten, and student life continued much as normal.

It was, perhaps fortunate, that Patti had grown up in a small community in Connecticut with a group of close and highly trusted friends. She was able to continue these friendships because each one of them had been sworn to secrecy about her true destination as an undergraduate. They went off to their several different universities and never introduced the subject of their friend Patricia to their new college friends and acquaintances. At Cambridge Patricia was able to talk freely and openly about her background, claiming that her mother was a prominent lawyer (which was true, if only partially so) and her father was a doctor (which was also true or had been). She could talk about her home and her school and not have to invent anything, except the false names allocated to her family, and a slightly distorted account of the location of her home.

A few articles appeared in the American press about whether the president elect's daughter looked a little paler and more drawn than in some previous press photographs, and there was speculation about her whereabouts at college. Pictures of the girls acting as Patti's double appeared in several different papers but, in the end, nobody could agree which of these girls was Patti, and nobody could determine where she was currently studying. As is always the case with the media, domestic and international events soon took over the headlines and, at least until the inauguration, Patti and her brothers were not entirely newsworthy.

Three adult children away from the central hub of Secret Service security, was too much of a dangling carrot for the many anti-American dissident groups. The two brothers were known about and well-guarded, and most groups soon gave up the thought of seeking to attack the president elect through the two young men. They, and Viktor Rubinsky's little band of terrorists was among them, were looking to identify the whereabouts of Patti and perhaps get some leverage through the first daughter.

It was at this point in his career that Jerry Gregory began to realise why his move away from Cambridge had been blocked. He had now been in Cambridge long enough to have become almost part of the fabric and was able to move around the city without attracting particular attention. He had an extensive network of acquaintances in the higher echelons of the society, and, through his two children, Audrey, and James, he had made contacts throughout the graduate student body. He was having another of his morning coffee sessions with Adrian.

"A former student of yours came to see me yesterday," said Jerry. "Can you guess who it might have been?"

There was no hesitation.

"Charles Hoi," said Adrian.

"Yes, and I'm really surprised that you hadn't given me any clue what it was going to be about."

"No you aren't," said Adrian. "You absolutely know I couldn't say a thing to you until I got clearance this morning from the Home Office and the Americans. I guess the fact you're talking to me means they've cleared you for that too."

"You know what they told me?" asked Jerry. "They told me that this had been on the cards for two years and that was why they kept me here and I'm to oversee the local surveillance. I must watch Patti Jones like a hawk and, if anything happens to her, they'll lock me in the tower and throw away the key. I expect the bastards will nick my pension too."

"Welcome to the club," said Adrian "I've been on that ticket for nearly a year now, only in my case it would be some seedy Fed penitentiary somewhere, after they kidnapped me. Let me tell you the good things about it, from my perspective. I get to work with you, I get coffee here at Savino's on CIA expenses whenever I want; Patti Jones is a worthwhile human being; and we'll get a year off when she goes to do her year abroad. From your perspective the pluses in this situation are obviously less clear."

They both burst out laughing. The Jerry Gregory continued: "First thing you must do is to introduce me to the girl and show me around again. I didn't really get to see the whole place when Jackson was strutting his stuff and I need a bit more detailed understanding of things. Charles said you have it sussed, and he has some lucky agents picking up PhDs at US government expense, but I'd like to know the lie of the land. How about one of your college meals this week?"

Adrian had held regular meetings with Patti during her time in Cambridge. It had been a little difficult because it was important for her not to stand out from the crowd, but most of the time the meetings had been virtual, using one of the online virtual meeting platforms with strong encryption. The meetings were not long but they had enabled Adrian to be confident that Patti's life in Cambridge at St Joseph's was proceeding along totally normal lines, and they also acted as a focal point when Patti needed a concession or special arrangement, such as that trip to the electoral announcement back in November.

Cambridge terms are very short and, almost before it had begun, Patti's first term was coming towards its end. She should be flying back to America in a week or so. Adrian wanted her to meet Jerry Gregory before the term ended so he spoke to her and suggested that she called on him in his rooms on the final Friday of term, the night on which the Fellowship had a rather splendid dinner, wearing dinner jackets, tuxedos as the Americans call them, and their best scarlet gowns. It was a guest night, so Adrian invited Jerry as his guest. Adrian, in his role as senior tutor, invited the choir, to which Patti belonged, for drinks beforehand in the long gallery which was part of the Wren Building. It was traditional to invite the choir to the dinner. They sang grace before and after the meal, and the dinner, a splendid affair, was a reward for all their hard work during the term. The Director of Music and the Master joined Adrian to host the reception. As Adrian's personal guest Jerry was also present, as were some of the other fellows who were regular chapel goers.

It was quite tricky at the reception to separate Patti from the Master, who had taken an instant liking to her during one of the cheese and wine parties he held during the Michaelmas Term for all the freshers. Adrian, not known as the most tactful of fellows, managed it by, almost rudely, breezing up to Lord Fairfield and saying bluntly that he, Adrian, wanted Patti to meet a friend of his who was married to a Frenchwoman and had two graduate children who had been through the college and were fluent in French. It put Fairfield's nose out of joint, but it worked, and Adrian steered Patti towards Jerry who was standing quietly in the shadows drinking yet another glass of the excellent champagne.

Patti had the impact on Jerry that she had on everyone. Her friendly manner had him interested and engaged in conversation almost instantly. He knew who she was, but he kept up the charade of asking her about her origins and her plans as if he had no idea at all of her back story, or, even, her made up new persona. Patti liked Jerry immediately. She had been pre-briefed by Adrian that Jerry was the head of the Special Branch detail in and around Cambridge and she knew that she might be having more contact with him after the inauguration of her mother as president of the USA. She was relieved that she liked him and that any meetings that had to take place would be in a cordial atmosphere. Jerry mentioned his French wife to Patti, and suggested that she might like to come round sometime to his house and meet Marianne, who, he said, was an excellent cook. Patti graciously accepted the invitation, for a date next term. There were plenty of others who overheard the conversation, including Professor Black, who was just a little jealous that this friend of Adrian's had gotten his invitation in first.

"I'm also married to a Frenchwoman," said Nigel Black, "and we have all our language students studying French round to dinner, so don't fill up all your evenings. Suzette is a superb cook." The rhetoric left Patti in no doubt that Professor Black was upping the ante in the food stakes!

Adrian was delighted that the contact had been made seamlessly and marvelled at the competence of the two conspirators in handling the arrangements in a way that left no suspicion that it was other than a casual invite. He left Jerry, Nigel Black, Patti, and several other linguists from the choir, chatting happily and went over to Elspeth Gray. He always enjoyed talking with her, she was with Simon Barnsley who had just returned to the college from a trip to Mexico where he had been guest of honour at a symposium in honour of Fuentes. The subject turned to theatre and Elspeth asked Adrian whether there was any indication that Patti Jones, an absolute bundle of energy, was doing too much.

"I gather she's 'teching' for a Lorca play at the Playroom," said Elspeth. "I love Lorca, and I'll go and see it, but surely nobody has the energy that Patti Jones has?"

"Patti Jones seems to have," said Adrian, and he shook his head indicating a level of disbelief.

At that moment Francesco the butler entered and rapped his gavel on one of the wooden benches at the side of the room.

"Master, Fellows, my Lords, Ladies, Gentlemen, dinner is served." And then, in his inimitable style, and pointing towards the doorway into the Hall: "This a way."

Jerry and Patti met up over coffee during the following weekend. It was a very brief meeting, seemingly casual, but they talked openly about Jerry's role in keeping Patti safe. To date Patti had no concerns. All had gone smoothly. Jerry believed that his present biggest worry, in terms of protection, was not Patti but rather Alexis Stanislowsky. He did not, of course, mention this to Patti. They simply arranged a dinner date for early in January at the start of term. Jerry was aware that Patti was flying back to America early the next week, on a commercial flight. That she would be met discretely at JFK airport he had no doubt, but it was not his concern. The US Secret Service would be taking care of her once she was safely back on the ground, and probably while she was still in the air. It was some comfort to Jerry that Patti had already been in Cambridge, without his specific knowledge, for three months with no untoward happenings.

It was a strong suggestion that the strategy around false identity was working. He did spend some time getting to grips with Patti's routine and told her that he would be thinking about it and how it might be tweaked to reduce risk, there was far too much routine in the week. It was probably the result of her packing so much into the time and therefore needing to be highly organised. Jerry promised to try to find a solution that removed none of the things that Patti wanted to do but did introduce more variability in her movements around the town. It was an easy promise to make but rather hard to deliver on.

Patti went home early in December. A black Mercedes, with an airport taxi logo painted on the side, turned up at the Porters' Lodge late one evening and collected Ms Jones. The taxi was, in fact, a specially adapted vehicle with bullet proof glass and armoured bodywork, and the driver was a member of the US Secret Service, but nobody would have realised that, had they not already been informed. Patti spent the night in the airport hotel at Heathrow and caught her flight to America the next morning at around 11am. She was in business class and chatted happily to the Air Marshall in the seat beside her.

There was nothing to challenge the perception that she was simply a relatively well-off young lady whose parents were paying for her to travel in comfort. It had been a long and busy term and she dozed quite a bit on the journey, choosing to tilt her seat rather than turn it into a fully reclined flat bed. Over the next few years this routine would become standard for her. Stay awake on the Westbound flight; fall asleep on a flatbed on the Eastbound flight.

Connecticut had not changed and, for a few weeks, in many ways all too brief, Patti again became Patti Howland. She continued to keep a low profile but there were press release photographs associated with the home life of the soon to be inaugurated president and her family. The brothers were also home for Christmas, or, as the Americans insist on calling it, the Holiday Season. It was a joyous time and, although Secret Service agents were crawling all over the town of Fairfield and its surroundings, it was one in which all the Howland family could, to a degree, let their guard down and relax. There was much to catch up on.

Patti had a very stylish brunette wig made and was given some tuition in make up so that she could pass for a brunette if necessary. She also needed tinted contact lenses; those green eyes were much too obvious otherwise. She tried out the disguise and her English accent when she met one or two of her former school friends at a concert and reception in the local Town Hall. They failed to recognise her until she came clean and owned up to who she really was. Although Patti was mainly taking part on the technical side in the ADC Theatre in Cambridge, she was a passable actress, and had developed her very English accent so that she could pass herself off as an Englishwoman to any stranger. She had a remarkable talent for mimicry and her spoken French and Spanish were rapidly becoming both fluent and authentic, in terms of pronunciation.

For Christmas itself, the family went to their cabin near Williamstown in upstate Massachusetts. There was skiing and snowboarding and a lot of family time. Patti met Thomas's girlfriend Sara, a young woman of Asian Indian descent, for the first time. Stephen brought some of his friends from med school. Cambridge was not mentioned.

The return to Cambridge in January of the following year was interrupted very early in the term by the necessary visit to Washington for the inauguration of the president. The inauguration, in the third week of January, meant that Patti had barely time to unpack at the start of the Lent Term before she was off again on one of the much more clandestine flights arranged in private aircraft by the Secret Service. Charles, rapidly becoming a friend as much as a bodyguard to Patti, escorted her throughout this trip.

There were lots of interviews for Patti to negotiate and she did so with aplomb and a strong Connecticut accent. It was all the boys could do to keep a straight face when they heard the exaggeration in her tones. Patti had never had a strong accent and now here she was laying down a false trail to the media pack, many of whom were still trying to locate where Patti was studying. There were lots of direct questions and the only thing that Patti did give them was that she was "majoring" in Spanish. She managed to tie that in with a comment about inclusivity in American Society and that went down well with the more liberal populace, on both sides of the political divide. She escaped unscathed from the intrusive questioning and returned to Cambridge with no one any the wiser about where she was studying.

Chapter 4

The Lent Term at Cambridge, the post-Christmas period that struggles through winter towards the earliest days of spring, is probably the engine room of degree study. Patti chafed a little at the darkness and the greyness of the January days; that short trip to the inauguration had been a brief interlude of relief. However, the involvement with the theatre proved to be a blessing in more than one way.

First came the pleasure of set design and construction. Building sets in the workshop and the yard at the ADC Theatre proved to be something at which Patti was quite excellent. She had manual dexterity and an eye for detail. The producer had a vision of the set in her mind when she called the crew together for the briefing. The play, Lorca's last one written before his assassination, "The House of Thomasa Alba," required the construction of a room, with "white, white walls" and several exits and entrances from other parts of the house. It was not demanding in technical terms, but it required an eye for detail, and a cleanliness of line. The production also required an excellent lighting scheme, with action at all times of day and into the night. Patti decided that this was a chance to develop her skills as a sound and lighting technician and she found herself working as an assistant to a young man from Brussels called Lucas Ndlovu, who was also a student at St Joe's. The two had noticed each other around college but had not really spoken much until they teched the same show.

Lucas's family had emigrated to Brussels from one of the many African Republics that had sprung up in post-colonial times. In his early years Lucas had begun his education at the Christian Brothers college in the capital, but his father had consistently challenged the oppressive policies of the government and had soon been forced to flee the country. Thembani Ndlovu had chosen Brussels in which to settle because of its centrality within the European Union and had enrolled his sons, Lucas, Vusi and Sifiso, and his daughter, Esther, in the British School at Woluwe-Saint-Lambert. They were enrolled in the bi-lingual programme of French and English and both Lucas and Esther sat the IB examinations. Esther was a year older than Lucas but had taken a year out of school during the resettlement in Belgium and so was in the same academic year as her brother. She was in her first year at Oxford reading law. Lucas was studying engineering, hence his interest in sound and lighting 'teching' at the ADC.

Lucas was charismatic. He was one of those people whose presence almost instantly commands attention. He had an athletic grace and the confidence that the backing of a loving and supportive family can give. He and Patti hit it off instantly and were soon taking every opportunity, after working on the production, to spend time together. It was not long before the relationship developed into a more physical one, they were soon an item.

It was quite tricky for Patti to deal with this relationship. Lucas wanted to know everything about her past, about her family, about her education, about her ambitions. The 'ambitions' part was easy enough, that was real and needed no deceit, but the history, all of it, required great attention to detail to make the story consistent. So complicated did things become that Patti was, eventually, forced to consult Charles Hoi, her Secret Service mentor, to discuss whether she might take just this one further person into her confidence. It was clearly a dangerous moment, and it would not be unfair to say that despite himself being a Chinese American, Charles found himself dealing with racial prejudice. It took an effort for him to return to a professional approach and he cautioned Patti to remain within character completely while he, Charles, investigated fully the background and politics of the Ndlovu family.

Patti found herself sitting, one Thursday morning in mid-February, on a bar stool in Savino's Coffee Bar, sandwiched between Charles Hoi on one side and Lucas Ndlovu on the other. She felt like the net in a tennis match. The conversation between the two young men almost excluded her. It was more of an inquisition by Charles than it was a conversation. About ten minutes of this was all she could put up with so Patti finished her doppio coffee and excused herself, saying that she had to go back to college, just across the road, to collect an essay for her supervision at noon. She would be back.

As soon as Patti had gone Charles began an even more in-depth inquisition. It was almost a parody of the sort of grilling that a parent might give to a prospective son-in-law.

Finally, Lucas became angry.

"What the hell is this about?" he asked.

"Have you no idea?" asked Charles.

"None at all," said Lucas. "I'm getting pissed off with your questioning. Who the hell *are* you to talk to me like this? I'm just going out with this fabulous young lady I met a few weeks ago and suddenly this elderly friend from America arrives and starts grilling me about everything, my beliefs, my politics, my religion, my family."

Charles bristled a bit at being called an elderly friend, and Lucas felt quite good about having scored a point.

"And, to make things worse," continued Lucas, "my family tell me that they've also had visits from American 'suits' and my dad says that his computer might even have been hacked. In fact, the family think they've been under surveillance for a week or two now, ever since I started going out with Patti Jones."

"Ok," said Charles. "I guess I do owe you an explanation; but I need us to go first and see your senior tutor so that he can witness the conversation."

At that moment Patti returned with her essay and this time sat next to Lucas at the Bar, with an espresso and a couple of Sara's amazing homemade *amore divinos*.

"If you two carry on with the aggressive questioning I'll make myself scarce again," she said.

"I came here for a peaceful coffee with a couple of friends and ended up in verbal World War Three!"

There was a very quick and thorough apology by Charles who said, at the end of the apology bit, that he was sure Patti knew why the grilling had taken place. Patti did not look amused.

"There's aggressive, and there's intelligent questioning," was all she would say for the time being.

Poor Lucas, by this time, was even more bewildered, but his natural good humour and poise took over and the conversation became general, about the play and about theatre in general.

It was eleven o'clock when Charles suddenly said: "Come on you two. We must go and See Adrian Armstrong. We have an appointment. All of us, now!"

Adrian had been forewarned by Charles who had briefed him during part of the ultra-vetting that Charles was doing on Lucas. He was waiting for them in his office at the foot of 'A' staircase in the Main Court, which was the first court that visitors entered when they came into St Joe's.

As if they had not had enough caffeine the three visitors joined Adrian in yet another cup of coffee, made with Adrian's hyper expensive bean-to-cup machine that he had insisted on having bought for him when he agreed to a further term as senior tutor.

The first item of business was to notify Lucas that he was now bound by the terms of the Official Secrets Act. It was pointed out to him that prison was the best that might happen if he broke the terms of the Act, and that life imprisonment was a possibility. It all seemed a bit over the top but, once Lucas had agreed to be bound by the Act, he quickly learnt exactly why it was necessary.

"You can walk away now," said Charles, "but if you do then we must insist that you end your relationship with Miss Jones and forget that this meeting ever took place. You'll need to stop asking Patti questions about her past and about her family. As far as you're concerned, she'll be an orphan who sprang to life fully formed on October 1st when she arrived at St Joe's last year."

There was a long pause while Lucas, looking as bewildered as ever, took that in and everyone drank their coffees, and Adrian ate his way through one of those small packets of very high-quality shortbread biscuits that the college served with its committee meeting coffee or tea. Those packets of biscuits were one of the reasons that Adrian had to go for a jog of about 8 kilometres each morning in order to ensure he could still fit into his trousers.

"If you do decide to continue this conversation then what we'll tell you could put your life in danger."

Lucas cleared his throat, took a deep breath, and then said: "I've no idea what's coming but it scares the hell out of me. I can't believe that it's anything bad about Patti, but I do hear what you're saying. I get the impression, if I say yes to all this, that I'm going to be faced with a responsibility that's currently well above my pay grade."

"Would I be right in thinking that what you are going to tell me, if I consent, is important for Patti's safety, as well as mine? Is there some threat, actual or potential, hanging over her?"

There was a nod from Charles, Adrian just looked on.

Lucas continued: "Three weeks ago, I hardly knew her. Over three weeks I got to know her, her family in Connecticut, her schooling in the States, her love of horse riding, her ambitions and everything else about her. I'm guessing that I'm about to be put back to how it was three weeks ago when I didn't know her at all. I'm guessing that what she's been telling me, except perhaps about loving horse riding, is all a fabrication. Do I want to know who Patti really is and where she's come from? I think that's what you're asking me. And if I say I don't want to know, what's my life expectancy?"

There was a sharp intake of breath from Charles. It had crossed Charles's mind that an accident might be necessary.

"Bloody hell," said Lucas, "I didn't see this one coming."

And he started to laugh, an ironic, confused, how the heck did I get into this, sort of laugh.

Lucas looked at Patti who smiled back at him.

"Sorry Lukey," she said, "I didn't mean this to happen, but we didn't know we were going to hit it off as big time as we have. If it helps, I really want you to say yes. I want to keep going out with you and I want to do theatre and university with you. I'll be really sad if you say no, but we'll both get over it and, Charles, whatever he decides, you will keep your grubby hands and your bloodhounds off Lucas."

That last statement was made with the kid gloves off.

There was another silence while Lucas sat there deep in thought, then he said: "Ok. I'm buying in."

Charles took out of his brief case a copy of the New York Times with a picture of the First Family standing together at the inauguration. He handed it silently over to Lucas and sat back in silence.

The look on Lucas's face when he recognised Patti Howland as Patti Jones was one of total incredulity.

"Oh shit!" he said.

Then he looked at Patti, smiled and said: "Let's tell these two geriatrics to clear off and we can start again!"

"We need to make a few things clear first," said Charles. "And then we'll leave you in peace. Nobody, not your family, not your friends, nobody, must know Patti's true identity. The two of you, if you stay together, will need to hide the true identity from all your friends in college, in the theatre, everywhere. I suggest you avoid any topics like family history and background and simply stick to the present and the future. Patti's done this brilliantly so far and I'm sure a smart guy like you, Lucas, can manage to follow her lead."

"Well," said Lucas, "this fucks up my life a bit, doesn't it."

"'Fraid so," said Charles. "And it's a ticking time bomb. What if you two bust up? What if Patti's mother does a second term. You're smart. I don't have to spell it out."

Patti looked at Lucas and gently took his hand.

"I'm sorry," she said, "but you were getting too close, and I just couldn't keep up the pretence with you any longer. Forgive me."

"Yeah," said Lucas. "I don't think I gave you any choice."

"Now, we're going to leave you alone for a minute or two and then we'll come back. There are some business matters we need to take care of," said Charles; and he and Adrian left the two of them together to take in what had just happened.

When he came back, Charles was all business: "Patti knows this shit," said Charles, "but you need some training. We'll want you to agree to come to London to the Secret Service HQ for some training about security and surveillance. We need you to be as aware as Patti about possible risky behaviours, both your own and those of people around you. You're a smart guy so I think you might even enjoy it. If Patti wants to, she can join you for a refresher. Maybe you'll get to see a West End show at CIA expense."

"I can't bloody wait," said Lucas, very sarcastically. He got up from his chair, looked very hard at the two men, then turned to Patti.

"Patti, meet you for lunch after your supervision."

And so Lucas came to know Patti's true identity. It would be difficult to overestimate the relief that Patti felt at being able to share her story with another person, especially Lucas. She had no apprehension about the future; what if they should fall out with each other? Patti was confident that Lucas would respect her privacy and help preserve her anonymity; besides which, youth does not always look for consequences. She was well aware that the relaxation engendered by having someone with whom to share her secret might lead her to slip up, but she found the opposite. The ability to relax with Lucas meant that the strain of keeping things from everyone else was somehow eased. The gloomy days of February and early March passed. Lucas and Patti became closer and closer, and when the term ended, Lucas invited Patti to his family home in Brussels. Rather than going back to America Patti decided to accept Lucas's invitation. What a fateful decision that proved to be.

Lucas's father, Thembani Ndlovu, was every bit as impressive as his son; perhaps, with the greater maturity and confidence that often comes with age, he was even more so. The two younger brothers, Vusi and Sifiso, and Lucas's sister Esther were all very welcoming and Mrs Ndlovu, Patricia, was the perfect hostess. Esther was home from Oxford for the vacation, the family lived in quite a large semi-detached house near the Woluwe Forest. The accommodation was on three floors, the third floor being a loft conversion, and there was a large double garage forming a basement. A typical Brussels town house.

The Ndlovus were Catholics, like so many of their countryfolk, and they asked Patti about her own religious beliefs. Patti confessed that she had been brought up in the protestant tradition but that she now rarely attended church. Little was made of that by either party and there was no issue made of the fact that, throughout her stay, Patti slept in on a Sunday when the Ndlovu family went together to attend Mass.

Patti shared a room with Esther; Lucas had his own room; the other two boys had bunk beds and study spaces in the loft conversion. The master bedroom at the back of the house, overlooking quite a surprisingly large garden, was that occupied by the parents. Vusi was in the final year of the IB programme and Sifiso was a couple of years behind him at school.

Patti was surprised to find that all the members of the family other than Lucas and Esther, spoke English with slight French accents, it was very attractive. All four children, and both parents, were fluent in French as well as English, and had a working knowledge of Flemish. Thembani and Patricia could also speak a little Xhosa, the language heavily punctuated with click sounds, and both Lucas and Esther had a smattering of that language too. This was a family of clever people.

Patti loved the furniture in the house. It was typically Flemish; dark wood, carved in simple lines; brown leather on the sofas and huge armchairs. Solid, reliable. She remarked on it to Patricia and was told that much of it had been in the house when they bought it, and the rest had been acquired from second hand furniture shops and auction sales. It had that patina that only age can give to really well-made things.

At the first meeting with the family Patti had been introduced as "my American friend from St Joe's" with no more explanation than that. Inevitably this lack of curiosity was never going to last. Patti wondered how long it would be before the barrage of questions began, but she resolved never to offer any information that she and Lucas had not already agreed on, and to try to confine conversations about her family background and life in America to moments when Lucas was also present. It was her hope that by doing this Lucas and she could continue to sing to the same hymn sheet and avoid any incongruities that might otherwise arise. Patti decided that her best plan was to take the initiative and find out as much as she could about Lucas's family, before they started to quiz her. It was partly a deliberate ploy, but it was also born out of a genuine desire to learn about the background and experiences of the first family of colour with which she had ever had meaningful conversation. She felt slightly ashamed that her background and upbringing had been so utterly white. Upper middle-class and upper-class American schools are not big on black history; Europe just about gets a mention, Africa almost never does. Patti herself had tried to learn where most of the countries are in the world; she had been given a huge globe of the world map when she was young and had lain awake at night sometimes, trying to identify countries by their outline in a puzzle book she had bought for herself at the local bookstore, but she had never, until Lucas came along, had a really meaningful conversation with a person of colour.

Lucas and Patti had arrived from Heathrow at Brussels Airport around noon on the Saturday and had been met by Thembani, in his green Peugeot hatchback. Themba', as his friends and family called him with affection, insisted on driving Patti and Lucas around the city to some of the main sights before calling briefly at a patisserie, to collect something for dessert, and then driving the two back to the family home. Patti was not only Lucas's first white girlfriend, but she was also his first ever true girlfriend. If this had been an English village the lace curtains would have twitched. As it was, the family, as much as Patti, found themselves challenged by the obvious racial and cultural differences and found, over the next few weeks and months, quite a lot of their attitudes changing as they came to know and understand each other's cultural backgrounds better.

That first Saturday evening meal was a chance for Patti to put into action her plan to divert attention from her own background. She was fortunate that the Ndlovus were polite and cultured hosts.

The family were originally from the capital city of their district. Dr Ndlovu had trained at the University of Pretoria Medical School and taken all the necessary examinations to be registered in the United States and Europe. He had returned home to practise medicine there, he was very committed to his country, but had gradually fallen foul of the ruling party. Thembani Ndlovu saw the writing on the wall and managed to smuggle out most of his resources. He sent his family to Brussels at the point when one of his school friends informed him that he had been put on the government's wanted list.

He disappeared from public life one afternoon in March, taking with him some money, and some survival gear. He knew the border crossing points would be watched, as would the rail and air terminals, and he trusted nobody for the five months it took him to find a way out of the country. He had friends within the opposition party who helped him to find places to hide out, but it was a difficult game staying ahead of his pursuers. He headed quickly south into Zimbabwe, taking his life in his hands as he swam across a crocodile infested river to get there. Once in Zimbabwe he avoided all routine, he never slept in the same place two nights in a row, he never decided where he was going to sleep until it was almost time to do so. Fortunately, he had gone underground in March and so, after an initial four or five weeks in which there was some rain, his homeless period was mainly dry and not too cold. That particular year the winter was relatively warm, the minimum temperature did not drop into single figures. For most of the time he was also in the part of the country where malaria risk was low to almost zero and it was only when he headed towards the border at Beitbridge, to cross the Limpopo and leave Zimbabwe, that he ran any malaria risk at all, and it was the dry season when he got there.

On August 16th he managed to bribe a guard at the Beitbridge border post leading into South Africa; it cost him five hundred US dollars to get the guy to delay, by half an hour, reporting having seen him, and it cost him another five hundred US dollars to get the loan of a small motorbike, from someone on the South African side, so that he could get well out of the reach of the pursuit before they knew he had gone. Once in South Africa it was not entirely easy going, but he had managed to keep his passport and other identity documents, and he decided that the motor bike was worth less than the five hundred dollars he had given to the owner so, somewhat against his principles, he stole it and rode it all the way to Johannesburg. One week later he was reunited with his immediate family in Brussels. He left behind his mother and father, and two siblings; he also had a grandfather, who had emigrated to South Africa at the peak of the civil strife, and now lived in a tin shack in Soweto.

By this point Patti's jaw had dropped open. She had had no idea about the background from which Lucas's family had come and what dangers had bedevilled Thembani Ndlovu's exit from his homeland.

"What might have happened to you if they'd caught you?" asked Patti.

"That's easy to answer," said Thembani. "Those friends of mine that they caught were tortured to extract information about the whereabouts of other dissidents. Some were killed, others were broken beyond repair. Even the very strongest among them were permanently damaged by their experiences of solitary confinement, water boarding, bastinado, and the like. Many could never walk properly again. I was one of the lucky ones, I got away."

There was a long silence after this as all the members of the family and Patti reflected on what Thembani had just said. The conversation that Charles had had with Lucas a few months ago seemed small beer compared with what surrounded Lucas's family.

"You never told us about all this before, Dad," said Lucas.

"I didn't think you were ready until now. But you mustn't dwell on it. I got away, and we now have our lives to lead. Perhaps someday our homeland will be an amazing place to go back to," said Thembani.

"How about you, Patti? How did you get to be sitting here with us this evening? What's your back story?"

"Very ordinary privileged upper middle-class American," said Patti. She was feeling a little in awe after what she had just heard.

"I was born in Connecticut in a large comfortable house in a town called Fairfield; I've never known a day's hunger in my life. Apart from self-inflicted danger with some extreme sports like rock-climbing, white-water rafting and skiing, my protected existence is all there is. I'm embarrassed to admit a life of utter privilege." Patti laughed.

"I suppose the most daring thing I've done is to defy the family wish for me to go to an Ivy League university and come here to Europe for my degree. Dad wanted me to go to Oxford, once he realised that he couldn't shake my ambition to cross the pond, but I wanted to go to Cambridge because I wanted to be taught by a particular Professor at St Joseph's, so there I am. Very dull I'm afraid, sir."

"You know, Patti," said Thembani, "that 'sir' at the end of the sentence is the first time you've sounded like an American!"

There was a happy sound of laughter around the room and because it was quite late, much to Patti's relief, that rather ended the conversation for the evening.

"Would you like a hot drink to take to your room with you anyone?" Patricia Ndlovu asked.

"I'll look after Patti," said Esther. "There's a lot I want to ask her, and it has to be done in the privacy of our shared room and without Lukey present. By the way Patti, we all call him Lukey so I guess you'd better do so too while you're here. And the other nicknames are Vus for Vusi, and Fiso for our little brother. I know Dad already told you to call him 'Themba' and I guess Mum will have to agree what you should call her."

"I find 'um' often works," said Patti.

Patricia laughed.

"You're here for a couple of weeks, I don't think 'um' is going to last that length of time. Themba calls me Trish, would that be OK by you?"

"I'd be honoured to call you Trish, thank you all for making me feel so welcome here. There were quite a few of us Patricia's in my class at high school so Trish is easy for me to remember. I'm a long way from home and being here is a privilege I shall treasure for ever. And what am I to call you Esther?"

"Hey, I'm just Esther. Nobody dares to shorten that," said Esther.

"What are you recommending as a hot drink, Esther," asked Patti.

"Chocolate," said Esther. "It's Brussels; what else?"

The two girls went out to the kitchen, made their hot chocolate drinks, and went up together to the room they were sharing.

"It's really good of you all to let me come here," said Patti. "Maybe you can visit me in the States one day."

"It's nice to have you here," said Esther, "and I hope we *will* be able to visit you someday. I've been dying to ask you. Is it serious between you and Lukey?"

"Too early to say," Patti said. "We really only met a couple of months ago, but we do get on well and I think it could get serious. But we're both very young and we both have serious academic ambitions. For the moment it's just great. Your brother's a fantastic guy and I love being with him. How about you? Have you got a special friend at Oxford?"

"Nothing romantic," said Esther. "I have a really good friend called Leah Shapiro. I met her at interview, and we corresponded afterwards and both got in. We've been really close friends since the start of the year."

"You'll have to bring her up to Cambridge to meet me and Lukey," said Patti. "Is she reading law too?"

"No, she's reading English and French, and she's the most amazing actress. She also writes, she's had her first novel published already. I have a copy if you want to read it. Actually, she's coming over at the end of next week to spend a long weekend here. She's been a couple of times already; she came even before we both got our places. It helps with her French to go out into the city and speak to the natives!"

"What's her novel called?" asked Patti.

"*Don't you like my cooking*," said Esther. "It's about a Jewish mother bringing up a family in Poland in the 1930s. She said it's based on stories she gathered from her London community."

"Well, I've got to read it," said Patti. "And I'm sorry if that means I could be in the way when she arrives. I can easily get a hotel room for a few days."

"No way," said Esther. "This bedroom is big enough for three beds. It seems to have escaped your notice that the sofa over there is a sofa bed. I think you'll like Leah. She describes herself as 'dead working class', and she comes from Bethnal Green. She says that makes her a genuine cockney. I think her great-grandfather escaped a pogrom in Russia in the last half of the nineteenth century and settled in the East End. She says a whole extensive family joined him just before the Second World War. I bet we have fun, and I bet we spend the whole night talking. But I reckon you must be very tired now. This must be all very strange for you. You've been travelling most of the day so I should let you go to sleep. I imagine when you close your eyes all the images of the day will come back. When I do something new that always happens to me, I go over and over in my mind's eye what I've not quite taken in. I'm glad you're here. I haven't seen Lukey so happy at home in years. Let's drink our chocolate and put the light out."

The next morning was a bright, clear, and cold day in Brussels. As it was a Sunday the Ndlovus went to Mass and came back hungry. There was a delicious breakfast of croissants, pains-aux-raisins, café au lait, baguettes, butter, and apricot confiture.

After breakfast the youngsters embarked on a tour of Brussels which, given that many of Brussels' major tourist attractions are large buildings with lots to see at each one, and quite a lot of walking, extended over quite a few days. They got into the habit of visiting an attraction or two in the morning, finding a café for lunch, and then taking some exercise in the afternoon before the light faded. It was still only March, and sunset was around 6.30 to 7 in the evening. Patti was an accomplished horse rider and was surprised to discover that Esther too liked riding. Lucas could ride, but it was not a passion of his, so the two girls went riding without him. When Esther had gone to school in Brussels she had made friends with a girl who had a large château style house in the nearby countryside, and a number of horses. Patti was about the same height and build as Therese, the friend, and was able to borrow riding clothes, including riding hat. A couple of other afternoons were spent at the swimming pool and, during the week, Patti continued her habit of going for a jog, around the Woluwe Parc.

Leah arrived Late on the Friday evening.

Chapter 5

Small, dark haired, dynamic, flamboyantly dressed in rainbow colours; Leah was impossible to ignore and impossible not to like. Leah had a cockney twang to her voice and, when she decided to get back into character, she had forgotten completely that the letter H existed in the English language.

"I done Eliza Doolittle in a production of My Fair Lady last term at Uni," she told Patti. "I must of bin the only actor what done the first 'alf of the play in me natural voice and the second 'alf in me put on one."

Where does the chemistry in relationships come from? The three girls became a unit almost immediately.

"I've never bin on a bloody 'orse," said Leah.

"We'll have to do something about that," said Esther.

And so they did.

Leah started off terrified and then gradually began to relax and enjoy the experience and by the time the afternoon was over she asked if they could come back the next afternoon.

"I've got me year abroad year after next," said Leah. "I was 'oping to come to Brussels and work 'ere. I wouldn't mind getting a job in one of the Theatres. Maybe at Theatre Royal du Parc. My college 'as an arrangement wiv the French free university 'ere, we exchange students, so I can get accommodation there."

They talked a bit about the plan for the year abroad.

Therese was from one of the very aristocratic families that make up the top tier of Brussels Society. It did not show in her demeanour or behaviour towards others, much in the same way that Patti's origins were not betrayed in her day-to-day dealings with people and events; what it did do was give her access to some happenings that were otherwise not generally available, in particular to something called the Ommegang.

All three of the young ladies were quickly intrigued by the whole concept of the Ommegang. Therese explained that the Ommegang happens every July in

Brussels. She told them about its history and how it was now modified for the twenty-first century.

It started in the fourteenth century with a devout local woman stealing a famous and important statue from Antwerp and bringing it back to Brussels. She placed it in the chapel of the Crossbowmen's Guild and in return the guild promised to hold an annual procession, called an Ommegang, in which they carried the statue through Brussels and into the Grand Place. The religious significance of the Ommegang gradually faded into the background and in the sixteenth century it began to commemorate the entry of the Holy Roman Emperor Charles V into the city.

Nowadays it is a great carnival, with jousting, horse riding, fireworks, stilt walkers, and bands playing loud traditional music. There are groups of minstrels, and Les Gilles, a group of men who help celebrate Mardi Gras in the Carnival at Binche but, in modern times, have come to join in the Ommegang procession in Brussels. They wear masks, colourful costumes, and huge hats adorned with ostrich feathers, and throw oranges to the crowd from long wicker baskets which they carry in their hands. Their drums beat out a rhythm to which they march in their heavy wooden clogs. Their wax masks fully cover their features.

"I really wanna be in that," said Leah when she heard about it. "Can you fix it for me, Therese?"

"I can get you involved," said Therese. "Especially if you learn to ride a horse properly."

"Watch this space," said Leah.

Leah left on the Monday afternoon. Thembani drove her to the airport after she had promised to visit Patti and Lucas, with Esther, in the next month or so.

Patti noticed that Lucas was sulking.

"What's the matter?" she asked.

"Nothing," said Lucas.

"Yes it is," said Patti. "You haven't said a word to me for almost a day now. What have I done wrong?"

"Nothing," said Lucas.

And then Patti realised what was going on.

"Will you come riding with me tomorrow and can we go to the cinema tonight? Just the two of us?" she asked.

"Are you sure you can spare the time?" asked Lucas.

"Probably," said Patti, and she went over to Lucas and kissed him. There was very little conversation for the next few minutes and, by the time they joined the others for an early supper, cinema tickets had been booked, a taxi ordered, and the *entente cordiale* had been re-established.

The next day summertime started in Brussels, and the extra hour of daylight gave them even more freedom to enjoy the city. From that point, until the pair of them returned to Cambridge, Patti was extra careful to make sure that she did not ignore Lucas. Esther and Patti still had their afternoon rides with Therese, but now Lucas joined them. Otherwise, it was always Lucas and Patti, and whoever else might come along.

"I had thought I would go to Spain for my year abroad," said Patti, "but I'm beginning to think that a year in Brussels might be interesting. I might be able to take some courses at the *Université libre de Bruxelles*, and I would love to get involved in the Ommegang. Do you think they'll need techies for it? I gather the centre piece in the Grand Place is more theatre than procession."

"I bet they will but remember it's over a year away and you could change your mind about Belgium. Apart from knowing that Audrey Hepburn, Hercule Poirot, and Tintin were Belgian, very few people know much about Belgium."

Back in England Patti and Lucas were able to keep their college rooms, as overseas students, throughout the vacation. No meals were provided, they were self-catering, but they enjoyed that; and cooked, ate, worked, and, occasionally, slept together. It had been a relief to Patti that they had kept so busy that questions about background had not been vigorously pursued by the Ndlovus.

Patti explained in more detail to Lucas exactly why she had to remain incognito. He was not unaware. Jerry Gregory was introduced to Lucas, and Lucas and Patti were invited to the Gregory home to meet Jerry's family and enjoy a rather good cassoulet cooked by Marianne Gregory, an authentic cassoulet which was slow and deliberate in the cooking.

As an Engineer Lucas was on a four-year course, just as Patti was, with her year abroad. They both did well in their first-year exams, comfortable first-class results, and so both were made scholars of the college. Patti's scholarship was the Wilson Scholarship for languages, named after a former professor of Spanish. Lucas's scholarship was the Cardwell Scholarship for engineering, named after a former head of the department of engineering. Patti was a little disappointed not to be able to share immediately with her family the pleasure of her result. Then came the issue of how to spend at least some of the long vacation together.

It would have been much easier for Patti and Lucas to visit America if Lucas had been white. He could have blended more easily into the Connecticut background. It would still not have been easy, just easier.

It was agreed that they would spend two weeks together on the west coast and in the nearby states. They would 'do' San Francisco, Yosemite, Grand Canyon, Bryce Canyon, Zion Canyon, and California State Route 1, taking in Big Sur, San Simeon, and other elements of the coastal route, before flying back to Washington, and thence to Camp David, where they could meet Patti's family in secret.

Lucas and Patti enjoyed every minute of the trip. After some years in Belgium and England, Lucas luxuriated in the California sunshine, the guaranteed sunshine of almost every waking day. They visited the Audubon Canyon Ranch near Stinson Beach, they saw the elephant seals, they saw pelicans, and even sighted whales off the coast further south. On the whole trip the only upsetting moment happened in Yosemite when Patti and Lucas went for a meal at the restaurant in the village and their service seemed to be delayed. It was as if someone had taken exception to this mixed-race relationship. Had she not been the president's daughter Patti would have gone ballistic about it but, in her difficult position of needing to remain incognito, all she could do was to apologise to Lucas for the behaviour of her countrymen and make a point of approaching the waiter to demand more rapid service. She did mention the word 'racist' in her conversation. The tone was gentle, but the rhetoric was biting. It had the desired result of getting service.

Lucas 'WhatsApped' his family telling them that he and Patti were off to the east coast for some horse riding and relaxation at the Jones family home.

"That should protect your cover," he said.

The flight from Los Angeles to Washington DC was unremarkable. Patti was aware of the Secret Service protection on the plane, but she tried not to let Lucas know about it. He had more than enough to deal with without realising that every journey was covered by security. The black Chevy Suburban SUV that had mysteriously followed the route driven by Patti all the way from San Francisco to LA airport had obviously been Secret Service, but, fortunately, Lucas had been so taken with the scenery and the buildings that he had not really noticed anybody else. Patti also knew that he had not realised that she herself had a Smith and Wesson M&P Shield 9mm handgun in the glove compartment, there was always the possibility that the Secret Service might get to her too late. The Ford Bronco hire car was specially modified with bullet proof glass, reinforced armoured panelling, and bullet proof tyres. Patti knew that, but Lucas had no idea.

The pair were met at the airport in Washington DC by members of the presidential bodyguard and escorted to a private helicopter which took them on the thirty-minute ride to Camp David, up in the Catoctin Mountain Park in Maryland. President Howland was not there when the two arrived, but the two boys were already there and required introduction.

Patti and Lucas were accommodated in one of the smaller cabins on the main site, relatively near to the main lodge, Aspen Lodge, in which Martha and Edward Howland would be sleeping. Thomas and Stephen, the two brothers, had separate cabins nearby. Each had arrived with friends; in Thomas's case his 'serious' girlfriend, in Stephen's case three of his fellow medical students, for Stephen had now moved on to medical studies at the University of California, San Francisco.

All the cabins were typical American real estate, constructed mainly of wood, and with a lot of whitewash around. It was impossible to miss the presence of several service personnel, Camp David is officially a military base. Originally built shortly before the Second World War as a retreat for federal employees it was effectively appropriated by Franklin D. Roosevelt as a residential retreat in 1942 and it has been used as such ever since. Roosevelt called it Shangri-La. How much resemblance it shows to James Hilton's mythical world is a moot point.

It was probably as well for Lucas that the president and her husband were not arriving for a few days. It's a long psychological trip from the English School in Brussels to the secluded retreat of the president of the United States, even if you are in love with the president's daughter, and she with you. The meeting of the Howland siblings and their friends was a little strained at first. It was due, more than anything else, to the three siblings having seen so little of each other over the previous few years. Initially Thomas's 'serious' girlfriend was not present when the others gathered in the large bar at Hickory Lodge. When Sara, the 'serious girlfriend' entered the room and went up to Patti and Lucas and gave them both a big hug, and continental style kisses on the cheek, the ice was broken. Did it have something to do with the fact that Sara was clearly of Indian heritage? There were two highly intelligent and charismatic 'significant others' in the room, with skin of a much darker shade.

Patti, for once, did not have to be on her guard. The three medical students had already been briefed about the need to keep Patti's college affiliation secret and so she and Lucas could talk freely about St Joseph's and life in Cambridge. All three medical students were Northern Californians, brought up in the bay area. All three were from families that were comfortably well-off. Not one of the three had the remotest connection to politics and so their association with Stephen was not going to trigger press interest and they were unlikely to be followed once back in their medical school routine. One of them, who seemed particularly close to Stephen, even remarked that it should be possible for them to visit Lucas and Patti in Cambridge without too much concern that such a visit would trigger discovery.

Sara was an Assistant Professor of Education at Yale, specialising in the understanding of the educational experience of underprivilege. She had gained her PhD looking at the education of ethnic minority students and had then gone on to investigate the impact of homelessness on education outcomes. She was petite, and dark, and lively, and Patti and Lucas warmed to her immediately. Just like Thembani, Sara's father was a refugee from conflict. He had escaped from Kashmir during the brief but brutal war of 1965. He was currently a surgeon at Yale New Haven Hospital, specialising in paediatric surgery in the West Pavilion. Thomas and Sara had met in New Haven when both of them took part in a fund raising half marathon organised on behalf of the children's wards.

Having a father who was a medic was a point in common for Sara and Lucas but, although it remained unstated, the shared experience of subliminal, and not always subliminal, racism was a further factor in common. Lucas could not help but admire the drive and ambition that had led Sara to her present post. He hoped very much that she might become part of his and Patti's long-term circle of friends. What he did not know at that stage was that Sara felt the same about Lucas and Patti.

It was after supper that Patti managed to corner Thomas quietly in the huge lounge.

"How serious, big brother?" asked Patti.

"What do you think, little sister?" asked Thomas.

There was a grin from each.

"Ok," said Thomas. "On my side very serious, but I really don't know about Sara. She's such a fantastic girl that I'm terrified to find out that she doesn't want me as much as I want her."

"Well ask her," said Patti rather loudly, much more loudly and impatiently than she had intended. Of course she was overheard.

"Ask her what?" asked Sara.

Thomas blushed.

"Nothing," he said.

"I don't believe you," said Sara.

She came over and sat on Thomas's lap. She put her arms round his neck. Seemingly oblivious to everyone else in the room, she kissed him passionately.

"Now ask me," she demanded.

"Will you marry me?" asked Thomas.

"About time," said Sara. "What took you so long. Of course!"

And, for the rest of the vacation, Thomas was there with his fiancée.

When they went back to the cabin Lucas and Patti were a little distant. Both of them were reflecting on what had just happened. They both knew it was far too soon for the two of them to consider the level of commitment that Thomas and Sara had just made to each other, but each of them wondered whether lack of that commitment was because the other was, in fact, less committed.

It's all very well for those two, thought Patti, *but Lukey and I have places to go, things to do, plans to fulfil, before we can make that sort of commitment. Just being here must be enough for Lukey to cope with without having relationship angst added to it.*

"They're old," said Patti. "We have plenty of time."

"Yeah," said Lucas, "I think I love you but—"

"You think?" asked Patti, in mock anger, interrupting him. "You think?"

"Well, alright, I know I love you but—"

Patti stopped him, kissed him passionately as they stood there on the porch, broke away and said: "See you for breakfast. Better put on something smart casual. Tomorrow, you meet the president of the United States."

And with that she moved quickly into the cabin and headed for her bedroom.

Lucas stood there for a while, looking up at the night sky. It was relatively free of light pollution, and you could see more stars that you could ever imagine existing.

Looking at stars like this is meant to make me feel insignificant but emotionally it doesn't. So, each of those dots is millions of miles away and massive, they tell me that anyway, but I don't feel that. All I see is a beautiful sky, beautifully black, with some little dots of light on it making miraculous patterns. I feel good. I have a great girlfriend, I am experiencing things I never dreamed of, I'm young, I'm healthy and I'm very happy. I feel grateful to be alive. Maybe I'll try feeling insignificant tomorrow.

And Lucas too went into the house, cleaned his teeth, had a pee, and went to bed.

Breakfast at Camp David was very American, how else could it be. There was a stack of pancakes with maple syrup and butter and cream, there was fresh pressed orange juice, good coffee, maple wood smoked bacon, the very fatty and crisp bacon strips that are peculiar to the North Americas, there were eggs, hash browns, bagels, cream cheese, gravadlax, French toast, waffles, and blueberry muffins. There were probably a few other things too, but the list so far is what Lucas noticed. He had a stack of pancakes with butter, maple syrup and bacon, a glass of orange juice, and several cups of coffee. It was a little while before Patti surfaced and when she did come into the breakfast room Lucas thought that she looked almost radiant. His heart just skipped a beat, and then he got on with eating his stack of pancakes.

"Good morning, Ma'am," he said, between mouthfuls.

Patti smiled.

"Hi Lukey," she said. "Let me grab some breakfast and then let's go for a long walk. Looking at your stack of pancakes you're going to need a good hike if you're going to stay slim and handsome."

Then she herself piled a plate at least as high as Lucas had, but she chose French toast rather than pancakes.

Everyone ate in the same large dining room, so, one by one, the other guests came in. Some of the officers on duty also came in and dined, although they sat separately from the official guests, and they talked quietly among themselves. Sara was wearing a curtain ring on the third finger of her left hand. It provoked lots of laughter and conversation. Last night it was only really Patti and Lucas who had realised that Thomas and Sara had got engaged, but this morning everyone joined in the excitement. Lucas and Patti were about to leave the table when a surprise visitor arrived. It was Charles Hoi.

"Hi guys," said Charles. "How's it going?"

"Good, Charley," said Patti and Lucas simultaneously.

"What are *you* doing here?" asked Patti.

"Let me get some breakfast first and then I'll tell you," said Charles.

Lucas and Patti, anxious to get on with the day, before the arrival of Madam President, sat there impatiently while Charles ate his way through a very large breakfast and then Charles asked: "Do you mind if we go onto the terrace, and I smoke a small cigar while we talk?"

"As long as you sit downwind," said Patti; she hated tobacco smoke.

They each took another cup of coffee with them and, when Charles had lit his cigar and had a couple of puffs he began to talk.

"When did you last talk to your father, Lucas?" asked Charles.

"About a week ago," said Lucas. "Just after the California trip. He said he had some important things going on and he would tell me about it when he could, but not to worry if there was a bit of radio silence for a week or so. What's the matter? Is he in trouble?"

"Yes and no," said Charles. "The fact is he's gone back to Africa to become deputy leader of the opposition party and there's a lot of civil unrest there. They know he's pro-western and there's a faction which is definitely anti-western and is partly aligned with the communists. We think he might be at risk because of his liberal views."

Lucas gaped like a fish gasping for air.

"You what?" he said.

Then he thought for a moment.

"Has the family gone with him?"

"No," said Charles. "Patricia and your brothers have stayed behind in Brussels, Esther is still at Oxford, and, as far as we know, there is no intention to move them back to join him. The two boys are happy in their schools and coming up to important exams and Esther's continuing her law degree, so I doubt they will be following Thembani Ndlovu very soon, if ever."

"Well," said Lucas, "I suppose that's one less thing to worry about. I worry for my dad but if he can survive for nearly six months on the run with people hunting him, I reckon he can last a little while in the urban jungle. Besides which I think he'll probably have a bodyguard and I doubt that anyone will gun him down in public. At least not until after the election, and that's just over a year away. At the moment the opposition isn't in a strong position, but you know what my dad's like; he's got charisma, and I reckon he just might stir things up enough to get them into contention. Then things might get nasty. Actually, things *will* get nasty."

"I wish we shared your optimism," said Charles, "but there are rumours of accidents, and arrests, and detentions, probably on the pretext of corruption. The main reason I've brought you this news is because it now seems to me that you've joined Patti on the list of at-risk persons because someone may want to use you to get at your father."

"Too bloody right," said Lucas. "And that's increased Patti's risk as well as adding me to the list. I expect that the people keeping a watch on me are going to be very curious about my white girlfriend and they're going to start digging around for her history too." Lucas became very thoughtful.

Patti looked at him.

"Don't you dare," she said.

"What?" said Lucas.

"You sure as hell know that I know what you're thinking," said Patti, who often reverted to American idioms when she was agitated.

"O.K. what am I thinking?" asked Lucas, looking a little sheepish.

"You're thinking about dumping me. How stupid can you get? Let's think this through. Do you have a bodyguard or anyone looking out for you? No, you don't. Does any of the opposition in your home country really care who your girlfriend is? Probably not. Will they connect a white girl at Cambridge to the president of the United States' daughter? Are they really that smart?"

"Yeah, but I do add to your risk," said Lucas.

"A few months ago, you took the decision to put your life at risk by continuing to go out with me," said Patti. "Now let me make my own decision; unless, that is, you want to use this as a convenient excuse to get rid of me. If you want to dump me, do it for the right reasons and not because you think you might put me in danger."

All this was said with anger and passion. Patti was no shrinking violet and Lucas, for the first time, felt the sharp end of her tongue, and his admiration of this woman grew even greater.

"Wow," said Lucas, "Charley, bugger off. Patti and I need to talk. Take that filthy cigar with you and go and pollute the woods. We'll call you when we want you again; if we ever want you again."

Charles grinned at them both, picked up his cigar, took a puff, blew a perfect smoke ring and a second one through the middle of the first, and went off to the woods.

Lucas and Patti looked at each other, moved round the table and stood facing each other. Lucas took both Patti's hands in his and leant forward and kissed her gently on the lips.

"That's another fine mess you've gotten us into Lukey," said Patti.

"Don't tell me," said Lucas, "Oliver Hardy and Stan Laurel?"

"Yeah. But seriously, I don't think it changes anything about my situation. I still just have to be ultra-careful to keep my identity secret and you and I have done an OK job on that since January so why shouldn't it continue? Besides which I think you can benefit from having my minders watching out for you. I'm sure Charley will brief them to be on the lookout for any danger to you, if nothing else because any danger to you will represent a danger to me."

Patti kissed him again, gently, but with real affection. Sometimes a gentle kiss speaks greater volumes than a passionate embrace.

"I do love you," said Lucas, folding Patti in his arms.

They stood like that for a moment and then broke off the embrace, went back into the dining room and poured themselves another cup of coffee, Lucas grabbed a blueberry muffin, and they went outside again to sit in the early morning sunshine.

Charles came back, without his cigar which he had tactfully finished during his walk. He too went and poured another coffee, grabbed two blueberry muffins, and came out to join them.

"So, what gives?" he asked.

"Not that it's really any of your business but we're staying together for now," said Patti. "Does that mean you'll brief your guys about the danger to Lukey, because it affects me?"

"Sure does," said Charles. "You get to piggyback on Patti's security. I'm glad about that. I can also recruit you to the protection team. You two seem to be on the same wavelength. Now I have to go and get ready for Madam President's arrival. But before I go just give me a proper briefing on your plans Lucas. What's your course now until you graduate? Have you any plans for vacations? Anything else I should know to be able to help with your security alongside Patti there?"

Lucas told him: "I'm sure you know most of this. You would have had friends doing engineering when you were at St Joe's. I'm the same year as Patti. We're about to start our second years. I'm doing engineering; probably going to specialise in electronics and nanotechnology. I get three more years in Cambridge because I'll take a master's after my bachelor's degree. I'll graduate and leave at the same time as Patti because she'll have her year abroad as her third year and then come back to finish off with Part 2 Languages."

"I'll probably spend every vacation with her if she'll have me. Either we'll go to Brussels, or we'll come back here to the USA, or we might even go and visit Europe and Africa and China if we can arrange suitable trips. God knows what'll happen if her mum stands for a second term as president. We graduate just before the next presidential election. Will we keep the secret that long? Will we still be together? And what if my dad's party gets elected and the opposition start running the country?"

"Ok," said Charles. "You're right. Nothing I didn't know but thanks for spelling it out."

"We don't intend to change our 'in Cambridge' behaviours," said Patti. "There'll still be sport and theatre for both of us, and we both have lots of friends. And we intend to keep in contact with Lucas's family, including Esther at Oxford. And our friend Leah."

"Who's Leah?" asked Charles.

They told him.

"With my dad away, I'll need to be there for my brothers. What else do you need to know?" said Lucas.

"Have you had firearms training? Have you had any security briefing? Would you like some?" asked Charles.

"This is a bit serious, isn't it?" asked Lucas, rhetorically. "I think I'd better say yes. You never fixed up the training in London you talked about when you scared me in Cambridge that day."

Charles was a bit embarrassed: "I guess I forgot. Sorry. We can do that over here, and give you the whole package, including a bit of unarmed combat and self-defence before you go back to Cambridge."

"Thanks," said Patti. "Lukey, you're going to love it. I assume I can have a refresher?"

It was early afternoon when the presidential helicopter touched down at Camp David. The flotilla of helicopters, all piloted by the Marine Security Corps, arrived over Camp David, and one of them landed. Martha and Edward Howland stepped down from the cabin and were met by their children at the helipad. The guests, the three medical students, Lucas, and Sara, were waiting somewhat nervously in the large bar at Hickory Lodge.

The family members went with their parents up to Aspen Lodge and took a little time out to bring the parents up to date with what they had been getting up to over the past few weeks. The biggest news, and that which was dealt with first, was Thomas's announcement of his engagement to Sara. Martha and Edward had known that Thomas was dating Sara, and deep down had known that this was probably serious, but they were pleasantly surprised that their eldest son had now formally asked Sara to marry him. It had been quite a short romance, Thomas had only known Sara for about eight months, but he had talked incessantly about her when he went to the inauguration and both the Howland parents were sufficiently astute to realise that this was someone with whom their elder son was really quite smitten.

"I can't wait to meet her," said Martha. "Does she know what she might be letting herself in for?"

"I think so, Mum," said Thomas. "I tried to explain about all the security and the protocol but, you know, the Secret Service guys have been great over the past few months, not too intrusive at all, and I think Sara and I can handle it. You know, the hardest thing is that I now have to go and ask her father's permission to marry her, and I know her parents were a bit worried about her marrying someone who was not Indian and could not speak Hindi. They've been lovely to me, but I think they were a bit surprised when I turned up! Sara's been great about not letting on that you're my mum. I think Sara's grandmother is really on my side, so I have a chance. Isn't life strange? It isn't prejudice, it's just that I think I'm not what they were expecting."

Patti smiled to herself inwardly. *I don't think Mum and Dad are expecting Lukey*, she thought. But she knew it wouldn't matter.

Stephen went next. He explained that his three friends were drinking and working pals with whom he got on particularly well and that the four of them were just taking a short break from study before getting stuck back into their clinical training. They talked a bit about the training and which parts of the course Stephen was enjoying most so far. He liked the physiology and the pharmacology most and was wondering if he might become an anaesthetist. He also liked working with children and paediatric anaesthesia, or anaesthesia with a paediatric specialist element to it, were the things he was planning to try to get residencies in. And, no, he did not have a steady boy or girl friend at the moment.

"And how about you Titch?" asked Edward, coming over to his daughter and giving her a big hug. The only people allowed to get away with calling Patti "Titch" were the immediate members of her family and Lavinia, the English nanny who had helped Martha with the children when they were young and who had remained as a sort of domestic overseer to the household when the children grew up. Lavinia was one of the reasons that Patti and the boys spoke American with almost an English accent, or was it English with almost an American accent?

The nickname had come when Patti, whose given name was, of course, Patricia, had tried to say Patricia as one of her very first words. It came out as "Titcha" and Edward had been unable to resist calling his gorgeous little toddler "Titch." Patti almost began to think that her name was "Titch," but she gradually came to realise that it was not, that her full name was Patricia Lindsey Howland, and that there were four other girls in her kindergarten called Patricia. The nicknames Pat, Trish and Tish had already gone so Patricia decided, having been introduced at the age of about four to the music of The Rolling Stones, that if Patti was good enough for Keith Richards's wife, it was good enough for her.

"Titch" smiled.

"I'm fine, Dad," she said. "I love what I'm doing, and I'm so grateful to you both for giving me my head and letting it happen. I really hope you'll be able to visit me in Cambridge sometime, but it might be difficult if I'm going to keep my identity and whereabouts secret. I guess you might be able to come to my graduation because that will be in the July of the last year of Mum's first term."

"Mum, if you go for a second term, I guess a week or so out of campaigning won't matter and if it's visiting your daughter in Cambridge, it might even help?"

"Anyway, I'm here with Lucas. Too early to do a Thomas on you, but I like him a lot, and I'm sure you'll like him. His dad is from Africa and is currently the deputy leader of the opposition party in his home country. Lukey lives in Belgium with his mother and three siblings. We do theatre together and we both do sport. And Lukey's sister and I rode with him a lot when I stayed with them in Belgium last Easter. He's an engineer and very smart. I think I'll let him tell you himself about all the other things you might want to know."

Martha came over to Patti and the two of them embraced each other.

"I miss you, Titch," said Martha. "My only daughter and you go off to the far side of the pond without a backward glance. I see many of my friends with their children still living clustered round them and there you are three thousand miles away, at least. I wonder what we did wrong, but your dad tells me to think of it as having done things right. Couldn't you call just a little bit more often?"

Patti felt guilty. She certainly *could* call a little more often.

"How do we set that up, Mum? Is there any time or any day when it would work for you? Time difference is five hours so maybe my lunchtime and your breakfast time would work? Let's sort it before you go back to work after this weekend. My best lunchtime is Sunday, unless we have a get-in at the theatre when Sunday is gone completely. My second best lunchtime is Saturday, except if I have a field hockey match or a mixed netball match or…"

Patti paused; her mother was laughing like a drain.

"So, Titch, I'm running the biggest democracy in the world, and *you* can't find a lunchtime to talk to me because you're too busy. I like it!"

"Come on guys. I can imagine your friends might all be a bit nervous and wondering where we've got to. Let's go and finish these conversations over at Hickory. It's a bit early for a drink but I asked Lavinia to arrange for an English afternoon tea for all of us and I can't wait to tuck into a cucumber sandwich and a cream cake."

"Lavinia is here?" Three synchronous voices shouted in pleasure. "Where has she been hiding?"

"Never you mind," said Martha. "I have to have some secrets from you. I may want to hide someone else here one day."

Back in the Hickory Lodge bar Lavinia had introduced herself to the waiting guests. Now stooped a little by age, Lavinia was a tall, elegant woman with blue rinse hair, an aquiline nose, high cheek bones, and piercing blue eyes. The daughter of a Viscount, trained at the Norland Agency in both early years and teenage care, she was a formidable woman, a real force of nature. The five nervous youngsters waiting to meet the president and Dr Howland were gently taken over by Lavinia, calmed, reassured, and prepared for the meeting.

Just as at the Aspen Lodge earlier, Thomas began the introductions: "Mum, Dad, this is Sara Acharya; Sara this is my mum, the president, and this is my dad."

"Pleased to meet you Madam President," said Sara, and she put out her hand to shake Martha's hand, but Martha would have none of it and instead gave Sara a big hug and said: "Martha to you, my dear, and please may I call you Sara and not Miss Acharya?"

"And I'm Teddy," said Edward Howland. "And I'd like a hug too please."

Thomas then introduced Stephen's three friends who were also instructed to call the Howlands Martha and Teddy.

"And who is this, Titch?" Martha asked Patti.

"This is my new best friend, Lucas Ndlovu," said Patti, "but if you ask him nicely, he might let you call him Lukey; and Lukey, if you call me Titch anywhere but around my family, you will be sent to Guantanamo."

"Hi Lukey," said Martha, giving him too a big hug; and she whispered in his ear, "I think my daughter is rather fond of you."

"Lukey, Teddy," said Edward, holding out his hand and shaking Lucas's hand warmly. "Thank you for looking after my daughter so very well in that strange land across the pond."

Just at that moment a couple of members of staff came into the bar with the pots of tea, sandwiches and cream cakes, and Lavinia, who had briefly gone out to organise the tea, re-entered the room. The three Howland youngsters immediately rushed to surround her, smothered her in kisses, and started talking to her nineteen to the dozen, not quite the way a Norland nanny expected to be treated. Lavinia loved it.

When, at last, Lavinia was allowed up for air they all went to sit around the huge table and smaller groups began to talk to each other. The Howland parents moved from group to group politely asking questions and skilfully finding out as much as they could about each of their children's guests.

The weekend passed in a welter of activity.

Lucas climbed back on a horse, he was beginning to enjoy riding, possibly because it was now always with Patti, and the advice he was getting from Patti and the stable hands helped him to handle a much livelier beast than the ones he had ridden in Belgium. The riding was hard work, the terrain at Camp David is mountainous and the paths and bridleways are steeply undulating. The weekend rides were tiring, and a good core body strength work out. The food was plain but healthy, and plenty of it. The other guests were good company. Patti and Lucas began to become very friendly with Sara and Thomas. Stephen's friends were a little overawed by Sara and Patti, at least it appeared that way, because they did seem particularly shy around the two of them.

It was quite late on the Sunday evening, just before Martha and Edward were due to depart for Washington, that the group got together for a photograph outside the lodge. Selena, the president's press secretary, thought that a group photograph at Camp David would be safe enough and provide some welcome publicity to begin the re-election campaign.

"It's nearly three years away from the first primaries," said Martha.

"Never too soon to start gathering material," said Selena, "but we probably won't use the photos for a year or so. It's just too good an opportunity with all of you here together to miss the chance to take the snaps. Getting you all together is such a rare event."

There were two sets of pictures taken, one with the family alone, and the other with the family, Lavinia, and the five guests. A couple of the Marines guarding the place took surreptitious snaps of the group on their smart phones. One of them had his android phone set to send snap shots to the cloud immediately. He had no intention of losing any photographs by mistakenly erasing them.

"What are your plans now Lukey?" asked Martha.

"I think Patti and I are planning to go back to Cambridge fairly soon and then we'll visit my family in Brussels. Nothing specific planned for the next couple of months. Term doesn't start until October."

"We have a little cabin in upstate Massachusetts, quite close to Williamstown." Martha turned to Patti. "Do you two want to go and spend some time up there together?"

"Thanks Mum, what do you think, Lukey?" asked Patti.

"Can we go later this summer?" asked Lukey. "I really want to check on my family in Brussels now that I know my dad has gone back to his homeland."

"Mum," said Patti, "could we take Lukey's family with us up there? There's plenty of space and it would be nice to be able to ride there with Esther, Lukey's sister. What do you think?"

"No problem about going there," said Martha. "We could just let the local stable know that you want the horses back in the meadow and have them exercise them a bit so that you get a good ride when you go. If you go, I suggest you fly into Albany and hire a car for the drive up there. If you give me the dates, I'll make sure the Secret Service know what you're doing. I think it'll need a Marine or two to be on duty for you. But it might compromise your anonymity with the Ndlovus."

Patti thought for a moment: "Oh. Darn it. You're right, Mum. Patti Jones wouldn't have US Marines guarding her at the family home. So nearly a mistake. So easy to make a mistake. I wasn't thinking."

The rest of the summer was beginning to fill up with exciting things to do but the trips planned so far were as nothing to the activity planned the minute Martha and Edward took off with their flotilla of escorts and returned to the capital.

Charles, who had been keeping a low profile, suddenly appeared out of the shadows.

"I need to talk to you two, Patti, Lukey," said Charles. "We can wait until the others leave but please don't plan anything specific until you've talked to me."

Lucas and Patti were intrigued and also a bit puzzled by this, but they agreed to wait. They guessed it was something to do with security and they were both now independently concerned about that.

One more evening meal, one more breakfast all together, and then the guests, other than Patti and Lucas, departed.

Charles came straight to the point.

"I think this would be a good chance to run the two of you through a security programme. Patti, I know you had a version of this before, but Lucas has never had any specific weapons or security alertness training, and I think you could benefit from a refresher course, so what do you say I set something up for you and we take you there from here in a couple of days? You get a few more days here in peace and safety, just the two of you. What d'ya think?"

With nothing pressing to draw them away the two youngsters agreed.

"How long do you reckon the course will be?" asked Lukey. "When can we fly back to Europe?"

"Today's Monday. How about we say next Monday to fly back? I reckon I can get things organised to start this Wednesday and five days should be enough. Boston will be the nearest airport to where the training is taking place, but we could take you to New York."

It proved easier to find non-stop flights from New York to London at convenient times, so the two decided to fly into London, from New York, and spend a couple of days sightseeing there, to get over jet lag, before heading off to Brussels by Eurostar.

A couple of days spent riding and walking and just being together at Camp David were followed by a short helicopter ride to a training base in New Hampshire. They took photographs to send to the family, photographs that could have been taken on any piece of east coast forest, in any stable, in any old east coast restaurant.

At the training base Lucas and Patti were given lectures and asked to take online tests for understanding and spotting hostile reconnaissance. They were given advice on personal security awareness, including cybersecurity; there were several video examples illustrating all the points made. They were given some self-defence training each day over the full five days. Both Patti and Lucas were fit young people, and the self-defence training was quickly assimilated; although they were advised to practise regularly to refresh the skills.

Finally, they were both given some training in the use of handguns and, more for fun than for self-defence, they spent some time target shooting with rifles. Although both understood the serious importance of the training, they enjoyed the interlude. It was very different and, for Lucas in particular, it was new to his way of thinking, and he came away from it feeling that, in a crisis, he might be more help to Patti than he would have been five days earlier.

Patti had written to Esther to give her a telling-off about not having visited Cambridge with Leah so when the New York flight touched down at Heathrow Esther and Leah were waiting to meet it. They still didn't get to Cambridge, too busy sightseeing around London, but they all left together for Brussels and spent time together there too. Lots of horse riding with Therese; and Leah and Lucas were getting to be almost as proficient as the other three riders. As Leah subsequently remarked: "Reckon I can ride in the Ommegang, if you can get me in Therese."

Much of the conversation in Brussels was about Thembani and his return home. There was no doubt that it was still a dangerous place, although the regional capital was less dangerous for Thembani than the national capital, which was in the centre of the ruling tribes' territory. There was so much anxiety around in the family that Lucas felt he could not really head off again to America, no matter how tempting the offer of a long summer holiday in Williamstown might appear.

Leah took the opportunity of being in Brussels to sound out the various theatre companies with a view to arranging her year abroad working in Belgian Theatre. Patti too was beginning to wonder about how she might spend her year abroad. Her previous visit to Belgium had derailed her thoughts about taking a year abroad in Spain and she was now certain that it would be Brussels for her; it would coincide with Leah's time there. Finding something to do that was acceptable to her college and the university, but would also be interesting, was never going to be easy. Yes, she could enrol in courses, but she also wanted to work. She began to think that her best bet would be to work in catering, perhaps as a waitress in one of the many restaurants just off the Grand Place. There was a charming little restaurant called Richard's in Petite Rue des Bouchers which caught her eye, the gang had eaten moules frites there one evening, and had, perhaps, a little too much wine to accompany it.

For both Leah and Patti, year-abroad plans were taking shape in their minds. Over the next year they would have to consolidate them.

Chapter 6

Lucas, Patti, Esther, and Leah were sitting at a table in the Grand Place one afternoon, having a coffee and a pastry, when Patti noticed Charles, Charles Hoi, of all people, wandering across towards the Town Hall. He was in animated conversation with a woman clearly of African ancestry. They were gesticulating and waving their arms about in a fairly agitated way. Charles appeared not to notice them on his way across the huge square and Patti, the only one of the group who had noticed Charles, decided, for the moment, to keep quiet. She watched him silently as he disappeared towards the Post Office, and she thought that Charles was probably aware of her attention. It was just something in the way he, seemingly deliberately, looked everywhere except towards where the group were sitting. The Post Office is to one side of the square and the street next to it has a lot of souvenir type shops, including excellent chocolateries. When Charles came back round the corner of the Town Hall, he was carrying several small boxes of confectionery in a little wicker basket.

Patti was right. Charles had seen them but, for some reason, probably connected with the woman who had been accompanying him, he had ignored them on his first pass through the square. Not this time. He came straight up to their table.

"Patti Jones," he said. "It is Patti Jones, isn't it. Charles Hoi. We met at your parents' place."

"So we did," said Patti. "Lukey, you remember?"

"Sure," said Lucas. "How are you, Charles?"

"Your parents' place" remained undefined. True to their brief, Lucas and Patti had not talked about Camp David after their visit there. As far as the Ndlovus and Leah knew, they had simply had a great holiday in America, on both coasts.

Patti introduced Charles to the group and then each of them in turn to Charles. Charles took out a cigarette, one of those strong French tobacco ones, and was about to light it when Patti gave him a withering look and he reached, instead, for an e-cigarette. He did not look happy, but Patti could 'do withering for America' and she had just done that. Charles ordered a coffee, and Patti and Lucas also asked for a refill. There was an uncomfortable silence for a moment and then Charles started to speak: "You're going to have to forgive me a minute. I'm a business associate of Patti's mother and she asked me to come and talk a couple of things over with Patti. I'm sorry but it's all a bit confidential so maybe we can just move over to the other table for a few minutes. It won't take long, then the next coffee is on me."

"Sure," said Patti. "Lukey, can you guard these cakes for me?"

"Sorry to be rude to you guys," said Charles. "I just need to get the business bit over and done with and then we'll be back before you know it."

They moved out of earshot of everyone, including Lucas, Leah and Esther.

"I guess I keep turning up in your life just when you really don't want to see me," Charles said. "It's fair to say that I wish I didn't have to keep bringing bad news, but… Why can't I just turn up and have a nice quiet drink with you all and not throw even more problems your way?"

Charles paused for a moment, puffed on his nicotine machine, sipped his double espresso, and then began to tell Patti just why he had been looking for them. He looked directly at Patti, held her gaze and held her attention.

"You remember that photograph session you had at Camp David?"

Patti nodded.

"Turns out that one of the staff took their own pictures of the event and used an android phone that automatically sends the pictures to the cloud. They then sent them to their mother with a message saying something like 'look who I've been working with'. The mother recognised the presidential family of course, but she wanted to know who the two people of colour were with the president's family at Camp David. The woman had dozens of Facebook friends, so the damn pictures are probably still out there somewhere. We've pulled them now but who knows how many downloads they had?"

"How concerned should we be, Charley?" asked Patti.

"You're probably going to be alright, but I couldn't take the risk of not raising the issue with you."

"Who was the woman you were with and why were you arguing?" asked Patti; she was the only member of the group who had taken any notice of that event.

"She was the woman who recruited the staff at Camp David, including the one who took the photograph. She'd just come over to tell me about it. I just happened to be here for another job, so they sent her to Brussels to tell me and they wanted me to tell you. I was just angry with her and giving her a hard time."

"Patti, in view of what's happened we'd like you and Lucas to commit to taking regular arms and self-defence refresher courses. We can fix that up for you in Cambridge. And you must both be extra careful. We're also going to ask you both to have GPS trackers on you at all times. They're small enough not to be obtrusive, but they'll give us an extra level of confidence that we know where you are."

"I'm gonna need you to explain all this to Lucas. It would have been too awkward to bring both of you over here to talk to me, but I reckon we can get away with my being a business associate and just wanting to talk to you. The others still don't suspect who you are?"

"No," said Patti, "Lucas has been just great keeping things quiet."

Charles heaved a big sigh: "You kids are showing us up. I'm sorry. I guess we sort of screwed up with those photos. I think it'll be ok, but you could do without this."

Charles handed two tiny boxes of chocolates to Patti.

"In each of these boxes, one for you and one for Lucas, you'll find half a dozen tiny GPS trackers. Conceal them any way you like but always try to have at least one of them with you. Ideally you would have two. One that a kidnapper might find and one that they're unlikely to find. They don't need activating; they're active already."

"Look Charley," said Patti, "we go back to Cambridge in a few weeks; if anyone finds out we're there they have access to our timetables, and they can find out where we're going to be, and when we're going to be there, very easily. The lecture timetable is online, university sports practices are open source, college sports practices are open source, theatre is at the theatre. Cambridge is very compact. It wasn't even a city until the second half of last century. There are very limited ways to get from A to B in Cambridge, and we all either walk or cycle. I suppose we'd just better hope that nobody identifies Lukey, and nobody connects us to St Joe's."

And then, letting out some of her anger and frustration: "Have you ever tried to give up smoking. It would be good for your complexion."

Charles gave a rueful grin: "Please don't shoot the messenger. There's a good chance that they won't find out about Lucas. I mean, how much social media presence does he have?"

"Almost none," said Patti. "If anything he's been even more security conscious than I have. I'm just trying to live a lie; he's trying to stay alive. His dad insists the family keeps a low profile. He's still worried about the enemies in his own country. The Ndlovus only do WhatsApp within the family, and that, and the university email, is all Lucas does; I think WhatsApp is encrypted."

"That's good. Might be very hard to do a photo match if there are no pictures out there to match with. We'll try not to screw it up again. Meanwhile there are some things you can do, sensible precautions for now anyway Patti."

"Go to the routine things with at least one other person. For theatre I guess you two can go together?"

"Not really," said Patti. "Sure, we can sometimes, but we might well be working on different bits of the project. Anyway, I usually go with someone else."

"How do you get to your lacrosse practices and games?"

"Cycle," said Patti. "I usually go with Vicky; she's at St Joe's, and we almost always meet up. With the other things, rowing; I think I might give that up. It doesn't float my boat."

Charles laughed. Patti continued: "As far as running is concerned, a girl was attacked on the tow path a couple of years ago so none of us ever runs alone; besides which it's good for training to run with a friend; you can't help being a bit competitive and the university cross-country team is quite a close-knit group, so we often meet up together. Some of those stooges you shoehorned into St Joe's often run along behind us too. There's also a Monday night fun run I can join in. It's a town thing: even though Cambridge became a city in 1951 they still talk about town and gown: they like the rhyme. It ends up with all of us at the pub. They call it Hash Harriers, or just 'The Hash'."

Charles was sitting there with his mouth hanging open.

"Do you ever do any work?" he asked.

"I got a goddamn first, Charley," she said. "You don't get that without work. I thought you would know that."

She was rapidly going off Charles, or maybe she was just grumpy. He went to reach for a cigarette.

"Don't you dare," she said, rather bossily, but very effectively.

Charles looked at the blonde curly haired, butter wouldn't melt in her mouth, young woman in front of him and could see, behind the façade, a steely determination and drive that he saw also in Madam President. A little bit of him thought *if some terrorist does get near her, they're going to get more than they bargain for,* and it gave him some comfort.

"Sorry," he said, getting to his feet, "I think I'd better leave you in peace before you leave me in pieces. Let's go back and re-join the others. I'll rely on you to talk to Lucas."

He gave a wry smile, got up from the table and accidentally knocked over Patti's purse. He picked it up and put it on the table apologising as he did so. It was quite heavy. He could feel that it contained a handgun. He said nothing but went away knowing that Patti, at least, was thinking seriously all the time about her own and Lucas's security. He looked at Patti and the glance they exchanged let her know that Charles knew what she was doing, and he approved. They went back and sat down again with the others.

"Sorry about that," said Charles. "It was something to do with some shares Patti has in some of the family investments in America."

Patti's attitude softened a little.

"Are you hanging out for a bit in Belgium?" she asked.

"I am," said Charles. "I have a few days leave and I haven't done Belgium much."

Lucas, Esther and Leah had said very little during the previous five or ten minutes. While Patti had been talking with Charles the others had been watching intently the interplay of expressions, trying to get a clue to what it was all about, but they had discerned nothing. They now did join in and suggested that Charles, who had got up to leave, sit down again and chat a little longer.

"Wanna come wiv us to Bruges?" asked Leah. "You won't be able to smoke or else Patti'll kill yer!"

Charles looked at Patti, he was beginning to be a bit wary of her, but Patti was smiling and looking quizzically at Leah who, in turn, was gazing intently at Charles.

"I'd like that Ma'am," said Charles.

It was arranged that they would meet next morning at Brussels Central, travel to Bruges, and spend a couple of days with hired bicycles, cycling and sightseeing.

On their first day there they did all the touristy things in Bruges, climbed the Belfry, went to the Markt, cruised the canal, visited the churches and the old hospital. They had moules frites; this close to the sea what else would they eat? They had booked for two nights into a private bed and breakfast place in one of the old streets of Bruges. There was a huge loft conversion with five beds in it and they all slept there looking up through the sky light at the stars. There was very little sleeping done that night. They were all too busy talking; Charles finding out more about Lucas and Esther; everyone, especially Leah, finding out more about Charles; Leah talking about her upbringing as a secular Jewish girl in the East End, and how she had come to write her novel. Shortly after midnight, Patti began to talk about her own wish to break free from family expectations. Not one of them in the room had come a simple route to this place. There had been very different physical, social, emotional, and intellectual challenges for each of them. The only thing they all had in common was the drive to do something, to make a difference, to make a mark on society.

The second day was spent on hired bicycles heading up the towpath by the canal towards Damme and then coming back along the coastal path by the North Sea. The working knowledge of Flemish that Lucas and Esther had was particularly useful. Assuming that northern Belgians speak French is a dumb mistake to make. Perfectly acceptable to apologise for not being able to speak Flemish, then ask if the person you are talking to speaks English and, as a final fall back, if they speak French. Otherwise, if you are seeking directions, and you ask in French without the preamble, you can end up a long way from your desired destination.

The afternoon was spent in more talking. Charles was very good. He had bought some nicotine gum and was relying on that to keep his cigarette cravings at bay. He had one moment when he nearly cracked, sitting at a café on the second evening, near to someone smoking a strong French cigarette; Leah gave him a beaming smile, shook her head gently, and Charles reached for some gum.

Patti's apparent hostility had faded. She had come to realise that, in the grand scheme of things, nothing had changed, at least for the time being. Even if her study location did become known to the paparazzi, they would have a hard time getting to her, and any publicity would be short-lived. She was more concerned about Lucas. Security in his African homeland was not likely to be as rigorous as in the US or England. It was a bigger country than England and much less densely populated, the police force was in the hands of the ruling party, and probably largely corruptible, the army was definitely under the control of the ruling party. She was going to have to have a long talk with Lucas once they got back to St Joe's.

On the kidnap front it was well known that America did not bow to ransom demands so kidnapping Patti to get to the president just was not going to work. Any attempt on Patti was likely to be simply malicious and would not provide political leverage. It might also be seen as a waste of resource and less valuable than other potential terrorist activities. Patti thought her greatest danger might come from an American source rather than from international terrorism.

By contrast an organised group of communists, either from within or outside his home country, might seek to gain political leverage over Themba Ndlovu by kidnapping Lucas and holding him to ransom. She thought it was Lucas who might be in greatest danger and the photograph at Camp David had increased his risk as much as hers. Only time would tell if her thinking was correct.

After another very restful evening sampling moules frites yet again, washed down with a delicious bottle of muscadet, or, rather, two delicious bottles of muscadet, the group retired to the loft and, this time, all fell asleep quite quickly, pleasantly tired from the seventy-kilometre bicycle ride they had undertaken earlier that day.

On the train back to Brussels Lucas fell asleep and Patti got up quietly and went to sit next to Charles, who had been sitting alone by the window on the opposite side of the central aisle.

"I need to talk to you," said Patti quietly. "I think Lucas is at just as big a risk I am, and I wanted to ask you about it."

Patti explained her logic to Charles who was nodding as she spoke.

"I agree with you," said Charles. "I think you're also at risk, but it's your association with Lucas that is probably your biggest risk factor right now, and that's for two reasons. The first obvious one is that you could be collateral damage in any attempt to kidnap or harm Lucas. Don't forget that someone might try to kill Lucas and then use a threat to kill Esther and the boys as a further leverage on Dr Ndlovu and his pro-western colleagues."

Patti nodded ruefully.

"But there's a second factor which you've only partly considered; white supremacists. True, Sara is not white but somehow Indian Asians are more accepted by the white supremacists than are Africans and African Americans. If someone finds out that the daughter of the president has an African boyfriend, it could light a slow burning fuse that means killing you is a serious option. It could also trigger a hate campaign against your mother. That's where the damn pictures come in."

"We just have to hope they don't make the connection. There's no evidence from that picture that you and Lucas are an item. Fortunately, there are three other white boys in the picture, and you're standing much nearer to all three of them than you are to Lucas."

"Thanks Charley." Patti sighed. "I suppose that's helpful. I hadn't considered it. It seems to me that Lucas is the key in this, and I wanted to know whether you, the CIA and Secret Service, have any eyes and ears on Dr Ndlovu. Are you watching out for Thembani? Is there any relevant intelligence coming out of Africa?"

"I wasn't quite honest with you when we talked in the Grand Place," said Charles. "In fact, I told a blatant lie. The lady I was talking to wasn't the one who had previously had a telling-off about recruitment. That all happened in Washington. No, the lady I was talking to, I'm sure you noticed she was a woman of colour, is a very smart cookie who coordinates our intelligence work in Africa. The heated discussion was about resources. She has very limited resources in southern Africa and she was reluctant to increase our presence and our activity there. I marched her through the square so that she could see you. I know she's a tough cookie, but I thought that seeing you there, sitting in the sunshine, might melt even her stony heart."

Charles paused and smiled.

"It did. You might have noticed the arm waving got less as we neared the Town Hall and by the time I got her into the chocolatery and bought her some Belgian chocolate she had agreed to send five more agents to see what they could do about Thembani and his family's security. I'll keep you posted if anything significant develops but you're more switched into security than Lucas is, so I have to rely on you to help keep him safe. We've briefed the career guys at your college to keep an eye out for him, but you're the one who sees him most."

Patti smiled. Lucas woke up. Patti went back to her seat.

"Thanks Charles," she said as she left. "And well done on the smoking. I bet you can do it. But next time I see you don't have put on ten kilos!"

Patti re-joined Lucas and the other two, and Leah decided to go and talk to Charles. Patti couldn't help but notice that Charles put his hands on Leah's as she sat there talking to him and when they got off the train at Brussels, they were openly holding hands. Charles said goodbye to them all and went off, presumably to the American embassy. The others caught the Metro from Brussels Central to Woluwe-Saint-Lambert and walked the rest of the way home.

"I quite like Charles," said Leah; as if that was going to be a surprise to anyone.

There was more horse riding and one day spent kayaking down the River Lesse near Dinant, but eventually the glorious long summer vacation came to an end. For the two linguists the time in Belgium might be seen as extra-curricular revision, for the lawyer and the engineer the vacation was just that. The beginning of October would be down to earth with a bump.

The mother of the wayward employee at Camp David did not have any African friends, and very few Africans would have known who Lucas was anyway, so, for the time being, Lucas's presence at Camp David and his connection to Patti Howland remained hidden from public awareness. This was to be the case for the next year, much to the relief of all the concerned parties.

Leah and Esther began to visit Cambridge on a regular basis and Lucas and Patti made more than one visit to the two young women at Oxford.

Chapter 7

The opposition party, of which Thembani Ndlovu was deputy leader, was making inroads into the support of the ruling party. Antipathy towards the former colonial power had faded with time and the political division in the country had refocussed on those who were pro-western and those who were very definitely against. The communists were strongly anti-western and aligned with that faction. For perhaps too long the western democracies had underestimated the importance of Africa and others had taken advantage of the opportunity to invest in and woo the regimes in power.

The eyes of the western world were, at last, beginning to turn towards the political conflict and the unrest and civil disorder that it was stirring up. The United Nations could no longer ignore the deteriorating situation there. A UN task force was set up and the blue berets were moved in to try to stabilise the country. It worked, to a point, but everyone knew that, as the election drew nearer, tensions would rise, and the violence might explode again, probably even more intensely than before.

Charles, true to his word, was keeping a watching brief and he reported regularly to Patti and Lucas about the situation on the ground. Each of the leading politicians in both factions, the UN needed to try to maintain some semblance of neutrality in the internal struggle, had been given a small detachment of soldiers to act as their personal bodyguards. This was especially important for the opposition leaders because they did not have the army to call upon. However, the number of troops deployed was relatively small, and the number of politicians involved was really quite large, so only the most prominent of the opposition leaders had protection, and the rank and file were still subjected to regular harassment, beatings and, sometimes, unexplained accidental death. There were far too many accidental deaths.

The message coming from Charles was that the pro-western groups now had significantly more popular support than the ruling party and it was highly likely that, if the election were held fairly, the opposition would form a majority government. The other message coming from Charles was that the election would almost certainly not be fair and there was already evidence of ballot rigging with the registration of several million people who simply did not exist but would almost certainly cast their votes for the status quo. President Jimmy Carter's foundation, the Carter Center, based at Emory University in Georgia, had requested access to monitor the elections and the government had refused that access.

Throughout the Michaelmas Term Jerry Gregory and Adrian met to exchange notes. It was a relatively quiet time for Jerry. Alexis Stanislowsky was getting on with a combination of married life and study, nearing the end of his PhD. His American wife, Sky, was now pregnant with their first child. Anton Stanislowsky, Alexis's oligarch father, visited for a week to see his son and his daughter-in-law. It was clear that the older man was delighted with this turn of events, the child would be his first grandchild, Alexis's siblings being a little younger than Alexis and none of them yet in serious relationships. The week-long visit went off without a hitch and its security arrangements were a welcome interlude of activity in what was proving to be a rather dull routine placement for Superintendent Gregory. Alexis's younger sister, Polina, had come to stay with Alexis and Sky in Cambridge and this added further to the security headaches of Superintendent Gregory. Polina was studying for a PhD in Development. She was specialising in the development of post-colonial Africa.

For Lucas, in regular telephone contact with his father, there was some comfort in knowing that Thembani did have armed guards protecting him, although the anxiety level was merely diminished and not completely abolished. At the end of the Michaelmas Term Patti, Lucas, Esther, and Leah all met up at St Pancras Station and took the Eurostar to Brussels.

The welcome in Woluwe was as warm as usual despite the obvious concern that the entire Ndlovu family were feeling. Thembani Ndlovu was keeping in touch with Patricia, as well as Lucas, using a satellite phone. The sort of places that Thembani was going to were often not covered by mobile networks. The government, headed by Jackson Ncube, had the capability of tracking satellite phones, but Thembani was hardly keeping a low profile and was relying more on his intelligence network, and the troops allocated to him, to keep him safe. Lucas spoke to his father on the first evening they were all together, and thereafter at least once a week while they remained at his home.

It was about a week after everyone arrived that they were sitting around in the lounge watching satellite tv. There was nothing anyone really wanted to watch so Patti suggested that they all ask Patricia to tell them what her life, and Thembani's life, was like as they were growing up; and during the immediate post-colonial era.

"Independence came quite late to our country," said Patricia. "I was very young when it came but, in the beginning, the old colonists still held most of the land. The soil is very fertile and there's a good rainy season and there's also a big reserve of fresh water in Lake Ngodi up in the mountains to the northwest of the country. There's also mineral wealth, which the western companies were exploiting. My grandfather and Themba's grandfather were both farmers with their own smallholdings for growing vegetables and other edible crops. They had cows, they had goats, they had pigs and they kept poultry for eggs, both duck and chicken eggs.

"The agriculture wasn't exactly traditional African pattern, it was strongly westernised. The influence of the European settlers, who had imported various breeds from Europe, was still very strong. Both Thembani and I were lucky that our grandfathers recognised quite early that we needed more than cooking and sewing and tending crops and livestock to give us a future, they got together and sent us to a local school which was run by the Catholic Mission. Our parents had been killed in the war leading up to independence, so we were each brought up by our grandparents.

"The school was a long way away. Thembani and I met each morning and walked seven kilometres to school and seven kilometres back each evening. School started promptly at eight in the morning, so it meant getting up and having breakfast, usually some sort of porridge or, if we had flour, we might have bread and milk, from either the goats or the cows, depending on which was producing most at the time. We might start our walk to school in the dark in the winter, but not for very long because the latitude wasn't very far south, and we had semitropical time zones. We never went hungry, but there wasn't a lot of money around and paying for our schooling was a significant sacrifice by our families."

"Sometimes we were needed to go into the fields to look out for the goats. Our country has lots of the wild animals you would expect in southern Africa; in fact, it has the big five and giraffes and elephants and crocodiles, and lots of other mammals too. It also has snakes, and I'm terrified of snakes. Most of the southern part of the country, the slightly cooler part, has been turned over to agriculture so the large mammals are mainly in the north, up into the mountains, along the central valley and over to the coastal plane. Until the troubles there was a lot of tourism there and it was a big money spinner. Our grandfathers took Themba and me there on a holiday once."

"It was magical, we saw all the large animals you could imagine, in quite large numbers, our homeland has a huge percentage of all these animals. There is a migration pattern for the herbivores, rather like the migration in the Serengeti, but on a smaller scale. Nevertheless, there are big crocodiles and there are wildebeest and zebra killed trying to cross a river. Occasionally, a lion would stray south towards our villages, but they never lasted long because the local farmers would hunt and kill them as soon as they were sighted and had made a kill of one of the domestic animals."

"Themba's grandfather had taken in an orphan, the son of one of the men who had fought for independence. The man had been in the same guerrilla unit as our two fathers, but had been killed, with his wife, by some looters during the troubles. Themba always referred to this lad, Mathula, as his brother, although he was not a blood relative. Themba's grandfather treated Mathula like a grandson and sent him to the school with us, but Mathula was less interested in study and quite quickly became more involved in helping the grandfather run the farm."

"It was a gentle but basic existence, and we might all have grown up together, gone peacefully on with our local existence, and taken over the family small holdings had the Catholic priests not started to notice us. Themba and I were good at our studies, good to a level where the priests decided to approach our grandfathers and ask if they might arrange for us to sit an examination to enter Catholic Boarding Schools near Gutare, a major town about fifty miles from our home. There was a lot of soul searching about it but in the end, it was decided that an education would serve us better than learning to manage a small holding. Mathula stayed at home to support his adoptive grandfather on the farm.

"From what Themba told me, the boys at the boarding school had a far harder time than we girls did. The Catholic boys school still had corporal punishment and they might be beaten for any minor misdemeanour. They also had to work hard on the large farm associated with the school, the farm was a major source of income for the priests and their charges. They had a long day, up at 6 to work in the fields, breakfast at 7:30, lessons from 8am until 3pm, with a short lunch break, then back out into the fields until dusk when the evening meal was served.

There were also services throughout the week. They weren't monks, but they might almost have been."

"We had a similar experience but there was more religion built into our day. Our Catholic school was run by nuns, some of whom were not very nice. We also had corporal punishment and I do believe that some of the nuns enjoyed inflicting it on us. There was one of the nuns, Sister Clare, who must have been a weightlifter in another life because getting the cane from her was likely to render you unable to sit down for at least a day."

"The residential blocks, the little chapel at each school, and the classrooms of the two schools were about two miles apart, so we developed ways of messaging between us. The Chapels had been built on slightly raised mounds so that the one was visible from the other. We all learnt Morse Code and some of the more scientifically minded pupils in each school built devices which enabled us to flash lights across the darkness. This worked for a while until one of the nuns saw the flashing lights and was smart enough to know what was going on. There was a search of both schools, and the equipment was confiscated. By then we had gotten an appetite for communication, and we didn't mean to waste the effort we had made to learn Morse Code so some of the girls organised themselves to smuggle in the necessary parts to make radio transmitters and receivers and smuggled them to the boys when there was a Sunday service at the Catholic Cathedral in Gutare."

"The Catholic Mission at Gutare was largely staffed by Americans so we followed an American curriculum and took SATs and APs, and we both did very well, which is how Themba ended up doing medicine at Pretoria; I ended up doing Economics there."

"When Themba and I went back home after finishing our training and, in my case, after working for a couple of years in South Africa, we'd lost touch completely with Mathula. Our grandfathers had both sold up and were living together in Soweto, eking out an existence in a considerable degree of squalor. The two farms had been merged by then and Themba's great-uncle was running them reasonably profitably."

"Themba and I moved into my grandfather's old house for a bit, we were fed and housed, and Themba set up practice there, but there was just not enough income, so we decided to move to the regional capital, and it was there that we started our family and Themba built up his practice, but also started to become involved in politics. Eventually, looking for additional training in his specialty and knowing that there were enemies looking to kill him, Themba arranged for our resources and the family to move to Europe. The rest of our story I guess you know."

There were six wide-eyed listeners staring at Patricia, sitting and listening, enthralled by the story.

"Mum, how come you never told us all this before?" asked Vusi.

"I guess you never asked, and, anyway, we were all too busy staying alive and then settling in here," said Patricia.

"You know," said Patricia, "before the troubles started our homeland was an amazing place to live. I think it could be again if the right people were running the country. I think that's what Themba believes too. Maybe he and his friends are the right people. Who knows?"

"I'd love to see the animals in their natural habitat," said Patti.

"Let's do it," said Lucas. "Let's plan a trip to see the animals next summer in the long vacation before you go off to do your year abroad."

"You can't do it in our homeland," said Patricia. "It's much too dangerous even in the north of the country where most of the animals are. I reckon you would have to do Tanzania and the Serengeti. If you can get away in late July and early August, you'll probably see the river crossing of the Mara River, they say that's absolutely spectacular. You need to go with an organised expedition because there are so many predators, and not just the crocodiles."

"I will have to clear it with my parents first," said Patti, "but I'd like to go."

Only Lucas, apart from Patti, knew what Patti was really talking about.

"Me too," said Leah, "but I'll have to work me arse off in the next couple of vacations and, even though you ain't supposed to do it, I reckon I'll need a term time job. I could be student bar manager at the college and wait tables at one of the other colleges. I reckon I can do a bit of silver service at one of the local restaurants too. Since Brexit they're always short of staff and yer get good tips."

"And how do you two propose to pay for this?" Patricia asked Lucas and Esther.

There was a bit of a pause.

Then Patricia grinned: "Just kidding," she said. "I'm sure your dad would want you to use some of your savings for something like this and I'll pay for the flights."

The two other boys, Vusi and Fiso, looked very disappointed.

"You're too young boys. Let these four go for now and I promise we'll go in a couple of years when you've finished school."

There was a reluctant acceptance on the part of the younger two, but they could see the logic. They argued a bit but, in the end, came round to it.

A lot of Google searches for the best deal took place over the next few days and Patti contacted her parents. They were quite enthusiastic about it and suggested that, if the group were making the trip to the Serengeti, they might also like to visit Zanzibar, and then fly to the base of Kilimanjaro before heading off on safari.

"I'll make sure that the embassy in Dar es Salaam knows that you're coming, and I'll get them to arrange a boat trip across to Zanzibar for you. You might just want to spend a day or so on the beach there," said Martha Howland.

Patti was aware that this would reduce the cost for her companions and so she acquiesced, but she felt uncomfortable about relying on privilege for herself.

They booked their trip a couple of days later. They decided to do the Zanzibar part of the journey on the way back from the Serengeti rather than at the start of the expedition.

While in Brussels that Christmas vacation both Leah and Patti firmed up on their placements for the year abroad. Patti organised a waitressing job at Richard's and Leah got her job helping to stage manage at the Theatre Royal du Parc. That both would also be enrolled in courses at the university was a given. Exchange arrangements for both Oxford and Cambridge students were firmly in place.

There was a question about where they were going to live during that year. The Ndlovus wanted them to come and live in Woluwe, but both Patti and Leah thought that it would be too much of an imposition and would also diminish the impact of the time spent in the Brussels community.

"Yeah. We'll see plenty of yer, but we 'ave to get totally immersed in living 'ere. We need to do our own shopping and cooking and washing and all that jazz," said Leah.

"Well, we can at least help you find a place to live," said Patricia Ndlovu.

Although they expressed their gratitude for the offer of help, in the end it was not needed. The three girls were riding with Therese in the Parc one afternoon and they got talking about the next year.

"I live in a flat with my friend Sandrine," said Therese. "And we'll be leaving it next summer to begin work. I'm going into law and Sandrine is going into medicine. I think we're a little older than you. If you like I can see whether the landlord will let you take over the lease. It's very good value. Two bedrooms, a sitting room, a kitchen, and a good bathroom. It is up three flights of stairs, but you're young!" Therese laughed.

"Come to supper tonight, I shall cook moules frites, and you can decide if you want the flat. Bring Lukey too if you like."

Never known for turning down moules frites, they went. They were introduced to Sandrine, Therese's flat mate. The flat was far grander than any student accommodation that you could ordinarily find and, after they had finished their moules and a couple of bottles of white wine, Therese admitted that it was her own flat, that her parents had helped her buy it to live in while at university, and that her flat mate paid rent which went towards the cost of the mortgage.

"I would be very happy if you shared the flat and paid the same total rent as Sandrine. I see this as an investment. I think it's already part of my pension fund! You'll pay the utilities and other bills, but I think you'll find it is *bon marché*. I don't think you will find anything cheaper so near to Woluwe."

Sometimes you get an offer you cannot refuse. This was one such offer. Leah and Patti would be flat mates next year.

"Therese," said Leah, "I know you're going but will you still be able to get us into the Ommegang and will we still be able to ride your 'orses."

"Of course," said Therese. "This place is my pension fund so I'm buying somewhere else to live next year and Sandrine will move in with me. We are, how do you say it in English, an item. We're buying a house together. Sandrine does not ride so I will hope to ride with you two sometimes, and both of us will be in the Ommegang, although Sandrine will be playing an instrument and not riding a horse."

A few days before Christmas, Leah and Patti departed for the airport very early in the morning, to go home to their respective families for Christmas itself. They said goodbye at the entrance and headed off to their respective check-in desks. At least, that is what Patti said she was doing when she left Leah checking her bags in at the British Airways desk. Leah checked her bags in, it was all a little slow, and was very puzzled when she wandered off around the terminal prior to going through security and saw what she thought was Patti, still with her bags, leave the terminal and get into a large Black SUV with a CD number plate.

I must be hallucinating, she thought to herself. Then she looked at the departures board and noticed that there were no standard flights to America for another three hours. *This is a bit odd*, she thought, *I reckon I'm going to 'ave to ask 'er about this. She didn't look distressed or anyfing so it must be alright, but somefin' funny's going on. And she never talks about her family much. I'm going to ask Lucas what 'e knows.*

Then she put the matter out of her mind, especially as Patti called her mobile a few minutes later and Leah asked her point blank what she had been doing and why she had come to the airport so early when her flight didn't go for hours.

"This nice American guy who knows my dad rang me last night and arranged to meet me at the airport to take me to pick up some presents for the family and for his family too, He works in the embassy, and he won't get home for Christmas. I didn't bother telling you and anyway, I wanted to come to the airport with you to say goodbye. If we're going to be flat mates next year… I just wanted to be friendly. Sorry if I worried you."

There was a bit more chit-chat and then Leah ended the call and went to get a cup of coffee. Patti breathed a sigh of relief, reminded herself to be more careful, especially around a sharp young street wise cockney, and wondered if sharing a flat with Leah next year was such a good idea after all. She determined to speak to Charles about whether she might take Leah into her confidence and whether Charles thought Esther and Patricia could also be brought into the circle of those who knew. She rather chuckled at the idea of Charles trying to put the frighteners on Leah, especially as Charles and Leah had obviously hit it off when they all went to Bruges last summer.

The black SUV took Patti to the Brussels Heliport and from there she was flown to Heathrow. She boarded a Virgin Upper Class flight to Boston and was met at Logan Airport by another black SUV which took her up state to the family cabin near Williamstown. Inevitably there were several Marines in the area providing security for the president and her family, but Patti enjoyed being able to relax in very familiar surroundings. The family had skied since they were little, and Patti took the opportunity to indulge in both some cross-country trail skiing and some classic downhill at the slopes on one of the many resorts nearby. Stephen had come with one of his friends, Graham, that Patti had met on her visit with Lucas to Camp David. Graham, and Sara, who had come with Thomas for the holiday, were relative novices at skiing so there was rather more cross-country and only a few gentle nursery slopes for them.

Two days after Christmas the others all went back to their day jobs, the medical students had very little time off at this stage of their training and the president can never be far from office. Patti was left alone in the house with Lavinia, the ever-present Lavinia, for company. Patti took the opportunity to work on the two long essays that she was submitting, instead of some of the end of year examination, as part of her Language Tripos study. One of these essays was to be handed in at the start of the next term, so this vacation was the last chance to complete it. She had been able to have some discussion with her supervisor, Professor Barnsley, about it before the end of the previous term and was incorporating some of the suggestions he had made in his inimitably perceptive analysis of her work.

Charles arrived to keep a watchful eye on her just as the other members of the family departed. Having had little opportunity to learn to ski Charles was limited to cross-country skiing which he thoroughly enjoyed. A mixture of study and skiing kept Patti's fitness levels up, and there was a small family gym with a cycle and rowing machine and some weights, which Charles also utilised over the next ten days. He also improved his skiing to a point where he could manage the occasional downhill run.

On one of their cross-country ski runs Patti broached the subject of widening the circle of people who knew about her identity. Patti explained what had happened with Leah and Charles listened intently, took a deep breath, and said: "I knew she was a smart cookie."

It was all Patti could do to keep from laughing. That statement was utter rubbish. He had hardly spoken to Leah, just gazed at her and made it obvious that he was interested. To be fair to Charles, Leah had made it equally obvious that she was interested in Charles.

Charles weighed things up in his mind. His initial thought was that the four students, Lucas, Esther, Leah, and Patti, were going to spend a lot of time together. But the more people that knew about Patti, the greater the risk that her identity would be discovered. He asked Patti to let him think about it a bit more.

"I guess you should know that we're planning to go on safari in Africa together this summer," said Patti.

Interesting, thought Charles.

"And I'm going to share a flat in Brussels for the whole of next year with Leah. Therese, Esther's friend, is letting us rent her flat for the year. We'll be studying together at the university, and I'll be working in a restaurant and Leah will be working in the Royal Theatre."

Well, that does it, thought Charles, *there is no way Patti will be able to duck the issue of identity if they're sharing a flat together.* Then, rather selfishly, he thought to himself, *If Leah knows then I can visit often without having to make up implausible excuses.*

"I think we can work this out," said Charles. "I think you'll find it impossible to have Leah not knowing about you and I think if Leah knows it doesn't make sense to keep Esther out of the loop. They're pretty good friends, and Esther will be very security conscious anyway, what with Themba and the African stuff. Thing is, in everyday conversation identity doesn't come up much, does it? It's more around when you have to go off for official trips and things, which you will do in you final year, at least a bit, if the president wants to run again for a second term."

"I think that Leah and Esther would be fine with the information," said Patti, "besides which I don't want to be deceiving them any longer. I like them both too much and I can see Lucas was having trouble talking about our trip to America without giving too much away. What about Patricia? Should she know too or is that a step too far?"

"I guess you're going to see a lot of Patricia next year when you live in Brussels," said Charles. "Can we wait and see as far as she's concerned? We can decide just before you go on your safari. By the way is there room for me on that safari?"

"No," said Patti, very firmly. "You must think we're all blind. If you came along, you would be all over Leah and Esther would be left out of things. So that is a definite no."

Charles went very red in the face.

"Is it that obvious?" he asked.

"Yes," said Patti. "But I'm sure Leah doesn't mind."

With mixed feelings Patti realised that her holiday just being her true self was coming to an end. On the one hand it was nice just to be able to relax about everything. Everyone she came into contact with knew who she was. Even the people working at the ski slopes knew her, but they were all sworn to secrecy and did not ask her any awkward questions. Casual visitors did not realise that the first daughter was skiing with them. Goggles, dark glasses, scarves, and ski clothing generally hide identity. On the other hand, she would soon be seeing Lucas and all her friends and colleagues at St Joseph's. Patti was surprised by how much she missed both Lucas and the college. She was quite proud of her first drafts of the long essays for her Tripos, and she was looking forward to seeing what both Professor Barnsley and Professor Black made of the attempts in the early supervisions that they had planned for the first week of term. For Barnsley the essay was on the use of birds as a metaphor for freedom in South American literature; for Black the essay was on the extent to which Guy de Maupassant's own experience with drugs influenced, and perhaps limited, his ability to explore the theme of drug abuse in his literature. Patti was aware that these were not original, they had been titles selected from a list offered by the faculty; they were not intended as chapters in a PhD thesis, nor even a master's; they were simply second year essays and what Patti was trying to do was to express her arguments clearly, with a word limit of four thousand words. The Barnsley essay was to be handed in in the first week of the Lent Term, so almost as soon as she got back. The second essay could wait for the next vacation to be completed; it was for the start of the third term, so was still very much a work in progress.

As she flew back to England, molly-coddled all the way, Patti reflected on the pampered life she led compared with so many others. The story of the Ndlovu's experience back home had made quite an impression on her. It was almost a relief to her to think that she would soon be back living a privileged, but slightly less privileged, existence at college. She slept on the plane back to Lakenheath. On this occasion, a USAF plane had been specially arranged to take her back and Lakenheath was the chosen destination. The usual black SUV drove her to Ely where she caught the train back to Cambridge and merged back into the way of life of an ordinary student. Lucas was at Cambridge Station to meet her. She was surprised by how pleased she was to see him.

It's growing on me, she thought, *I don't really know if it's love but I do get this funny feeling in my stomach, the butterflies they talk about, and sometimes I find it hard to catch my breath when I hold him. That hollowness in the pit of my stomach. I don't get that with anyone else.*

Lucas did take hold of Patti Jones, and he kissed her gently on the lips, but held the embrace for a long time.

Lucas helped Patti with her bags. She had gotten used to travelling relatively light. She, as an overseas student, was allowed to store her belongings in the basement of the conference building, so relatively little needed to be moved to and fro between the States and England.

A quick trip to the store to collect the belongings and then the pair went out across the road to Savino's Coffee Bar, the place where the idea of Patti coming to St Josephs had first been mooted nearly three years ago now.

"They still do great coffee," said Patti. "Sara still makes those amazing amoretti biscuits."

Chapter 8

Term passed in a welter of activity. The play that both Lucas and Patti opted for was the Lent Term musical, a great tradition of the Cambridge University Musical Theatre Society. The club had been founded in the late nineteen nineties by a group of people who wanted to raise the profile of musical theatre. There had been a Gilbert and Sullivan Society for some thirty years before a small group, wanting greater variety of theatrical performance, broke away. The particular play chosen for this Lent Term was *Singin' in the Rain*. There were two or three reasons for the choice. The first was that there were one or two particularly good dancers in the club that year, the second was that they could get the performance rights, the third was that, as one of the techies put it, "we want to make it rain on stage."

Adding in the sport that both Lucas and Patti did, the visits to Oxford, and from Oxford, socialising, and studying, meant a full-on flat-out charge through term for Lucas and Patti. Elspeth and Leah were equally full-on at Oxford.

The elections in Africa were still over a year away and Dr Thembani Ndlovu, definitely charismatic and an outstanding orator, was moving up the opposition pecking order. He had already been appointed Shadow Health Secretary and was generally seen as a likely deputy president if they won the election. With the increased campaigning came an increased danger, both to Ndlovu himself and to his family. Charles reported that his contacts believed there to be no immediate danger to the family but thought that something might be tried next year, in the last month or two before the election, especially if Dr Ndlovu's rise up the hierarchy continued, as seemed likely.

Charles took the opportunity of coming to see *Singin' in the Rain* to visit Cambridge and, at the same time talk to Esther and Leah. Patti was looking forward to the conversation between Charles and Leah; Charles was not looking forward to it.

Charles may have been a rising superstar in the intelligence world, he probably had a very high IQ, but he was singularly lacking in the EQ department when it came to dealing with non-Americans. He chose the morning after the closing party of the musical, a party at which far too much alcohol was consumed. Everyone was hungover and tired.

St Joe's served a buffet brunch on a Saturday, at around 11am, and the five of them went together to sit in the hall and eat as much as they wanted. Charles, who had given up smoking, was clearly very tense and was ignoring Leah, who felt quite hurt by it. Finally, being Leah, she met the concern she had head on. As always when she got worked up the cockney upbringing shone through.

"Listen Charles Hoi. You are pissin' me off. You 'adn't been in touch wiv me since Bruges. You ain't spoken a bleedin' word to me all mornin' and every time I look at you, you look away. Now I reckoned I quite fancied you and you quite fancied me, but if I'm wrong just effing say so and you can bugger off. I'm trying to be a lady so I'm restrainin' my language, and I shall get on with my life, just like I done before."

Leah looked down at her hands, picked up her coffee and started to sip it.

For the first time that morning Charles looked at Leah and smiled; a somewhat rueful smile.

"Listen Leah Shapiro. You are so wrong." Charles paused a moment and then went on: "Patti, it's quite nice outside so can we all go and sit in the garden and then I can talk to everyone without worrying about being overheard."

Ever since the Covid lockdown in 2020, some of the picnicking tables, which had been essential during the periods of social distancing, had remained on the part of 'the meadow' nearest to the Cumberland Building. 'The meadow' was the big open area of grass within the college between the pond and the ancient wall, that was used for tennis courts, croquet, and volleyball, in the summer and just as somewhere to walk and sit with a coffee in the autumn and spring.

They each filled their reusable mugs with more coffee and duly followed Charles out to a table big enough for the five of them to sit around in comfort. The tall buildings and the magnificent trees sheltered them from any wind and there was a clear blue sky with just a sprinkling of cloud. The wind was from the southwest, bringing the warm air across from the gulf stream; it was a perfect late winter's day. Patti was the only one who knew what was coming.

Charles looked at Lucas first.

"You're only here as a witness," he said. "You went through this last year. Round about the same time I think, maybe a little earlier?"

Now Lucas too knew what was coming. He too found himself wondering how Charles was going to handle the situation with Leah and how Leah would handle it in return.

Then Leah surprised them all.

"I know what you're goin' to tell us Charley. I've known ever since I saw Patti leave the terminal at Brussels and get into that black CIA or Secret Service Chevy Suburban SUV. She gave me some bullshit about collecting presents with a friend of 'er father's and I sort of knew that it was important for me not to worry 'er by telling 'er I didn't believe 'er. I spent an hour on the internet in the café while I was waiting for me flight, and I looked up black Chevy Suburban SUV and I found out that it was Secret Service and that the president of the United States travels in a special one. I dunno why but I decided to google the inauguration, and I got a YouTube video of it and, bugger-me, there was Patti Jones standing next to her mother who, mysteriously, had the surname Howland and was the president of the bloody United States."

Leah Shapiro paused to let it sink in. It would be true to say that she revelled in every minute of the stunned silence that followed.

"I told Esther too, didn't I, Esther? I wanted 'er to look at the video and make the connection and she agreed that our lovely friend Patti Jones is really the first daughter. We 'ad a long debate about whether we should let 'er know that we knew who she was, but we decided that it was more important that she didn't worry about us, and anyway, it makes no difference to 'ow we behave. We didn't tell Lucas that we knew because we didn't want to worry 'im. Looks like he's known all along. Lukey, bloody well done for keepin' us in the dark."

There was a stunned and amazed silence for a bit. Then Patti said: "I guess that solves a lot of my problems. You guys are amazing, just awesome."

Charles took hold of Leah's hands.

"You're very smart," he said. "I have to swear you to secrecy, both you and Esther, but from what you've told me I guess I don't really have any worries. Patti asked me if she could tell you immediately after that incident with the black Chevy Suburban and the plane times. I suppose I had better tell you two now what I told Lucas and Patti that day in Belgium when I was arguing with the lady in the Grand Place."

When Charles had finished talking Leah's comment was simply: "You jammy bugger, Lukey. You got to Camp David and you actually met Patti's mum and dad. How did you keep a straight face that day just before Christmas when she said she would have to ask 'er parents if she could go on safari?"

Patti looked at Charles.

"Charley," said Patti, "Leah and Esther are very bright but there are things they teach you on the security awareness courses that aren't entirely obvious. Do you reckon the four of us could go on a course together this Easter? I was thinking that the place near Camp David was pretty good, and I don't think my parents are going to be there much."

Then turning to the other three: "That's if you want to come."

"OK," said Charles, "I'm sure my budget will run to it; after all. If I have to fly *you* there I might as well fly three more people. And I suppose you want these other two to have some small arms training and unarmed combat."

"Oh wicked," said Leah and Esther in chorus.

"When do you have to go back, Charley?" asked Leah. Now that she had calmed down, there was more Miss Doolittle than Eliza in her voice.

"Late tonight. A car's picking me up to take me to the airfield."

"Right," said Leah. "Amuse yourselves, you lot, Charley and me have some catchin' up to do. Patti, can I borrow your room for an hour? Actually, make it two."

Once Charles and Leah had disappeared to Patti's room to set about repairing their relationship the other three sat around a little longer in the pale winter sunshine. Esther and Lucas, now that Patti's identity was out in the open, had lots of questions for her. The obvious one was why she had chosen to remain incognito; the reply was slightly surprising. It wasn't about security, it was about identity, but not in the way they all might have expected.

"I wanted to study in England. I wanted to choose my own university to come to. I wanted not to waste these precious years in being an add-on to the First Family. I didn't want the fuss and palaver that Chelsea Clinton had when she arrived at Stanford. I got to ask her about life there and she told me that, apart from having a lot of Secret Service agents in her dorm, and bullet proof glass put into her dorm windows, things were not so intrusive. Being America any ceremony she went to, like graduation, everyone had to go through a metal detector, so many guns around, but she said it was ok. She said she felt that people treated her differently. She tried to be super nice with folks, but she was never sure whether people were being friendly because of who she was or because of what she was."

"In all my own growing up, I never had that worry. My mum and dad were just smart professionals, a lawyer, and a doctor, and we were very wealthy upper middle class and so were all my friends. What I did miss out on was meeting people of a different background and I really wanted to do that at university. And then, somehow, my mother became a candidate for president, and I knew that I didn't want that to define my life. I love and respect them, and I'm very proud of what they do, but I'm twenty years old and I want a career of my own. I've seen what being part of a dynasty does to some families, the Kennedys for example."

"I decided to ask all my family to let me just go somewhere without being the First Daughter. I guess I even hoped my mother might lose the election. Not really, but you can understand what I mean."

"Do you think it was a good choice?" asked Esther.

"I do," said Patti. "It gave me all of you. Tell me, Lukey, would you have gone out with me if you knew who I was? Didn't the fact that you got to know me first mean that it was not so much of an issue between us? Even now, tell me, is the knowledge of what I am, the elephant in the rowing boat?"

"It's there in the background," said Lucas, "but because I know you so well now it *is* only in the background."

"And all the fun we've had Esther. Could that have happened if I was the First Daughter all the time? How would your family have reacted if the First Daughter arrived at their home in Woluwe? I know you and your family are all truly great human beings, but surely it would have put a damper on things. Moules frites in the back streets off the Grand Place? A train ride to Bruges? A cycle ride in North Belgium? I think probably not. There would have been half a dozen Secret Service guys tagging along everywhere."

There was quite a long silence, everyone lost a little in thought, then Lucas said: "I've been thinking about this on and off ever since I found out what you are. I didn't find it hard to find out who you are, because you were always, with me at any rate, yourself, just Patti. Even at Camp David you were still you. Yes, there were all the trappings of power but somehow you kept it at arm's length, and we were hardly aware of the security. And then, oddly enough, some of the things I had to do, like the security course and the weapons training was such fun that I just thought I would go with the flow. What was happening between us was so good."

"Would it have made a difference if I knew you were Patti Howland when we first met? I'll be honest, I think I would have run a mile. As for inviting you home, if I hadn't been able to get to know you as I do, that would never have happened."

Esther chipped in at that point, "I only know you as Patti, my friend. I think I might never have gotten that chance if you had been Patti First Daughter. I think you're doing an amazing job of just being you. I think it's interesting that you could come to university and just be whatever you wanted, Patti studying languages and looking to the future, and your past was made irrelevant by the way that you've handled things. But I have a question for you too. Does it make life harder for you that Lucas and I are black?"

Patti paused and thought.

"Personally, no. Socially and politically, probably yes. We know it doesn't bother my parents or my siblings but there are a lot of white supremacists still, and a lot of guns, in the USA. As Charley pointed out to us, if anyone finds the picture of Lucas, and my brother Thomas's girlfriend Sara, at Camp David, it could trigger a nasty reaction, especially if they identify the unknown black person in the photograph."

"What are we going to tell Mum?" asked Lucas.

"Charles and I talked about that," said Patti. "We thought we should wait a little and see whether she might need to know at some point, but for now perhaps we could keep it quiet. She has enough to worry about with your father being away. We think she might need to know before Leah and I turn up in Brussels this autumn."

That made sense to Lucas and Esther.

The sun was beginning to go down behind the tall oriental plane tree that dominated the skyline to the west. It was still winter, just, and the air began to turn quite cool.

"I reckon those two have had long enough to sort out their affairs," said Patti. She took out her phone and called Leah.

"We're coming over now. Why don't you put the kettle on and toast some of those crumpets," said Patti, and she ended the call.

"Put the kettle on," laughed Lucas. "What First Daughter ever said that? I can imagine the Queen of England saying it, but the president or the first daughter? Do they even have kettles in America?"

It was not a long walk to the first part of West Court where Patti was living, for the second year in a row. As they got onto the second floor landing the smell of toasting crumpets was wafting out of the gyp room and Charley, his hair a bit of a mess, and Leah her hair a lot of a mess, were standing there grinning sheepishly as they hovered over cups and a large enamel teapot.

"Well," said Esther, a little impishly, "hope you two had a good rest."

There was a slightly modest blush from Leah and a much bigger one from Charles.

"The funny thing is," said Patti, "if your dad keeps on the way he's going, it could be that you two are First Daughter and First Son of a President. That would be one for the books."

The five sat around in Patti's room eating crumpets, lavishly buttered and with plenty of locally made blackcurrant jam which Patti had purchased from a stall in the market square. The bed had been carefully made, neat and tidy with 'hospital corners', when Patti had left it and now it was in an utter mess.

"While we talk, you can make my darn bed," said Patti.

The conversation turned to Tanzania and Zanzibar and Charles looked so crestfallen that Esther took pity on him.

"Charley, if the others don't mind you can come with us," she said.

"But that would leave you as the odd one out," said Leah immediately.

"Might not," said Esther. "I could ask someone else to join us."

"And who might that be?" asked Lucas.

"Therese's twin brother Raphael," said Esther. "I sort of got to know him quite well when Lucas and Patti were travelling around America, and we keep in touch on Facebook. He asked if he could join us sometimes on our horse rides, but I wasn't sure how everyone would react, so I tended to see less of him when you were all around."

"Hey," said Leah, "was 'e that gorgeous hunk who visited you a couple of weeks ago and you were too busy to see me all weekend?"

This time it was Esther's turn to blush. "Might have been," she said.

Charles had to be practical.

"Before you ask him, do you mind if I check him out, a bit of vetting to protect Patti? If that's alright by you, I'll need his full name and his home address. Sorry to ask, it makes me feel bad, but I am supposed to be looking out for Patti."

"Don't feel bad, Charley," said Esther. "We all know why you have to do these things, and we love you anyway. He's Raphael Gabriel Henri du Bois de Mons," said Esther. "He lives at Château de La Lesse near Woluwe."

"Is that the big chateau we see when we go on them 'orses?" asked Leah.

"Yes," said Esther. "The stables belong to them, and all those horses we get to ride, and the ones we don't."

"Worth a bob or two then," said Leah.

"Yes," said Esther. "He's worth a bob or two."

"If he's going to come with us, he needs to know that there's a bit of a risk," said Charles. "And we'll need to get him some training. Patti, how do you feel about someone else knowing who you really are?"

"What do you think, Esther?" asked Patti.

"I would trust him with my life," said Esther.

"Well," said Patti, sharp of tongue, "that is exactly what Charley is planning to do, trust him with our lives."

"Oh look. Just go for it, Charley."

The five went together to the canteen for an evening meal and shortly after that the car came to collect Charles and take him to the airport. The other three gave Charles and Leah some privacy to say their goodbyes and then Lucas and Patti escorted Leah and Esther to the train station where they caught the train to London. Annoyingly the journey between Oxford and Cambridge, if you are relying on public transport, is tortuous. Mr Beeching closed the direct rail line in the 1950s. There is no direct bus link anymore, you change at Bedford, and it takes well over four hours. Alternatively, you can go via London and it takes about 3 hours, first to King's Cross and then, after a short underground journey, from Paddington to Oxford.

On the journey from Cambridge to Paddington Leah was grilling Esther about Raphael and Esther was interested to know how far things had moved on with Charles. On the journey from Paddington to Oxford the two youngsters got out their laptops and used the time to do a little work.

Charles visited Raphael whose credentials proved impeccable. From one of the noble families, his father was a Viscount, and he would inherit that title one day. His great-grandfather had been part of the Belgian resistance during the

Second World War. His grandfather had also worked for the resistance, although he had been very young at the time.

Raphael was well liked by his peers and everyone who dealt with him. Discrete enquiries among his friends at university, he was studying at the Sorbonne, indicated that he was a strong supporter of democracy and very pro-Europe. He had been disappointed by the decision of the United Kingdom to leave the EU but had not developed any antipathy towards the British, just a sorrow at their departure. He had never expressed any anti-American sentiments and he was strongly critical of homophobia, racism, and any other form of discriminatory prejudice. Charles sent the team the word that Raphael had passed the vetting and was now fully in the picture about the Ndlovus and Patti.

Esther immediately asked Raphael if he would like to come with her and some friends on a safari this summer and he was delighted to say yes. He stopped short of declaring undying love for her, but it was obvious that he really liked her, and was looking forward to spending his summer vacation with her. The next weekend he came over to Oxford via St Pancras on the Eurostar and all six of them met up at Esther and Leah's college. There was instant rapport and Patti was totally confident that her secret was still safe in Raphael's hands. Patti took responsibility for organising what was now six places on the trip to Zanzibar and Tanzania.

Arrangements were made over the next couple of weeks for Esther, Lucas, and Leah, to join Patti in America for part of the Easter vacation.

It was right at the end of the term, and just before the organised trip to Williamstown, via Camp David, that the first of a number of alarm bells rang for Patti and Lucas.

Patti had just come back from her morning run with her friend Vicky, had a shower and changed into her day clothes. She was sitting in the new coffee bar in the student centre in the college, having breakfast. She had a croissant, a Danish pastry, and a very large cup of coffee. Patti had a lot of friends, nobody particularly close, apart from Lucas, but lots of people with whom she hung out and with whom she talked on a regular basis. There were the other linguists; the people with whom she had rowed, before she decided life had more to it than freezing your backside off on a river in winter; the lacrosse players; the field hockey team; the thespians and the techie thespians; the other students on her staircase, both from last year and this. It probably amounted to about sixty or seventy people who she would talk to most, if not all, days.

She had just finished the croissant and was starting on the pastry when one of the other linguists, Iris White, came up and asked if she could join her.

"Sure," said Patti, and took a bite out of the pastry.

Iris put some brown sugar into her cappuccino and stirred it gently.

"I swear you are the spitting image of the president of the United States's daughter, and she has the same name as you," said Iris.

Patti nearly choked on her pastry.

"Sorry," she said, when she had finished coughing, "some crumbs went down the wrong way."

Iris reached into her bag and took out a copy of the New York Times.

"I mean," she said, "just look at this picture. I bet you get mistaken for her all the time."

"It happened once," said Patti. "I was in Boston for a friend's birthday party, we were going to a Red Sox baseball game at Fenway, and someone asked me outright if I was Patti Howland, but my friend started to laugh so that was that. I hear there are half a dozen girls who look like Patti Howland, someone said they have been coached to be doubles so that she can keep her privacy. The press is always discovering them. From what I hear Patti is studying at Yale, Brown, Vanderbilt, Harvard and Stanford and even Berkeley. She must have one of those time machines that Hermione Grainger had in Harry Potter."

Both girls laughed.

"She is very beautiful," said Iris. "You are lucky to look like her."

Patti was beginning to relax about this conversation.

"That's so kind of you to say so," said Patti. "Can I get you another cappuccino? A compliment like that deserves at least a coffee. Pastry too if you like."

The conversation over the second cups of coffee turned to less challenging themes. Iris and Patti discussed which of the long essays they were doing for their degrees. Would Patti be going home to the States for Easter; would Lucas be going with her, where was Iris going for Easter. What was Iris doing for her year abroad.

Iris and Patti had a class together that morning, one of the French classes entitled Revolutions in Writing, the nineteenth century. It made sense for them to walk together but Patti began to feel uncomfortable. Iris was pressing too hard the physical similarity between Patti Howland and Patti Jones. Patti Jones was afraid that Iris White would look harder into this and find something which unveiled her identity. Iris was as dark as Patti was fair, and she was an attractive young woman, so Patti decided to ask Iris if she had ever been mistaken for someone.

"Is there anyone you do think I look like?" asked Iris.

"Yes," said Patti, "I think you look like Ana de Armas. You have that same heart-shaped face and those lovely green eyes with a touch of brown."

Flattery will get you anywhere. For the moment, Iris was purring enough to let Patti off the hook.

Patti might have thought that the whole incident would go away but Iris was a garrulous and gregarious member of the college and, once the likeness was pointed out, several other students came up to Patti and mentioned it. It did not feel dangerous, but it became tiresome, and Patti was hard pushed not to snap when the fiftieth or sixtieth person came up and talked about it.

Lucas was more worried than Patti; Charles, when Lucas informed him, was also concerned. Charles took the step of finding one of the girls they had used as decoys, the one who most closely resembled Patti, and persuaded Patti's brothers and Sara to attend a function with 'their sister' at the Boston Children's Hospital, with full press coverage. Charles told Patti what was happening.

Patti made sure that the event was showing, live on the news channel, in the college bar as she and lots of others sat in front of the television having a drink before formal hall. There was a lot of amusement and conversation about the similarity but no more thought about identity.

After that, the issue went away, and the Easter vacation began.

Esther and Leah met Lucas and Patti at Heathrow in the Virgin Atlantic Lounge. Charles had arranged the flights and sent each of them an e-ticket. It was the first time that Esther and Leah had flown Upper Class.

The weather in Camp David, and in Williamstown, is a little cold in March so Patti had persuaded Charles to let them all go to California for the security training and then come back to the east coast in the first week of April, for about ten days, before going back to school.

They were going to take the opportunity to visit Stephen at Stanford University and, when he knew that Patti Jones was going to San Francisco, Adrian asked Patti to take a couple of presents to Ceci and Martha; two former students, who were now in their final year of med school. Patti was delighted that it gave her an excuse to take her friends to San Francisco. They would spend three or four days in San Francisco, and a day in Palo Alto with Stephen, before going to Travis Air force base for the security and small arms training.

"Bloomin' 'eck," said Leah, "I could get used to this," as she ordered another gin and tonic from the bar and tucked into a bacon butty, alongside a cappuccino.

"Wot?" she said, dripping brown sauce from the corners of her mouth and looking challengingly at the others who were all watching her with somewhat querulous expressions. "Is it the bacon?" she asked. Then she added: "I said I wasn't orthodox!"

The other three, behaving with exaggerated decorum, sipped their lattes and nibbled their Biscoff Caramelised biscuits. Leah shrugged her shoulders. Free food is free food, especially when you are hungry.

When they went through the boarding gate and turned left at the doorway, Leah and Esther both remarked that it was the first time they had turned left on boarding. Patti noticed the air marshal that Charles had clearly assigned to watch over them, sitting quietly in the seat next to the rear toilets. The configuration of seating allowed Leah and Esther, and Lucas and Patti, to sit together in pairs. The purple colour scheme and the brand-new A350 Upper Class layout was somehow very soothing and yet, as Leah put it, "cool and exciting."

Patti had particularly wanted to fly in the A350 so the team were heading for Los Angeles on the outward flight and would be flying from New York on the return leg of their journey. The flight they were on, the 10.30am flight, meant that they would be arriving in the early afternoon, and they were planning to spend a little time that day as tourists, visit Disneyland at Anaheim the next day and then head up the coast along the pacific highway to San Simeon, staying overnight in Moro Bay.

They would pass through Palo Alto the next morning and Patti would spend a little time with her brother. There was no urgency about this because Stephen was planning to fly over to join them in Williamstown, after they had completed their security training. The four students would then go on to San Francisco. Martha McArthy, Adrian had put them in touch with Martha and Cecilia Tan, would meet them and take them out to her home in Mill Valley, where she and Cecilia were going to join them for a long weekend break from their medical studies. Martha's brother, Vinnie, was away at Grad School and her parents were on a long trip to Europe so it would just be the six youngsters in the place.

It all went according to plan, and they met up with Martha and Cecilia on the Friday, at about mid-morning. The rendezvous was the car park on the Marin Headland, just over the Golden Gate Bridge as you head north out of the city.

Martha led them in convoy to her home in Mill Valley and they left their luggage there. The two medical students had a full programme of activities planned for them, starting with a cycle ride around the bay, including crossing the Golden Gate Bridge.

Martha's first ever boyfriend, Jonny, had worked in a cycle shop during their school days and Martha had managed to borrow enough bicycles for all of them. They cycled to the ferry terminal at Larkspur and took the ferry into the city.

The Larkspur ferry trip is a great way to get into the city and gives an amazing view, from the water, of most of the major landmarks in the bay. The ferry building is very close to the foot of the Bay Bridge, the other major bridge out of the heart of San Francisco. From there they cycled past Pier 39, Ghirardelli Square, stopping only to purchase some of the famous chocolates, the marina, and the presidio, and then over the bridge. It was perfect cycling weather, still and not too warm. The view towards the city from the bridge is stunning. Alcatraz, Angel Island, the city itself.

"I'm glad we done that," Leah said. "I might never come back 'ere again."

They made a detour into Sausalito and had an ice cream at the café on the waterfront. Then they cycled back into Mill Valley. They had coffee and sandwiches at the bookshop in the centre of the town and then cycled gently up West Blithedale Avenue towards Martha's home.

The second alarm bell rang that evening. They were sitting quietly in the large lounge with the huge picture window, when Patti noticed Martha and Cecilia looking at her and talking quietly together. Her hair stood on end. She was pretty sure she knew what they were talking about. Sure enough, a few seconds later, Martha spoke up: "We don't want to alarm you, but we think we know who you are," said Martha. "Please don't worry, we won't put you in any danger and we really won't tell anyone, but…" she paused: "You're Patti Howland, aren't you?"

There was a sort of deathly hush.

"What makes you think that?" said Patti.

"Well, you look like her, and you're wearing that cool T-shirt," said Cecilia.

Patti realised that she was wearing a Jefferson Airplane White Rabbit T-shirt that her mother had given her before she went off to Cambridge. It was one of the few things that she had taken with her and still wore regularly.

"Goddam," said Patti. "How did you know that?"

Martha said nothing but went to her room and came back with an identical T-shirt.

"I saw a picture of you in that T-shirt when you were about sixteen and because they are San Francisco I went and bought one, and then Cecilia got one when we went to Cambridge."

Patti smiled a rueful smile: "My first mistake in two years," she said.

"Bollocks," said Leah. "Your second. I got yer in Brussels."

They explained what Leah meant and then Patti explained to Martha and Cecilia why she had chosen to go incognito to St Joseph's.

"Look, don't worry," said Martha. "We won't say anything at all about this visit and we certainly won't let anyone know that you are at St Joe's. But would you mind if we called on you there if we come and visit out old haunts. It's pretty likely, because we still have some friends there, doing PhDs and post-docs."

"Would you have guessed who I was if I hadn't been wearing this Tee?" asked Patti.

"Nope," said the two women, almost simultaneously.

"Then I'd better make a note to leave it at home along with anything else that might trigger a memory," said Patti. "I'll get one of those vacuum pack things and preserve it for my old age."

A combination of jet lag catching up with her and slight anxiety that there were more people in on her secret meant that Patti slept badly, and she had to remind herself to be very careful not to snap at everyone in the morning. She knew that she could be very irritable when she was tired.

After breakfast Martha suggested they spend the morning at Muir Woods, the giant redwoods over by the Pacific Coast. Spectacular, mind blowing.

"Big brothers and sisters of the tree in St Joe's," said Lucas.

That afternoon they returned their hire car to the airport and were met by another of those black Chevy Suburbans which took them to the USAF base from whence they were flown to Albany airport and then driven to Williamstown. Charles had been unable to arrange the security and small arms training in California, so they were going to do it back on the east coast. He had promised enough warm clothing if it got colder.

Lavinia was waiting at the Howland home and Charles had also turned up.

There was a debrief on the trip and Charles was surprisingly laid back about the revelation that Martha and Cecilia had identified Patti.

"They are not the kind of people who talk. They have a back story too[2], which maybe, sometime, you can get the senior tutor to tell you. Or Jerry Gregory, he could tell you."

Williamstown ski resorts still had plenty of snow when the group arrived there. Only Patti and Charles had skied before, Charles had been practising since his last visit to Williamstown, so, while Charles and Patti took to slightly more adventurous downhills, all the others enjoyed the nursery slopes, and skiing lessons from a Marine ski instructor, sent to look after them by Charles. The whole group did go cross-country skiing together, although some of the lower trails had begun to melt and only those deepest in the woods and hidden from the gradually strengthening sun were genuinely easy to use. They had about a week of letting their hair down and then they were air lifted to the training base that Lucas and Patti had been to previously. Some of the staff were still there and they welcomed Lucas and Patti back as if they were old friends. Leah and Esther were greatly surprised by the familiarity in the tone of the staff when talking to Patti. They did call her Miss Howland when they were not conducting the training but during the training it was no holds barred and "shift your arse Patti" was heard on more than one occasion.

There were assault courses, training in concealment, weapons training, and unarmed combat. In the evenings there were lectures on security awareness. Charles was made to join in, which suited him very well as he was, by now, clearly besotted with Leah.

They were all surprisingly good at the physical aspects of the training and all had good marksmanship skills. Leah was the surprise package. Small, wiry, tough as old boots; the highlight of the unarmed combat training was seeing her throw, first Charles, and then an instructor at least two and a half times her size, almost the full length of the judo mat.

"I bloody love this," she said. "When I get back I'm goin' to join the Army Cadets and the Judo Club."

Charles looked up to the sky with raised eyebrows and said: "God help me."

---

[2] See "Karma" by Richard Barnes.

Charles made one mistake in the organisation of this trip. He took the group back to Camp David for Easter Weekend. The short visit to the camp was enjoyable and Madam President and Edward Howland were charming as hosts. The other family members, including Sara, came for Easter Saturday and Easter Day. Selena took some more photographs, and this time there was no confusion about the relationship between Patti Howland and Lucas Ndlovu. It was a hostage to fortune, and that, later, proved to be a mistake.

Leah, Esther, Lucas, and Patti all took photographs, but all knew that these were not to be put on social media or the web in any way. It might be quite a few years before they could be made public.

Sometimes, especially at times like this weekend at Camp David, Patti wondered if she was making too much of the need for anonymity, but it was too late to go back on that now, and the pleasure she was deriving from her studies and her friendships more than outweighed the concerns that she had, even the concern that she might be being ridiculous and overstating her case for privacy.

For Leah, the flat bed flight home was a highlight.

"Everywhere else I've bin 'as bin knees up yer nose," she said, as she put out her seat light and drifted quietly off to sleep.

Patti had been working at her second long essay throughout the trip, sneaking the odd hour or two here and there and working on her laptop on all the flights. She had also worked, after the morning skiing, either in the afternoon or evening, in her study bedroom at Williamstown. She had been glad that she had broken the back of the task during her sojourn there alone during the Christmas break.

Lavinia had the habit of "popping in to see that you are alright" and, on one occasion, had asked her point blank how serious the relationship was with Lucas. Patti had told her she thought it was very important and that they both thought it had a future and Lavinia, aristocratic, Norland trained, Lavinia had said: "I'm glad you are serious my dear, I know he is, and I thought and hoped that you were too. If you'll pardon my saying so, I really like him. He has something about him. I would call it charisma. I think he might just be a match for you. In fact, my dear, all your friends are a bit special. I think you did the right thing going over there and striking out on your own."

And with that she went over and, as she had done since Patricia Howland had been a baby, she kissed her on top of the head and said goodnight.

Chapter 9

Lucas and Patti turned up at the Porters' Lodge at St Joseph's just before the start of the Easter term. They both found dinner invitations from Jerry Gregory waiting for them. James and Audrey, Jerry and Marianne's children, were coming for the weekend, with their partners and the new Gregory grandchild, and Jerry wanted Lucas and Patti to meet them. Both James and Audrey had studied at Cambridge. James was now an Associate Professor of Physics at Oxford and Audrey was currently in a show in the West End and worked regularly with the National and the RSC. Audrey had been one of the actors mentioned in an article about up-and-coming talent in one of the Sunday papers. Patti did not know but the biggest alarm bell of all was about to ring.

Jerry and Marianne still lived in Hampstead, so the dinner invitation involved the two St Joe's students getting on the train down to London late on the Saturday afternoon. They had intended to catch a bus out to Hampstead, but Jerry asked them to let him know which train they would be catching and arranged to pick them up from King's Cross. They received one or two odd looks as they sat opposite each other holding hands across a table in the standard fare section, but they were used to that. A white woman with a man of colour, or the other way round, was still a little bit of a stretch for some people to accept. What might have caused Patti and Lucas to raise an eyebrow, had they been less concerned with looking at and talking to each other, was that one of the other passengers was taking quite a few photographs and obviously eaves dropping on their conversation. Patti had been aware of the man when she entered the carriage but had no reason to give him any more thought. Fortunately, all the eaves dropper picked up was that they were going to Hampstead for a dinner and that they were both at St Joseph's. That they were at St Joe's he could have gotten from the fact they were both wearing St Joseph's College scarves and Patti was carrying the St Joe's bag, with its crossed hammer and pliers, that was one of two that all St Joe's freshers were presented with on arrival.

The photographer was a member of the Rubinsky gang, and he was in the United Kingdom on reconnaissance. There was another interested party in the same carriage as Patti and Lucas; Jenny Taylor, Detective Inspector Taylor, who had been the first to pick up the information that was leading to the surveillance, was sitting just a few seats away from Patti and Lucas.

About three months earlier, during the height of the Southern African summer, Marine Lusinga, the CIA agent with whom Charles had been talking in the Grand Place the previous summer, had observed the arrival at Jackson Ncube Airport of a small group of Eastern Europeans. This, in itself, was not unusual, but the group had been met at the airport by a convoy of government owned vehicles and had been immediately driven away in the direction of the presidential palace. Ms Lusinga had managed to take photographs of these men as they left the terminal building and had sent them to Langley for identification. Two of the four were unknown but the other two were identified as members of Viktor Rubinsky's terrorist cell.

Inspector Jenny Taylor had been following the trail of the Rubinsky gang but had lost it in Brussels after they fled from the United Kingdom. Recently close contacts with the European police forces had indicated that several members of the gang were living in the Anderlecht and Molenbeek districts of Brussels as illegal immigrants. Other members had gone further afield, but what they all had in common was a desire to overthrow the more liberal Government of Anton Stanislowsky back in their home state. In order to do that they needed money for arms and, to recruit mercenaries and to raise the money, they had started two new lines of business; kidnap, and assassination to order.

This change of tactic had first come to Jenny's notice when the opposition leader in one of the new republics was shot during a religious festival at his local church, and his bodyguard managed to capture the assailant. The photograph of the assailant was circulated to all police forces in Interpol and Jenny recognised the man as one of Viktor Rubinsky's gang who had been involved in the Semtex bombings in the United Kingdom a couple of years earlier. From that time forward surveillance suggested strongly that a number of other killings and kidnappings could be traced back to Viktor Rubinsky. The kidnap victims almost always came back safely, but they could only speculate that a large ransom had been paid into the Rubinsky war chest. And there would have been other kidnaps that never came onto the radar. The assassinations were thought to have been contract killings, again with large sums paid to Rubinsky by one or more of the parties that stood to gain most from the death.

The report of the arrival of four members of Rubinsky's gang did not immediately cross Jenny Taylor's desk. The analysts at Langley did not pick up on it immediately. It was one of those moments of inattention which might have cost someone dear but, fortunately, Marine Lusinga was developing a network in the capital of Thembani's homeland and the surrounding countryside, which was both active and effective. Sometimes serendipity plays a hand in espionage and the development of Marine's network was, indeed, serendipitous.

Quite soon after Thembani Ndlovu's return home he had visited the farm, now run by his great-uncle, Nomusa Ndlovu. This had come to the notice of the government, and they had sent Horatio Madiba, the finance minister, with a small group of party thugs, to talk to Nomusa. It was meant to be an inquisition, to intimidate, but Minister Madiba was not a thug, he was not an unreasonable man, he was a patriot, and an idealist. As a child he had been brought up under colonial rule at a time when all the indigenous population were oppressed, and all worked together to resist the excesses of the colonial power. When the uprising came that threw out the colonists, Madiba had fought alongside warriors of all the different factions, united in a common cause. Unlike many of his parliamentary colleagues Madiba had remained committed to a society that respected all people and he had a vision of a country that, with all working together, could be prosperous and peaceful. He had a particular reason to go to the Ndlovu farm. The father of Mathula, Ndlovu's adopted grandson, had been in Madiba's guerrilla group and had, on more than one occasion, shown courage and intelligence in the battles that eventually helped to overthrow the colonial regime. Madiba believed he had a debt to pay and was relieved that he, and not some hard liner, was sent to make the enquiries about Thembani Ndlovu's visit.

Horatio Madiba, as finance minister, knew that the seizure of the farms from the descendants of the colonial power, and the period of insecurity and change which followed independence, had led to a serious diminution in productivity. Only a few farms, farms that had been run by the same families for many generations, were proving profitable and adding to the export capacity of the nation. Madiba had his own ideas on why so many of the other farms were not making the same progress. He attributed some of it to government subsidies, which were largely unregulated, and allowed the farmers to simply sit on the land and live off government money. There was an unfairness about the distribution of the government subsidies; the subsidies were given for "the improvement of farms previously neglected by the colonial powers." The one saving grace of this political nonsense was that it was only the farms of the colonialists that had been seized. The existing African farmers had been allowed to keep their farms, and, without subsidies to sustain them, they had been forced to continue or develop sustainable farming practices themselves. Not only had they maintained their farms, but they had also improved on the western farming methods, exploiting their own knowledge and understanding of the climate and the environment. A consortium of farmers from many different backgrounds had begun breeding programmes for livestock, for drought and pest resistant crops, and for new crops, harvested from the diversity of the flora within the forest areas. Some of the children of these farmers had gone to foreign universities where they had begun to research on compounds obtained from traditional medicine plants with a view to turning them into even more effective medicines. In particular antibiotics, a new generation of antibiotics, were a hope for the future.

Horatio Madiba was not about to throw away a potential catalyst for the economic growth of his country. Resurrecting his feelings of comradeship with those with whom he had fought for freedom, he sought information from this wise older man. The minister sat down with Nomusa, and Nomusa waxed lyrical about the economic potential of the country. The growing conditions, with the warmth, and the water supply, both rainfall and from Lake Ngodi, meant that their homeland should be the food basket of Africa. Prior to taking over the farm, Nomusa had been a miner up in the mountains surrounding Lake Ngodi. Nomusa decried the state of these mines.

"We have so much mineral wealth in those mountains," he said. "Not just precious stones and gold, but chrome, and platinum, and lithium, and other elements needed for modern industry. If only we could stop our internal battles and concentrate on improving the economy. But I fear that some of us have come to believe that they are 'entitled' to rest on their laurels and the laziness is infectious."

The minister listened and warmed to this man who clearly cared passionately about his country and the poverty of his fellow countrymen. Madiba asked Nomusa about Mathula, but Nomusa, ever wary, informed Madiba that Mathula had too many enemies and had fled the country. Nobody, outside a very small circle of friends, of which even Nomusa was not a member, knew where Mathula was in hiding.

"I think you fought alongside my nephew," said Nomusa. "He was the father of my great-nephew, Thembani Ndlovu."

"He died bravely," said Madiba. "Yes, I fought with him, and with another man from this part of the country."

"That would, perhaps, have been Ntando Mafana. He had the farm which is now merged with mine. His daughter Patricia married my nephew," said Nomusa.

"Yes, I knew him. I loved him too like a brother. We were all very close."

Madiba paused, lost in memories, for a moment. Then he said: "Mathula's father was also our brother, our comrade in arms. I wish his son no harm and hope that we will, one day, once again have a country fit for him, and other heroes, to live in."

It was a brave thing to say but, fortunately, it was heard only by Nomusa and Horatio, and they both knew the implications of the statement.

The visit to the farm made Madiba even more certain that he had a duty to his country to try to remain in power. The only hope, in his opinion, was to resolve the internal tensions, to remove the disincentives to hard work, and to rebuild an economy. Perhaps they would start slowly; develop a base of sustainable agriculture and mining, the infrastructure for which was already in place. Then they might attract foreign investment and who knows where it might lead. Madiba was not a saint. He was ambitious. He was a natural leader. He would bide his time and start to build alliances. He knew that there were those who would make the connections with the Eastern Bloc, or with China, as well as those who, like Madiba himself, would prefer to build connections with Europe, Australasia, and the Americas. Hanging on in power would not be easy but Madiba saw it as his duty to try.

Nomusa knew a lot more than he had told Madiba. A first meeting with a fairly high ranking official of the ruling party was not the time to start to reveal all the opposition secrets.

Mathula Ndlovu had fled the farm shortly after an incident in which he and a group of his friends had ambushed and killed members of a criminal gang that had been escorting a car containing a lot of money to the private residence of one of the most corrupt officials in the government. The friends had taken the money and used it to escape the country. They went first to South Africa, by much the same route as Thembani himself had taken; but then they had decided, as a group, to seek military training in France. The first stage of their journey took them to Madagascar. Miraculously they managed to become Madagascan citizens; passports, identity cards, everything else it took. It used up more than half their cash reserves. A further small bribe helped them to obtain visitors' visas for France. Once in France they disappeared into the Foreign Legion.

They had a long-term plan. It corresponded in its objective to the plan of Thembani and Horatio and other opposition leaders. Both groups wanted the overthrow of the existing government and the establishment of a government of reform and change, a government of economic development and welfare; the difference was that Mathula and his group hoped to achieve regime change by a military coup, while the political leaders planned a political route to government.

Nomusa sent a message to Mathula, who responded by saying that Madiba was a good man, had been an outstanding guerrilla commander, and, in most circumstances, could be trusted. Mathula urged a cautious but cordial relationship with his father's old comrade but asked that his own whereabouts not be revealed to anyone. In his note Mathula remarked that, if the opposition ever came close to power, Horatio Madiba should be included in any coalition, he might even lead it. Years in exile had taught Mathula that a military coup alone would not achieve a stable government. He was more of the mind that he and his friends might support and sustain a democratically returned parliament, if ever it came to exist.

In his message to Nomusa, Mathula indicated that he and his fellow exiles were almost ready to return and help. Should Nomusa think the time right, he should send a simple code word to Mathula and Mathula would be there, with his friends, to facilitate the establishment of a coalition force to help restore prosperity to the country.

Marine Lusinga was gradually extending her circle within the capital. She herself was of local heritage, but she was conscious that her existing contacts were from a limited cross section of society and she was anxious to extend her circle of informants to include those from across the whole political spectrum. She had begun by getting herself press accreditation as an overseas correspondent of the New York Times. It had not been difficult for the CIA to arrange for her to have that cover. It did mean that she wrote a regular column on African politics for the paper, perhaps an article every two to three weeks, and many of these were based on local politics and the upcoming elections.

The press pass gave her access to the press gallery in the National Parliament Building. This old building, in the style of the grand palaces of the home colonial power, housed the senate. It was really too small to act as the seat of government, but it could just accommodate the hundred and twenty senators who made up the upper house. The lower house, the Federated Council of Deputies, had more than three hundred members and met in the converted opera house. The committee rooms and the working offices of the deputies were accommodated in the converted barracks that had previously been the military headquarters of the colonial power.

Marine spent some time listening to the speeches of the leading politicians, concentrating first on the senators. She gradually came to realise that there was a nucleus of perhaps twenty senators within the ruling party who were more liberal and open to cross party cooperation than the remaining eighty or so party members. She also came to realise that many of the opposition senators in the house were only token opposition and were there for their own benefit. They each had an expensive government car, a luxurious government apartment, a generous staffing and expenses allowance, and a salary which was about fifty times the national average wage. This section of the opposition party was not about to rock the boat anytime soon. Marine was aware that the non-parliamentary members of the opposition party, the group to which Thembani Ndlovu belonged, formed an entirely different group. They truly were a party looking for reform.

It was quite natural for Marine to follow certain members of parliament when they left the building during the day. One of these was Horatio Madiba, the finance minister.

Madiba had a habit of taking a morning stroll to a coffee stall at one of the many street markets near the parliament building, where he would sit in the sunshine and drink a coffee and eat a crunchie, one of those South African oatmeal bars that are so much more than oatmeal, while he read the daily newspaper. He sometimes met friends there, and sometimes talked to other people who happened to be sitting by the coffee stall, asking their views on all sorts of political matters. It was Madiba's way of keeping his ear to the ground. Marine heard views expressed by some of these casual acquaintances of Madiba which were not favourable to the government. She noted that Madiba listened patiently, occasionally corrected errors of fact, but never condemned the opinions being expressed. He seemed to listen equally attentively to both pro- and anti-government speakers.

Marine did not rush things. She befriended the stall holder over the next few weeks and gradually came to be known to him as a regular customer. She declared herself completely addicted to the coffee, she declared it to be nectar, and she started to come every day. After the first few days of following Madiba to the coffee stall Marine came to realise that the visit was a daily habit and so, in order not to be too obvious, she started to come for her morning coffee at rather more random times. Sometimes her visit coincided with Madiba's and sometimes not.

Marine noted those to whom Madiba talked regularly and she began to take an interest in them. Quite soon some of them were talking about Marine to Madiba, telling him about this interesting woman who had been born in the capital, but had lived abroad until recently, and was now trying to understand the political landscape in order to represent it to the western world. Madiba became intrigued, he wondered who this woman might be. His colleagues in government were becoming more hawkish, especially as the opposition was beginning to establish itself in public estimation as a feasible alternative government. The ruling party was on notice that the opposition soft belly in the senate and among the deputies did not truly represent the political views of the wider opposition party.

Marine's patience paid off. It was Madiba who, overcome by curiosity, approached Marine one day, started a conversation, and continued to meet her for coffee at least a couple of times a week from that time on. Marine showed no signs of pumping Madiba for information. He was, for her, a long-term prospect. The conversations were kept general, non-partisan and more about political theory and Madiba's plans for the economy than about the politics of power.

It was fortunate that Marine had managed to establish these contacts by the time some of the Rubinsky thugs arrived in the capital. Marine finally decided to ask directly for information. She did not know whether Madiba was aware of the arrival of the gang members, she had formed the impression that he was holding office because of his intellect and his strategic skills and not because he was a dedicated ruling party member. Marine thought it quite likely that he had not been involved in hiring Rubinsky's thugs. Nevertheless, she decided to approach him.

She first explained that one of her friends who worked at the airport had seen a group of Eastern Europeans arriving a few days ago and wondered what they were doing there. Marine said that she knew that they were terrorists because one of her colleagues at the New York Times had investigated them previously in connection with a bomb outrage in Belgium. Marine wondered what their business was. She was just warning Madiba because they might be there to attack the government and try to destabilise the country. She was just offering a friendly warning. Maybe he could find out and then put both their minds at rest. She really didn't want to see her new friend hurt in any attack that might occur. Madiba seemed to take her concern at its face value.

It was three days later that Madiba reported back. He had no idea that this report was going to the CIA and, via them, to Special Branch.

Madiba had mentioned to the Foreign Minister, one of Ncube's closest allies, that a friend of his had seen some western terrorists arriving at the airport and had mentioned it to him because she was worried for the safety of the government. The Foreign Minister had laughed; when he stopped laughing, he took hold of Madiba's arm and leant forward very confidentially and whispered in Madiba's ear that the terrorists were there to negotiate a price for a mission that Jackson Ncube wanted them to perform for him.

"See. You don't need to worry, comrade. Those guys are going to deal with that irritating bastard Thembani Ndlovu. Not directly, this time anyway, that would be too obvious, but he does have a family, and one of our men in Brussels, where Ndlovu lives, has managed to discover that Ndlovu's eldest son is at Cambridge University, and his daughter is at Oxford. From what I gather the gang think they have some unfinished business to settle in the United Kingdom, so we have a mutual interest. Ndlovu is far too pro-western for our liking, eh comrade?"

It was this conversation that Marine reported to her CIA contacts, and it had, via Charles, been reported to Detective Superintendent Jerry Gregory and Detective Inspector Jenny Taylor. Surveillance had been started on Esther at Oxford; that was exclusively by Special Branch because there was no immediate connection to Patti Howland. Special Branch and the CIA collaborated on the surveillance for Lucas and Patti.

DI Jenny Taylor had wasted no time in starting to take precautions to protect Esther, Lucas, and Patti. And that was why Superintendent Gregory was waiting to collect the two undergraduates from the station.

As he sat in his car waiting to drive to pick up the two guests Jerry Gregory was on the telephone to the British Railway Police.

"Have you got the surveillance tapes from the carriage my two young guests are in?" asked Jerry.

"Yes sir, we have. We have a good set of images of the suspect, and we have pictures of him taking the photographs. We'll download them and send them up to you in Cambridge tomorrow morning. Do you want us to follow him when he gets off the train?"

"Please," said Jerry. It was as well to have belt and braces on this. Jerry knew that Jenny had arranged for someone to follow the man anyway, but a second person following would reduce the risk of their losing him. Jerry felt bad that there was the ulterior motive behind his invitation to the two youngsters, he would have enjoyed having them to dinner anyway, they had been to his flat in Cambridge and it had been a very good evening, but the news from Marine Lusinga had given a sense of urgency to the proceedings. He needed to bait a trap and find out who might be tasked with collecting information on, and, perhaps, ultimately making some sort of move on Lucas.

Until the train journey that Saturday evening all bets were on, but the detection of the stranger monitoring Lucas's journey started to focus minds on the strong possibility that Lucas was a target for the ruling party in his homeland, and Rubinsky was involved. It was difficult to know the best way to approach this. It was awkward for both Special Branch and the American's. Professional surveillance teams and kidnap squads would be alert to any protection surrounding their potential victims, so, for the time being, the decision had been made not to change any of the current arrangements. Jerry Gregory, Jenny Taylor, and Charles had met together as soon as the news from Ms Lusinga came through. They had decided to wait until the dinner party in London before talking directly to the three youngsters.

DI Jenny Taylor got off the train at King's Cross and followed Patti and Lucas out into the main concourse. She took a taxi to Jerry's house where Marianne, James and Audrey were already awaiting the arrival of the guests. James's wife, Annie, was holding the new granddaughter, Juliette; Audrey's partner, Justine, was also there.

Jenny was introduced to the others, she had not met them previously because James, Annie, and Audrey had all completed their PhDs and, in James's case, research fellowship, and had moved away before Jenny had been posted to

Cambridge, her previous posting before the Special Branch duties in Peterborough.

"I've prepared a bouillabaisse," said Marianne. "I asked Jerry and he said that you had no food allergies and I know the others don't because we have entertained them before. A good bouillabaisse needs at least eight people to do it honour and tonight we will be nine, a good number."

Shortly after Jenny arrived Jerry came in with Patti and Lucas and they were also introduced.

"Weren't you in our carriage?" asked Patti.

Jenny grinned a little sheepishly. *She doesn't miss a bloody thing, does she?* she thought.

"Yes, I was," she said. "Of course, I noticed you, you were the most handsome couple on the train."

Patti blushed.

"What a pity we didn't know," she said. "We could have got Jerry to give you a ride."

Annie, dark and beautiful, went over and sat on the sofa.

"Please excuse me," she said. "Juliette needs a feed and, if I feed her now, we may get through the meal without interruption."

There was a lot of talking about the baby, the usual questions; how much did she weigh, how was your labour, does she go through the night, how much sleep do you get?

The conversation flowed through dinner. There were lots of questions to both Patti and Lucas about their families and where they had lived previously. Lucas was able to be honest and talk about his homeland, his father, and life in Brussels. Patti stayed entirely in character and deflected everything towards talking about the future as soon as she could twist the conversation that way. By now the Connecticut upbringing with two upper middle-class professional parents was so routine that even Patti herself could almost believe it.

"Have you ever met any famous Americans?" asked Annie.

"I met Paul Newman once in the local drug store," said Patti. "He lived in the next town from Fairfield."

Marianne had prepared a wonderful bouillabaisse; not the poor relation that so many pretentious restaurants serve, but a proper Marseilles bouillabaisse prepared over two days. It was served with the ritual that the Gregory family always followed, handed down from Marianne's '*de Marsay*' grandmother.

Toasted French bread, rubbed with garlic, was placed in the bowls, covered in grated Gruyere cheese, and topped with a dab of rouille, the rouille made with olive oil, garlic, saffron, and cayenne pepper. The steaming hot fish stock was then ladled into the bowls and the first course was consumed.

Then Marianne served the fish, brought whole to the table. It was then sliced or picked from the bones, with more of the saffron, garlic, and tomato soup, garlic bread, more rouille, and some potatoes.

A superb tarte au citron was the pudding, and some delicious cheeses, all French regional cheeses that Marianne had brought back on one of her recent trips to visit her mother in Marseilles.

It was while they were drinking a coffee and sipping at a cognac, after the meal, that Jerry asked them if they had noticed anything strange in the carriage.

"Not really," said Lucas. "There was another guy in the carriage, and he did keep looking at us. I thought he was looking at Patti, people quite often look at her. Now you mention it Jenny here seemed to be watching that guy, but he didn't bother us and, to be quite honest, we were too busy catching up with each other to be looking around much."

"Ok," said Jerry. "What you've mentioned is highly significant. We didn't want to alarm you, but I think we now have to tell you, and someone is down at Oxford telling your sister, that we're a bit concerned by some intelligence that has come our way. We think the guy was looking at you and not Patti."

"Why would he be doing that?" asked Lucas.

"Long story, I'm afraid." Jerry paused, thinking about how best to tell the tale.

"A few years back, we crossed swords with a nasty terrorist group from Eastern Europe. At the time they were into bombs and trying to destabilise their own home country. Recently, they have started to build up funds by undertaking contracts for other dissident groups or political factions; sometimes governments wishing to destroy opposition, sometimes individuals with a lot of money and a score to settle."

"So, what's that got to do with me?" asked Lucas, knowing full well where this might be going.

"Our intelligence, from that woman Patti saw arguing with Charles when you were in Brussels, is that some of the members of that gang have recently visited your country and met with the anti-western government there. From what we can gather they've been commissioned to help to undermine the opposition and that may involve an attack or a kidnapping of either you, Lucas, or your sister."

"Ok. So that's what the guy in the train was all about?" asked Lucas.

Jerry nodded: "We think so. Jenny here isn't just a friend, she's Detective Inspector Jenny Taylor, a colleague of mine, very experienced and very good. Sorry Jen, but you know I think that about you. Nobody knows more about Viktor Rubinsky's gang, he's their leader, than Jenny. When I knew you were able to come tonight, I arranged for her to be on the train to keep a look out for you. What she saw, well, I'll let Jenny tell you yourself."

"The guy was taking photos of you," said Jenny. "He had a wrist camera which he kept looking down at and pointing at you. Must have taken at least a dozen photos so I think he was just making sure he had something to give back to the team for id purposes."

"We have a couple of people following him tonight so we may find out if there is a cell in London that he's working with and whether it's Rubinsky focussed. I do think there is a serious threat, but it may not be immediate. Rubinsky's gang never rushes things. They were slow and deliberate over the last set of bombings, and they used an intermediary to try to achieve their end. We may be watching for some time but perhaps we should give you and Esther, and Patti too, a refresher on security. Perhaps we could contextualise it for university life, as you know there are a lot of constraints around routine; although post-Covid there is much more that you can do online. Anything you want to ask at this point?"

Jenny paused and there was a short silence.

"Not so much a question as a statement," said Patti. "I'm at university for more than just sitting in front of a monitor watching some professor deliver her lecture notes at me. Whatever you come up with as security advice has to allow us to be real students and not virtual ones. Do you agree Lukey?"

Lucas nodded his assent.

"I do. If we can't do theatre and sport, we might just as well go home. We have our trackers so you can follow us. Maybe we should just send you our daytime schedules and you can monitor our movements during the day. As for the evenings, apart from theatre, monitoring us would seem to me to be far too intrusive. We can be careful about the unscheduled time; Patti and I can both vary our behaviour patterns; and we'll try not to go alone to anywhere deserted or sparsely populated."

"I get it," said Jenny. "You need some privacy. We can set the tracker alert parameters to a 3-kilometre radius of St Joe's, and we'll note if you are planning a run which goes further away from St Joe's than that. How would you feel about being armed?"

"I carry a handgun in my purse, Charles discovered that in Brussels," said Patti.

Lucas looked startled.

"I'm black. If I carry a gun I might just get stop and searched," said Lucas. "I've been stopped and searched a couple of times in Cambridge already and even on one of the few occasions when I came up to London. Stop and search is still racially biased over here, but I guess you know that."

Jenny pulled a face and nodded in acknowledgment.

"I even had to argue about my Swiss army knife, had to convince the beat copper that I was not going to stab someone with the 3cm spike for getting stones out of horses' hooves. Doesn't happen when I'm with Patti but when I'm by myself, I'm just another black kid walking around the streets at night and probably up to no good."

Disgust and sympathy spread across the faces surrounding Lucas. Nobody else there had realised that Lucas had been the victim of racial profiling in that way.

"I would still prefer that you were armed," said Jerry, who to this point had been sitting quietly letting Jenny run the show. "We can deal with the aftermath of an arrest for carrying concealed firearms. I suppose the only danger is that the police might rough you up when they arrest you; unfortunately, that's a high probability."

Jenny reverted to detective mode: "Guv, we could give him a false warrant card identifying him as an undercover officer. We can arrange that, can't we."

"Great idea, Jenny," said Jerry. "In fact, I think we should give both of you warrant cards to carry, just to be on the safe side. What names do you want on them?"

"Let's take our second names and a corruption of our surnames," said Patti. "I could be Katherine Howard."

The English people in the room burst out laughing. For a moment Patti did not realise why, and then it dawned on her. She and Lucas had been with Leah and Esther to see "Six," the musical about the wives of Henry the Eighth and

Patti remembered that Katheryn Howard lost her head, fifth in the sequence. That had probably been in the back of Patti's mind when she came up with the idea.

"So what?" she said. And Katherine Howard, undercover agent, she became, at least for the purposes of avoiding arrest.

Lucas decided to take his grandfather's name and his mother's maiden name. He became George Mafana, George had been king at the time of the grandfather's birth.

"I'll get those warrant cards to you very soon," said Jerry. "Patti, can I see your gun?"

It was a Smith and Wesson M&P Shield, 9mm handgun, weighing about 500g when fully loaded. Jerry noted, with approval, that the safety catch was on and there was no round in the chamber. Patti clearly knew how to handle her weapons.

"Have you fired one of these?" he asked Lucas.

"No Jerry, I haven't," said Lucas, still a bit stunned by Patti's revelation.

"I think it might be our best option for you," said Jerry. "I'll arrange to get one, and for you to have some training in using it as soon as I can. I'll do the same for your sister, and she can have a warrant card too."

The whole family, apart from Annie and Juliette, who were 'doing a somewhat late bedtime', was sitting around with its collective mouth open.

"Why were you carrying a gun, Patti?" asked James.

"How shall I say it? Force of habit. My parents had me carry a gun for protection in the USA as there were a few kidnappings for ransom in our part of Connecticut and a couple of girls were abducted and raped, one was murdered."

"Bullshit," said James, somewhat impolitely. "I've just remembered who you are. It's been bugging me all evening. Sorry about the swearing, but I know who you really are. I saw you once when you were a good bit younger. You came to see your brother at Stanford when I was there. He was doing a physics class as part of pre-med and I was teaching it as a visiting fellow. Bloody hell. You're the First Daughter. You're Patti Howland."

There was a stunned silence and then Jenny stepped in to take control.

"Ok, now you know. I'm sure you're all smart enough to realise that the Patti Jones aka Howland identity is currently a side show, even if it's an important one. I suggest you don't tell Annie when she comes back, and Audrey, Justine, you're sworn to secrecy too. Too bloody smart by half your kids are Jerry and Marianne. Still, what did I expect from a Detective Superintendent's son?"

"Don't worry, Jenny," said James. "We all have our secrets, and I think it would be as well to tell Annie. I have a feeling that we may be seeing a bit of Patti and Lucas before too long. I've just been offered a full professorship at Cambridge and I would naturally be going back to St Joe's. I think we might need a bit of babysitting. Besides which I could tell that Annie and Patti were getting on particularly well and given how sociable Annie is, and how much music she does in her spare time, I think we would be meeting at the theatre before too long. Sorry."

At that moment Annie came back into the room, sat down, looked around, sensed something was going on and said, rather defensively: "What?"

It was typical Annie, resolute, determined, intelligent and competent, but taking no prisoners[3].

"Patti is President Howland's daughter," said James.

"Took you a while to work that out, didn't it?" said Annie. "What got you there?"

"Her gun," said James. "What got you there?"

Annie turned to Patti: "I saw you when you came to see your brother at Stanford that time when James was doing his visiting fellowship at Stanford, and I remember thinking how beautiful and composed you looked and wishing I was blonde! Don't worry. I can keep a secret."

Annie looked around the room. *'You have no idea how I can keep a secret'* she thought to herself. Several years on and neither James nor his dad knew what the secret was that Annie was keeping, nor, if she could help it, would they ever know.

Audrey and Justine had been very much in the background during the past half hour or so when the security conversations were taking place, but, from this point on, the conversation became more general and Patti was asked lots of questions, about why she was studying incognito and about the reality rather than the artificial construct of her life. Audrey and Justine also talked about their own life plans. At this stage Audrey had made a significant breakthrough in a Chekhov play at the Harold Pinter Theatre in the West End. She had also been given a leading role in a drama series based around the unsung women heroes of the Second World War who were working in the munitions factories.

---

[3] See "An Ideal Daughter," by Richard Barnes.

Justine was an artist. A little younger than Audrey, she had obtained her first degree in Art History at the Courtauld Institute and was now planning a career move into theatre as a costume and set designer. She was studying for an MA in Design for Performance at the Bristol Old Vic Theatre School. That common point of interest for Justine. Lucas, and Patti helped to drive away the anxiety and concern engendered by the earlier discussion and led to Justine and Audrey promising to visit the undergraduates during one of their next ADC Theatre productions. Audrey owned up to having spent a lot of time in leading roles at the ADC during the time that she was completing her PhD in English at Cambridge. It was no revelation to Jerry and Marianne; they had always maintained that Audrey had done a PhD in theatre with English as a side line.

By the end of the evening, although another five people and a baby now knew that Patti was not who she claimed to be, nobody considered that this was likely to add an additional threat to Patti or Lucas. It was the gentleman on the train, and his contacts, who were the current threat, and that would be a threat that might come Patti's way indirectly, through the interest being shown in Lucas.

Jerry drove Patti, Lucas, and Jenny back to King's Cross to catch the train. Although her working life was based in Peterborough Jenny, had kept her flat in Cambridge. Her involvement in the bombings a few years earlier had given her many friends among the graduate community, especially at St Joe's, and she was currently in a relationship that made living in Cambridge very much to her taste.

Now that contact had been made Jenny was in a position to become more involved in the security of the two youngsters and Jerry decided that most future communication with the two would be through Jenny, a much more natural seeming route than through a much older police Superintendent.

The journey back to Cambridge was uneventful but Jenny insisted on escorting her new charges back to St Joe's. They invited her in for coffee and she accepted.

"Would you like tea, coffee, or hot chocolate?" asked Patti.

Jenny started to laugh, and then she told them the story of the last time she had drunk hot chocolate in St Joe's, over in the Cumberland Building, and how it had been laced with Rohypnol and what that was all about.[4] It was not a short story, but it was fascinating, and it was well after 2am before Jenny went off to her flat.

---

[4] "Karma," by Richard Barnes.

Chapter 10

Once lectures began both Patti and Lucas started to faithfully indicate their daily routine to Jenny Taylor, and she set up the perimeter detection facility for their trackers. All the trackers they had been given were monitored. Four of each remained stationary in the relevant student room but the other two moved around as Patti and Lucas did. They were not continuously monitored, but they left a trail, and they triggered alarms if the two strayed outside the detection perimeter. When the pair ran to Baits Bite an alarm would sound, but it was always a scheduled run, on the calendar, and was therefore ignored by Jenny and the team. There was one false alarm when the two decided to cycle to Wandlebury Ring, because Patti wanted to see where the Godolphin Arabian was buried, she had a genuine interest in horses and the Godolphin was one the three horses credited with starting the United Kingdom thoroughbred lines. Fortunately, it was the middle of the day and Jenny was able to look at the CCTV footage on Hill's Road leading out of Cambridge in the direction of the Ring and so hold back from sending in a serious incident team, something that would have blown the cover of everyone concerned.

Meanwhile Jenny had received the report from the detective who had tailed the photographer after he alighted from the train at King's Cross. The man had taken the tube to Finsbury Park and got off there. He had then walked to a slightly scruffy flat above a hair salon in Stroud Green Road. He rang the doorbell and the person who answered was a woman. The tail managed to get a photograph of the woman. Jenny recognised her. It was the woman who had acted as housekeeper for the Rubinsky gang when they holed up in the farmhouse up near Somersham while they plotted to kill Stanislowsky. If proof were needed that there was a serious threat, to Lucas and Esther in particular, this was it.

From that moment surveillance teams watched the comings and goings from the flat and gradually built up a picture of the occupants and their activities. In addition to the woman, identified as Natasha Rubinsky, Viktor's sister, there were two other members of the gang there, and two other males, probably African, unknown to Jenny and the team. Surveillance obtained photographs of all the occupants and Jenny arranged, through Charles, for Marine to see the photographs of both the African men. She also gave Charles the names of the Rubinsky team, including Natasha.

Marine took about five minutes to get back to Charles with the names of the two Africans. They were prominent members of the government's secret police and had track records of bravery during the campaign for independence, followed by track records of cruelty and criminality in the period after it. Very dangerous and very skilful fighters, not to be treated lightly. Just like the Rubinsky team, these two gentlemen were well capable of taking out almost anyone in single, and unarmed, combat.

Jenny accelerated the training, for Lucas in particular. Patti was already a very good shot with her Smith and Wesson and Lucas quickly improved his marksmanship. They also had a bit of practice with full bore rifles at the range out at Barton. It was offered as a treat to soften the tension of the handgun training. The two also had some time riding horses out at the stables nearby, Patti still wanted to ride in the Ommegang in Brussels during her year abroad.

Meanwhile, in Oxford, Esther was being subjected to a similar hike in security. She too received weapons training and she too was given a handgun and a warrant card in a false name. It was decided to include Leah Shapiro in the training because she was already in the know about the true identity of Patti and also understood the potential danger to all three of her friends.

Leah was in her element. She laughed like a drain when she got the warrant card. Small she may have been, but tough as old boots she certainly was. Esther felt strangely comforted that Leah too was armed and prepared, should any attempt to attack Esther be made. Charles handed over one of his famous boxes of chocolates with the tracker devices to each of the girls when he made a flying visit to their Oxford College. He did not see much of Esther, but he saw a lot of Leah. Esther wondered if the security was for her or for Leah, but she did not really mind either way.

For six months nothing happened; that is to say, no danger arose. No further alarm bells rang. Theatre happened, the Lent Term musical, 'Singin' in the Rain', happened, and everyone agreed it was a techie masterpiece. It really did rain on stage. The trip to Tanzania and Zanzibar was arranged, and Raphael visited several times as the group of friends built up their relationships. As both Patti and Lucas had expected, anyone that Esther was likely to find attractive was going to be worth knowing, and Raphael was certainly that. Gentle, generous, open minded, athletic, and intelligent; all were convinced that he would make a great addition to the team.

Exams took place in May, as always. Since Covid many exams were taken online, each person bringing their own laptop to the examination hall where, for most of the exams, a software programme blocking access to the internet was installed; other exams were open book and did not need special isolating software but did require an examination platform that the university had committed to several years earlier. 'Turnitin', plagiarism checking software, was used in all exams.

During some of the early examinations, before Lucas and Patti's examinations started, having the computers fitted with the upgraded software began to show up a number of difficulties. It turned out that the upgrade to the programme introduced a vulnerability to hacking. There was evidence that some of the computers had indeed been hacked and that key stroke software, so called spyware, had been introduced. It was the conflict between the spyware and the lock out of the internet that caused the computers to crash.

Patti heard about this from some of her friends who had been victims of this clash, having to abort their attempts to sit their exams and instead sit in isolation for several hours while new computers from a loan pool were found for them. Patti and Lucas spent a lot of time comforting highly stressed friends who felt their careers might just have been derailed. To be fair to the university the examiners were made fully cognisant of what had happened and did their best to compensate for the stress and anxiety caused. They operated a no-detriment policy for those taking second-, third- and fourth-year exams. Nobody would get a lower degree result than their best previous showing, but they could get better than that.

Patti and Lucas were not bothered by it but began to wonder about their own computers. Lucas had remarked that sometimes, recently, his computer had seemed a bit slow, and it had frozen a couple of times, but he had put that down to bandwidth and a huge overload on the college network. Now he was not so sure.

Lucas and Patti met Jenny Taylor as soon as they heard about the problem with the computers and Jenny consulted a forensic software analyst at Special Branch. She, in turn, took them and their computers to GCHQ in London where the members of the National Cyber Security Centre analysed both the machines. Meanwhile Lucas and Patti were lent identical laptops to their own, guaranteed squeaky clean, to take their exams.

Lucas's machine had been compromised. This was a potential problem because, although all the detailed arrangements for the safari had been made by Patti using her computer, on Lucas's computer there were a few messages indicating the time of the trip and the destination. Fortunately, all these communications were first names only, Patti, Leah, Raphael, Esther, Lukey, and Charley. There was no communication that gave any clue to Patti's true identity and Lucas had not had anything directly to do with booking the safari or the trip to Zanzibar; the false names under which they intending to travel were not obtained by the hackers.

At the time it had seemed like overkill, but Charles had insisted that the bookings be made using false names and addresses. It turned out to be very fortunate that he had. Patti used her Katherine Howard identity and Lucas's George Mafana alias. Charles gave her false names for the four other travellers; they were given American diplomatic passports under the assumed names. As far as the company was concerned there was an American called Katheryn who had booked various flights, and a safari, for six people, including herself, for a few weeks in the summer. The National Cyber Security Centre was currently trying to locate the source of the spyware, and the destination of the logged keystrokes, but they had very little to go on.

It was quite possible that this was a cyber-attack for money by a criminal gang.

There was a long debate between Special Branch and the CIA about whether to stop the six going on the safari but the fact that a few hundred machines had been targeted and the fact that there was no obvious link to Africa or the Eastern Bloc helped them make the decision to allow the expedition to go ahead. An investigation in Oxford showed that no Oxford machines had been compromised, and this was taken as further proof that the targeting had been opportunistic and malicious and not aimed at Lucas. A couple of attempted fraudulent transactions on Lucas's credit card, and on cards of several other people whose machines had been hacked, tended to support the analysis.

Patti and Lucas kept their new machines. They had already saved anything academically important to the cloud, so the transition to the new computers was seamless.

It was Viktor Rubinsky who had arranged the hack, through a Russian criminal gang with which he had links. He was disappointed that he had obtained so little useful information, but he did now know that Lucas Ndlovu was going in a party of six to the Serengeti and to Zanzibar. He knew the dates of their trip because Lucas had mentioned them in his communications with the others; he knew the first names of all the travellers; he did not know their surnames. Most importantly, he did not know the names under which they were travelling. The company was well-known and reliable, and it provided sample itineraries on its website. Rubinsky had no reason to believe that the six would deviate from the general pattern of the company's holidays. He could expect them, at some point, to head for Lake Manyara and one of the three safari camps that the company used in that region of the Serengeti. The one thing Viktor did have at his disposal was an extensive network of thugs. Viktor arranged for extra surveillance on Lucas. He knew that a KLM flight towards the end of July was going to have six young passengers on board, one of which would be Lucas Ndlovu. Viktor was not particularly interested in the other passengers. He was a little intrigued to know who this Patti was that Lucas was in email correspondence with, but there were a few other young ladies, mainly connected with the theatre, that Lucas had sent emails to, so Viktor just assumed that Lucas was 'playing the field'. Viktor would make sure that some of his people would be on the same KLM flight. There could not be that many groups of six youngsters heading for Dar es Salaam on the date in question.

The examination results came out at the usual time. For the second year in a row, both Patti and Lucas had first-class results and Leah and Esther, in the true Oxford tradition, would have to wait until their final year before having any further examination results to show for their studies.

Full term ended on the Friday of the third week of June and Patti and Lucas went to the St Joseph's May Ball on the Sunday. In addition to their studies and to helping with the scenery for one of the Easter term plays Patti and Lucas had both been involved in designing and constructing the decorations for the ball. The theme of the ball had been 'Paradise' and, taking cognisance of the Chinese saying "above, there is heaven; below, there are Suzhou and Hangzhou" they had built a mock-up of one of the bridges in the garden of the humble administrator in Suzhou, and turned the island in the middle of the pond, not usually accessible, into a teahouse. There were beautiful Chinese lanterns and colourful drapes and lots of little Chinese snacks. Ordinarily the head gardener would not have allowed this to happen, but he had made plans to reclaim this part of the garden for a special arrangement of his own design, he thought the island was an underexploited feature of the grounds, and so he was not unhappy to have helped to clear the way for the planting that he had planned for the autumn. An intelligent and knowledgeable man, the college governing body was happy to give him his head and knew that something special would come from it.

On the Thursday after the May Ball Patti flew home to America. It was one of those flights that Charles had arranged; secret and private, using USAF aircraft flying out of Mildenhall. She spent a week with her brothers at the Williamstown property, generally relaxing; hiking, fishing, and camping out on one of the trails in the woods to the north of their home. Thomas and Sara, who were now planning their wedding day, were waiting for Patti when she arrived on the Thursday evening, and Stephen and Graham joined the others for the last seven days. It was, by now, becoming more obvious that the relationship between Stephen and Graham was a little more than just friendship and the other members of the family, including Madam President and Edward, were pleased for them both. Martha and Edward joined the family for the last weekend of Patti's stay.

Chapter 11

For both Patti and Leah, the arrangement to spend the third year of their studies in Brussels had been confirmed. When Patti flew back from New York she travelled with Charles as an escort and they caught the Eurostar from St Pancras to Brussels, meeting up with the other members of the expedition at the Gare Bruxelles Central. Leah, Lucas, and Esther, having travelled to Woluwe earlier that week, had already collected Raphael, and it was he who drove them all to the Château de La Lesse, his family home. Therese and Sandrine were also staying at the château, and it was from there that the expedition would leave in the last week of July. They were flying KLM from Amsterdam, intending to take the train to Amsterdam and spend a couple of days there before their departure; Patti wanted to see the Anne Frank Museum, the Van Gogh Museum, and take a canal cruise, and do anything else they had time to fit in. The flight would touch down at the base of Kilimanjaro on the way out, the return trip would be via Nairobi.

During the time in the Serengeti there would be a couple of transfers by light aircraft between Dar es Salaam and Arusha, at the foot of Mount Kilimanjaro and then Arusha to an airfield near the northern end of Lake Manyara. From there they would explore the Ngorongoro Crater and then head into the Serengeti National Park for a few days before flying back to Dar es Salaam by light plane from the Manyara Airport. The trip to Zanzibar, with relaxation on the beach, would follow the safari.

Charles was very concerned about the difficulties of maintaining security; in particular it would not be easy to ensure that the group was armed and Charles, cautious in a sensible way, was sure that this was necessary. He was not worried about the wild animals, that was the remit of the safari organisers, but he was worried that they might not have covered all the angles after discovering the problems with the computers in Cambridge. He was not yet convinced that no harm had been done by the breach of security; he was not convinced that it was an entirely random event; and in this he was correct.

In the flat over the hair salon in Stroud Green Road the Rubinsky and African conspirators were digesting the information they had received from Lucas's computer. They now had a good idea of the complete itinerary for the trip and were trying to decide where the best point of attack to try to kidnap Lucas might be. The Ngorongoro Crater has limited ways in and out and therefore did not look promising as a kidnap venue. The obvious place to attempt a kidnap would be during the time when the group were staying in the Serengeti National Park in a camp with canvas tents. There were good reasons for this choice. The first one was that there were many routes away from the camp leading to some dirt airstrips nearby; a light plane could remove Lucas and his captors before those on the ground could move quickly enough to close off their escape routes. The second reason was that the group were planning to spend several days in the park, exploring the region in their vehicles, but also taking one or two opportunities to walk, with Maasai guides, across the Serengeti scrub land. Finally, there were lots of tourists around in their Land Cruisers: another Land Cruiser in the area would not attract attention, especially if it were to be driven by an African and carried touristy looking white passengers.

Charles arranged for Smith and Wesson pistols for each of the members of the expedition to be taken to the camp in the Serengeti National Park. He also arranged, with Marine Lusinga, for two assault rifles to be available to the group once they left the Ngorongoro Crater. Charles would take one and Patti the other, as they both had the most experience with weapons. The decision not to arm the group before Ngorongoro was based on the same logic as was used by the potential kidnappers, too many people, too few exit routes.

Back in Brussels Leah and Patti had already moved many of their somewhat limited belongings into the flat in Rue des Erables in Etterbeek. Sandrine and Therese showed them around, showed them how everything worked, including all the appliances. They also learnt where the nearest supermarkets and other essential shops were and rehearsed their journeys to the Theatre Royal du Parc, the university, and Richard's restaurant, where Patti would be working. This part of their lives was then put on hold until the return in the autumn.

Charles took Patti by herself one day to the USAF base and gave her some practice with the particular model of assault rifle that was going to be left for her in the Serengeti. He had her practice with a special sniper's sight that could be attached to the weapon if needed. He also, not wishing to alarm Lucas, suggested to Patti that there might be more danger than previously anticipated and told her to assume that every part of their itinerary was known to a potential kidnapper.

"Ok," said Patti. "What's the profile of the likely attackers? Is there any help you can give me so that I can help you look out for trouble?"

"Not really," said Charles. "I'll get you photographs of the people we know are in London in the house where that photographer guy lives. I'll get you pictures of all the known members of the Rubinsky gang, since we think it might be they who've taken a commission to kidnap Lukey. I seem to recall you're pretty darn good at remembering faces. The other thing is that I don't expect trouble until you get into the Serengeti itself, or until you get back to Zanzibar. In the Serengeti there's scrub and some nearby dirt airstrips, and Zanzibar has a long coastline, so a quick getaway from either of those places is possible. Ngorongoro is too contained to allow easy kidnapping, and it's kidnapping that we are anticipating, although some of the others may get hurt in the process."

Patti thought about it and put it into her memory banks. She would relax until they got to the Serengeti and Lake Manyara.

So that is how they left it. They decided not to say anything too much to the others, except to warn them to be extra careful. They decided to come clean about the *possibility* that the entire itinerary had been leaked and could be in the hands of a potential enemy, but to play down the *probability* that this was the case.

With growing excitement, the six youngsters rode horses, went out to dine together, often with Therese and Sandrine along too, and simply enjoyed each other's company. They spent quite a bit of time with Patricia and the two younger siblings at the house in Woluwe. The two younger boys still did not know the true identity of Patti and it was comforting to her to find that there was no slip up with regard to identity from those who did know. Therese, and Sandrine were also unaware of the true family connections of their riding companion.

At last, the time came for the train journey to Amsterdam, complete with soft frame bags of quite limited size. There was more efficiency in packing than any of the youngsters were used to. Lots of the clothing was that special fabric which is said to wick moisture away from the body and which contains antibacterial treatments to reduce the odours of fermenting body sweat. Good hiking boots, with high ankles to protect from sprains, and suitable double layers of socks for blister protection, were also the order of the day. In addition to the soft frame bags, that were destined for the cargo bay, each of the group had a sensible sized rucksack, with a couple of changes of light clothing, and enough of the essentials to get them through a few days if their bags were to go missing. All young, fit, and healthy, they did not need medicines, apart from the antimalarials that they were required to take for the safari part of their trip. They did all have DEET wipes in their rucksacks; they had packed the DEET spray, along with the mosquito nets, in their main luggage.

The couple of days they spent in Amsterdam passed pleasantly enough. The touristy things they had planned to do were enjoyed by all of them. Patti went to the museum shop, just a few minutes' walk from the Anne Frank house, and arranged to send some special double tulips back to her parents for the house in Connecticut, using a postal address that was a CIA safe house. Charles would arrange for the tulips to reach their destination. She also sent some very beautiful delftware for Thomas and Sara as an early wedding gift, and some vintage Gouda and Edam to Stephen and Graham, just because medical students are always hungry.

Waiting at the airport for the flight to Dar was no chore. They were travelling business class and so had the ability to sit in the comfortable KLM lounge, relax, and talk, prior to boarding the flight. The flight was not full; particularly in the business class seats there were lots of gaps. There were two large and stern looking gentlemen sitting together either side of the aisle at the back of the cabin and Patti did wonder if they were air marshals put in place by Charles, but Charles said not. Even so Patti was suspicious of them and observed them carefully, committing their faces to memory, you can never be too careful.

The journey from Europe to Africa involves minimal time zone shifts so the arrival in Dar es Salaam did not involve a major element of jetlag, just a bit of travel weariness. The flight touched down in Nairobi, doubling as a service to both of the East African capital cities, but the passengers to Tanzania remained on the plane, and felt only the heat from the tarmac as the door was opened to allow the passengers remaining in Nairobi to disembark.

For most travellers the visas for Tanzania and Zanzibar are obtained at the airport by paying the relevant visa fee. Passengers wait in a long queue to pay their dollars and get the stamp. In the queue, just in front of the group of six, were the two large men that had attracted Patti's attention. She noted, with interest, that they had Russian passports. Patti was not near enough to see their names, but she did manage, when they were not looking, to get a photograph. When they compared notes afterwards Charles had also managed to get a photograph of the men, so they sent both versions off to the CIA and Special Branch to see if their identities were known to the intelligence agencies. At the CIA end this request for identification was not given a high priority. It is difficult to say whether, if it had been, things might have turned out differently.

There is no word in Swahili which conveys the urgency of the word 'mañana' in Spanish. Fortunately, Patti and the others had diplomatic passports, and had obtained eVisas in advance. It was very late when the group had finally collected their baggage and left the airport. Some of the ordinary passengers were still queuing to get their single-entry visas issued on the spot!

The friends were staying at the home of one of the American diplomats based in Dar and she had nobly waited up for them.

"I expect you observed the usual highly efficient and high-speed processing of visas at the airport?" The Deputy Chief of Mission, for that was her rank, posed it as a question, but it was very much rhetorical.

The American embassy is about a kilometre inland and in the morning the six woke early and, before it became too hot, shook off their travel legs by going for a brisk run along the beach and looping back along a parallel road. There was a day to kill before the light aircraft would fly them off to Arusha so they took a boat ride out to Changuu Island to see the giant tortoises and enjoy some seafood at the beach barbecue.

The tortoises came first, huge, and very old. The oldest on the island was believed to be over 140 years old but there were several similar aged veterans. Slow, deliberate in their movements, eating their way steadily through the vegetation; it was impossible not to admire these giant reptiles and their persistent hold on life.

The group moved to the beach on the north of the island, to relax under the canopies and eat fresh cooked, and very cheap, lobster and chips.

"You don't want to look into the kitchen," said Lucas, who had just done so, "but I'm thinking that the hot oil and the grill will deal with any issue, I just wouldn't eat the salad."

Sure enough, the chips were tasty, and the lobster was remarkable; but maybe any sea food that has hardly had time to get its feet dry and is eaten as you sit under a clear blue sky, sipping ice cold lemonade and looking at a turquoise ocean, maybe any food eaten like that is just a little special.

The rickety island ferry returned just as the sun was going down and they took the short journey back to the Harbour as one of the most glorious of sunsets lit the sky with orange and red tones. Patti and Lucas sat together in the bow experiencing the cooling spray as the boat dipped up and down in the ocean swell. It was a good moment; it was a memory that would last.

They were given a light supper in the embassy dining room and turned in early for the night. The flight next morning was at 7am and, although it was an internal flight, they were still required to be at the airport two hours before the flight was due to take off. The airport is not an easy ride out of Dar, although some of the worst bottle necks on the road from the centre have been more recently dealt with, so they would be getting breakfast, or at least a cup of coffee, at about 4.00am. They would be rising in the dark, quite a contrast from the European summer they had just come from.

Some of the smart casual items in their luggage were left at the embassy for collection upon their return from the trip. They were travelling as light as possible. They all had those Tilley hats, khaki and in the original style, to keep the sun off their heads and Patti, the lightest skinned among them, had a lot of sunblock packed away in her rucksack, factor 50-plus. The plane was a fourteen-seater, the modified version of a Cessna Grand Caravan 208b. It was noisy and exciting, and seemed constantly very close to the ground, but the land it flew over had not many features and the views from the airplane were dominated, in the last half of the journey, by the towering peak of Mount Kilimanjaro, still topped in white from the most recent snow falls. Patti, mentally, added Kilimanjaro to her 'to do' list.

Touch down and disembarkation was swift and, perhaps unusually, the GlobalAir connection to Lake Manyara was loaded and the passengers transferred within the hour. The second half of the journey was much more interesting. They flew over the terrain they would be exploring in a few days' time and saw many thousands of the migrating wildebeest and zebras that they would see much more closely during the days to come.

The landing on the dirt air strip at Lake Manyara was not as smooth as the landing of your average Jumbo Jet but it was no worse than a slightly bumpy traverse of an English road after a bad winter. They transferred to a Land Cruiser and were driven to a lodge on the rim of the Ngorongoro Crater where they settled down for the evening with a gin and tonic, or two, and a pleasant enough evening meal, picking selectively from five courses; catering for the richer and older tourists who would be tackling this experience rather as if they were on a cruise in the Mediterranean. Driving around the crater the next day was a carefully choreographed experience. The tour guides were all in radio contact pointing out to each other where a particular type of animal had been seen. That way everybody on the crater floor managed to see the full catalogue of animals. The rarer species, the leopard, and the wild dogs, for example, were seen by everyone because of the radio contact. The majority of the groups managed to see two lionesses dragging a wildebeest that they had killed out into the shallows of the lake on the crater floor to keep their kill away from the jackals and hyenas that were eyeing up a free meal. Only Patti's group saw the dramatically exciting chase and kill; it was their courier who called it in for the other guides.

That evening, as they sat contemplating the next stage of their journey, they all agreed that it had been interesting, but they also felt that it had been more like sitting in a three-dimensional version of a National Geographical documentary than going on safari. They hoped that the next stage of their journey would bring a more realistic view of the ecosystems in the Serengeti. Be careful what you wish for; be very careful.

The next morning the journey onward to the tented camp was made in another Land Cruiser; the driver headed northwest into the Serengeti National Park along unmetalled dirt roads. The large vehicles kicked up dust behind them as they travelled. The youngsters were not quite sure why, but it all felt more real than the Ngorongoro experience. It seemed to them that the crater of the Ngorongoro volcano had created a partially isolated environment in which the ecosystem had somehow come into balance; it was rather a stable ecosystem. Out in the plains of the Serengeti the seasonal changes and the mass migration presented a much more dynamic picture of life in pre-colonial Africa. The occurrence, intermittently, of Maasai villages added to the sense of reality that this part of the journey imparted.

The first sight of large herds of elephants or a great tower of giraffes is quite mind blowing. The group spent the rest of the journey trying to outdo each other in sighting the next interesting mammal or bird, nobody was that keen on watching out for reptiles. Part of the game they played was to try to remember, and then, if necessary, look up, the collective noun for each animal group. It was confusing that several different collective nouns might refer to a single species and sometimes two species shared a collective noun.

It was all still very armchair tourism, and the group was beginning to become impatient, wanting some physical activity to offset the sitting in the vehicle. It was small wonder then that, when they arrived at Camp Kilimana, having dumped their belongings in their relevant tents, they looked for something to do.

There were several other tourists at the camp. Most of these tourists were older Americans, ticking off one of their bucket list 'to-dos'. There was one young American couple on their honeymoon. To say that the young bride was inappropriately dressed would be an understatement. Fortunately, the camp manager was able to sell her a pair of canvas walking boots, for an exorbitant price, which enabled her to reserve her stiletto shoes for evening use in the camp canteen. and her flip-flops for use in her own bedroom. A list of possible activities was posted on the camp noticeboard and one which appealed to the European group was a hike, through the scrub terrain, with a Maasai guide, to a Maasai village about 10 kilometres distant. Not surprisingly it was only the six youngsters who signed up for this for the following day. The warmth of the midday sun meant that they would start early and rest up in the Maasai village before walking back by a slightly shorter route in the late afternoon.

Charles disappeared briefly into the manager's office and collected a parcel that had been left for him. It contained, as everyone guessed it would, the weapons and ammunition that Marine Lusinga had arranged to have deposited there. These weapons were checked, loaded, and placed into everyone's small backpacks, along with some energy bars and water bottles for the hike the next day. The two rifles were specially modified semiautomatics, with detachable snipers' sights, which could be folded small and were light weight, small enough to go into Patti's and Charles's back packs.

The next morning, while the early mist was beginning to clear, they set out with their Maasai guide and an armed escort, also a Maasai. The Maasai guide was tall and elegant and spoke excellent English. He carried a traditional Maasai spear for protection and wore the bright red robe which is the traditional garment of his tribe. As they walked through the scrub it soon became clear that these rather low woody plants formed a serious obstacle to progress since they had no real distinguishing features, one bush from another, and were sufficiently densely packed to prevent anyone walking amongst them getting a clear idea of the terrain. It seemed to them all that the Maasai guide had a miraculous understanding of the pathway, he clearly knew where he was going, and they simply followed. At several points the guide stopped to point out some of the trees and shrubs important to his tribe and what uses they were put to. There seemed to be four main uses for these trees and shrubs. Plants used for medicine were pointed out by Nampazo, the Maasai guide. That some of the rather thorny acacias were used for fencing to deter predatory animals seemed a sensible option to the eagerly listening tourists. On the subject of the medicinal uses Nampazo explained that the roots of various plants were most used, followed by bark and leaves, and that they were often pounded and crushed and then prepared by boiling in water. Sometimes they were burnt before use, and sometimes they were added, almost like herbs, to meat stews prepared partly as food and partly for medicinal reasons. The names of the plants, which Nampazo told them in the Maa language, were soon lost to them, but it was nevertheless clear that the Maasai had a great respect for these traditional medicines, not only because of tradition but also because distances to get western style treatments, and the poor availability of and high cost of western style drugs, made that sort of medicine almost inaccessible. Nampazo pointed out a particular tree the leaves of which, when properly prepared, could make a tea which relieved pain. Patti tried to remember what it looked like, but retaining the name was beyond even her linguistic capability.

All the while, as they walked, they found evidence that animals had been along the trails they were following. Both Nampazo and the Maasai soldier following in his army uniform were constantly warning the group to stay closely bunched and to make enough noise to frighten away any large predators. There was evidence that lions had been through this route in the very early morning and the two Maasai were anxious to reach the village and impart this news to their fellow villagers, warning them to be careful not to stray too far from the village with their cattle in search of grazing.

The walking was moderately challenging but not severe. There were only a couple of very steep descents to small streams at the foot of narrow valleys carved in the gentle hillsides, followed by equally steep ascents back onto the ridges along which most of the journey took them. Patti, Charles, and Leah had compasses. Leah had said: "I was in the army cadets at school, and we would never go walking without a map and a bloody compass."

Patti and Charles also had maps. Not paper maps, but ones downloaded to their satellite phones, which also had GPS capability. Charles and Patti had spare power banks and Leah was carrying a solar powered charger. It all seemed overkill, especially when they reached the Maasai village without incident. The general direction of their walk had been south and east, south along the ridges and east across the valleys.

The arrival of groups of tourists was clearly very important in the economic life of the village. The group were aware that later in the afternoon several of the more sedate tourists, and probably the young honeymoon couple, would arrive by Land Cruiser to experience "life in a Maasai village" and take lots of photographs to bore their families and friends witless with on their return to their homelands.

Somehow the hikers were greeted differently. There was a little more respect for those who had walked the ten kilometres through the scrublands. True, the Maasai children regularly walked six kilometres each way to school, when school was running, but this was not about bragging rights; it was about making money. Respect went a long way to gaining friendship, and friendship went a long way to extracting a greater contribution from their visitors. Even so, the prices charged to those who 'walked the walk' were a little lower, and the items offered to them were especially beautiful.

The ritual upon arrival was for Nampazo to distribute the six in pairs to three of the Maasai homes to enter the Maasai huts and see the women preparing the evening meal. It was very dark inside the huts, made of mud and cow dung, and the smoke from the fires stung the eyes. The sleeping areas and the eating areas were explained. The small, cramped space was challenging to the Western sense of fairness. Why did these noble and generous people live in such circumstances? How little they had and yet how appreciative they seemed of what the earth was giving them.

The next part of the routine was for the tourists to reassemble as a group and be taken round the various huts in the village. Outside each of the huts was a young woman selling her wares. The Maasai traditionally make beadwork, sometimes now with glass beads, but originally with seeds, dried and hardened, and dyed with locally sourced pigments. The tourists are expected to purchase some of these and all six of the group obliged, taking only small beadwork objects like bracelets and necklaces. Traditionally red is the major colour of Maasai clothing, they believe it frightens away wild animals, and each of the young women bought Maasai cloaks in the brightest red fabric, to wear on the journey back to base camp, and to give as gifts on their return home.

The Maasai children were fascinated by Patti's blonde hair and fair skin and lined up to hold her hand as she walked round the village. All the children wanted photographs taken with her and she promised to print out copies that evening at the camp, there was a printer there, and have them sent back with the next tourist visitors.

Two large Land Cruisers turned up shortly after this and the Maasai put on a dancing and singing display for the whole group. The traditional Maasai men's jumping display happened, and all six of the young visitors were persuaded to join in, much to the undisguised amusement of the indigenous population; but there was good-humoured banter and, before the later arrivals went on their shopping expedition around the village, the hikers began their return journey. While the souvenir hunters were about their business a third Land Cruiser came past the village and headed off in roughly the direction that the hikers had taken.

The six hikers and their escort were deep into the scrub about two kilometres from the village and, according to Nampazo, about seven kilometres from Camp Kilimana when the first shot rang out. The Maasai soldier dropped dead instantly and the whole party threw itself on the ground. Lucas crawled over to the dead guard and took his rifle. The girls, wearing their bright red cloaks, removed them immediately and put them into the camouflage fabric rucksacks that all had been carrying. Nampazo moved, once too often, and he too was shot dead by a volley from an assault rifle.

The six hikers were alone. Deep in the bush, unable to pinpoint the direction of the enemy, and debating among themselves exactly how they were going to get back to civilisation. The obvious thing was to go back to the Maasai village and hide out there, but the attackers had clearly followed the group from that direction, they had shot the rear-guard first, so going in that direction was probably not the number one choice. Going forward would lead to a longer journey to safety but might, indeed almost certainly would, be a better option. But before going anywhere they needed to regroup and find somewhere out of rifle shot to talk and plan. They had noted earlier the peculiar character of the terrain, the long ridges all running north south with the steep, water eroded, valleys between the ridges. The obvious thing to do was to move east or west into a different river valley and pick up a different north south ridge to move carefully along. Charles signalled to the others to move in the westerly direction, and they crawled on their bellies up the hillside and over into the next valley. Before he left Lucas went over again to the body of the dead soldier and went through all his pockets looking for anything useful. There was a good Swiss army style knife, a machete, some matches, a torch, a compass, and some more ammunition, all of which Lucas gathered into his rucksack and, conscious that he now had a higher profile than he would like, he too crawled on his belly over into the next valley.

The shocked party met at the bottom of that valley by the tiny stream flowing there. Both Patti and Charles unpacked and assembled their rifles, there were now three rifles and six handguns making up the armoury of the group. They had no idea how many attackers there were, and they had not caught sight of any one of them.

"We have to get back to the camp," said Charles. "Patti, you have a rifle. While the rest of us work out a route back to the camp will you climb up to the top of the valley and keep a look out. Everyone, make sure your satellite phones are on silent. Patti, if you see anyone coming call us but stay up on the ridge if you can and cover us. We'll pinpoint our position using the GPS; we'll make a satellite call to the embassy and to the local ranger force: and we'll plot a route back to the camp. Once we have that sorted, we'll come up to join you. We were heading west when Nampazo was shot so go to the west side of this valley and take first watch. Leave the safety catch off once you get in position."

Patti climbed quickly up the hillside and settled herself, with her back to a deserted termite mound, looking out over the length of the valley. She could see the others poring over the mobile phone map and she watched Charles make a number of telephone calls. There was no obvious movement elsewhere in the bush.

After about five minutes the group of five gathered up their belongings and formed a line three in front, two behind, about five metres between each person. They climbed the hillside in that formation, maintaining their separation and constantly checking up on each other. They found Patti at the top of the ridge.

"The embassy says they have no ground forces here, other than the small embassy guard in Dar, and there are no goddam US helicopters nearer than Djibouti, and it'll take about 24 hours to get the necessary flight path clearances to get to us, so, until then, we're on our own as far as the USA is concerned. The local police force and the park rangers are all out in the park hunting poachers. They're in various all-terrain vehicles and are pretty unlikely to get to us before the helicopters. I gave our current position, and they asked us to report in every hour with our new position. Looks like getting back to the camp is our only option. So, let's get moving. I suggest we move in two groups. Leah, you go with Lukey and Patti; Raphael and Esther, you come with me. I have the route on my phone so I'll lead. Leah, you have the route on your phone too so, if we get separated, you just follow it. I reckon we have four hours to darkness, and we have about six or seven kilometres to safety. It's going to be tight. Have you all got head torches?"

There was a general murmured acknowledgement that they all had their head torches and that they had not so far used them. It should give them an extra hour of walking if needed.

There was no more action on the route back towards the camp. Charles's group led and Leah's group followed about ten yards behind. They were moving mostly from east to west so that they met up on the top of each ridge. It was slow going but necessary. They did not want to get separated, nor did they want to form a single group that might have been ambushed.

The GPS navigation proved essential; one bit of scrubland looked like any other bit of scrubland. They ate some of their power bars as they walked, and they drank most of their water by the time the camp came into sight. It was becoming dusk and yet there were no lights on in the camp and the sundowners were not sitting on the veranda downing their gin and tonics.

"I wonder why the ambushers decided not to try to attack us again?" said Charles, as they paused before approaching nearer to the camp.

"I think they probably thought we would try to go back to the Maasai village," said Patti. "That would have been the obvious thing to do."

"I think you're right," said Charles.

"What would they do then do you think, when we didn't go back?" asked Esther. "They certainly didn't come after us."

"They'll be in the fucking camp waiting fer us," said Leah. "Either in the fucking place or lined up down the side of the road waiting to ambush us."

They all knew that what Leah was saying had to be right.

"How many Land Cruisers can you see?" asked Charles.

Raphael, who had a pair of binoculars, said that he could see three of them.

"Goddam," said Charles. "The bastards got here first."

They were still several hundred yards away and not yet visible from the camp. Charles borrowed Rafael's binoculars. What he saw was not good. There were dead bodies lying on the ground near to the camp restaurant and there were three or four men armed with assault rifles lying in wait.

"They've massacred everyone," said Charles. "They're hiding out waiting to ambush us."

There was a collective groan and a general slumping to the ground.

"Shit. 'Ow many are there?" asked Leah.

"I counted four on a quick inspection, but there may be others watching the other side of the camp," said Charles.

"You're right Leah, we need to know how many there are, and we need to decide whether we're going to take them out or try to hide for the 24 hours it will take for the rescue teams to arrive, if they do arrive."

"My guess is that they won't know that we're properly armed," said Patti. "They'll probably guess that we took the dead soldier's gun, in fact I expect they'll have gone and checked the bodies before coming after us. They also won't know that we've had military training, so they'll be expecting a bunch of untrained kids to be coming back, all unsuspecting, and walking into an ambush."

There must have been some Celtic blood somewhere in the ancestry, despite the connection to the Mayflower. The hair was blonde, with a touch of ginger!

"I vote we take the bastards out," said Patti.

"Yeah," said Leah. "Me too."

"I'm hungry," said Lucas. "If we wait until its dark and take the bastards out quickly, we can have supper before we go to bed."

"Leah," said Charles, "do you think you and I could manage to sneak up on the camp and find out the disposition of the bastards and how many there are?"

"Yeah," said Leah. "I fink we can do that."

"Be careful," said Patti. "It's not a game. They've killed a lot of people already. Lucas and I have rifles. Charles, you don't need your rifle if you're going to be crawling around up there trying to do a recce. Give it to Elspeth, she was one of the best shots of all of us with the rifles at Barton Range. The three of us will find a slightly higher bit of ground to cover you from. Rafael has the binoculars so he can come with us and let us know what's happening. I wish there were some proper goddam trees around here."

She looked around. The only vantage point was the water tower, about a hundred metres from the encampment. For some reason there was no vehicle anywhere near the tower and nobody guarding it.

Patti looked at the route to the tower. There was just about enough cover.

"I think the four of us can get up that tower and cover you from up there," said Patti. "I know they tell snipers not to go for obvious high points like that, but this lot won't know we're coming after them, so I reckon it's the only sensible option for us. I'll go first and you come one at a time once I get up there. Charley and Leah, I suggest you wait until we're in position before you make your moves."

And with that the four of them were off and, without incident, were on top of the tower looking down on the camp within another ten minutes.

It was just as well they had got there under the cover of the gathering gloom because, no sooner had they settled in position, than someone finally worked out how to start the generator and all the lights in the camp came on at once. The carnage in the camp was immediately starkly revealed. All the staff had been shot and the bodies had been left where they lay. The extra light made it easy to see exactly where the attackers were. The four that they had seen on first arrival back at the edge of the bush were still in position but there were two others on the roof of the restaurant, also facing the likely route of the returning hikers.

The four in the water tower watched as Charles and Leah went right round the encampment and came in from the opposite direction, getting very close and looking into every building. They used standard FBI and CIA search tactics, with gun held out in front and remembering to look behind the door as well as into the room. They also looked into all the tents, quietly unzipping the flaps of the tents, only to reveal a lot of dead elderly tourists and one honeymoon couple lying, clasped together, dead.

They signalled their withdrawal and headed back to the rendezvous point. Those on the watch tower descended carefully without making any noise and, careful to keep the base of the tower between them and the waiting killers, rejoined the others a few moments later.

"There are six of them," said Raphael.

"Yes," said Charles, "and a lot of dead tourists."

He described what they had seen, and it was immediately obvious to all that the only solution to this quandary was to kill the attackers before they could be killed by them.

"They're not that smart," said Patti. "As I said I think they don't believe that we're armed, nor do they believe that we'd be able to organise a significant attack. They've regrouped, from what we could see. They're lying there close together in pairs. We need three of us to take the rifles and get up on the tower. We need to kill the terrorists. I suggest Charles takes the two on the roof, Lukey, you take the two to the right as we look at the restaurant and reception building, and I take the two on the left. Now that they've turned the lights on, we can't miss the bastards. We should get up that bloody tower again and get into position and then all fire simultaneously."

"I don't think I can do this," said Lucas.

"I fucking can," said Leah. "I didn't come here to die."

And she took the rifle from him and joined Charles and Patti heading for the tower.

It took about twenty minutes, now that the lights were on, to move undiscovered into position on the roof of the water tower.

"I'll count down three, two, one, fire," said Charles.

And he did.

And six would-be attackers lay dead a few seconds later.

They each put an extra round or two into the bodies lying there and when they were confident that there was no more threat, the six moved into the remains of the camp. Patti and Charles looked at the bodies of their attackers. Among them they recognised three of the faces they had seen in the surveillance photographs from the Stroud Green Road flat. One was the photographer, the other two were from the Rubinsky gang. Patti also recognised two of the dead as the men who had been on the plane with them and come through Dar es Salaam airport on the same flight. The sixth man was unknown to them; about thirty years old. The men were carrying more arms and ammunition than had at first appeared. In particular they were carrying grenades.

"Why didn't they use the grenades?" asked Charles. Then he answered his own question: "They wanted some of us alive. I think it must have been Lukey and Esther that they were intending to capture. They would certainly have killed the rest of us."

And then to Patti: "As far as we can tell your identity is still secret. How ironic that it's your association with Lukey that brings you danger. They weren't after you, they just didn't know who you are."

Charles telephoned through to the embassy and explained what had happened. He also sent through photographs of the six dead men, four Caucasians and two Africans. He was patched through to the USAF base in Djibouti, and they advised absolute discretion, no further communication with the outside world unless there were an emergency, and to simply sit and await rescue.

"It's clearly a terrorist attack, and we need to work with the Tanzanian authorities to present it as such. Really tragic that those innocent elderly citizens got wiped out, and the young honeymoon couple; but my advice is that you six were never there and the terrorists were killed by the security guards at the camp before the rest of the terrorists finished them off and escaped. By the time we get to you we should have a story."

When he came off the satellite phone Charles called them all together and explained what was happening. The generator was still running, and had clearly not been off for long, because the food in the refrigerators and freezers was all still fresh and they were able to make themselves a decent meal, albeit with minimal culinary artistry. They were surprised that the events of the day had not spoilt their appetites, quite the reverse. While two of them prepared the food the others removed the bodies of the staff that were in the restaurant area and put them into one of the nearby sleeping tents. Most of the tourists had been killed in their tents, changing for dinner after their trip to the Maasai village, so only two or three of the bodies needed to be moved.

"We need to keep watch overnight in case there were other attackers who did escape, and we need to keep scavengers like hyenas away from the dead bodies," said Charles. "I know some of us would like to get a bit drunk, but I don't think that wise. A couple of bottles of wine between the six of us shouldn't do any harm but no more than that."

"Lukey and I will take first watch," said Patti. "It's 10pm now, I reckon we wake the next group, Esther and Raphael, at 2am and then they wake the last group, that will be you, Charley, and Leah, at 6am; does that work for everyone?"

It was agreed. To be fair to Lukey and Patti, they did stay awake, but were far too occupied with each other to be especially observant of what was going on around them. It was about midnight when they heard some rustling in the undergrowth nearby. Their senses were immediately on high alert and they both reached for their rifles, training them on the bush in the direction from which the noise had come. Fingers on triggers they waited, ready to shoot on sight.

A family of crested porcupines emerged from the gloom, bumbling along making a lot of noise and oblivious to the world around them. The tension diffused away.

A small herd of zebras came through the camp at about 3am, giving Esther and Raphael a little bit of alarm. They were followed not long after by a pair of lionesses, who were clearly on the trail of the zebras, and the two sentries kept their fingers on the trigger of the rifles, which had been handed over to them at the changing of the guard. The lions were intent on the zebra and ignored the humans and the human remains.

Even those who were not on watch slept badly. The slightest sound alerted the senses, and fitful rest was all that was achieved. By the morning they were all exhausted.

Charles and Leah prepared breakfast for the group and everyone went into the restaurant for coffee, orange juice, American pancakes, and eggs and bacon, at about 10am.

Over breakfast the group had discussed what they would do next.

"I think the best thing would be if we'd never been here," said Charles. "The terrorists clearly managed to tap into the communications and knew which camp we would be in, but nobody else really knows, and the Rubinsky gang are not going to want this failure broadcast throughout the world. Beaten by a load of undergraduates isn't going to make them particularly saleable in their line of business. No. I think we find a way to carry on with our safari if you guys can stand that. I cannot believe how well you're all taking this. Most kids would be a jabbering mess by now. Raphael, how are you feeling?"

"I'm shocked at what's happened, but I'm also deeply relieved that we survived. Charles warned me that there were people who could try to kidnap Lukey and Esther. I came with my eyes open. I didn't think it would happen, but it has."

Charles spoke to them all: "In many ways it's good that all this has happened away from your homes and regular life. It means that it will be in a compartment, an adventure, perhaps more dangerous and distressing than you might have liked, but you'll move on. Raphael, I think everyone here probably feels similar to you about the innocent bystanders."

Then Charles turned to Leah and Patti who, like Charles, had pulled the triggers.

"What about you two?"

"We 'ad no choice," said Leah. "And we're all still alive. I don't think of it as 'aving killed some people, they were scum anyway; I think about it as 'aving made sure that my friends and I survived. I don't think it's going to haunt me."

"Nor do I," said Patti. "I had the training for just this sort of eventuality, and I'm grateful that the training paid off. I want to see the Mara and I want us to make this whole episode disappear as far below the world's radar as we can.

Those Land Cruisers work. We have fuel. We have provisions. There has been no damage to the camp. I say we stick it out if we're allowed to."

They all agreed that they wanted to go on. They needed the time to process what had happened.

The flight of helicopters, there were two Chinook size copters with about a dozen special forces personnel on board, arrived at about 11am. They had arranged refuelling stops at various airfields on the way down from Djibouti. They also had on board a complete replacement team of staff for the camp itself, picked up from an airfield near Nairobi on the way down.

The replacement staff sat quietly in the restaurant until the troops had cleared away the bodies into the cargo holds of the helicopters, then they set about making the camp appear as normal as possible. At about noon a new group of tourists arrived, totally unaware of what had happened to the previous occupants of the camp. The total deaths among tourists had been sixteen, about the load of two Land Cruisers. The story was going to involve an ambush by poachers of two Land Cruisers that had been travelling in convoy towards the Mara River. The tourists had been killed in the crossfire between ranger patrols and the poachers. The dead African camp personnel would be passed off as rangers who had also perished. The escaping poachers, and many had escaped, had taken their dead with them.

It was a very flaky story, but it was the best they could come up with, there was nobody left alive who might tell a different tale, and nobody was going to dig too deeply. The rest of the world tends to ignore atrocities in Africa; it was a continent good for exploitation during colonial days, and often ignored after independence. The families of the dead camp staff would get a pension from the government, funded by America, in recognition of the service that their dead relatives had given. The dead Americans would get Insurance pay-outs, or compensation in some form. The dead honeymoon couple would be mourned for a long time by their families. It was not pretty, it was very ugly, but it would have been far harder to allow a story out which involved political motives. It was almost certain that Patti's identity would have been uncovered and that was still a concern for Charles, and it would have put far more heat on Dr Thembani Ndlovu; the violence surrounding him would undoubtedly have escalated. Putting it bluntly, the cover-up stank, but the alternative was worse.

The American troops began a thorough search of the area where the first ambush had taken place, combed the brush between there and the camp and searched the surrounding area very carefully. There were no traces of any other terrorists so they concluded that the threat was now over and that the incoming Americans could have their safari adventure without danger.

Patti and the others felt sick. Sixteen dead American tourists, including the honeymoon couple, fifteen dead Africans, six dead attackers. All the lives surrounding the dead would be changed for ever.

Once the adrenaline fuelled activity of survival had burnt itself out there was nothing to do but attempt to enjoy a holiday that had gone completely sour.

But there is something about watching a truly ancient ecosystem in action, something about Africa in particular that demonstrates how small a niche in evolution humankind occupies; seeing the cradle of human evolution in all its glory is very healing. All six of the youngsters knew Sophie, the giraffe; Sophie's real live cousins were the most healing of all the sights they saw that first day of the resumed safari. And they saw two lionesses take down a zebra. They reflected on the difference between that kill and the senseless kills of the previous twenty-four hours. Animals killing for food is one thing, humans killing for political gain is quite another.

It would not be true to say that by the time they reached the Mara River they were over the events. Those events would never leave them, although they would gradually recede into the background, overtaken by the exigencies of existence. An army jeep was trailing the three Land Cruisers, the explanation given to the unknowing tourists in the other two vehicles was that there had been some poaching activity in the area, and they were taking all precautions. The sense of excitement that this engendered in the tourists was upsetting.

"What an adventure we're having. Just wait until we get home and tell George and Mildred."

Florida society was going to have a lot to listen to, especially when the fake news of the firefight between the rangers and the poachers broke in the Florida papers.

But no matter how emotionally drained they were, sitting on a cliff top watching a huge herd of wildebeest and zebra massing on the southern bank, trying to pluck up the courage to cross, trying to assess the danger from the giant crocodiles, trying to make the pastures of the promised land on the northern side of the river: It got to them. First one or two of the wildebeest approached the edge of the cliff and looked into the water, then more and more closed up behind them. The first few adventurers drew back and moved a little way along the bank;

they approached the water again. The pressure behind was building up. This time the withdrawal was harder, the pioneers had to push their way back up onto the safety of the cliff top. But the urge for pastures new was too strong and they tried again and this time the sheer weight of thousands of animals behind pushed the leaders into the water and suddenly the air was filled with the sound of drumming hooves and the whole herd stampeded across the river. The giant crocodiles moved in for the kill.

The whole crossing on this occasion took twenty minutes, it was a massive herd. It was not until the last of the stragglers climbed up the bank on the northern side that the watchers could see the aftermath of death. The price paid by the crossing herds was the loss of a tiny fraction of their number. There were crocodiles clinging on to their prey. Wildebeest, trying to claw their way up the bank, while the jaws of the monsters were firmly clamped on their hind quarters, until, exhausted, one by one, the wildebeest sank beneath the muddy churned up waters of the Mara River; and the crocodiles tucked their prey away under an overhanging shelf, to rot and tenderise; breakfast, lunch, and dinner, for another day. This was the gift from the herd to the great god Sobek. It was renewal of life for the crocodiles of the Mara River.

"You were lucky to see that," said their guide. "We'd not had a crossing for five days and the herd had been building up. Sometimes people don't get to see a crossing and then they go home very disappointed. Let's go a little further east and see what we can find."

It was a lucky choice for the group. A little further east the group came across a slightly shallower crossing point and saw a family of elephants with one baby crossing the river. They were surrounded by half a dozen big crocodiles and one of the crocs decided to have a go for the baby elephant. It was a huge mistake; it might have been the crocodiles last mistake; the group would never find out. The crocodile grabbed the hind leg of the baby elephant; the mother, or the nearest relative, trod on the crocodile. There was some blood in the water. The crocodile floated off downstream. The baby elephant moved back very close to the mother and the crossing was safely negotiated. The other crocodiles, probably thinking themselves lucky that they had not also attacked, dispersed to wait for another crossing, perhaps of something a little less dangerous than a mother elephant and her family.

The convoy returned to the camp, arriving long after dusk. A meal was waiting, and lots of cold beer. The Americans were interested in the young people, as older people often are. It was quite therapeutic for the group to mix with the others, although there was one very nervous moment when a large American lady suddenly said to Patti: "Gee, sweetheart, you sure look like that daughter of our marvellous Lady President. I bet loads of people tell you that."

But she meant nothing more than the words conveyed, and it was soon forgotten in the third or fourth large glass of cabernet sauvignon that the lady consumed with her 'ten-ounce steak, medium rare and I would like a double helping of fries'.

As Charles had predicted the report of the gunfight between the poachers and the rangers made the front pages of the press worldwide. In America President Howland condemned the cowardice of the poachers, commended the courage of the rangers, and sent telegrams of sympathy to the bereaved families. There was a short-lived reduction in the tourist trade to Tanzania and Kenya, but, just as with the other terrorist actions in the East African countries, the effect was short-lived and those who had the Serengeti on their bucket list continued to tick off that item. The honeymoon couple achieved the sort of fame that might have eluded them had they lived.

Apart from the honeymooners there was no mention of young tourists on that trip. They did not exist; they had never existed.

The group of six returned to Dar es Salaam directly from the airfield at Lake Manyara. It involved one more long and exciting safari drive through the Serengeti plains and the briefest of waits at the airfield. Another plane load from Arusha arrived in the plane, disembarked and then Patti and the others went on board. The rifles and pistols had been folded up and put in the luggage; there was no baggage security check on this occasion; presumably there was a thought that the passengers from the Serengeti tours were unlikely to have access to guns, and the presence of terrorists in the Serengeti was not a high probability.

Chapter 12

The Deputy Chief of Mission met them at the airport in Dar. She looked a little less at ease than the last time they had seen her. Imogen Shirley, the Deputy Chief, had been Charles Hoi's first point of contact when the attack had taken place and it was she who had patched them through to Djibouti to arrange the helicopter rescue flight. On the journey from the airport to the US Embassy Imogen was assessing the mood of the group. Leah led the responses as Imogen began the debrief, others chipped in from time to time. By the time they were back in the dining room at 686, Old Bagamoyo Road, Imogen was no longer worried. *These kids*, she thought, *they seem to have come through this OK. I guess the training we gave them helped but some of it is just that these are intelligent and fit youngsters, and they could hack it physically and mentally.*

"Are you still on for Zanzibar?" asked Imogen.

"As long as we get to keep our Smith and Wesson's," said Raphael.

After a good night's sleep in the embassy and a very big American breakfast, the six were driven to the ferry terminal and took the two-hour boat ride across to Zanzibar. The boat came in at the northern end of Zanzibar city and they spent a few hours wandering around Stone Town and the old slave market. The heat was not as intense as in the Serengeti, the proximity of the beautiful blue ocean saw to that, but after a few hours in the city they resumed their journey by taxi to the northern tip of the island, to a resort in a part of the island known as Nungwi. The poverty of Zanzibar contrasted even with the poverty of Dar es Salaam. There were ribbon developments along the main road in the centre of the island. Mango trees were everywhere. Mango trees and other tropical fruit trees, and large fields of cassava plants. There was a major contrast between this lush green vegetation and the dusty roads, the tin shacks that passed for shops and housing, and the open sewers alongside each and every main road. All along the road were the open topped vehicles which carried people and goods and were known as *dala dala*. These were a sort of minibus for the population and were almost always heavily overloaded.

The resort hotel was comfortable enough. Four-star luxury in Zanzibar is not quite what it is in a major western city; but clean sheets, comfortable beds, ceiling fans, Wi-Fi, a clean if basic restaurant, and running hot and cold water, go a long way to creating comfort, and, when there are stunning ocean views and beautiful sandy beaches, most people would probably give a four-star grading too.

They swam every day, they sat by the pool at the resort, they snorkelled on one day, they ate, and relaxed, and played cards and board games. They debriefed themselves on the events in the Serengeti. That this was primarily an attack on Lucas and Esther was obvious, but the reason for it, and the likelihood of a repetition, was not far from their minds.

As they sat out on the balcony at the hotel on the second evening, drinking light beers and looking out over the ocean at the darkening horizon they began to discuss the future.

"This will not ever really go away until the situation in my home country resolves itself," said Lucas.

They all agreed.

"What's the situation on the ground there?" asked Esther. Charles knew that the question was aimed at him.

"Marine Lusinga says that the intelligence she's gathering suggests that there are increasing numbers of the ruling party who recognise that they have exhausted almost all the reserves left over from colonial times and that the country needs to start paying its way in the world once again. They recognise that too many corrupt politicians since independence have salted away personal wealth in foreign countries, notably Switzerland and the Cayman Islands, and there is now little left to be stolen, or looted, or however you want to describe it. It seems that the contact she made with Horatio Madiba is beginning to bear fruit. Madiba is quietly, much below the radar, making overtures to members of the opposition. Madiba seems to have been greatly influenced by his conversation with Nomusa Ndlovu and is talking to your father, very secretly, about a coalition with Madiba as president and your father as prime minister. It's all very secret, and it's not going to happen while the current president is still clinging to power. One of your father's friends is a doctor to the president and has reported to Thembani that all is not great with the president's health. It seems that he's suffering from prostate cancer, and it's known that prostate cancer in Africans is more common and often more aggressive than in Caucasians. The president refused westernised treatment initially and relied on the shaman, or sangoma, and herbal concoctions. He did himself no favours and is now very ill, with metastases everywhere. The estimate is that he'll be dead within six months and that means he'll be dead before the next elections take place."

Charles paused and took a drink of beer.

"It's a tightrope that everyone's walking," he continued. "Even some of the members of the ruling party want a new leader because the civil unrest since Thembani Ndlovu came back has been growing almost exponentially, and the old guard, the freedom fighters who fought with the president, are themselves ageing and weighing up their options. Several have already left the country and gone to their tax haven exile, and many of the ruling tribe are remembering that they were once friends with opposition leaders, perhaps fought alongside them against the colonial military, and they're putting out feelers to restore the pre-independence sense of national unity. The ruling party will have to reinvent itself; the opposition party will have to convince everyone that it can be a party of government and not a party of protest. Marine tells me that Thembani Ndlovu and Horatio Madiba are meeting secretly at every opportunity and have developed a programme of social, economic, and political, reform which they will roll out to the electorate in a couple of months as soon as the president succumbs to his disease. The tightrope they are walking is that the army is still behind the government and there's nobody obvious from the opposition side, or a dove on the ruling side, who's capable of taking over the role of Chief of Staff. Any attempt to expedite change would almost certainly be met by a coup and would worsen the human rights situation and possibly lead to civil war."

"So, folks. Sorry I went on, but I think you guys need to be extra careful for a month or two, and then we'll see what happens. Marine is optimistic and we now have a very good line on the possible thugs who might try to enter the UK and try to abduct or kill either Lucas or Esther."

"What about Rubinsky," asked Lucas.

"He's there still, but we think he'll have pocketed the money from the attempt you've just endured and will move on to fresh targets. Stanislowsky is making friends with the USA, his human rights record is beginning to win him allies, and we think Rubinsky may try to undermine the relationship between the eastern republic and the US. We actually think that Patti is now a more feasible target for Rubinsky than Lucas and Esther. And there are also Alexis Stanislowsky and his sister Polina as juicy targets in Cambridge."

"Well, thank you, Charles," said Patti. And then, with heavy sarcasm in her tone. "Just what we need to know on a beautiful evening in Zanzibar. Are you always such a party pooper?"

"It's the job," said Charles.

"You know," said Leah, coming to Charles's defence, "a lot of what Charles said is a bit encouraging. If the two main factions in your homeland can find peace, then that country could be amazing. It could become the market garden of the world with all that water and all that sunshine; and I read somewhere that is has huge mineral resources in the northwest of the country. I think your mum told me that your great-uncle once worked in those mines and I do remember they've recently discovered that it has lots of lithium, and everyone wants lithium for batteries."

There were lots of nods of approval.

"From what Charles said the fighting between factions could soon be over and then human rights and poverty issues can be dealt with, and I'm betting that there will be great checks on corruption if your dad gets his way."

It produced a more optimistic feel around the table. Each of those who had experienced the ambush and taken part in the killing still had flashbacks and each one had had at least one nightmare associated with the attack. A few more days in peace and quiet, with lots of physical exercise and with a partner to whom they were very close, were going to help a lot to wash away the bad memories. Waking from a nightmare to a familiar cuddle is a whole heap better than waking alone.

The ferry trip back from Zanzibar and the flight back to Amsterdam were pleasant and uneventful. Despite the trauma in the Serengeti, they all arrived back in reasonable spirits and the students went off to their respective homes to spend the final four weeks of the long vacation before taking up the third year of their courses. They were trying to put the events of the past few weeks firmly out of their minds.

Charles flew out to meet Marine Lusinga and get an even more up to date briefing.

Patti's flight was the usual clandestine operation involving a mixture of civil and military aircraft, but she ended up back in Connecticut with her family. It was a shock-horror conversation that followed the reunion with her parents.

There was an initial gut reaction from Edward that Patti should now cut her losses and come back to finish a degree at a US institution; quite understandable, but Patti was having none of it.

"Dad, we fought the bastards off and, I'm sorry to say, we killed them. It was not targeted at me; it was aimed at Lukey and Esther. As far as we know my true identity is still secret, apart from the immediate circle of friends and a handful of others, and for the next year I'm going to be in Brussels with Leah. I'll hardly see Lukey; he has a lot of project work when he's not studying. I suppose I'll see him when he comes home to his family in the vacations, but what makes you think I would be any safer here in the US? Think about the gun laws here. Any idiot with a gun licence could take a shot at me. At least over there I'm usually the one with the gun. Besides which I want to do the Ommegang and I do want to make my French totally fluent. If people haven't come for me already, why should they come for me now. Nobody even knows that I was there in the Serengeti."

There was a bit of toing and froing in the argument, but Edward Howland had spent far too much of his life being bested by determined ladies, young and old, and he knew that his chance of winning the argument was almost negligeable. He eventually gave in with a good grace but added the proviso that someone from the Secret Service would be required to live in the block of flats that Patti and Leah were moving into, and that Patti would listen to any warnings or guidance that might be given by that agent.

There was a frantic month while the flat beneath Therese and Sandrine's was 'requisitioned'. One happy couple moved into temporary accommodation in an even more luxurious neighbourhood, rent-free and 'just for a year'. The couple were also paid a fair rent for the property, considerably more than Patti and Leah were paying, but the rent being charged the two girls was definitely not market, more like grace and favour.

Lucas and Esther went home to Brussels, and Leah, who had no reason not to, joined them at their home in Woluwe for the last three weeks. Leah's mother and father, and her siblings, were regaled with tales of the Serengeti and Zanzibar and Leah's father, Itzhak, was very proud that his daughter had been able to do things that he and his parents could never even have dreamed about. The account did not include the events of the ambush and the killing of the attackers.

"Your grandmother, she would be so proud, God rest her soul."

Leah knew that the love from her family, even though the upbringing had been tough, had given her a platform from which to grow and spread her wings. She missed her grandmother, and she missed her grandfather. She was glad that her grandfather at least had lived to know that his granddaughter was going to Oxford.

Lucas saw relatively little of Esther; he spent more time talking to his mother. Esther was now very close to Raphael, and she went with him to Paris at the start of the first semester, a good three weeks before her own term began. It was a sign of the times, a good sign of the times, that someone whose family pedigree was recorded in the Almanach de Gotha, the heir to the family titles, should now be very strongly in love, and planning a life together, with a young woman of African descent. When Raphael told his family they were delighted and welcomed Esther into their family circle with obvious delight.

"I like her," said Raphael's mother. "You need to hang onto this one!"

Before Esther went back to Oxford Raphael proposed to her and she accepted.

Lucas and his mother were now in frequent contact with Thembani. They heard how the plans for a new government were progressing; plans for reform of the education system; the health and welfare provision; the economy; agriculture; industry; and accommodation for the homeless. The plans were very ambitious. The water from Lake Ngodi would power industry while irrigating fields and providing clean water for the millions of citizens. The lithium would not just be exported for others to use but would be value added 'in house' by foreign investment employing local labour to make batteries for all sorts of appliances from IT stuff to motor cars. That should encourage local spin-offs. There were similar plans to utilise the remaining mineral wealth to grow jobs. The diamond and gold mines would be re-opened, and the proceeds would be used to provide a serious economic reserve for the National Treasury.

"What are the biggest obstacles to all this Dad?" asked Lucas.

"The people, and time," said Thembani. "For too long the people have lived on handouts. They've eaten the seed corn. It's a ten-year project that we're putting forward, and people tend to want instant results. We're going to have to find a way to get a few quick wins."

"Realistically, we have to start with education. The children currently in primary school, and even before primary school, are going to have to learn that nothing comes for free, you have to earn your daily bread.

"We're determined to do this carbon neutral. With the hydro-electric power and the sunshine we have, we ought to be able to do this without using all those coal reserves we have in the mountains around Lake Ngodi. We want to make our country not only the market garden for the world but also an example of how development can occur without creating more greenhouse gases and adding to the problems of global warming. Our climate and our resources put us in a unique position to do that."

"We're lucky the population isn't huge. Wars and subsistence-level existence for many years have seen to that. I hope there'll be a place back here one day soon for you and your engineering skills. Anything you can pick up on environmentally friendly energy generation would be very welcome. I worry that the people will want us to move too quickly, but that they won't themselves move quickly enough; I worry that they won't share our ambition; I worry that we might fail because we're too bold in our plan and they can't cope with our high expectations. To be honest, I sometimes just worry because I always have!"

Lucas and his dad laughed at that.

"My God, Dad, you have such a vision. If you don't have a vision, then what do you aim for? How are you going to buy yourselves the time?"

"I wish I knew. We can end the corrupt practices, the subsidies and handouts. Even at our present low ebb the economy can support our population if the wealth is more evenly distributed. But how we do it without provoking an armed revolt, that's a big question. We need an army loyal to us and committed to democracy. Goodness knows where we get that from."

Chapter 13

After the intense danger and excitement of the Serengeti the return to normal life was tough for all of them. But life is not always to be led in the fast lane and the six youngsters, or five youngsters and Charley, as Leah remarked one evening, all had sufficiently interesting options ahead of them that they could eventually come off the adrenaline high and settle down.

Lucas was still in Brussels when Patti returned for the start of her year abroad. Leah, Lucas, and Therese met Patti at the airport and drove her to the flat in Rue des Erables in Etterbeek; a reasonably comfortable part of Brussels. The flat was on the top floor, and there was no lift, or as Patti still often called it, elevator. The house had a red brick frontage; it was quite a wide building, and the ground floor had a large double garage and a small single garage. There was a broad staircase, accessed through a rather ugly double width wooden door that had seen better days, and up that staircase the occupants of the flats on the three upper storeys dragged their shopping, their belongings, and any additional furniture that they wished to use to brighten the interior of their home.

Therese and Sandrine had made the upper floor flat very comfortable. It was spacious, with a huge living room, a generous kitchen, two large bedrooms, and a box room. The flat was fully furnished, with lots of modern appliances, and essential Belgian things, like waffle makers, three or four different ways to make coffee, and a well-stocked wine rack. There was an extensive collection of Le Creuset cookware, Sabatier knives, crockery, cutlery, table ware, and glasses. A note on the wine rack, in very scruffy handwriting, pinned there with a corkscrew, simply said: 'Thank you two for saving my brother's life. If you run out of decent wine let us know, and please invite us to supper very soon, with love, Therese, and Sandrine.'

Although Therese and Sandrine had described everything to Patti and Leah at the start of the summer, when the two girls had moved their belongings into storage there, it was inevitable that the girls had forgotten most of what they had been told. There was a guide to all the appliances, including the heater and the kitchen white goods. There was a guide to the neighbourhood, written in a beautiful clear hand. It described the route to the Metro, useful bus stops, a wine merchant, an upmarket supermarket, a local patisserie, charcuterie, chocolaterie, boucherie, and coffee bar. It also contained detailed information about recycling and garbage disposal and a list of tradespeople to call in case of emergency with the plumbing, including the heating, the lighting, and anything else that needed fixing that the two youngsters had neither the skill nor the time to fix themselves.

At the end of the guide Sandrine had written: "Sandrine wrote this. Not every doctor has bad handwriting."

And as if to emphasise the point Therese had written, in her appallingly bad hand: "It is true; if I had written the guide, you would have found nothing, ever, at all."

The weather was kind in the few days that all of them were together. Leah went off to work first, the theatre schedule was almost continuous throughout the summer and autumn and then there would be the build up to the big events in December. To Leah it did not feel like work. She was doing something she loved, exploring every facet of a language she loved, living in a city for which she was developing a growing affection, and sharing accommodation with a friend for whom she had nothing but love and admiration, a love and admiration that was reciprocated.

The Theatre Royal du Parc is located in a white neo-classical building, accessed from La Rue de La Loi, and backing onto the highly anachronistic all-male club 'Cercle Royal Gaulois Artistique et Littéraire'. It became a progressive source of annoyance to Leah and Patti that they were unable to access some of the resources of this male only facility when it was so conveniently located in relation to Leah's working day.

"If this was England someone would bloody sort it," said Leah.

"If this was the USA, someone would bloody graffiti it," said Patti.

The theatre, over 200 years old, was a delight to work in. The auditorium seats over 500 people in some comfort. There is a splendid central chandelier and a marble entrance foyer. Very eighteenth century. For Leah, the highlight was that much of the drama was a showcase for young performers, and she was constantly meeting young Belgians with the same sort of ambition for theatre as that which she herself displayed. She had been aware that many of the performances were concerts rather than drama, but that did not detract from the experience. She learnt about administration; she learnt about technical matters; she learnt about catering and cleaning and maintaining a two hundred-and-fifty-year-old theatre. There was variety, and there was useful knowledge, and, all the time, in the background, there was fluency in the French language.

Leah worked a typical theatre shift day. On most days work started at around 11am and would go through to 11pm or later. She had time in the morning to attend a number of classes at the university. She had one weekday off completely, usually the Monday, a half day in the week, and one at the weekend, usually on the Sunday, so that she worked a shift from 6pm on that day. It gave her time to explore the city and to ride. Therese was still looking for an opportunity for Leah and Patti to take part in the Ommegang.

Patti started work at the restaurant a couple of days after Leah began her job. Patti's work pattern was very flexible. The restaurant was open from 8am for breakfast, through until midnight. Patti, once she knew the schedule at the university, was able to work out a rota with the owner that suited her perfectly. There was another girl working in the restaurant who was relying on the income from the job to support herself and her child, she was a single mother, and so she was always willing to take on extra shifts if Patti had something urgent to do. Patti did not abuse that willingness, Michelle was far too nice for that, but tips were greater in the evening and, whenever possible, Patti tried to make sure that Michelle received the larger share of those tips.

It was inevitable that an attractive young woman like Patti would have to deal with a sometimes subliminal but sometimes overt level of sexual harassment. There were a number of regular customers at Richard's and these soon recognised that such behaviour was not acceptable, and Patti was not going to put up with it. It was mainly tourists, often middle aged, and with exaggerated opinions of their own attractiveness to the opposite, or, perhaps, even the same sex, who could be a little troublesome. Patti took to wearing a wedding ring to deflect the unwelcome attentions; it was successful more often than not; but if it failed then she was not averse to knocking over a glass of water and apologising profusely. Only on one occasion, when a hand started to track up her leg, did she resort to tipping the clients dinner into his lap.

"I am so sorry, monsieur, but when you put your hand on my *derriere* it made me jump."

It was said very loudly in perfect French and the client apologised to Patti and left a much too generous tip after he had cleaned himself down in the restaurant toilets and consumed a replated meal. He probably thought himself lucky that he had not ordered the oversized helping of moules mariniere, in a gigantic pot of boiling stock and wine.

The two young women had been happily following their academic and domestic paths for about a month when, on one of the evenings when they were both at home together, Leah decided to go out to the local wine merchant who, on this particular evening, stayed open until 8pm. Meanwhile Patti, who was not a bad cook, was busy putting the finishing touches to *carbonnade Flamande*, the rich Belgian stew with the beef cooked in beer. The beef had been marinaded overnight in the strong Belgian ale, with garlic and bay leaf. That morning, before going off to her early shift at the restaurant, Patti had fried the beef, some pancetta, onions, carrots, and leeks and put them in the heavy Le Creuset casserole dish to await her return. She came back from her shift at about 5pm and returned the marinade, some tomato puree, beef stock and a bouquet garni to the casserole dish which she then put into the oven to cook slowly for slightly more than two hours. It was about 7pm when Leah went out to the wine merchant to get a good Burgundy to go with the casserole, although she also purchased a few bottles of beer, in case, on the spur of the moment, the two of them decided to go for beer rather than wine. While Leah was out Patti was preparing a very creamy mash, with potato and celeriac and lashings of butter, and some savoy cabbage, to accompany the *carbonnade*. She also tested and adjusted the seasoning and prepared some chopped parsley to sprinkle on the *carbonnade*.

Patti heard Leah come back into the building because, as often happened with Leah in the evenings, she had gone out without her key and rang the bell to be buzzed in. Fifteen minutes later Leah had still not come back to the flat and Patti was beginning to be a little worried. There was a knock on the door. Patti went swiftly to the bedroom and got her Smith and Wesson out of its safe place, checked that it was loaded, took off the safety catch and went to answer the door.

"Who is it?" asked Patti.

"Who do you bloody think it is?" asked Leah.

Patti reapplied the safety catch. She looked through the spyhole and noticed that Leah was standing there, but that there was a man standing behind her. She took off the safety catch again and slowly opened the door, taking care not to allow herself to be caught off guard by a sudden assault from the man outside.

"Hi Patti," said Charles, briefly unwrapping himself from Leah.

"I bloody nearly shot you," said Patti. "You would have deserved it. You bastard."

"Glad to see you are still your charming self and alert to any danger," said Charles, not at all disturbed by the proximity of a loaded gun with safety catch off.

"You can put that away now if you like. Supper smells good, is there room for two more?"

"I know you're getting fat," said Patti, "but you don't count as two."

Leah and Charles were both grinning and Patti thought that her joke had not been worth a grin.

At that moment Lucas came up the last few stairs to the landing, walked over to Patti and kissed her. Now Patti knew why the other two had been grinning like Cheshire cats.

It was a really pleasant evening, but there were several questions to be answered before they settled down to the serious business of drinking themselves to sleep.

"Charley's here to keep an eye on us," said Leah. "Apparently, the CIA bribed the couple who lived in the flat below to bugger off for a year while we stay 'ere and they've put a young American couple, CIA agents, in the flat, to watch over us. Charley gets to stay in their spare room whenever he wants."

Patti looked at him, looked at Leah, and thought, *Yeah, right, like he's going to stay in the flat below when Leah's up here.*

Charles stirred uncomfortably in his chair: "I thought it might be unfair to come over here and see Leah without bringing a friend for you to play with," he said.

Patti was not really amused by that comment.

"I suppose you're planning on staying the night here?" she asked. "Or are you going to go downstairs and take up your option of the spare room?"

"Would like to," said Charles. "Stay here, I mean."

Lucas looked towards Patti.

"We could go to Woluwe," he said. "Mum would be really pleased to see you. Not that sure she's all that bothered to see me, but she really likes you."

"Ok," said Patti, "but try not to make this a habit, Charley Hoi."

"Let me brief you first," said Charles, "and then we can get a bit more smashed, and I'll get you an Uber to Lucas's place."

"You can do the briefing, but you won't get an Uber. Brussels has banned Uber. I'll settle for an ordinary taxi, there and back."

Charles's briefing added little to what they already knew about the situation surrounding Thembani. Marine Lusinga was saying that the new alliance, of the opposition and the more open minded ruling party politicians, was already planning for the next government. At the present time the biggest issue they faced was the possibility of an army led coup if the ruling party were, as now seemed likely, to be defeated.

"That will be when your dad will be at greatest risk," said Charles.

Patti knew that this was not worth Charles coming to Brussels to talk to them about, and even the added attraction of a night or two with Leah could not explain his arrival.

"Listen, you bullshitting bastard," said Patti, "what have you really come for? We pretty much already knew everything you just told us so there must be something else that's worrying you. Cut to the chase."

Charles was struggling. He was not sure how to break this news, especially as it had the potential to completely derail Patti's chosen career path; but he had a duty to protect the First Daughter, so it left him no choice.

"Have you been following US politics?" he asked.

"Sure," said Patti. "Mum has the highest midterm rating of any president since Eisenhower."

"Overall, that's true," said Charles, "but there's something else going on. Our intel suggests that a section of the public is very upset with her and is looking to stop a second term, if necessary, by assassination. There's an organisation called Anarchy for America, a new group, that's trying to do what it says on the tin, create anarchy in the USA. They recently killed one of our agents who was trying to infiltrate them, but not before he'd told us that one of the group was a veteran, with access to vast quantities of ordinance, including grenades, machine guns and AK-47s. The other thing our guy said was that the particular person he was talking about seemed to be a loner, seemed to be well travelled, and seemed to be much better educated than some of the people he was associating with. In fact, our guy thought he was a really smart and dangerous man. He thought he might be passing on secrets to Anarchy for America members. We found our guy shot dead in a motel in Gilroy. We know that the man he was investigating is well connected and has some inside information about security. We think he may even be a member of the Secret Service; if not, he certainly has contacts. We can think of no other way in which our guy would have been identified and taken out."

"We all know the most dangerous terrorist is a loner, working entirely by him or herself. There's no weak link, hard to get close to them. They stay under the radar. Look at the Unabomber. Brilliant loner."

"At the moment we don't think you're under threat, but any sort of leak about your identity and the game changes. I just needed to give you a heads up that there's a potential threat; we think it's one man working alone, and he'd be directly targeting you or your family. But he could involve others, directly or indirectly. Our nightmare would be if our loner links in a significant way with Rubinsky."

"Rubinsky's ramping up his activity. The hard liners in his government are always looking at ways to attack the USA. Our analysts say that Rubinsky's masters are probably going to lose the next election and there's a real chance that Andre Stanislowsky will be elected in six months' time when the general election takes place."

Charles took a huge gulp of the Gevrey-Chambertin.

"Stanislowsky and our government are getting on very well. Your mother Patti, our beloved Madam President, is key to that. I reckon that makes her US target number 1 for Rubinsky. That probably puts you and your siblings high on his hit list too."

Another huge swig, and a refill, from the Gevrey-Chambertin.

"Bugger, it's a mess? We have Lucas's dad heading for government, and the ruling party wanting to take him out; we have Andre Stanislowsky being friends with the president and people in his own country wanting to take him out, along with the president of the USA, to stop any more close ties forming with the West; finally we have a madman, a very clever madman, wanting to stop President Howland from getting a second term in office. Why did I ever join the Secret Service?"

"Is anything really that different?" said Patti. "With mum's liberal policies there was always going to be an issue. Wait till they discover Stephen's gay and I'm going out with a 'man of colour'."

"I think there's a significant change in the danger level," said Charles. "The fanatic in the Secret Service is a very dangerous add-on. He, we know this person is male, could be almost any one of several thousand people, and that's all we know."

"We know the threats around Lucas are real, we've seen one acted out already, so we continue to deal with that," said Patti. Then she continued: "But it may be that those threats are time limited. It seems to me that any further danger to us, either from Rubinsky or the madman, is likely to come if, and when, we're in contact with my family. That isn't going to happen for a while. Probably not until the next democratic convention, and that's two years away. We have no plans for a family get together outside the US and I'm assuming that the Marines at Camp David, and guarding us around Williamstown and Connecticut, are all carefully vetted. I'm going to enjoy this year, take sensible precautions, and shoot the eyes out of you if you ever come here sneakily again."

"Sorry," said Charles, "I should have warned you I was coming, and I will next time, but the guys in the flat below are CIA and they're there to protect you and I was checking up on them."

Patti looked sceptical. "You just came because you were missing Leah," she said.

Charles grinned: "That too. But we do need to take Rubinsky seriously. He'll be wounded after what happened in the Serengeti and his masters will really want him to have a go at the Howlands. Make no mistake, he's a dangerous bastard."

"Well, I'm sure your friends in the flat below will protect me; and I'm sure they'll let you use their spare room because I have to get up for a class tomorrow, and an early shift, and I'm not lying here awake all night while you two make love noisily."

Charles looked surprised, almost shocked.

Lucas looked a little anxiously in Patti's direction, but Patti winked at him, and he knew that she was just teasing Charles.

Just then the taxi arrived outside.

"Its's ok, Charley," said Patti. "Just teasing you. Lukey and I are going over to his place, and you can have the run of the apartment. But the last time I lent you two my room it took me a week to clear up. Better not happen this time or I might just shoot you anyway, and 'Hotel Etterbeek' will no longer accept you as a non-paying guest. I'll go and pack my overnight bag and we'll leave you two lovebirds to it. I think we'll take the wine with us; if you drink any more of it we'll have to get you a stomach pump."

"You rat," said Charles. "You had me going there a bit."

"Leah's not the only one who does theatre," said Patti, going over to Charles and giving him a hug and one of those continental kisses, on both cheeks.

"Get some sleep, Leah," she said. "We do have a class in the morning, and I have a feeling that Charley, now he's made contact, is going to be around quite a bit more than he has for the past few weeks."

In the car on the way over to his family home Lucas explained to Patti that Cambridge University had finally introduced a reading week in the middle of the Michaelmas Term and that he, Lucas, was planning to spend most of it here in Brussels. He had plenty of work to do but he would be able to see her every day, fitting in around her schedule, and he would certainly come riding with her on her afternoon off. He couldn't stay the whole week because he had to get back for the "get-in" at the theatre over the weekend, he was teching for 'She Loves Me', the musical by Joe Masteroff, based in a perfumery in Budapest in the 1930s.

"I'm sorry you're missing it," said Lucas. "It's gentle and generous and such fun."

Lucas was missing Patti more than Patti was missing him. This was probably inevitable because Lucas was spending time in a place where he had spent a great deal of every day with Patti, and everything reminded him of her absence. Patti, by contrast, was living in a place where she had spent some time with Lucas, but she was doing vastly different things, mostly new and exciting, and so only now and again did she become acutely aware of the physical distance between them. They did video call regularly, but both had busy lives and, unlike very young teenagers in the throes of first love, they did not speak every day.

Patti had begun to wonder if she had moved on and if the relationship was sliding towards a natural end, but the frisson she felt when she saw Lucas come round the corner of the staircase, that skip of the heartbeat, that emptiness in the stomach, the catch of her breath; these had let her know that this was not the end. She still wanted Lucas, and, when she thought about it, she did miss him very much.

The next few days were important for them both, but they were over far too quickly, and Lucas and Patti knew that it would be the middle of December before they could meet again.

Meanwhile the first steps to getting Patti and Leah into the Ommegang had taken place. Someone whose name was included in the Almanach de Gotha was always going to have a pull with the organisers of the event, and the fact that Patti and Leah were more than competent horsewomen certainly aided their acceptance into the group which would be preparing for the mounted entry of the

Emperor Charles Vth into the Grand Place. There were costumes to be found, medieval costumes for noble ladies, and there was a decision about which horses the two would ride. Therese and Sandrine were also part of the parade, Sandrine as a musician, and they had already set to work to find, or tailor, suitable costumes. During the last couple of months of the year they met frequently in a social way with many of the other noble families of Brussels, since it was largely the noble families that took part in the mounted procession. The other elements of the Ommegang, the musicians and Les Gilles, had their own meetings and their own traditions. Many of the Gilles had handed down the role from father to son. The Gilles were not based in Brussels. Their base was in the town of Binche, where they would enact the festival that starts in January and leads, over the period of about six weeks to a grand climax on Mardi Gras, the Tuesday before Ash Wednesday. The dancing and the drumming are then borrowed for other events, notably the Ommegang in the Grand Place in Brussels.

The origin of the Gilles and their costumes is lost in the mists of time. Many believe that the Gilles represent the way that seventeenth century Belgium thought of the citizens of the New World, especially the Incas. The bright costumes of red and gold and black, with white head covers over the whole of the head and the shoulders, often topped with dramatic ostrich feather headdresses, were thought to represent the way that the Incas dressed in those middle centuries of the last millennium. The Gilles are anonymous, in that they wear very solid wax masks; features like black eyebrows and rosy cheeks are painted boldly on the masks and there is always a moustache painted on the visage; the whole thing is often topped off with green lens glasses with very heavy black frames.

As they dance their peculiar rhythmic dance to the Gilles drums and the ancient instruments, they throw oranges to the crowds from long wicker baskets which are slung around their necks. The ritual is precise, the dance rehearsed over and over again.

Patti and Leah, as young women, were excluded from any involvement with Les Gilles.

The musicians practised their instruments all year round, but gathered together to support the Gilles in Binche, and in other cities and towns where the Gilles tradition held sway.

The biggest thing that Leah and Patti had to do, as far as the riding was concerned, was to learn to ride side saddle. Noble ladies of the Middle Ages rode side saddle. It was different, but when you are young, and athletic, and determined, anything like riding side saddle comes easily to you. It was fun and it extended the social circle of the two girls so that they met a wide range of native Belgians, both French and Flemish in background.

Sandrine introduced Patti and Leah to her brother Allain, who like generations of Sandrine's family before him, was a Gilles. Although he would have been in trouble if anyone had found out, Allain, having developed rather a crush on Patti, offered to teach the two girls the basic Gilles dances, he even let them borrow spare clothes and a mask.

It was fortunate that Lucas came back to Brussels for Christmas, just as Allain was beginning to become a little emboldened and was plucking up the courage to ask Patti out on a date. It soon became obvious to Allain that Lucas and Patti were 'an item', and he decided that, if friendship with Patti was all he could hope for, it was better than nothing. Charles had been in and out of Brussels over this period and so there was no thought on Allain's part of diverting his attention to Leah. Allain was a little younger than the others and so he rather enjoyed the pain and anguish of unrequited love. He was kind and generous, and Patti, who was not unaware of the situation, was gentle with him and treated him kindly, almost as a much-loved younger brother. She also kept an eye open at the university for someone a little nearer to Allain's age who might just provide a diversion; perhaps in the spring?

Patti and Leah enjoyed learning the dances of the Gilles. The exact sequence of dancing varies a little from festival to festival, there is much spontaneity, but it is fair to say that, by the time the Ommegang came round, both of the girls knew the play book by heart.

Things might have gone on very peacefully and without incident had it not been for something that happened, back in America, in early December.

It was the birthday of the young American woman who had been the new bride on honeymoon during the Serengeti killings. The father of the bride was a prominent local businessman in Independence, Missouri, and he asked the local paper, 'The Examiner', to make a special edition to honour his daughter who had been so cruelly taken from them. The paper obtained the back catalogue of social media photographs from the accounts of both the bride and groom. They did a full colour special edition culminating in a huge centre spread of the photographs taken at the airport and the camp *before* that fateful trip which led to the ambush. Two things stood out. The first was the radiant happiness of the bride and groom, the second was that there were six other young people at the airport, among a relatively large number of much older folk. Those six younger people, who had never previously been mentioned, included one very attractive blonde girl who looked a lot like the daughter of the president of the United States. She was sitting next to a young black man who had his arm around her waist. The six were not in any of the other pictures which had been taken on the safari itself.

Charles, alert to any reference to the Serengeti or any follow-up articles on the massacre, was on tenterhooks, but nowhere in his network of agents did anything turn up that suggested the link had been made that this young blonde American girl was the president's daughter. He wrote a memo to his team of agents: *'The Howlands' daughter has been inadvertently photographed and displayed in The Examiner, a newspaper published in Independence, Missouri. So far, the girl in the photograph has not been identified as Patti Howland, but please be alert. There has also not been identification of Lucas Ndlovu, but he is seen to be close to the blonde girl in the photograph. There is no indication in the article or the photograph that the two are now in Europe.'*

It was a specially encrypted message, and it had a very limited circulation. Unfortunately, that circulation included the mercenary mole in the CIA. He knew the history and the background of the failed kidnap attempt on Ndlovu in the Serengeti; he had not realised that Patti Howland had also been there, but, now that he did, he decided that the link between Ndlovu and Howland was a good opportunity to make a lot of money. Surely Rubinsky would want revenge. One million dollars later and a little more rooting around by the mole and Rubinsky had the information that Patti Howland was somehow associated with Lucas Ndlovu and that she was somewhere in Europe studying under an alias. The mole did not know the alias.

Rubinsky already knew that Ndlovu had a blonde girlfriend. In the lead up to the attack in the Serengeti the two men who had travelled with the group, and subsequently been eliminated at the safari camp, had reported it to him. What he had not known was that the blonde girl was the president's daughter. This upped the ante considerably. The next thing to do was to find out exactly where the two, Ndlovu and Howland, were now, and see whether there was a possibility of using the knowledge to get at the presidents of two important countries.

Brussels is a city where many immigrants have settled. It was not just a coincidence that some of the Rubinsky gang had remained there after their escape from the United Kingdom. The Rubinsky members who had occupied the flat in

Stroud Green Road had already provided the information that the Ndlovu son and daughter were at Cambridge and Oxford respectively so the first thing Victor did was to send in fresh agents to scout around Cambridge and Oxford and find out as much as they could about the routines and contacts of both Lucas and Esther. Working in catering is a common thing for eastern European immigrant workers and does not attract attention. It was not difficult for Viktor to find out that the blonde girl associated with Lucas Ndlovu was studying French on her year abroad in Brussels and that her name was Patti Jones. A friend of Esther Ndlovu, Leah Shapiro, was studying with that girlfriend in the same city. It took a little longer to identify where exactly they were living in Brussels.

For the time being Rubinsky lost interest in Lucas, he had tried once and needed time to think about how to try again. He was now focussing on this new information. He was focussing on Patti Howland. The relationship between the United States and the political party of Andre Stanislowsky was developing strongly and Rubinsky wanted to destroy that. It was a long game that needed playing. Simply kidnapping or killing the president's daughter would not lead to a major crisis. It would be nasty, but it would be of little overall impact. What Rubinsky really wanted was to find a way to get at the president, and that was going to need a more subtle approach. He reasoned that the First Daughter would surely find ways to meet with her mother, and that could be the weak point in the president's security.

He needed to confirm the alias of the First Daughter and he needed to know where she was living in Brussels. He could perhaps wait for Lucas Ndlovu to go home to Brussels and call on his blonde girlfriend, that would be one way to find her, but Viktor thought he had a better idea.

Patti, working in the hospitality industry, could not get away for Christmas. It would have placed too large a burden on Michelle, the single mother with whom Patti worked. Instead, she arranged to take a fortnight's holiday in early January. There was academic work to do for the year abroad project, but she could meet up with the family back in Williamstown, where they would all arrive just after New Year for the skiing. She asked Leah if Leah would like to join her, but Leah had arranged to spend all the holiday time she could with Charles and the Ndlovus. Patti wondered about asking Lucas, but somehow the time went by, and arrangements for Lucas to join her would have been cumbersome, to say the least.

There was the usual car ride in the black bulletproof Chevy Suburban, followed by the flight in the US Airforce plane to Albany Airport There Patti was met, very discreetly, by Thomas and Sara in their own private Mercedes. The wedding was now planned for September at the Harvard Memorial Church in Cambridge Massachusetts. The conversation most of the way back to Williamstown, a relatively short trip of about 50 kilometres, was taken up with chatter about the wedding and with Sara Acharya asking Patti Howland to be her chief bridesmaid.

"I know you won't be able to help much with the wedding planning, but I would so like you to be there on the day to support me and, as I see it, you won't be at university at that time of year, your term doesn't start until 3rd October. Is that right?"

It was very quickly a done deal. Patti asked which of the family were going to be at the house in Williamstown and was delighted to find that everyone, including Mum and Dad, was going to be there; indeed, they were already there and waiting for her.

It was the first time that her family had seen Patti for about four months. Following the incident in the Serengeti Patti had insisted on getting back to her course and, in the end, the family had agreed. However there had been very little follow-up after that and Patti was feeling a little aggrieved about it. Sometimes 'important families' have too much to do in their lives to spend time on worrying about or even supporting their children. The Howlands made sure Patti was safe and then got on with their own lives.

"As you can see, I survived," said Patti. Now that she was back in the fold, she was a little angry about the lack of contact. She quite ignored the fact that she herself seemed to have forgotten how to use the telephone to family members. However, she soon realised, as the others talked, just how busy every member of the family had been. It turned out that the Secret Service had completely downplayed the incident when reporting to the president, so Patti's family had simply thought that she had been in the group when the ambush had occurred, and they had had no idea that it was she who had masterminded the killing of the attackers and pulled the trigger herself to kill two of them.

Patti told the full story to a hushed assembly of Howlands and partners, Stephen and Graham were there with the others. The full horror of the event came home to them for the first time.

"My God," said Stephen, "so you had to deal with it yourselves? The troops didn't arrive until you had killed the attackers?"

"That's right," said Patti. "We had no choice. Thank goodness we'd all been so very well trained. I couldn't understand why none of you tried to contact me after the event. I can see now that you thought I'd been a passenger in the actual incident. When did you start to think it might be different?"

"Well, we didn't really until you just told us. When the photos in the 'Independence Examiner' came out and we recognised you in one of the photographs that they showed of the unfortunate couple who got killed, we did wonder if there was something more to it than what was in the media," said Thomas.

"You were there, and Lucas too was there, and your other friends. That's when we started to talk among ourselves about what might really have happened, but we only just now realised, as you told us, just how big an involvement you had. So proud of you Titch."

The President and Edward Howland arrived on the Sunday after New Year's Day. When they heard the story, they too were a little shamefaced.

"The Secret Service played it down completely," said Martha Howland. "Jeez baby, I am so sorry we didn't react more to what had happened. How can we make it up to you?"

"No need, Mum," said Patti. "But you could come and visit me in Brussels and see the Ommegang next summer. I'll have almost finished my year abroad then. It's on for three days around the end of June. I think this year it is 30th June to 2nd July. Surely you can find an official reason to visit Brussels then. Europe's a big ally. And perhaps we can do a visit to Cambridge just before that. I intend to finish my year abroad around the end of June so I could show you St Joseph's, and maybe we can go and visit some other places? Don't worry about what happened in the Serengeti; we handled it."

Patti had quite forgotten what she had told Charles only a month or so earlier. The meeting in Brussels, if it took place, would be only about six months away; not the two years that she had suggested to Charles. The invitation would prove to be important.

Martha summoned her Private Secretary: "Davelle, please can you look into the possibility of a visit to Brussels between 30th June and 2nd July? Edward and I would like to be able to see Patti and her friends in the Ommegang. If I'm not wrong the senate isn't in session then, I think we could be back for 4th of July. If we can fix a few days in England, and some official state business around it, before the Ommegang, that would be good. We can do some official stuff in Europe, and in the United Kingdom too, now that they're out of Europe. Would you liaise with Patti about it? Can you do it fast?"

Within 2 hours he came back to them with a tentative schedule which included visits to London, Paris, Berlin, Amsterdam, and Luxembourg, with a final meeting in Brussels on the 2nd of July, and tickets for the Ommegang on that Friday evening. A visit to Cambridge the weekend before was also included on the tentative itinerary.

"We can sort the details of the trip to England later, Madam President," he said.

"Thank you, Davelle, I don't know what we would do without you," said Martha.

There was plenty of time over the next few days, between the skiing, and the swimming in the local country club indoor pool, for Patti to plan the trip to England with Davelle. St Joseph's May Ball was on the Sunday at the end of the second week in June, and Patti had already been asked by Lucas to partner him to it. In addition, Lucas was taking part in the May Week musical production being put on by CUMTS, the Cambridge University Musical Theatre Society. The choice of musical had not yet been decided but this particular slot, from the Tuesday through to the Saturday, the day before the St Joe's May Ball, was always allocated to CUMTS. It was light relief after exams, and a good money spinner for both the theatre and the club. Davelle agreed to arrange for the Howlands to be there for the Saturday evening performance of the show. Lucas and Patti would make sure everyone had tickets, including, of course, the Secret Service agents who would be accompanying them, and tickets for Leah, Charles, Esther, Raphael, and, if they were free, Therese and Sandrine. It would involve booking the whole of row "I" in the relatively small theatre.

Relaxing and catching up with the family was a pleasant relief for Patti. She was, as she had previously mentioned to Charles, by now, totally convinced that Stephen and Graham were more than just friends and, at breakfast one morning, over a stack of pancakes, Stephen came out to her. He started to speak, and was getting himself into all sorts of embarrassed knots; Patti just got to her feet, came round the table, kissed Stephen very gently on the forehead and said: "So happy for you. If you love him, I am sure we will love him too."

Stephen teared up, blew his nose, and said: "Well, that gives Mum quite a ticket for the next election. A gay son, an Indian daughter-in-law, an African boyfriend for the youngest child. Might make for an interesting campaign!"

"Don't you worry about Mum," said Patti. "She's so amazing as president that she'll get in. She wouldn't want to be elected on a wave of intolerance; she'll leave that to the opposition. I bet she told you that."

"She did. Mum and Dad were so supportive when I told them. I shouldn't have expected anything less, but I did worry a bit. Like most countries, as a nation we're less far down the road of intolerance towards homophobia than we are towards intolerance of racism; and goodness knows we have miles to go, even on racism."

"We'll get there, we have to," said Patti. "The younger generation are generally better at accepting people for who they are. I guess we're a bit luckier than some people because most of our friends are open minded. Must be much harder to be open minded when you are struggling just to put food on the table and clothes on your back."

At that moment Thomas and Sara came into the breakfast room. Sara looked at the two sitting there: "Lighten up," she said. "Now my guess is that you just told Patti about you and Graham, and my other guess is that she had already worked it out and all your angst was wasted energy."

Sara walked over to Stephen and gave him a hug and a rather sisterly sort of kiss.

There was a sort of wry smile from Stephen: "You two are smart cookies, aren't you," he said.

There were no other major pronouncements during the remaining few days of the winter break. Sara and Patti went for a dress fitting at a bridal shop in Albany. That took up the best part of one of the relatively short days. The September wedding at Harvard was now definite, Patti was to be chief bridesmaid, one of Sara's friends from high school was to be a sort of executive chair, and the other bridesmaids were some of the younger cousins from Sara's side of the family. There would be a Christian wedding ceremony in the morning followed by a Hindu ceremony later the same day. The reception would be a full-blown Hindu celebration. There would be amazing Indian food cooked by the best Indian chefs. There would be dancing and feasting well into the next morning.

"What an amazing summer we've got planned," said Patti. "I'll be glad to get back to Cambridge for my final year, it'll be a rest!"

The information about the intended visit of the president and her husband to Europe the following summer made its way back to the White House staff. The Secret Service and the CIA group under Charles Hoi, the group, looking after Patti, heard about it too. One well-placed undercover agent is all you need, especially if she or he is greedy, so Viktor knew almost as soon as it had been decided that the event would take place.

"How much Semtex have we got left?" asked Viktor.

His quartermaster, Ludovic Fedorov, told him. It was more than enough to blow up the Albert Hall.

"Where is it?" asked Viktor.

"Brussels mostly, and about a few kilos buried under the hedgerow at the farm near Somersham."

Viktor still had access to further explosives if he needed them, and to the type of electronic detonators that had been used to in the abortive attempts to destroy Stanislowsky in Cambridge. He had a plan. The next thing to do was to find out where Howlands' daughter was living in Brussels.

Chapter 14

Viktor arranged for one of his associates to visit the Modern Languages Faculty at Cambridge University to ask if there might be a student, studying in Brussels, who would like to earn some money tutoring a young girl, living in Brussels, in English. The receptionist was very good, she did not give out any of the names; but she undertook to email all the students studying abroad in Brussels with a request that, if they were interested, they should contact Mr Ludovic Kransky; she would include the telephone number.

"Is it your daughter, Mr Kransky?" asked the receptionist.

"It is my daughter," said Ludovic.

"What's her name?" asked the receptionist.

Ludovic was a little slow to reply but when he did reply he pulled his mobile phone out of his pocket and fiddled with it for a moment, then showed the picture of his cousin's daughter, aged about ten, and declared that the name was Natasha.

It seemed to settle any anxiety on the part of the receptionist, and she promptly ran a search for 'student destination Brussels' on her computer. Ludovic had remained near the desk and could see the four names that came up, and their colleges. He talked to her while she completed the search and showed her yet another picture, this time of the little girl in a swimming pool. There was still some work to do finding out which of the students in Brussels were blonde, but, given that Lucas Ndlovu had been with a blonde girl in the Serengeti, and was at St Joseph's College, Ludovic was going to start by making enquiries at St Joseph's.

It did not take him long to find out that a blonde young American woman was reading modern languages at St Joe's. He went to the pigeonhole room, the room where all the students receive their mail. A label with each student's name, alphabetical, but colour coded by year, is placed in a little holder at the base of the compartment into which that student's mail is put. When students are away their name label is turned round so that a blank card marks the space. Ludo' had remembered the names of the four girls, so he looked at the array of pigeonholes in front of him and noted the ones with the names turned round. He had brought with him a whole collection of leaflets for an animal liberation meeting which he had picked up from a stall in the market square and, under the pretence of distributing them into specific cubby holes, he looked in turn at the labels which had been turned round. It did not take him long because, although students were constantly in and out checking for post, he had only three letters of the alphabet to work with and the second of these was the letter J. Patricia Jones was a student at St Joseph's, away at the moment.

Now Rubinsky knew that Patricia Jones was the alias for Patricia Howland. He had pictures of the blonde girl who had been with Lucas Ndlovu in the Serengeti. It was no problem to identify that blonde girl as the First Daughter.

Viktor had always loved plans which enabled him to take out two targets with one attack. He had a very good feeling about the coming June. Surely Lucas Ndlovu, Patricia Howland, possibly Thembani Ndlovu, and the president of the United States, would find themselves together in Cambridge on the visit that was to precede the official state visit to much of the rest of Europe? If not, then the visit to Europe was a further possibility. He could plan for both contingencies.

Viktor didn't bear grudges, at least he thought he didn't, but he had lost a couple of his best men at the safari camp, and he thought it might be nice to avenge them. *Maybe the other students will join them? That would be nice*, he thought to himself.

Viktor's planning for the attacks he hoped to make was confined, for the moment, to the generalities. He knew they would involve bombs; he knew that they would need to be ready for the end of June and the start of July; he did not know where he was going to have to plant the bombs. There was little he could do to plan in detail until the spy in the CIA came up with a more detailed itinerary.

Ludovic was ordered to remain in and around Cambridge. Ever since Brexit there had been a shortage of staff prepared to work in the catering industry, an industry to which Eastern Europeans had contributed so much. They were sorely missed. It was not just that they had been there in numbers; it was also that they had such a strong work ethic and an outstanding idea of how to provide excellent customer service. Ludovic was not really in that mould, Ludo's idea of customer service was more likely to be a short range shot with a Luger; but orders are orders, and so Ludovic practised his silver service, brushed up his manners, and applied for a job on the catering staff at St Joseph's College. He was taken on under the assumed name of Ludovic Andreev; as with many choosing an alias he kept his first name and just changed his surname. Rubinsky was well enough connected to provide the necessary documentation for the employment to go through. Ludovic also looked around for accommodation and settled on a fairly upmarket two-bedroom flat in one of the new developments overlooking the River Cam down on Riverside. It was expensive, too expensive for someone on the sort of salary that St Joseph's paid, but Ludovic was not relying on his income from the job to support himself in the lifestyle to which he was accustomed and from which he was not going to budge.

For both Patti and Leah their colloquial French improved beyond recognition. Patti had received the communication sent by the receptionist at the Modern Language Faculty requesting that she might contact M. Kransky about coaching his daughter in English and she had dialled the number that she had been given and put it on speaker phone. The person who answered was clearly not French nor, as far as she could tell from his accent, was he Flemish. His knowledge of English was also very limited. Patti and Leah were trying to acquire some understanding of Flemish. Both, being good linguists, were taking classes in the language, and when she tried a little of her recently acquired Flemish on 'M. Kransky' Patti received no intelligent responses, it was clear he had not got a clue about what she was saying. In the end Patti resorted to talking in English, even though Kransky's English was severely limited, because this incarnation of Kransky had no significant knowledge of French either. In hindsight Patti perhaps should have been surprised about this, but she asked to speak to the daughter and a very young sounding voice came on the telephone and was able to speak in French, knew a few words of Flemish and spoke limited English. As it turned out the girl said, in rather broken English, that she had already found a tutor; then she started talking in French and after some general talk about Brussels and why they had come there to learn French she thanked them for calling and asked if she might have their address and telephone number, just in case the appointed tutor let her down. Who knows what instinct triggered Patti's response? Was it that the French was too perfect for someone who was supposed to be an immigrant and only about ten years old?

"How long have you been in Belgium?" Patti asked.

"About one year," replied the 'girl'.

"Where did you come here from?" asked Patti.

The 'girl' ended the call.

"Oh shit," said Leah, who often swore when things got tricky. "Who the f' was that? What made you suspicious? Are we in trouble?"

"She was using the subjunctive and her tenses were too perfect for a newly arrived ten-year-old little girl," said Patti. "No harm done; they didn't even get our telephone number because Charles insisted that we have 'number withheld' on our call plan. Goodness knows what would have happened if we had given them our address. I'm going to call Charles and I'm also going to contact the faculty and ask them about M. Kransky and the tutoring job."

That ploy used by the Rubinsky gang to try to obtain the address and telephone number was not really necessary. It was just a slightly lazy way of doing things. The gang knew that Patti would be attending classes at the Université, and they could easily have picked up the trail from there. Not only was it lazy, and unsuccessful, but it also triggered a greater level of alertness on the part of the two girls. It was definitely counterproductive. They finally tried the less lazy method.

Armed with a photograph from the Indianapolis Examiner, members of the gang lay in wait for Patti Jones at the Université and eventually identified her and followed her home. Once the home street was known it was but a short while before they were able to identify the building, and the precise flat, in which the two girls lived. They identified the flat number by ringing the doorbells of the flats one afternoon, before the girls returned, and seeing which flats did not answer. As it happened, all the residents were out. Then, five minutes after the girls had returned, they rang the bells again. This time only the top flat answered, and it was a young sounding woman's voice which said, "*Qui est là?*"

There was no shortage of Rubinsky gang members to follow Patti about her business and the Rubinsky gang very quickly knew all there was to know about her daily routine, and that of Leah Shapiro. They also knew that these two went, very regularly, and especially at weekends, to ride horses with a group of aristocratic Belgian citizens, preparing for the Ommegang.

Rubinsky could not immediately see how the Ommegang might help him attack the president, but he did reason that Patti and Leah were rather heavily committed to Ommegang rehearsals and so would almost certainly be riding in the procession. The mole in the security services had indicated that the Howlands would be visiting Brussels at some time; It seemed quite possible that President Howland and her husband would want to watch their daughter in the procession.

Viktor's people searched the archives of the Brussels papers and magazines for pictures of the Ommegang in the Grand Place. They noted the disposition of stands and vantage points within that large and famous square. It seemed to Viktor highly likely that the presidential party, if it were to attend the event, would sit in the VIP stand which was always located in central position in the square at the very front of the many tiers of seats. The performance area in front of the Hotel de Ville was about twenty-five metres wide, so the presidential party would be perhaps a further five metres back and raised about five metres above ground level. There would be one or two rows of seats at ground level, but not in front of the VIP stand. A ten-metre-wide gangway into the performance area from La Rue de la Tête d'Or would allow for the entrance or exit of performers; and another ten-metre-wide gangway into and out of Rue Charles Buls would provide further access. There was a mock-up of the Grand Place performance area at the Chateau de La Lesse; it took all these measurements into account. There would be many possible locations for a bomb in the Grand Place, but Viktor knew that the security around the construction of the stands and the staging would be set at the highest level, and a bomb plot there would be very unlikely to succeed.

Knowledge that Patti was likely to be taking part in the Ommegang meant, to Viktor, only that the presidential party would be likely to combine seeing the First Daughter with visits to various of the important European offices in Brussels. The European parliament buildings, and other centres of administration, would almost certainly occur on the presidents itinerary and might offer opportunities for effective use of pre-planted bombs. The team in Brussels was set the task of planning a bomb attack at every one of the possible administrative sites that the president might visit. It was not a trivial task, but there was plenty of explosive, and Rubinsky was determined not to let this opportunity be missed.

Rubinsky also reasoned that the president might want to visit the United Kingdom officially on her trip, not just Cambridge. The United Kingdom was still an important ally of the United States and the president had not yet made an official visit to one of her country's oldest allies. He reiterated his instructions to Ludovic to make sure that he was prepared to deal with the presidential party, should it come to visit Cambridge; and he instructed those in the flat in Stroud Green Road to seek any information they could about a possible State visit by President Howland to either the Royal Family or the government.

Meanwhile a totally independent and convergent process was taking place in a small town somewhere in the mid-west of America. The photograph taken at the airport just before the massacre had included Lucas and Patti. The photographs posted on his mother's Facebook pages by the Marine at Camp David had never actually been erased from view because too many people had downloaded them before the National Security Agency had got to know about it. The guy who was the mole for Rubinsky had access to those photographs and had put them together into a small pdf. As a white supremacist and anarchist, the guy posted the pictures to a group of his friends in Kansas City, with a note to the effect that two of the president's children were dating non-white partners, indeed the president's eldest son was about to marry a non-white woman. He added, for good measure, that the president's younger son was gay. The actual words he used to describe Stephen, Sara and, especially, Lucas, were much less acceptable; traditional foul expressions used by bigots throughout the ages.

The communication, with the pdf, was enough to trigger one member of the white supremacist group into an apoplectic rage. Zacchary Hutchins, for that was the name of the Kansas supremacist, decided there and then that the president had to die, and he knew just the person to recruit to achieve that task. Zach worked as a prison guard at the high security Military Prison at Leavenworth. He had befriended an inmate of the prison, a university graduate and former officer in the Marines, who had been convicted of torturing and killing a prisoner during a tour of duty in Iraq. Now in his mid-forties, and alienated by his imprisonment, which he saw as his government letting him down and throwing him to the wolves, that prisoner held strong views about the governance of the United States and subscribed to almost every conspiracy theory that criticised racial minorities and liberal policies. He was due for release in late April and Zach was going to set him up with a passport, money, and contacts, to head for Europe and lie in wait for the president. Like Viktor, Zach thought that Belgium or London would offer the best chances to take out the Howlands. At this time Zach did not know how former Marine Major Corland was going to take out the president, but Zach had a lot of faith in Corland and, ever since the Unabomber, everyone knew that a man working alone can inflict a lot of damage. When he handed over the money, the documents, and the plane tickets, on Corland's release, Zach knew that something dramatic was going to happen. Lee Corland left the country within four hours of his release from prison. It was a parole violation, of course, but Corland had no intention of ever resurfacing as himself. From now on he would assume the identity in the false papers he had been given and, when he returned to America, after killing the president and her family, he would take up a position running a shooting range, gun shop, and outdoor training centre, somewhere in the Appalachian Mountains just off highway 81.

For the next few months Ludovic saw Lucas almost every day. He recruited a second member of the Rubinsky gang from among the small group that had remained in Brussels and that young woman moved in with Ludo. It suited Ludo' to have an attractive young colleague living with him. It was also easier for the young woman to follow Lucas about his daily business. She was a very young looking 28, and could easily pass for a second- or third-year undergraduate.

Within a very few weeks Lucas's complete routine had been worked out. Without Patti there to remind him continually of his need for caution he dropped into a very fixed pattern of behaviour. Irina, for that was the young woman's name, knew which route Lucas took to lectures, practical classes, sporting activities and, very importantly, the theatre. She also knew that Lucas was taking part as a techie in the Lent Term musical, 'Assassins'. The irony was not lost on Irina; and Ludovic and Irina sometimes sat around together in the evenings composing a mock-up of an extra number, in which the assassination of President Howland featured very strongly. They borrowed the tune from a popular Russian school song and simply added the words, in Russian of course. All that really mattered to them was that, at the end of the song, President Martha Howland was dead.

Once the theatre had been established as a central pivot in Lucas's existence Irina got herself a job working for the cleaning company that the university contracted to keep the place clean. It meant cleaning lots of other buildings too, but it gave her almost unrestricted access to the auditorium and the bar of the theatre, at a time when very few other people were around. It also gave her most of the late morning and the whole of the afternoon and evening to keep an eye on Lucas.

Chapter 15

Superintendent Jerry Gregory had been enjoying a relatively quiet time back in Cambridge; or, rather, he had not been enjoying it. Quite simply Jerry was bored out of his mind. You could tell that because he was ratty with his subordinates and he was, again, combing the situations vacant columns of national newspapers, and crawling all over LinkedIn and other social media sources, looking for some sort of job that might interest him. He was even looking at opportunities abroad, with police forces and with private security firms. Inspector Jenny Taylor was also bored. Rubinsky had gone under the radar, after the disaster in the Serengeti, and Jenny was desperately trying to update her files on the gang members and discover what new targets they might be looking at.

Patti's telephone call to the Modern and Medieval Languages reception on the Monday morning after the fiasco with the 'Kransky daughter' was to stir up quite a hornet's nest. Patti reported to the receptionist that they had contacted Kransky and he had not appeared genuine. She asked about Kransky, what sort of English accent did he have, how good was his English. When the receptionist said that Kransky's English had been very good, he just had a fairly strong East European accent, Patti knew for certain something was wrong. The "Kransky" she had spoken to in Brussels was definitely not the same man. The receptionist agreed to telephone, immediately, the other three girls doing their year abroad in Brussels and warn them that this was a scam of some sort, and she also agreed to contact the local police. The immediate thought was that this might have been a scam designed to pick up a few girls for sex trafficking; there had been a recent high-profile case of girls arriving in Brussels being picked up at the airport and abducted. Patti was not so sure. She wondered if it might not have been targeted at her. So far, she had been lucky, she was still largely incognito, but there was no guarantee that this situation would hold forever. She was certainly going to talk to Charles.

About ten minutes after Patti had rung off the receptionist called back and said that all three of the other girls had called the Kransky number and had each been told that the position was already filled. Now it was looking even more likely to Patti that this *had* been a device to find out her whereabouts.

Charles received the information very calmly. He agreed with Patti's assessment of the situation. Someone was looking for Patti Jones, and that probably meant that they knew who Patti Jones really was. If they knew that Patti Jones was a student in Brussels, as they clearly did, that would mean they must now know where she lived. It was not rocket-science to get a picture and find the girl going about her daily business, then follow her home. Whoever was looking for her had contacts in Cambridge. Adrian Armstrong and Jerry Gregory were due another visit. Meanwhile, what to do about the girls in the flat on the Rue des Erables? There was good security; the young CIA couple in the flat below were always on duty; Patti and Leah were smart cookies. There was no immediate reason to pull the plug on Patti's year abroad. The thing to do was to find out who now knew the identity, and, more importantly, how they had discovered it. Then they could think what the implications might be.

Meanwhile Charles would just remind everyone, including Lucas and Esther, to be extra cautious and break their routines again. No point in inviting trouble. In terms of threat levels, on a scale of one to five, this had now moved up to at least level three. Charles made the relevant telephone calls to raise the alert levels of everyone concerned.

Brussels; Cambridge; was the only link Patti, or was there something else?

It was about a week later that Charles visited Cambridge. The first thing he did was to go to the Modern and Medieval Languages Faculty and interview the receptionist. She was adamant that she had not given Kransky any of the names and contact details of the girls on their year abroad.

"Was there any way he could have seen those names?" asked Charles.

The receptionist gasped; her cheeks coloured with embarrassment.

"The clever bastard," she said. "He showed me a picture of his daughter and when I did the search on the computer he came over and showed me another picture of the same girl, and while I was looking at it, he was probably looking at the screen."

"What could he have seen?" asked Charles.

"The four names and their colleges, I guess. Couldn't have seen the photographs because they are on the individual files and not on the year abroad database."

"So, he would have had four names and four colleges to go and investigate?"

"Yes. I'm so sorry. Actually, it was three colleges because two of the girls are at the same college. It never occurred to me that there was anything wrong and if he hadn't leant over my counter to show me the picture, he could never have seen the names."

"Please don't worry," said Charles. "No harm done, and he's clearly a very devious character."

"Funnily enough, I think I saw him again a few days later walking around Cambridge," said the receptionist. "I thought it was a little odd, but I presumed he hadn't yet gone home to Brussels; I just ignored it."

"Can you give us a description?" asked Charles.

"He was big," said the receptionist. "Not fat, just massive. I would say well over 6 foot, and very muscular looking. He was slightly balding at the temples, and he had very dark hair. I would think he was about thirty-five to forty years old. He had nice teeth; he was clean shaven; he had very piercing grey eyes. Oh, one thing I did notice was that he had a scar on his forehead, just a little one, over the left eyebrow."

Charles thanked the receptionist and reassured her yet again that she had done nothing wrong, and she was not to worry. He then headed towards his old college, St Joseph's, for a group conference with several important players on the right side of the game.

Adrian Armstrong, Jerry Gregory, and Jenny Taylor were sat down together in Adrian's office in St Joseph's when Charles was ushered in by Adrian's P.A.

Adrian, as usual, made lots of high-quality coffees using his private high-tech machine. They were offered the usual packets of three posh biscuits in wasteful, environmentally unfriendly, plasticated paper wraps. Once everyone was settled with a coffee Charles opened the discussion: "I think I ought to let you know something we've kept under wraps until now. The president and her husband are planning to visit Cambridge in late June on their way to Europe to meet various heads of state, attend the European Parliament, and watch their daughter take part in the Ommegang."

"What's the Ommegang?" asked Jenny, much to the relief of everyone else in the room; only Charles knew what it was. He explained.

"So, the Ommegang is outdoors in the Grand Place?" asked Jenny.

"Yes," said Charles. "Probably the safest bit of the whole trip," he smiled "Certainly the easiest bit to do security for. A big open space with well established businesses and official buildings around it. Contractors who have put up the staging for decades. Sniffer dogs, ultrasound, all the modern state of the art detection stuff."

"I guess the Secret Service will be liaising with the local police forces in Europe," said Jerry. "So we only need to think about our end of the trip. About Cambridge and St Joe's?"

"I wonder," said Jenny.

"What!" said Jerry.

"Nothing," said Jenny. "Just thinking you can't ever be sure with terrorists."

"Right," said Charles. "There seems to have been some intelligence gathering going on in Cambridge, because we think that's where someone managed to connect Patti Jones with Brussels and set up a phishing operation to try to suck her into their net. We think information was leaked from the Washington end of things. The Cambridge link was through Lucas because some photographs published in America showed him with the First Daughter and one of the terror gangs knew that Lucas had a blonde girlfriend who he'd been with in Africa."

He explained what had happened with the Kransky affair. They all agreed that this was a targeted event and not a general attempt to try to kidnap random girls for trafficking.

"There's a good chance that the person who called himself Kransky is still here," said Charles.

"From what Patti said the man who answered the telephone in Brussels was not the same as the one who spoke to the receptionist here. I do just wonder if we're seeing a return of the Rubinsky gang. They missed out on Lucas Ndlovu in the Serengeti so maybe they're having another go and Patti Howland is just caught up in it serendipitously. Should we advise the president not to come? If she does come it'll be a very quiet and unofficial visit because she still wants to allow Patti to remain incognito for the final year of her degree. At least as far as that's now possible. I'm sure the gang will now know Patti's Brussels whereabouts. Given that she has to attend classes at the university, and they have a picture of her, they would have to be stupid not to follow her home."

"Why now?" asked Adrian.

"That's the puzzle," said Charles. "What suddenly triggered this interest in Patti, and does whoever it is know about the possible visit? We shouldn't assume the visit, and the trying to identify Patti, are connected, but it does seem quite likely that they are. As far as I know, only President Howlands' staff and key people in the National Security Agency, the CIA, and the Secret Service, know about the potential visit. So why is someone sniffing around Patti Howland at this time? Is it just a coincidence? Could it still be linked to Lucas?"

"Do you think the publication of the photograph in the American papers just before Christmas could have had anything to do with it?" asked Jenny.

"We had no evidence that there was any follow-up on that," said Charles.

"But I bet you put a memo out about it, some sort of alert," said Jerry.

"Heavily encrypted, limited distribution," said Charles.

"How limited?" asked Jerry.

"Maybe 50 people," said Charles. He was beginning to get a very hollow feeling in the pit of his stomach.

"So, 50 people would have decrypted their messages and read them. And what then?" Jenny continued her cross examination.

"Would it have cascaded down from there? Could someone have seen a decrypted hard copy?"

"I think it's very unlikely," said Charles.

"Was there any indication that anyone in the press or the social media had worked out the connection between the white girl with Lucas in the picture and the Howlands? From what you're saying it seems not and, in that case, 'Houston, I think you have a problem'."

Charles though for a minute. He too was beginning to think that his problem might be closer to home than he had previously believed.

"There is absolutely no indication that any of the American press took any interest in any part of the story except the death of the poor young kids who had just got married."

"Well, then," said Jerry. "Just thinking about this from an outsider's point of view, I reckon you must have a mole somewhere within your organisation. I reckon it's someone on your distribution list. If there's been no public follow-up to the airport picture it must surely be an internal affair? I reckon someone in one of your organisations recognised Patti Howland; was that in your memo?"

"Oh damn," said Charles. He had remembered.

"There was a memo that left no doubt that the girl in the airport photograph was Patti Howland. It might have mentioned her alias too. It certainly mentioned Lucas Ndlovu."

"How about the visit?" asked Jenny. "Any memos about the visit?"

"One," said Charles.

"Same 50 people?" asked Jenny.

"Yep," said Charles.

"So, if there is a mole, it will be in the public domain, at least the terrorist domain, that Patti Jones and Patti Howland are one and the same and that a presidential visit to Europe is planned for next summer."

There was a deathly hush in the room. It was logical, it made complete sense. How to find the leak? That was the multimillion-dollar question. The Jerry spoke: "You need to find the mole before the details of the visit are worked out otherwise it's an open invitation to finish off Martha Howland and her family, and probably the Ndlovus as collateral damage."

Charles looked very worried.

"Meanwhile," said Jenny, "what do we do here in the UK? I still put my money on Viktor wanting to finish the job with Ndlovu. His corrupt government has a lot to lose if Thembani Ndlovu and the Movement for Democratic Reform are elected, whenever it is that those darned elections are taking place. The MDR is making overtures to the USA; the ruling party is totally in bed with the communists, including Rubinsky's bosses."

"From an American perspective," said Charles, "Rubinsky's bosses are also losing out as Stanislowsky makes friends with the USA, and Howland, for these purposes, could be seen as the USA."

"How, and where, are we going to find Rubinsky's people?" said Jenny. "Could the mole have been leaking information to them? They wouldn't need to do that for Rubinsky to target Ndlovu but, when you put the whole picture together, Ndlovu, Howland, the USA, Stanislowsky; it all just makes a juicy target. Rubinsky has got to be thinking about taking out the president."

"When are they all going to be together on this trip, if it's allowed to go ahead?" asked Jerry.

"The first place they're all going to be together is here in the UK, and probably here in Cambridge," said Adrian; until that moment he had just sat there patiently listening, but now he was going to have something to say about likely movements around the college and the city during the visit.

"I think you have to see the whole trip as a continuum, every part of the visit is vulnerable. You need to be careful to liaise fully and not leave gaps in planning the protection."

"Tell you what," Adrian added. "Once we know what Patti, Lucas, and the presidential party have in mind as their itinerary I think I just might be able to contribute to working out the pinch points. Until then I don't think I'm much use, except," he paused, "anyone want another cup of coffee?"

Half an hour later, they each left the meeting with a large to-do list but by far the two most important were, first, for Charles to investigate the possible presence of a mole, and, if possible, identify that person, and second, for Jerry and Jenny to locate any members of the Rubinsky gang in the UK and try to neutralise the gang's activities before they could come to fruition.

There is a fairly standard procedure for trying to plug a leak in an organisation; you simply give different bits of information to different people and see which bit of information actually does get leaked. The trick lies in making the evidence credible for each person and deciding where the leak needs to come out. Charles went off to set about doing just that.

What information to spread? Charles thought long and hard about this. In the end he decided that the easiest thing to do, since he needed about fifty pieces of information to distribute, individually, to fifty 'need to knows' was the location where President Howland and her husband would be staying incognito on the first night of their trip to Europe. The detailed planning for the trip was beginning to emerge, and this made it essential to find the mole before the plans were finalised.

Each of the fifty people fed information was individually given the name of a hotel or stately home at which the presidential party had been "booked in." It was impressed upon them that they should not tell anyone else; they alone were party to this particular detail which would only be made known to the general team once the rest of the plans had been formalised. Each person was reminded of the importance of keeping this little detail secret.

****

After the Serengeti disaster Rubinsky had repopulated the flat above the scruffy hair salon in Stroud Green Road. It had made sense to both the British and the Americans not to let Rubinsky know that his safe house in London had been uncovered. There was no reason for him to be suspicious because the incident in Africa had been entirely unconnected to anything going on in London. That flat was clearly going to be the place where the leak should emerge. That was the easy part. It was coupled with the second major plan, the plan to identify and limit Rubinsky's gang's capabilities.

It was about five days after Charles had spread his information that the team watching in Stroud Green Road saw two of the occupants of the flat get into an Uber car and visit The Montcalm Royal London House in Finsbury Square. The two men got out and started to walk around the outside of the hotel, and then they entered the building and went to the bar, as if meeting someone for a drink. If there had been no other reason to be suspicious, the behaviour of the two men would not have attracted attention. As it was, Charles now knew the identity of the mole in the CIA. There was a debate about whether to pull the guy in immediately, or to simply exclude him from further deliberations until they wanted to leak false information. The false information brigade won. Meanwhile Charles set some of his best investigators to monitor every aspect of the mole's activity. All his IT activities were analysed, his phone records and his bank account were investigated. His phone and computer were bugged, his apartment was bugged, even his car was bugged. Not only the mole was going to get his comeuppance, but also some of the people to whom he was leaking information were going to be caught. Charles was unable to resist taking a walk past the guy's desk and he noted that the young man was far better dressed than his pay grade would normally allow for. There was almost certainly a mercenary rather than an ideological motive for the betrayal of trust; although the first indication, based on one or two of the recipients of the leaked information, at least within America, was that white supremacists and Anarchy for America were likely to be involved; as well as Rubinsky.

Meanwhile life went on pretty much the same as before in both Brussels and Cambridge.

In Brussels the rehearsals for the Ommegang were gradually building momentum. Following the scare about the Kransky incident Patti had taken to keeping her Smith and Wesson with her on almost every occasion and she and Leah were randomly varying the route of their journey to the university, and to their places of work. Some of Leah's young contacts at the Theatre Royal du Parc were also in the Ommegang, many as musicians, and just a few as Gilles. The riders in the Ommegang procession were largely drawn from the aristocracy and the upper middle classes of Belgian society. That was how Therese had become involved. Patti and Leah were exceptions, allowed partly out of curiosity value for the Belgian nobles, and partly because Therese's family were so important that she and Raphael could have almost anything they wanted, and they wanted the two girls on the team. The procession would begin some distance from the Grand Place and ride through the streets, but the final part of the pageant was within the Grand Place and was highly organised to a traditional script. The inclusion of Leah and Patti was probably helped by the fact that, in order to make the rehearsals as realistic as possible, the rehearsals used the huge mock-up of the Grand Place on the estate associated with the Château de La Lesse, the du Bois de Mons' family home. Raphael often joined for the rehearsals; it was a short train ride from Paris, only an hour and half on average, and with a regular hourly schedule. More than once Esther, who, since their engagement, was now very much part of Raphael's life, came over to Brussels by Eurostar and joined them for a long weekend.

The riding and the procession were very carefully rehearsed but it was not until the end of May that the entire assembly of musicians, Les Gilles, and the riders, came together for the final refinement of the proceedings. In the meantime, Patti and Leah were still fascinated by the Gilles; under an invitation from Allain, Sandrine's brother, they were able to observe the Gilles preparing their dance routines for the ceremony. Allain, just over two metres tall, despite now knowing that Lucas was Patti's steady boyfriend, still had his crush on her, and so he was prepared, despite the risk of discovery and expulsion from the Gilles movement, to teach the girls the dance routines. By the time the Ommegang came round Patti and Leah knew the routines as well as, if not better than, most of the participants; *o fortunata!*

From March onwards the activity in the restaurant had become very hectic. Brussels is not only on the tourist route, but it has so many aspect of European governance that there is always a heavy throughput of tourists and visitors, and many of these find themselves dining at the restaurants in the Petite Rue des Bouchers. It would have been impossible for Patti to notice any suspicious strangers taking an interest in her as she went about her waitressing. Charles had a CCTV camera installed to observe all customers entering the restaurant, and he had facial recognition software run the rule over every one of those entering. The extremely fast computers involved checked for a match with known criminals and terrorists on the relevant databases, but nothing triggered any alarms.

There were no exams in May this year for either Patti or Leah so they simply worked at their language acquisition and the projects associated with their years abroad. Having spent so much of their lives being busy outside their academic studies both Leah and Patti were well capable of keeping up with their study schedules while taking full advantage of the other things available to them.

In Cambridge Lucas was doing his best not to miss Patti too much. Lucas spent more and more time at the ADC theatre and on his project in the engineering department. His project involved graphene and an attempt by his supervisor to create a more effective way of converting solar energy into a stored form. The project was technically difficult and conceptually challenging, and he was enjoying it; but he still spent some time sitting at his computer gazing wistfully at the pictures from the Serengeti trip and, especially, the Zanzibar part of the summer break.

At the theatre he became almost a permanent fixture. He was either the Technical Director, or the Assistant Technical Director, for one show every week in the Lent Term, the term that includes most of January and February and half of March. The third-year engineering exams take place very early in the Easter term, the term that includes much of April, the whole of May and some of the month of June. This meant that during the Easter term Lucas could again throw himself wholeheartedly into the technical production of plays at the ADC and the associated small theatre, the Corpus Playroom. He had lots of offers of dates, he had a number of very attractive and lively young people, of both sexes, taking an interest in him and hoping for more than just friendship, but he just sighed, and looked forward to the end of June when normal service, as far as he and Patti were concerned, ought to be able to resume.

Whether the absence of Patti lulled Lucas into a false sense of security, or whether his sense of self-preservation was not as highly tuned as Patti's; whatever the reason, Lucas remained unaware of the constant observation of his routines. Inspector Jenny Taylor came to see him, shortly after the conference in Adrian Armstrong's room, and she warned him that he might be in danger, that he ought to vary his routines, that he needed to be on the lookout for anything unusual happening in his life, but he took note for a short while, varied his routine for a day or two, and then he slipped back into old habits. He no longer carried his gun around with him either.

Ludovic and Irina had not found it difficult to add detail to their dossier of Lucas's movements. It helped them that whenever Lucas had visitors (his mother and brothers visited on one occasion, a couple of his schoolfriends from Brussels came on another occasion, and there were others), whenever these visitors came they had Saturday evening tickets for that week's ADC show, they had a pre-show snack at Patisserie Valerie, and they stayed in the ADC bar until the very early hours of the morning, enjoying the post show party. The other absolute given was the seat numbers that Lucas always booked. It was always row I and the seats were I1 up to whatever number it was he had to accommodate. He was well organised, and he always booked early, so Ludovic and Irina would go onto the website almost as soon as the seats were released, pretending to look for tickets. A block of seats booked from I1 upwards, booked early, almost certainly meant that Lucas and friends would be there at the theatre on the Saturday evening. There was no real debate about where bombs would need to be if they were to take out Lucas and guests. Under row I in the auditorium or under the staging in the bar area. If nobody was alert to the possibility of an attack, putting bombs in either of those places would be very easy. Detonation would also be easy; the theatre is an old building without any element of Faraday Cage like steel reinforcement in the walls, so there are no significant reception blind spots. A couple of Viktor's electronic triggers and a few hundred people would go up in smoke.

It was Irina who did most of the following around and the leg work, her job at the cleaning firm left her plenty of time, and Ludovic was busy making himself popular with the staff, fellows, and students at St Joseph's. What Ludovic was doing can best be described as 'hiding in full view'. Later on, Adrian Armstrong would kick himself for not having noticed the piercing grey eyes and the scar, but, for the moment, he had no reason to interact significantly with Ludovic; catering is the province of the Bursar and not the Senior Tutor. Ludo' would come up behind Adrian as Adrian sat there chatting to his colleagues over lunch; Ludo' would ask what Adrian wanted for his next course; Adrian would respond, with hardly a glance at the waiter; the food would arrive; Adrian would continue doing business.

There were numerous pinch points around the college where a party of visitors being shown around would come close together, and Ludovic reported to Viktor about these possible ambush sites; but Viktor, already less enamoured with face to face attacks on people, if only because of the difficulty of getting away, had had his fingers burnt in the Serengeti and his imagination led him to consider that the 'little blonde bitch' might be carrying a gun, possibly even a machine gun. The intel from the CIA mole had made Viktor very wary of Patti, possibly even a little afraid. His reasoning led him to shy away from a frontal attack in the college and to think, instead, about using explosives in either the theatre or the hotel or residence in which the president might stay during her time in Cambridge. He would need more intelligence from the mole at Langley, or directly from Ludovic, before he could decide where to plant his bombs, but for the bombs in the UK, wherever they were to be placed, he would need to recover the explosives he had left in Somersham, the little village just north of Cambridge.

Irina planted a couple of dummy bombs in the theatre at various times throughout the next few months. There was one carefully levered into the seat cushion of seat I1. She also planted one under the staging in the corner of the bar area. The mock bombs were left there for several days and remained undiscovered until Irina returned to remove them surreptitiously after they had served their purpose.

Once Viktor knew what it was that he was going to do he had to put his plans into action. He had to get hold of the explosives and make the bombs. Ludovic and Irina were too valuable to Viktor for him to risk their going up to Somersham to recover the material that had been left there so, fortunately for Jenny and Jerry, the gang decided to use two of the people from the Stroud Green Road cell. The same two who had gone to The Montcalm Royal London House left the flat early one morning and collected a hire car from the local Hertz Rental car depot. The surveillance team had been replaced by a camera trained on the front door of the flat. It was a sophisticated camera system which detected the opening and closing of the door and triggered an alert. A signal sent to the local police station allowed the team to track the movement of the two men and, once the destination was known, an unmarked car was despatched to pick up the duo and follow them to wherever they were going. Once the car was followed onto the M11 Jenny Taylor took a punt that this car was heading towards Ely, and she arranged to meet Superintendent Gregory at Ely station and to take over the pursuit of the hire car to wherever it led them.

"I bet they are going to recover more explosives and bomb making stuff," said Jenny, as Jerry settled himself into the passenger seat of the souped up, but very ordinary looking, Ford Focus.

"I want a surveillance team in place near that Somersham farm as soon as possible," said Jerry. He got on the radio and called Special Branch and a small detachment of the SAS was deployed to the farm, dropped by helicopter, within minutes.

"We may look stupid if they don't go there," said Jerry, "but if we pick them up when they leave the A10 we can cover the possibility that they are going somewhere else and, if they do go to the farm, we can see what they do without arousing their suspicions. I bet they buried the rest of the Semtex, and probably a selection of other arms and ammunition, somewhere in one of the hedgerows around the place. It wasn't worth our while trying to find it at the time, but I sort of wish now that we had."

"No Sir," said Jenny, "it really wasn't worth it. I think I always kind of knew that we would be on to them if they tried to reactivate the cell, and here we are… lucky; or what?"

"Are you always so bloody optimistic, Jenny? How does anyone live with you?"

"At the moment they don't, sir, But I'm ever hopeful."

"That's what I mean. Ever hopeful."

And with that remark, Jerry gave Jenny a fist bump and they settled back to watch out for the black VW Golf with the two terrorists in it. They chatted a little, they ate a few snacks. It was about fifteen minutes after Jerry got into the car that the target vehicle came past them. Jenny waited for a few more cars to pass and then pulled out to follow. It was not difficult, the occupants of the Golf had no idea that they were being followed and, to Jenny's surprise, seemed remarkably lazy about their security. Having travelled this route previously, the two detectives knew very soon after leaving Ely that they were heading for the Somersham farm and took the risk of dropping back even further and simply moving at their own leisurely pace in the same direction as the black VW. Jerry got back onto the radio and asked the SAS commander to ensure that observation was thorough. He wanted to know what munitions the terrorists laid their hands on; but Jerry insisted that the terrorists could not know that they had been watched.

The countryside just north of Ely is very old-style farm country, lots of hedges and small fields, and winding, narrow, roads; Jerry noted that Jenny was an excellent driver, that knowledge might come in useful sometime.

After about fifteen minutes the commander of the SAS unit reported that the VW had arrived at the farm and the two men had walked down a bridle path to a single ash tree standing proud of the hedgerow lining the path. They had taken spades with them and had, after a little digging, retrieved a small black box, about 25 by 25 by 50cm in size. They paused to fill the hole back in and to sprinkle some dead grass and twigs over the ground to disguise the fact of their digging.

They had then walked a little further along the bridle path and had dismantled a small dry-stone wall that replaced a bit of the hedgerow. From underneath the last few stones they had removed a package wrapped in waterproof material, possibly oilskin. They had unwrapped the package and inspected a couple of what looked like AK47 rifles, some handguns and a packet of something that the observers could not identify. There was also a significant quantity of ammunition that they fished out of a slightly deeper recess under the wall. The two men had loaded the items into their backpacks, apart from the rifles which they laid on the ground while they filled the hole back in and replaced the stones in the wall. Within twenty minutes or so they were back at the farm, loaded their spoils into the boot, and were heading back down the road towards London. They seemed in high spirits, laughing and joking together as they went.

Jerry arranged a tag team of unmarked vehicles to take over from Cambridge and follow the pair back to their lair. The terrorists made a detour into Cambridge, parking in the car park at the large Tesco Supermarket at the junction of the A10 and the A14. They waited about ten minutes, during which time they took some items out of the boot of the car and got them ready to hand over to a contact. One of the men went into the store and came out with three cups of coffee in disposable cups. About ten minutes after their arrival a young blonde woman on a bicycle rode up to their car. She had come on the cycle path from the centre of the city. The hand over was of a couple of items from the package of guns and ammunition, something from the small package that the SAS had not been able to identify, and a rectangular parcel, about the size of a 1 litre carton of orange juice, which they had removed from the black box that had been the first item they dug up. The three chatted for about another ten minutes while they drank their coffees.

By the time the transfer of goods had taken place and the coffee had been drunk Jenny Taylor had identified a bicycle that she would like to ride, arranged with the owner of that bicycle that she could, indeed 'borrow' it, changed into a pair of shorts and a long-sleeved sports top, and moved towards the cycle path entrance at the far side of the car park. She fiddled with her chain, loaded, and unloaded a couple of panniers, and got ready to ride over the cycle bridge. Jenny followed the woman, it was Irina, back into town and discovered that she was living in a fairly luxurious apartment on the Riverside. Jenny could work out which entrance the woman used but she could not determine the precise address. Nevertheless, she had some excellent photographs of Irina and would be able to pass those to members of the surveillance teams so that they could follow Irina's movements around Cambridge. Given the contact it was clear that this woman was up to no good and further follow-up was essential.

Nor was that the end of the good fortune. The tag team took up the trail as far as the service station at the Stanstead Airport turn-off. The men stopped there for another coffee and, when they came out, they were talking to a third man who looked to the tag team as if he was of African origin. They transferred all the remaining packages to this man's car, a rather upmarket black Mercedes. The tag team then made a very brave decision, they decided to follow the Mercedes rather than the VW. The tracking of the Merc took longer than anticipated; it drove down beyond the M25 and moved onto the north circular road, eventually reaching the Chalkhill Estate in the Wembley Park area. There the Mercedes parked up at one of the addresses on the estate and the man got out and began to transfer the items in his car boot into the lock up garage next to his house. The Mercedes seemed a little out of place. The area was known as a very high crime area, lots of drug dealing and violent crime. That the Mercedes looked in very good order was a clear indication that this gentleman was towards the top end of the food chain. When he walked up the path to the front door two very 'heavy' looking gentlemen opened the door to him and greeted him very deferentially.

As they sat together back at the Cambridge police station Jenny Taylor and Jerry Gregory could look back on a highly successful day. They had not only confirmed the presence of Viktor's terrorists in the Stroud Green Road flat; they had also identified a young woman involved in the gang at the Cambridge end of things, and a further possible terrorist house in a high crime area of North London. It felt very much as if they were no longer fishing in the dark. Someone had turned the light on.

It was not long before the team in Cambridge had seen Irina in the company of Ludovic and had managed to get a good photograph of him too.

For the second half of the month of April Lucas returned home to Brussels and spent a lot of time with Patti, Leah, Esther, and Raphael. Esther had also gone home for the vacation but, unlike the other three, this was her final year of undergraduate study, she had her law final exam in the summer. She had applied to study for the BCL, the one-year Bachelor of Civil Law degree. This is a highly competitive course to get into and, despite her record so far, she would need an outstanding result in her final year to make the cut. The application to admittance ratio was close to ten to one and every applicant was well qualified. Esther had more sense than just to sit there studying non-stop. Her organisation skills and her quick and retentive memory gave her enough of an edge that she could join the others riding and relaxing for quite a bit of the time. She did not attend the Ommegang rehearsals, but she rode with Raphael and the others at weekends.

It was at the end of April that Lee Corland, under his new alias, arrived in Brussels and moved into a small apartment in the Molenbeek area of the city. He did not know about Patti Howland, only that the president of the United States was planning a visit sometime in late June or early July. He was waiting for additional information from his mentor, Zacchary Hutchins, about the likely movements of the president and the exact timing of the visit. The information came to him in dribs and drabs. He knew that the president was going to visit England on her way to Brussels, but he decided that there was little point in risking another border crossing now that the United Kingdom was outside the EU. Instead, he, like Viktor, was looking at all the possible places in Brussels the president might visit.

It might all have come to nothing had the security at Langley not been accidentally breached. It was just one of those things that can happen anywhere. Davelle, the president's private secretary, had just finalised the details of the trip and had shared those details, on a very secure line, with Charles and one or two others. The mole in the organisation had not been included in the circulation but he was in the office of one of his colleagues when the information came through. The person whose office the mole was in had been called away suddenly to collect a sick child from their school and had forgotten, in their anxiety over their child, to turn off the computer before leaving. Viktor, who paid for the information, and Lee Corland, who shared an ideological dream, received information that the sequence of visits would be London, Paris, Berlin, Brussels, Ommegang; that was the sequence that was presented to them. They also had dates and approximate times.

Chapter 16

Neither Patti nor Lucas was making total sense of the way their relationship was working out. It would be a bit strong to say it was going through a rocky patch, but it lacked the sure conviction of the relationship that they had enjoyed during their time together in Cambridge. They clearly liked each other's company and were still quite happily physical in their relationship with each other, but the future was much too uncertain for either of them to think about longer term commitment.

Lucas spent quite a bit of time making sure he was ready for the exams that would happen almost immediately on his return to Cambridge. With Patti and Leah working and the others studying hard the relationships were much less carefree, and more adult, than they had been used to. Patti, on a weekend visit to Cambridge, noticed that Lucas was less security conscious than he had been, and they had quite a strong argument about it.

"You know as well as I do that the Rubinsky gang has been commissioned to get your father, directly or indirectly, and yet you've stopped being careful. Leah and I nearly got caught by them with that scam they tried earlier this year. My mum and dad are probably coming to visit next summer. Without better security awareness on our part," Patti was trying to be firm but gentle, "we're putting that visit in danger and I do want them to come. I miss them and I'm certainly going back to America to be nearer them when I finish at Cambridge. Please start being careful again. You don't even look over your shoulder when a car comes round the corner, or someone walks up behind you."

Lucas looked a little embarrassed: "I keep forgetting that I'm supposed to be an important target," he said. "I keep thinking I'm just another engineering student at Cambridge, and I also keep forgetting what you are. I think I know *who* you are but that isn't what this is all about. I'm sorry. I'll try to do better."

"Not good enough Lukey. You will not *try* to do better; you *will* do better. I don't want to end up dead and the way you're behaving means that you're opening the door to terrorists, especially the Rubinsky gang, to take any of us out. I think we have to assume they know who we are and where we are, so it's a case of making sure they can't get to us. Have you got your gun with you?"

"No," said Lucas, "I haven't. Have you?"

Two seconds later, Lucas felt the barrel of a Smith and Wesson M&P Shield digging into his ribs.

"Oi! That bloody well hurts."

"Tough," said Patti. "Give me your phone. Lock it."

Lucas handed over the phone.

"Have you changed your PIN?"

"Yes."

Patti tapped in six numbers, the phone remained locked, she tapped in six more, the phone unlocked.

"You know why I was able to do that," she said. "Your PIN was Vusi's birthday. I tried Esther's first, but you had at least gone for one that the Rubinsky gang would be less likely to go for. But honestly Lukey, high security, and it's a member of the family's birthday. How many other devices do you have the same pin for?"

Lucas started to get cross, but Patti shut him up.

"Don't get cross. I'm not getting at you; I'm just as bad. I'm trying to show you how vulnerable we are. You know my PIN, it's your bloody birthday. Let's make a pact to upgrade our security arrangements, both you and me, and let me telephone Charles and get us on a refresher course. We can do it the weekend after your exams finish; before that it would be too distracting. Besides which we can get absolutely drunk after your exams and I fancy getting absolutely drunk with you, I haven't been able to do that for a long time. Too long."

"When is the May Week musical? What are they doing?" asked Patti.

"It's still strictly hush hush," said Lucas, "but they're planning to do a two-week run of 'Chicago'. We have two brilliant women to play Roxie and Velma; Justin is a brilliant dancer, and he can play Billy, and Josef will make a wonderful Mr Cellophane! Oh, and Marielle will be Mama."

"That's great. I think there's a lot of scope for some good tech in there too. I bet you're going to enjoy it. I think it's time to tighten up on our dates for all this. You just make damn sure you have row I1 to I14 booked for the final Saturday evening performance. I want us all to come to the party too."

"Will your parents be incognito?" asked Lucas.

"Yes, I believe so. I think that 'officially' they're planning to go to Camp David for a long weekend, back to Washington for a week, and then fly from there to London, then Paris, then Berlin and finally end up in Brussels, miraculously just in time for the Ommegang. In reality they are coming to England via the USAF base at Mildenhall and are going to have two or three days in Cambridge, including the play on the Saturday and the May Ball on the Sunday. They should arrive in Cambridge on the Thursday evening, so we have the Friday to do things like punting and showing them round St Joe's. The college shuts down on the Saturday morning so that it can prepare for the May Ball, so the play's timing is perfect, and I already have tickets for them for the May Ball on the Sunday. I believe they'll fly back to the US on the Monday. The next Monday they fly back to England and begin their official visit by addressing the United Kingdom parliament."

"So, we have a week after the show before the official visit?" asked Lucas.

"Yes," said Patti. "Back to Brussels and lots of rehearsals. I have special permission from the Ommegang team to miss the rehearsals over the ball weekend, but I need to be back for the rest of the week, and the week leading up to the Ommegang. Full dress rehearsal the Thursday before the Ommegang and then three days of performance. No rehearsals over the actual weekend before; the vets said it was important for the horses to get a rest; some of the horses are going to be used for jousting, and animal welfare's important. I guess that was lucky for us, we can spend some time together."

Patti and Lucas had no idea that they were organising, or planning to organise, exactly what Rubinsky had anticipated.

Lee Corland started to explore the likely 'official visit' sites at about the same time as the Rubinsky gang increased their effort in that direction. Anyone involved in terrorist activities becomes very suspicious when they find the same old faces cropping up in their lives. Lee saw, on numerous occasions, members of the Rubinsky gang at the critical venues. At first, when he did an initial inspection of the potential sites, he thought only that there was a group of tourists who happened to have the same itinerary as he did.

After the initial inspection he contacted Zacchary back in Kansas and asked him for help in acquiring suitable explosives and detonators. One of Zacchary's group of contacts was of Irish American ancestry, and he knew some former members of the provisional IRA who still had access to arms and ammunition, bombs, and detonators. Zacchary arranged for one of these Provisionals to send some explosives, and some other munitions, to Lee in Brussels. The Irish Republic was still in the European Union so the sending of these materials, suitably concealed, by courier, was quite straightforward. Lee spent a happy couple of weeks reorganising some of the contents of the three parcels that arrived at the apartment in Molenbeek into parcel bombs that would be relatively hard to detect by conventional gas chromatography and sniffer dog methods. They were sealed, with only the electronic detonators protruding from the packages. These could be set off by mobile phone signals or by radio signals from a special handheld transmitter. He made three such bombs. He was waiting for more information before deciding where he might place them.

About two weeks later he again made the rounds of the sites he had been inspecting and this time he noticed that the same people he had seen a few weeks previously were following a similar itinerary. He decided that this was too much of a coincidence. Tourists do not usually go to the same tourist destinations, especially tourist destinations as dull as the European parliament buildings, and the other places of governance, more than once. They also do not tend to stay two weeks in the same place.

That evening one of Rubinsky's men was walking back to his apartment, also, by coincidence, in Molenbeek, when someone stepped out of the shadows, stuck a gun in his ribs and said, in very bad French with a strong American twang: "Say anything, or shout, and I will kill you. You and I need to have a little talk. When I tell you to move you will walk to the corner and turn left. From the corner you will see a gate into an alleyway. You will go down that alley way and stop when I tell you."

The French may have been bad, but the message was clear enough. Laslo froze. Lee Corland, for it was he with the gun in the man's ribs, expertly frisked Laslo, found and removed both his concealed weapons, the one in his shoulder holster and the one in his thigh holster, and tapped him fairly hard on the back of the neck, just for emphasis. He also removed the man's wallet.

"Now move; walk steadily and don't look round."

Lee had done his homework. Halfway down the alley there was a gate into the backyard of a garage business. It was deserted at this time of the evening, the garage being closed and all the employees, mechanics, and customers, having long departed.

"Put your hands together behind your back," said Lee.

Laslo did as he was told.

Lee looped one of those 15mm wide cable ties, the heavy duty ones that are used to tie up thick cables and pipes, put it over the man's wrists, and pulled it tight. This was not one of those parcel ties that even children, with the right training, can break out of.

"Lie on your stomach," said Lee.

The man did so.

"Bend your knees and lift your feet together in the air."

Another large cable tie was fastened around the ankles and pulled uncomfortably tight.

Lee pulled the man to his feet by grabbing his collar and unceremoniously hoisting him upright. He then turned the man round and sat him on a large block of concrete that had been dumped in the yard.

"Let's see who you are," said Lee; and he reached into his pocket and brought out the wallet that he had previously removed from the man's jacket.

"Laslo Meszaros; is that you?"

Laslo nodded.

"Why have you and your friends been following me? Are you police?"

"No. Not police. We have not been following you. Where did you think I was following you?" Laslo spoke for the first time, and he sounded very afraid.

"You were at the parliament buildings about four weeks ago, and then, again, this week, and you were at several other government buildings when I was there; and there were some others with you. It was the same people each time," said Lee.

"Who are you? Are *you* police or security?" asked Laslo.

"I ask the questions," said Lee, "but for your information I'm not police or security, far from it."

Laslo thought for a minute and decided he was going to end up dead if he didn't do something a bit radical.

"Were you looking at possible bomb sites too?" asked Laslo.

Lee Corland was not expecting that. It took him a moment to process.

"What do you mean, too?" he asked.

"We want to kill the president of the United States," said Laslo.

"You're shitting me," said Lee.

"No, is the truth. We think the president is coming to Brussels in June and we want to kill her, with a bomb," said Laslo.

"Do you have any proof of anything you are saying?" asked Lee.

"I can call the other members of our gang and they will tell you it is true," said Laslo.

Then Laslo, realising that he had not been killed and that his captor had taken the statement rather at its face value had a eureka moment.

"That's why you were going round the same sites too, wasn't it?" asked Laslo.

"Maybe," said Lee.

"Perhaps we could work together?" said Laslo. "How did you know the president is coming to Brussels?"

"I might ask you the same thing," said Lee.

"We have inside information from the CIA," said Laslo; gradually becoming emboldened by the way this conversation was going.

"Me too," said Lee; beginning to think that this encounter was likely to be more useful than he had feared it might. He had thought that, however improbable it seemed, the local police were onto him. Now it appeared that there was a gang in the city intent upon the same mission as he was. This kidnapping had been to find out what the local police knew; and how they knew it. It now appeared that he was still completely unknown to local law enforcement and security. It also meant that he might be able to find an ally, and allies are always useful in military situations.

"If you are who you say you are, and you are what you say you are, can you get the leader of your gang to come and rescue you? He or she is to come without a gun and bring proof that you are planning a bomb. Some detonators and some explosive will do. And they must come alone, or I will shoot you, and them, as soon as they come through the door in the alley way."

"My brother is our leader," said Laslo. "I will call him."

Laslo made the telephone call and arranged the meeting. Lee gave him the precise address and then left Laslo sitting there on the concrete block while he himself hid in a carefully chosen vantage point, from which he could cover the gate and the concrete block, and from which no part of the yard was hidden.

It was about fifteen minutes later that the gang leader came through the gate into the backyard.

"Put the objects on the ground over by the water tap," called out Lee.

The man obliged.

"Now take off all your clothes except your underpants and put them on the ground next to the explosives and the detonators."

The man did so.

"Tell me why you were at the parliament building on the 17th last month and the 3rd this month," ordered Lee.

The explanation given tallied completely with what Laslo had told Lee.

"Do you want to work together, or shall we just forget that each other exists?" asked the guy in the underpants.

"Get dressed, you dumb klutz," said Lee, in his usual charming and endearing manner. He moved into view, took out a very large and very sharp pocketknife, and cut the parcel ties from around Laslo's wrists and ankles. Laslo spent about five minutes rubbing his wrists and ankles to restore the circulation.

"You did not have to pull them so tight," said Laslo.

"Bullshit," said Lee. "I was going to kill you if you were police, and I didn't want you turning the tables on me. I'll make up for it. Let me buy you both a drink and we can talk this over."

They headed together, the three of them, for the nearest bar. Michu Meszaros, the gang leader, called the others, who had been loitering about a hundred metres away, and the rest of Rubinsky's gang joined Lee in the bar. Michu spoke good English with a very strong accent.

"My name is Michu Meszaros," he said. "You have been hosting my little brother. I'm glad you did not seriously hurt him."

Michu Meszaros asked Lee why he wanted to kill the president. Inwardly Michu was not impressed. He was a criminal with a money motive. He had been converted to a terrorist with a political motive simply by Viktor offering opportunities to earn large amounts of money. Michu had been involved in people trafficking, including sex trafficking, but he was not homophobic, nor was he racist. He was not a misogynist, just a chauvinist who didn't really think of most women as anything more than sex objects. Had he been recruiting he might have considered Lee too obsessional and too unbalanced for the gang. However, Michu was not recruiting, and he could see that Lee's ability to identify a threat to his own security and take action to neutralise it might make him an asset worth courting. It all depended on whether Lee could be managed, and Michu had some ideas about how that might be achieved.

Michu decided to tell Lee about the gang, the extent of the network and the resources at its disposal. Lee did not interest himself in the reasoning behind the Rubinsky plans, only in the thought that here might be another ally in destroying the president and the president's 'corrupt and decadent' administration.

"I'll talk to you, and we can share intelligence, but I still want to work alone," said Lee.

"I think that is sensible," said Michu. "That way, we have two different cells working to the same end. The only thing we mustn't do is blow each other up, eh little brother?" He turned to his younger brother Laslo and smiled.

Over several very good Belgian beers, the gang and Lee agreed that they would keep each other informed of their detailed plans for the explosions and they would also pass on any information that they received from their sources about the presidential movements. It had not occurred to them that their sources might be identical, especially as Lee, until his meeting with the Rubinsky gang, had no idea about the presence in Brussels of Patti Howland. When Michu told him that the president's daughter was studying at the university and working at Richard's restaurant, somehow Lee knew that this young lady, who had an African boyfriend, was going to have to figure in his plans for the takeout of the president. He needed a backup to make sure that he got her too, all the better if he could get the boyfriend at the same time.

"Where do you eat?" asked Michu.

"I move around," said Lee, "but there are many good and cheap halal restaurants in Molenbeek, and I often go there. There is one called the Kasbah, and that, and the Maharajah Tandoori are my favourites. Why do you ask?"

"Zsofia, one of our group, who did not come with us tonight, she is a very good cook. If you would like to eat with us sometimes that would be a very nice way of keeping in touch."

Michu smiled. Lee smiled back.

"Here is my card," said Michu.

He handed over a very dirty piece of card cut from a plain postcard and with the address and telephone number written on it.

Lee took a pen out of his pocket.

"Do you have another one of those?" he asked. Michu handed one over and Lee wrote his address and his telephone number on the back of the card and returned it to him. There was a lot of back slapping, embracing and fist bumping; since Covid, fist bumping had largely replaced the handshake as a regular form of friendly acknowledgment.

"How about tomorrow evening?" asked Michu. "About 8pm?"

"That would be my pleasure," said Lee. "I will not come empty handed. Red, or white, or beer?"

"Why not all three?" said Michu.

That night, back in his apartment, Lee decided that his next action should be to find this Patti girl and start to work out her movements.

The next morning Lee decided to stake out Richard's restaurant to see if a blonde girl came into work. He was intending to take lunch there; his dinner plans were already in place.

Patti was working an early shift that particular day and Lee soon spotted her arriving at the restaurant mid-morning to prepare for her shift. He could not resist taking lunch at Richard's, if only to get a closer look at the girl and see if he could recognise her as the Howland daughter. He did.

When Patti left at about 4pm Lee followed her. She met up with Leah and the pair of them headed off towards the chateau, to meet up with some of the others and ride their horses. It just happened that when they arrived at the stables Sandrine and Therese were waiting there with some of the costumes that the girls might be wearing for the parade. It was a sort of dress try-on for the two latest additions to the pageant. Moat of the regulars already had their costumes, but Leah and Patti were novices, and needed to get something appropriate sorted out well in advance. Lee was fascinated by this but had no idea what it was all about. He resolved to ask the Meszaros brothers when he dined with them that evening.

It was not late, only about 7pm when Patti and Leah returned home, and Lee followed them to their apartment. He was not intending to use the knowledge of their base in any of his assassination plans, but he did like to develop a complete dossier on his potential victims when he could. A relatively short journey from their apartment to the Meszaros base meant that at about 7.30pm he was sitting down with the gang, drinking red wine, and anticipating a delicious smelling meal that Zsofia was preparing in the kitchen. Lee noted, with approval, that the apartment, although not lavishly furnished, was clean and tidy and spacious enough to accommodate all the gang members in comfort. The meal began with a cold meat jelly, the nearest thing Lee had seen to it before was the English dish of brawn, and some pickled vegetables. The main dish was a goulash, served with some potato cakes. The pudding was honey cake, sprinkled with walnuts. The wine flowed freely throughout.

It was halfway through his second portion of honey cake that Lee asked Michu about the girls' costumes.

"They are doing something in the Ommegang," said Michu.

"The what?" asked Lee.

"The Ommegang. It's an event that is held every year in the Grand Place and it has a pageant with horse riding and jousting and bands of travelling musicians, and people called Gilles who dress up and throw oranges into the crowd and play all sorts of funny music, very loudly."

Lee's ears pricked up. The Howland girl in a procession through the Grand Place.

"When does it happen?" he asked.

"End of June, start of July," said Michu.

"The president is going to be here then, isn't she," said Lee.

"We think that's right," said Michu.

"How do we bomb the Grand Place?" asked Lee. "If I can get hold of some mortars, can we use mortars? What do you think?"

There was a long debate and they all agreed to go away and think about it. The Meszaros and the gang had almost dismissed the idea of an attack in the Grand Place, but they had not thought of using mortars and it was an idea worth following up, especially if Lee could get them the ordnance to actually do the job. Lee was curious about the Ommegang.

At the end of the evening, they all parted on good terms. Lee's somewhat harsh treatment of Laslo had been forgiven, even by Laslo, who now saw Lee as a fellow soldier in the fight against the American president and the pro-Stanislowsky regime. Zsofia had taken quite a liking to Lee, he was a very handsome man and clearly had maintained his level of fitness, even during the years in prison. She slipped him a note with her private cell phone number on it and a suggestion, in English, that they might meet one afternoon for some recreation. Lee was not averse to the idea; he had been a long time in prison and a long time without a girlfriend. Michu was delighted that his plan to handle Lee was working out.

Over the next few days Lee looked in great detail at all the information he could glean from the internet about the Ommegang. He became fascinated by the Gilles. The macabre face masks, with their little moustaches, their green spectacles, and their rosy cheeks, appealed to him. It was almost like old-fashioned vaudeville theatre; it was loud, it was brash, and, given the instruments involved, it was genuinely brassy.

Back in England both Lucas and Esther were coming to the end of their third undergraduate years. Lucas knew he would be studying for a further year at St

Joseph's. Esther was sweating a bit on her exam result. She needed a very good result to get onto the highly competitive BCL programme.

Jerry Gregory, Jenny Taylor, and the team in Cambridge had been given a lot more detail about the itinerary for the presidential visit. They had continued their surveillance of the Rubinsky gang in London. They knew, from the previous surveillance, that the gang now had quite a stock of explosives and they were thinking again about where the explosives might be deployed. The obvious places in Cambridge where an attack might occur were the ADC theatre and the Vice Chancellor's residence, where the president would be staying overnight after the performance, before heading back to the local United States Airforce base and flying into Heathrow.

Special Branch in London were taking care of that end of the operation. There was no point in showing their hand. There were surveillance cameras on the Chalkhill Estate and on Stroud Green Road.

In Cambridge Jerry and Jenny had identified Irina as a person of interest. They had shown Ludovic's picture to the receptionist at the Modern and Medieval Languages building and she had made a tentative identification of him as the man who had come and asked her to help him find a tutor for his daughter. CCTV cameras were all over Cambridge and the software was programmed to identify and signal any movements of Irina and Ludovic, with particular emphasis on any times when they went near to the theatre or to the Vice-Chancellor's residence out on the Madingley Road. It took less than a week for them to discover that Ludovic now had a job in catering at St Joseph's.

There was an interesting conversation when Jenny confronted Adrian with the news that his charming new high table waiter was a member of the Rubinsky gang.

"Oh shit," said Adrian. "Are you quite sure."

Jenny showed him the picture.

"Yep," said Adrian. "That's Ludo'."

"He was also Kransky," said Jenny. "The guy who tried to find Patti Howland by setting up that false job teaching English to his non-existent daughter. His real name is Ludovic Fedorov, and we think he was, and maybe still is, Viktor Rubinsky's quartermaster."

"Do we sack him?" Adrian asked.

"No. I don't think so. I think we watch him," Jenny said. "We watch him, and you let us know if he takes any long holidays or disappears from the scene.

Can you also see who he talks to and whether he tries to pump anyone for information about either Lucas or Patti. The gang are still after Lucas as far as we can see."

"Oh, and this is his girlfriend, Irina Semionova. She has a job working for a cleaning company which gives her access to a lot of central university buildings, including the theatre. We arranged for one of our Russian speaking officers to get a job at the same cleaning company and he works in the same team as Irina."

Patient surveillance was always inclined to bring its reward and by a long period of observation of Irina and Ludovic entering the Riverside block and then noting movement in the flats, the turning on and off of light switches, they were able to pin down the precise flat which the two terrorists occupied. Inspection of the rental agreements for the flats confirmed their observations. There was a debate about whether to round up the two at this stage or to let the thing run a little longer. In the end it was decided that pulling in Irina and Ludovic would simply lead to replacement of a known threat with an unknown one; a new team drafted in to complete the task. Observation remained the name of the game.

The one thing that Jenny did arrange was for one of the IT team to enter and bug the unoccupied flat, and to put some tracker software into the laptop and the desk top computer that they found there. The two hacked devices became a very useful source of information. There was a lot of contact with both of the London Rubinsky groups, and Jenny and Jerry always knew exactly how up to date was the gang's intelligence information, particularly when there were planned changes in the presidential visit.

Chapter 17

Back at Langley, now that Charles knew the identity of the mole in the CIA, a constant stream of plausible, but inaccurate, information was being fed to the Rubinsky gang. Most of the inaccuracy concerned timing. The sequence of visits was also sent misleadingly. But the Rubinsky gang were not taken in by any of this, and, in conversation with them, neither was Lee.

"One thing we know for sure is that they are going to be in Brussels for the Ommegang," said Lee.

"Yes, and that's not a moveable feast. It has to be between the 30th June and 2nd July," said Michu.

"The other fixed points are the theatre visit and the May Ball," said Lee.

"If we're going to do something at the Ommegang it's got to be flexible, and we need to work out how we get to know which one of the days to do it."

"We need to be able to watch the Grand Place and *see* the president arrive, then we know which day to do things," said Lee. "What do you reckon. Can we set up mini surveillance cameras somewhere? Any other ideas about how we do this?"

"Little cameras seem a great idea to me," said Michu. "We need to work out where we can site the mortars, and maybe we also try to put some bombs in place in advance. If we get lucky, we may be able to use them and if they get discovered the police may think they've dealt with the threat. I'm sure they know there's a potential for trouble."

"Do you have anyone in Interpol or the European Intelligence services who can tell us if the authorities are expecting particular trouble?" Lee asked. "I mean, is there anything that singles this visit out from any other visit the president might make to a foreign country?"

"I don't think so," said Michu. "We don't have anyone in the administration or the local police but I reckon the thing that might make them specially careful is that this is the first time the president has visited Europe and they are going to worry about her being a target."

"I hope we can keep it that way, not give them anything specific to stir them up," said Lee. "If they start to get specific, we might be in trouble. What about your guys in London? And do you have some in Paris or Berlin?"

"We do have guys there. We're not planning on doing anything anywhere else in Europe, as far as I know. London is different and, because we think she is going to Cambridge, we do have a couple of people there looking at possibilities."

"My contact told me they were planning to visit Cambridge," Lee said.

"There was a suggestion from my contact that they would go to see the theatre and also go to the May Ball at their daughter's college. But that would be a couple of weeks before the Ommegang. I can't imagine the president spending nearly three weeks out of the country, so maybe it will be two separate visits? What do you think?"

"Two visits, that sounds about right," said Michu. "We have a couple of people in Cambridge. They are keeping an eye on the Ndlovu boy, we still want him out of the way. In fact, we got paid to take him out and failed, so we have that job to finish."

"We need more detail," said Lee, "and we need it fast."

"Do they know about your gang?" Lee asked.

"They do," said Michu, and he went on to tell Lee about the failed attempt to destroy Stanislowsky, the failed attempt to capture Lucas and Esther Ndlovu, and the raid on the Somersham farmhouse that he himself and others of the gang had only just managed to get away from.

"Gee, that's all kinda tough," said Lee; but he thought to himself *these guys really fucked up. Maybe I need a plan B that they know nothing about.*

He resolved to go away and work on it. He was not going to try to cross into the United Kingdom, although he knew that the president would be visiting there, mainly because there was free movement within the EU but, since the UK had left the European Union, there would be passport checks for Lee at the EU and UK borders. No; plan B had to be based in Brussels around the time of the Ommegang.

Michu, on the other hand, was wondering if a second plan based around Cambridge might be a good idea. Certainly, finishing the Ndlovu job and taking the president out at the same time would be a coup. Irina had already tried out the dummy bombs, maybe real ones would work?

Ludovic, working in St Joseph's College, was becoming very aware of the timetable for the end of year celebrations. He knew the timing of the May Ball, not difficult to find out since it was widely advertised, and he also knew that Ndlovu was involved in the Cambridge University Musical Theatre Society production of "Chicago." He had to think that the visit of the president would coincide with one or other of these events. Semtex is very stable, until it is not. Sometime towards the end of May Irina replaced the dummy bombs, which were still where she had put them, with real bombs which had electronic detonators embedded ready to receive an appropriate signal. There were 12 small bombs embedded in the first twelve seats in row I and a relatively large bomb under the staging in the ADC bar.

Irina and Ludovic were now confident that, if the president and her party visited the theatre, they could kill her and everyone else in the building. On one of her morning cleaner's visits Irina put surveillance cameras on the wall of the auditorium and above the bar. They pointed at row I, the stage in the corner of the bar area, and at all the entrances into the bar. It was belt and braces. Blow them up in the theatre itself or wait until they came for interval drinks and blast them out of existence then. It was perhaps fortunate that Irina was unaware of the existing surveillance cameras that Jenny Taylor had placed a few months earlier. There was almost a smug satisfaction as the two police officers watched the tapes of Irina placing her bombs and her cameras. But there was no need to move on the matter at this stage.

The group in London still believed that the president and her entourage were intending to stay at The Montcalm Royal London House. Over the next few weeks Special Branch watched, almost with amusement, as the previously identified gang members put their own bombs in place. There would be plenty of time to remove them when the visit did actually occur, although there was no intention of allowing the president to get anywhere near the danger. As was often the case with visiting dignitaries, the official part of the tour would involve the president staying at Chequers as a guest of the prime minister.

Chapter 18

Lee Corland was very busy. He was watching Patti and Leah, mostly Patti, and becoming familiar with their routines. Despite varying the routes between the things that they were doing they did, nevertheless, have several fixed points in their days. The morning classes at the university, the work shifts, and the rehearsals for the Ommegang, were in fixed locations so Lee did not bother too much about following them between those locations; instead, he picked one or two of them each day to simply turn up at. He did, however, almost always turn up at the chateau and observe the Ommegang rehearsals. It was usually at a sensible distance and from a concealed vantage point, he had powerful binoculars. He was not learning much from these rehearsals except that he had seen the costumes that the two girls would be wearing, and he noted that they always rode side by side in the procession. He was confident that he could recognise them in the pageant. It might be important for the plan that was beginning to form in his mind.

Allain, Sandrine's younger brother, was very caught up in the rehearsals for the Ommegang. The Gilles were part of the procession, but the Ommegang was only one of the events that they were rehearsing for. There was the Carnival de Binche, and there were other appearances throughout Belgium.

Lee Corland just happened to be observing one of the rehearsals by Les Gilles. He was very busy photographing with his camera phone and took a short video of the dancing. He went home most evenings and practised the dance steps, not completely choreographed, but clearly stylised. On this occasion, he noticed Allain because Allain was such a similar height and build to himself, and because both Patti and Leah went up to Allain and embraced him, continental style. Allain was one of the tallest of the Gilles and, judging from the dancing, one of the most energetic. When they formed up into the procession for the carnival Allain was always on the right side at the back of the group. On this particular occasion, when they had finished the dance rehearsal, the leader of the group called them into an assembly and presented them with a huge crate of large Jaffa oranges. Lee wondered what this was all about, but it was not long before he realised that they were having an orange throwing competition. Some of the throws were impressive, several tens of metres. And all the oranges were large, not satsumas and mandarins, just big juicy fruits. Lee was aware that part of the Ommegang involved the Gilles throwing these oranges from the big wicker baskets they carried around with them. As might be expected from such a diverse group some of the Gilles managed only a relatively short distance and, indeed, one of the gentlemen manged a single throw before clutching his shoulder and deciding to take no more part in the event, much to Lee's amusement.

A review of the situation by the Rubinsky hierarchy suggested that all the bombs were in place in Cambridge and London. They were blissfully unaware that these bombs had all been identified and marked for removal. In Brussels they had decided on two approaches. They were going to find a way to put explosives into the Grand Place, at the key points where the spectator stands were likely to be set up, and they were going to try to find a suitable roof top near the Grand Place from which they could fire their mortars. True to his word Lee Corland had managed to obtain significant ordnance, including mortars and additional explosives, from his contacts in Germany.

The availability of apartments in the vicinity of the Grand Place was extremely limited, to the point where this was not an option. It would have to be the roof top of a hotel nearby from which the mortars were to be fired, and there were plenty of options for nearby hotels. Viktor took the decision to send a couple of the United Kingdom based gang members over as tourists to Brussels, to book into various hotels and begin to establish a profile as visiting businesspeople.

Irina and Ludovic booked their trip to Brussels on Eurostar and booked into the Marriott Hotel, just a short distance from the Grand Place. They were using false passports, in the name of Mr and Mrs Kransky. Not a smart move as it turned out, but imagination sometimes takes a holiday, even for highly dangerous professional criminals. The hacks that Jenny had arranged on the computers in the Riverside apartment flagged up all the details of the trip, including the hotel reservations. Ludovic had claimed a family bereavement which he needed to go home for. Adrian guessed it was a lie, but he allowed it nevertheless, and informed Jenny and Jerry. Knowing that Charles had well established agents in

Brussels Jenny suggested that they also inform him immediately. Jerry called him.

"I've sent you some pictures of a couple of terrorists from the Rubinsky gang. They are living and working in Cambridge," Jerry said.

"Why now?" Charles asked.

"They're on their way over to Brussels and we think they may know about the presidential trip in the summer," said Jerry. "They've been in contact with the guys who responded to your leak. We have them all under surveillance. We think they may be going to Brussels to organise some sort of unpleasant reception for the Howlands when they visit their daughter. Let's hope we can keep on top of this."

"You got any more details?" Charles asked.

Jerry gave him the couples booked itinerary.

"We'll meet the bastards off the train at Brussels Central," said Charles.

"Watch out for Jenny. She's having a holiday in Brussels at police expense at exactly the same time as these two."

Charles chuckled.

"Does she need a gun?" He asked.

"You bloody Americans feel naked without one," Jerry said. "She has one waiting at Brussels Central."

"D'you think this visit is important?" Charles asked.

"Bloody important," said Jerry. "We had intelligence that some of Viktor's gang had gone to ground in Brussels, but we have no idea where they are, or who they are. If we can get a lead on that then we can start to do something about the safety of all the kiddos, and you can do something about the safety of the president. There are the obvious things, the places we need to look at, but it would help a heck of a lot if we knew not only the places but the who we ought to be looking at."

"Leave it to me," said Charles.

"No way," Jerry said. "I bet Jenny finds them before you do."

Inspector Jenny Taylor and Mr and Mrs Kransky arrived in Brussels on the same Eurostar service, at around mid-morning one Thursday in late May, and both checked into the same hotel near the Grand Place. The Kransky's were not expecting surveillance and failed to notice the progression of agents who picked them up on their journey. Not so Jenny, she was looking for it and soon noticed the clean-cut young agents who, rather naïvely, followed the two to their hotel.

Jenny entered the lift slightly behind the pair, acknowledged them with a smile, and noted the floor on which their room was situated. She herself stopped at a floor below her own and walked up the stairs the single flight to her room. This was not a holiday, so she immediately went back out, back to Brussels Central, and retrieved the gun which had been placed in a left luggage locker there. She went straight back to the hotel. She was firearms trained, as many members of Special Branch are, so she carefully cleaned and checked the gun, loaded it, and applied the safety. As she re-entered the hotel, she had seen Irina and Ludovic standing at the bar talking to a tall man with dark, slightly thinning, hair and a woman with very blonde hair, who appeared to be his companion. There were a few others in the group, standing a little further back from these four. It was Michu and Zsofia, and a few others from the Rubinsky group. Photographs were quickly taken and as soon as she got back to her room, she sent them off to Jerry and Charles.

Jenny was ultra-cautious. Clearly, one of the security team needed to follow Irina and Ludovic, but she thought that the other two talking there might offer a better lead to the whereabouts of the Rubinsky gang within the city. She left to the Americans the task of tailing Irina and Ludovic. She made herself a takeaway coffee at the coffee machine in the lounge and went outside to sit patiently until Michu and Zsofia left. It was late when they left the hotel, she thought for a moment that she might have made a mistake. Zsofia left Michu, and walked over to a very tall man, with athletic build, reached up, and, as he bent down from his height of about 2 metres, she gave him a fairly passionate kiss. Jenny found it hard to get a good look at the man, because of the lighting in the street; he was silhouetted against a very strong light from a shop window; but for some reason she thought he might be American, his clothes had a sort of mid-west feel about them. Then she looked back towards Michu, who blew the other two a kiss, and went off in a different direction. Her instinct told her to follow Michu, but before she did, she looked back at the couple walking off and managed to get some photographs as they turned to watch Michu walking away.

Michu was unaware of Jenny following him. She tracked him back to Molenbeek. Michu went to the bar where he had previously taken Lee, it was a regular hangout for them, and, in that bar, Jenny recognised one of the gang. She knew at once that she had struck gold. She ordered a small glass of white wine and picked up a copy of one of the local free papers that was lying on a window table. She sat down and pretended to read it. She sipped her wine.

Michu and the others, including Laslo, began to get drunk and Jenny decided that discretion was the better part of valour. She knew where she could pick up the trail on another occasion and she also recognised that she looked rather out of place in this particular setting. It had been a mistake to go in. Jenny asked the proprietor where the ladies' lavatory was and rather hastily went into the lavatory and then left, without re-entering the part of the bar where the gang were beginning to be a bit boisterous. It was clear to her that they were regulars because the barman was not at all perturbed, just told them to cool it a bit, and called them by name. The two names she definitely recalled were Michu and Laslo, she also thought there was a Stefan. No surnames, but all very eastern European or even Russian sounding first names.

On the way back to the hotel Jenny was glad that she had her gun with her. It was dark, several streetlamps were broken, the whole area was dirty, full of street rubbish; it felt totally unsafe. Every scruffily dressed smelly drunk that came past, every small group of men shuffling along the street, every street corner, alleyway, and doorway was a threat. Maybe she was just tired, but she had never felt so scared. When she got back to the hotel she went to the bar and ordered a very large brandy and a decaf coffee. *I'm a bloody fool,* she thought, *this isn't my home territory, I don't really know where is safe and where is not. This bit of the surveillance is for the CIA boys. Do something like that again and I expect Jerry will kill me, even if I do survive.*

The next morning Charles and Jenny met together over a café au lait in the restaurant at Jenny's hotel. The CIA boys had followed Zsofia and the tall man she had gone with. They too went into Molenbeek, but they had made their way to Lee Corland's apartment.

"I don't know whether this guy is significant," said Charles, "but it's my experience that terrorists don't tend to risk relationships with ordinary citizens."

"Yes," said Jenny, "I go along with that. I would put this tall guy into the category of person of interest and I think we should keep an eye on him until we know what he's up to."

"Might be totally innocent," said Charles.

"I put my money on his not being," said Jenny.

"You gonna take him on or shall I get one of my boys to do it?"

"I'll do it," said Jenny. "There's a bar and a group of Rubinsky's boys and girls to follow up. Could I leave that to you? That area was not a place for a woman on her own. I got very scared and was glad I had a gun."

Jenny shared the address of the bar, and a whole lot of photographs she had managed to take, with Charles. Charles gave Jenny a photograph of Lee Corland, and the address of his apartment. He sent the photograph of Lee to Langley to ask them if this was someone they knew.

He was amazed when the answer came back that this was a convicted criminal, recently released on parole from federal prison. That he had been serving a sentence at Leavenworth and clearly had a lot of expertise in munitions was a further warning flag. Jenny was informed immediately.

"D'you think that this Corland guy and the Rubinsky lot are working together?" Jenny asked.

"Maybe," said Charles. "I think we should assume that anyway."

Later that morning Jenny was waiting outside the Corland apartment when Lee emerged with Zsofia on his arm, still in yesterday's clothes. She followed them discreetly back towards the bar where she had had the scare the night before. They walked past it and on to the Rubinsky gang's apartment where Lee dropped Zsofia off and then continued his afternoon journey. He went to the chateau where yet another Ommegang rehearsal was taking place. He watched carefully and appeared to be making a video of the Gilles and the horse riders. For a moment Jenny wondered if Lee Corland was after all totally legitimate, but then she remembered that he was on a parole violation, that he had disappeared off the radar in Kansas, and that he had a history of violence going back quite a long way. The odds on his being a simple tourist were pretty long. Why the interest in the Ommegang? Then, suddenly Jenny noticed the striking blonde hair of one of the riders. It was Patti Howland. And was that Leah Shapiro? Yes, it was.

It did not make any sense to her at this moment. If he had designs on doing something to Patti Howland it was going to be easy enough. Then she thought a little more about it. Patti Howland and Leah were in the Ommegang, the president and her husband were coming to observe the Ommegang. It surely had to be that which was causing Lee Corland to take such an interest in a few horses and crazily dressed musicians. As she watched the rehearsal, the Gilles, who were now coming regularly to rehearse with the riders, had their regular orange throwing competition and Jenny, like many others benefitted by picking up a stray orange and peeling and eating it in segments on her way back to the hotel.

The Ommegang was happening in about three weeks and the preparations at the company erecting the stands for the audience were in full swing. There had been a few difficult months for the scaffolding firm since the end of March. One of the most experienced teams, the one destined to put up the scaffolding in the Grand Place had been working on a building next to a shallow rat-infested canal; scaffolding was required to allow repointing of ancient walls and restoration of rotted woodwork, from the canal side of the walls. Several of the men became ill with leptospirosis. This was difficult to understand since they were all very careful about cleaning their hands before eating or drinking anything, but it did not arouse suspicion of foul play. But foul play it was. The building site had one of those water coolers with the large water reservoirs, and the hot and cold tap. Most of the men took their own cups with them and drank water from the large containers. Had the containers been tested it would have been found that the Leptospira bacterium was in all the drinking containers used on that particular building site. Many of those infected had, as is always the case, quite mild disease, but three men, including two of the most experienced men who regularly headed scaffolding teams, became really very ill and it was obvious that they might not be back to work for some time.

The company, Access Echafaudage de Molenbeek, thought itself remarkably fortunate to find a number of experience scaffolders from among the immigrant population. The first recruit was a gentleman called Laslo Meszaros. He arrived fortuitously right at the beginning of the problem with the disease and was rapidly integrated into the scaffolding gang. It soon became clear that he knew his stuff. To the others he seemed very finickity. He drank only cold tea, from a huge two litre flask that he brought with him each day, and he ate only special flat breads smothered in a sort of garlic oil, cheese and sour cream mixture that turned the stomach of most of the Belgian workers. It did not seem out of place that Laslo never drank the water provided on site.

Laslo had been working in the gang for a week or so when the next few serious cases happened. There had been a few of the men who had taken a couple of days off with an upset stomach or a mild flu like illness; they had returned to work shortly after. But about a week or so after Laslo arrived another four men developed much more serious symptoms and were more fully investigated. At first the doctors suspected food poisoning but when they realised that the workers were all wading in shallow canal water each day it suddenly dawned on them that this might be leptospirosis. Precautions on the site were immediately tightened but the cases continued to appear.

With so many men off work Access Echafaudage de Molenbeek was desperate for more experienced hands, and the firm was overwhelmingly grateful to Laslo for offering to recruit experienced scaffolders from among his immigrant friends. A quick message to Viktor Rubinsky soon led to a number of new Brussels immigrants, all with scaffolding experience and impeccable credentials, arriving in the capital and presenting themselves for work. As the regular team recovered Access Echafaudage took the opportunity to take on more work, welcoming back the recovered staff, but keeping on the new blood. Some were sent to other gangs, some to join Laslo, but Laslo's new recruits proved to be such competent and hard workers that all were eventually picked for the Grand Place scaffolding job.

The end of the canal work marked the end of the run of cases of leptospirosis. By that stage the Rubinsky gang had very effectively infiltrated the scaffolding firm.

It was against that background that the Rubinsky gang had acquired the quantities of plastic explosive that they were planning to insert into the structure at key places, including under the VIP stand. Over the two weeks directly preceding the Ommegang the scaffolding poles for the stands in the Grand Place were slowly recovered from sites all over Belgium and were stored in a special corner of the yard at Access.

It was fairly obvious to the team that putting explosives into the scaffolding or the seating for the stand would not be a sensible option. There would be others handling the scaffolding poles and it would be too much of a job to try to keep tabs on the ones containing the explosive. Their common language meant that they were often put together as a gang working on jobs, a team of maybe six or eight of them. This was going to happen for the construction of the Ommegang stand.

"The Grand Place has many cobbles," said Laslo. "We must just make sure when we check the stand that some areas of cobbles have been damaged. We will need to replace them and when we do, we will make a place to put our explosives."

There was a general murmur of approval, a few very sly grins, and a smug sense of satisfaction. A very big bang was going to happen.

Meanwhile Lee had been making his own plans and they were well advanced. His observations at the chateau had helped him to confirm his intentions.

Patti and Leah took the Eurostar back to Cambridge at about the same time as the Rubinsky gang started work on the stand. For no particular reason, except to provide background for future thinking, Jenny decided to go and take a look at the beginning of the preparations in the Grand Place before she too boarded the Eurostar back to the UK. She watched the various groups of workers going about the early stages of marking out the perimeter of the stand and her hair suddenly stood on end.

Three of those scaffolders were in the bar that night when I followed the guy from the hotel. She had recognised Laslo and some of the others, and they were all working in a group together. It was too much of a coincidence. Jenny called Charles on his mobile.

"Charley boy," said Jenny. "I know how they plan to take out the president, and they are going to take out several hundred others with her, including everyone attending the Ommegang."

"Goddam," said Charles. "Shall we meet and talk this over?"

"I'm on my way to the Eurostar at Brussels Central," said Jenny. "I need breakfast. Can you meet me at Tonton Garby, the restaurant, in fifteen?"

"Copy that," said Charles.

Jenny was already sitting at a table when Charles arrived. She had a large cup of café late and was waiting for Tchoutchouka, a wholemeal baguette with eggs, tomatoes and chilli. It was too much for Charles to resist. He had already had breakfast but was still suffering a little from his increased appetite, having given up smoking. A second baguette, the appropriately named Baguette Charley, with a brie omelette and honey, was duly ordered and arrived with another large cup of coffee.

"So, what have you got?" asked Charles. Jenny told him.

"! don't think we move now," said Charles. "If we stop them now, they'll just shift to a different site and there are so many possibilities. We sort of know they've been casing the city for likely pinch points where they can kill Howland. We know they have loads of explosives and we know that they have plenty of people around Europe that they could bring in to complete the job. I'll let the Belgian police know and we can let them get right through to the end before we pick them up. That way there'll be too little time for them to make further arrangements."

"Sounds good to me," said Jenny. "I'll let Jerry and Special Branch in London know what's happening. I don't think Rubinsky even knows that I exist but, in the unlikely event I don't get home, you call Jerry. If you don't get a call from me this evening, call him."

There was a pause while they each ate some of their food and then Jenny added: "The tall guy, Lee Corland, the one who you followed home, and I followed the next day. He doesn't seem to be involved in this bomb plot, but his girlfriend arrived at the hotel with one of the terrorists and Lee has been taking a big interest in the preparations for the parade. I saw him out at the chateau where they rehearse, and I swear he was filming it. I think he was watching Patti and Leah and making sure he got them on film. I thought he was also filming the Gilles."

"Ok," said Charles. "We have him watched too."

They finished their baguettes, Jenny ordered another take away baguette for the train journey, and they went their separate ways.

Chapter 19

The American Secret Service in Washington was finalising the arrangements for the presidential trip. The whole of the official end was carefully worked out and regular sweeps were made of all the venues where Martha Howland and her family, or Martha Howland and her official entourage, were going to visit in London, Paris, Berlin, and Brussels. The previous long-term surveillance had not shown any bomb making activity in Paris or Berlin and the regular sweeps revealed nothing new. They would continue right up until the visit itself, intensifying as the time drew nearer.

One extra complication had been added to the itinerary of the visit. The State Department, anxious to revive their interest in Africa and counter the rapidly growing influx of aid and influence from both the Eastern Bloc and China, asked the Howlands to arrange to meet Thembani Ndlovu and his companions during one of their stops in one of the capitals. Given the close relationship between Lucas and Patti the obvious place chosen was Brussels. The information about this meeting was intended to be kept secret, in particular the mole in the CIA was not meant to know, but one of the clerks at Langley, carrying messages to and from Marine Lusinga, dropped his folder with the day's messages on the floor and, by a really unfortunate chance, the mole helped him to pick up the papers and saw the relevant memorandum. Speed reading is a useful skill, and enough information was acquired, not complete details, but enough for him to alert both the Rubinsky gang and the white supremacists. It did not really change the plans of either the gang or Lee Corland. It just gave both of them an extra incentive to get the whole of the US presidential party, including those recently added to the guest list.

Rubinsky reported the likely meeting to the ruling party in Africa, and requested an extra sum of money to make sure that Ndlovu was taken out. At this stage no mention had been made of Madiba, it was still a well-kept secret that it was not just opposition members who were seeking a regime change.

Lucas, back in Cambridge, was quite unaware of how things were really going in his homeland. Thembani had decided, now that things were moving so very fast, to exclude his family from further contact with the reform movement. He hoped that, by doing so, he would be keeping them safe. He reasoned that, if it appeared that he was estranged from his family, his opponents would lose interest in Patricia and the children.

The build up to the elections was accelerating in its intensity. The president, despite the prostate cancer, was defying probability and still clinging to power. Behind the scenes, the planning for a coalition government was evolving rapidly. The opposition party and the ruling party were neck and neck in the polls, but both the opposition candidates and the more liberal members of the ruling party were under no illusion about what might happen in the aftermath of a close fought election. It had been decided among the political leaders of the opposition coalition that Horatio Madiba would become the president and Thembani Ndlovu would become the prime minister. The rest of the posts would be divided according to talent among the remaining supporters of the coalition. Inevitably there were disaffected members of the opposition party who would, even if elected, try to veto any association with the ruling party, and there were many more members of the ruling party who were determined to cling to power. Fearful for their freedom, and even their lives, the hard liners recognised the strong possibility of trials under international law at the court of justice in The Hague. There was plenty of evidence of corruption, and worse, that would be uncovered if ever observers were allowed into the country to investigate possible crimes committed by the government.

Awareness of impending disaster caused something of a crackdown. What at first was a series of very selective arrests of important opposition leaders suddenly blew up into a full-scale emergency when a public rally in the capital, at which Thembani Ndlovu was speaking, was broken up by members of the armed forces firing, first rubber bullets, and then live rounds, killing over seventy supporters of the coalition. Horatio Madiba, who was quietly there in the background, and Thembani Ndlovu, only just got away.

That evening the coalition planning party sat around a campfire deep in the forest, unable to return to their normal residences which had been surrounded by members of the armed forces loyal to the government. Madiba, who had previously managed to keep secret his involvement in the coalition cause, was now recognised as an enemy. Many of the government's soldiers were afraid of what might happen to them if there were a change of regime. Self-preservation is a powerful motive for any form of action.

"We still don't have a military leader," said Thembani. "Our resistance fighters are scattered all over the place, hiding more than acting."

"We have assault rifles, grenades, no armour, no artillery, no planes. If we try a full-scale fight, we will be annihilated," said Horatio.

"Maybe," said Thembani, "but the government has only one military airfield, that's up near Lotanga. All their armour is concentrated around the capital. They're very vulnerable in that sense. We need to think how we can steal the weapons. We don't have the resources to buy armour and planes, we'll either have to steal them, or destroy them on the ground and in their depots."

"What have they got?" asked Horatio.

"15 fairly old fighter jets, a few helicopters, and some trainers and transport aircraft; about 50 tanks; and probably a hundred armoured personnel carriers. They also have some artillery, but that won't be as relevant for the sort of attacks we might plan. It's the tanks, helicopters, and the fighter aircraft that we need to take out or capture."

"We don't have trained pilots or properly trained soldiers," said Thembani. "We wouldn't be able to use the planes, 'copters, tanks, or artillery, even if we captured them. We'll probably have to just disable everything that we can, destroy on the ground anything that flies, and, wreck the tanks. It's not going to be easy."

"And we don't have a military leader. Who do we have that might plan this and how do we organise?" asked Horatio.

There was a long silence as the two political leaders and their closest associates pondered that question. Who had the strategic and tactical expertise in guerrilla warfare, and the gravitas, to lead a rebel military force? It had to be someone already capable of taking that role. There was no time to train someone up.

"You have a brother, Mathula. Right?" said Horatio. "He served with me. Even though he was very young. He was brave and, if he's anything like his father, he'll have a good tactical brain. I wonder what he's been up to during the past few years. He still has a price on his head. Where is he?"

"I don't know," said Thembani. "'Thula and I lost touch with each other. I don't even know how to contact him."

"You know, I think I might be able to help there," said Horatio. "I remember that when I went to see your great-uncle, Nomusa, on his farm, I got the distinct impression that he knew where Mathula was. I didn't press him to tell me where Mathula was hiding out, but I think this might be the right time for us to have another chat. Will you come with me to see Nomusa? If you come, we might get more out of him. He was quite rightly a bit defensive about location last time I went. I don't blame him. He probably thought I was on the government team, which, strictly, I was."

The opposition channels sent out a message to all their supporters to halt sabotage and other activity for the time being and to conserve their ammunition and limited weaponry for something big, as yet undisclosed. The members were told that their priority was to stay safe and wait for further orders.

Thembani found it very strange going back to his grandfather's farm. The memories came flooding in. The walk to school, the building was still there; the first meeting with Mathula, the orphan that his grandfather had adopted as Themba's brother; the meeting with Patricia; the hard labour in the fields and the surrounding countryside. It was sad to see so much of the area non-productive. Not the Ndlovu farm, that was doing well, but the other farms around were much neglected.

Thembani had sent word in advance that he and Madiba would be coming to talk. He sent reassurance that this was a friendly visit and not a hostile one.

Nomusa met the tiny party, Thembani, Horatio Madiba, and three armed guards, in the yard behind the main house. He had set out a table, and some benches for them to sit on, and had started a kettle barbecue burning, so that the charcoal was hot and ready to receive the traditional vast quantity of meat, without which a barbecue in Africa was never complete.

There was a warm embrace between the two blood relatives and, perhaps surprisingly to Horatio, he too received a more friendly welcome than simple protocol would have dictated.

"My friend," said Nomusa, "I remember you. I thank you for respecting me and listening to my opinions. You are welcome in my home."

"Man," said Horatio. "It is I who must thank you. You gave me the benefit of your wisdom and I saw the truth in what you said. Your nephew and I are simple slaves to your vision. We *will* make our country the food basket of Africa once again."

Such formal conversation soon dissolves in even small amounts of excellent beer and, with full stomachs, and sitting comfortably in the warm sunshine, Thembani and Horatio came quickly to the point.

"Uncle," said Thembani, "we need to find Mathula. We need him to lead our soldiers. Do you know where we can find him?"

A wise and pleasured smile spread across his great-uncle's face.

"I know, and you will be very pleased when you know," said Nomusa. "Hey, Themba, you and he will be able to talk to each other in French, or is it Belgian?"

Thembani knew then that his great-uncle was teasing him. He put his elbows on the table and his face into his hands. He opened his fingers and looked hard at Nomusa.

"Come on, Uncle," he said, "put us out of our misery. Where is my brother?"

"I think he's in Djibouti," said Nomusa. "That's where his last message came from."

There was a long pause while Thembani and Horatio took it in.

"What's he doing there?" Horatio finally broke the silence.

"He's the Colonel in charge of the French Garrison there," said Nomusa.

The looks on the faces of the two visitors had to be seen to be believed. How had Mathula become a Colonel in the French Army? Then it dawned on them, he must have joined the Foreign Legion.

Sure enough, Nomusa confirmed to them that Mathula had fled from the farm and found his way to Madagascar where he had quickly learnt French. From there he had made his way to France, with a group of about fifty of his fellow guerrillas, and all had joined the Foreign Legion.

"From his letters to me I think he and his friends were very well trained. Thula's very high up among the engineers, some of his friends are in infantry and transport. He tells me half a dozen of them are in a section of the armoured corps. Some of his friends became French citizens and joined the air force."

Thembani and Horatio were like a couple of children who had opened a chocolate selection box and could just not believe the range of delicacies displayed before them.

"We have our leader."

"We don't have to destroy the tanks and planes; we can just steal them."

****

Talking later with his brother Thembani would come to realise how carefully Thula and his comrades had planned for a military take over. They had given several years of their lives to preparing. They had known that they would need pilots, tank drivers, engineers; above all they would need leaders. French citizenship can be granted to Foreign Legionnaires if they apply after three years of service. Several of the group had become French citizens and then, after discharge from the Legion, had joined the French Air Force. They had their pilots, engineers, and tank commanders. After ten years, for it had taken ten years of exile to reach this point, they also had leaders.

Thembani Ndlovu had known nothing of this before he went to meet his great-uncle. He knew nothing of the determination and drive and suffering that had gone into creating Mathula's small, but deadly, force of comrades. All he knew at this point was that he needed to have a meeting.

"Uncle," said Thembani, "can you arrange for me to talk to him?"

"I think so," said Nomusa. "I think so. I'll send a message. How can we reach you?"

"I'll give you my email address. Get Thula to use a VPN. Tell him to suggest somewhere we might meet. I'll gladly go to see him. And give him these numbers for a credit card, to book any flight he needs. Tell him that Madiba and I will both come; and tell him that we are not looking for a military coup; we want support for a Democratic regime."

"Done," said Nomusa. "Now there's a lot more food and a lot more beer, and the day is still warm."

And that afternoon meeting began the process of planning the end game for the restoration of true democracy and unity in the homeland.

Chapter 20

The Rubinsky gang in the United Kingdom, in London, and in Cambridge, had placed their bombs.

The London group hid theirs at the hotel that they thought the Howlands were going to stay in. They were observed planting the bombs, they were observed going back to the Stroud Green Road flat and the Chalkhill Estate. Arrangements were put in place to jam the radio signals around the bomb sites and to pick up the terrorists on the morning of the arrival of the Howlands in the UK.

Shortly after Jenny arrived back in Britain Ludovic and Irina returned to their Cambridge jobs from their 'holiday'. The bombs that Irina had placed at the Amateur Dramatic Club Theatre were all real. If they exploded there would almost certainly be 100% casualties in the theatre and quite a swathe of destruction in the area around. The surveillance cameras that Jerry had had installed in the theatre, actually illegally, since he had not sought permission from anyone, had shown Irina inserting small explosive packages under each seat in row I and a very big load of explosive under the raised area next to the bar. Like the team in London the local Secret Service guys were going to use jamming techniques and pick up the terrorists at the last minute. It would not be long now.

Lucas was busy with rehearsals, but not too busy to miss out on greeting Patti and Leah as they came off the London Train at Cambridge Central. It was a very passionate and emotional reunion for Patti and Lucas who had not seen each other for so many weeks. Esther came up from Oxford, Raphael came over from Paris, and Patti's brothers and their partners also arrived on the Thursday of the second week of the Easter term musical. "Chicago" had been given rave five-star reviews by all the student press and every seat was sold for every performance. Patti sneaked into the Thursday evening performance, sitting on the stewards' seat on the right of the auditorium, right next to row C. Leah spent the time with Charles, who was over in Cambridge awaiting the arrival of the Howlands.

On the Thursday evening the Howlands arrived in Cambridge and were taken to the Vice-Chancellors residence where they were to spend the night. This detail of the itinerary had not been leaked, and everyone was confident that the Howlands were safe in the hands of the Vice Chancellor.

The next day they went to St Joseph's and Adrian Armstrong greeted them, and the rest of the family, as they visited Patti's college and were given a tour. Edward Howland couldn't help himself comparing St Joseph's with his old college at Oxford, but it was more a nostalgia trip for him than anything critical.

The Master, Lord Fairfield, entertained the entire entourage at the Master's Lodge for lunch and the Vice Chancellor and her wife also turned up. The Vice Chancellor, as had happened so often in recent years, was from an American university and was relatively new in office. There was a very amused look on Patti Howland's face when the Vice Chancellor recognised that Patti Jones, for the place name at the table still bore the name Patti Jones, was actually the First Daughter! Lucas was also invited, and Esther, Raphael, and Leah.

Dinner that evening was a private affair at the college, in the Fellow's Breakfast Room where Charles had first held the meeting with Adrian about bringing Patti to St Joe's. It was catch-up and chat between the parents, the siblings, and the significant others. The new member of the group was Raphael, and he was welcomed with open arms; within minutes it was as if he had always been there.

The next morning all the youngsters moved into temporary accommodation, into rooms which would be theirs for the night of the May Ball. Martha and Edward Howland also moved into temporary accommodation with the youngsters. The group took over the building in which Patti had spent the first two years of her time at St Joe's. It was easy to secure the whole building and, as it was not on the main site, it was little disturbed by the preparations for the ball.

In mid-afternoon a small group of armed policemen visited the apartment on Riverside where Ludovic and Irina were living, and the two terrorists soon found themselves enjoying the hospitality of the Cambridge Constabulary. A team of disposal experts moved in on the ADC theatre and quickly and safely dismantled the explosive in the seats and under the elevated platform in the bar.

So it was that the president of the United States, her entire family, their significant others, and half a dozen Secret Service agents watched, in absolute peace and safety, "Chicago" performed by a group of amateur student actors. As far as the British Secret Service was concerned the UK end of the presidential visit was secure, free from any further danger. So secure did they all feel that many of them got a little more drunk than they should have done at the end of show party. Martha and Edward Howland sat together talking late into the morning, free of the burdens of office for the first time in two and a half years.

The next morning, after a leisurely punt down the river to Grantchester, and a ploughman's lunch at the pub, the group returned to get ready for the ball. It was a nostalgia trip for Martha and Edward, something that they had not done since Edward's year in Oxford. For the youngsters it was a fairy tale. There was no threat. All the Rubinsky eggs had been put in the theatre basket. As Jenny said, in one of her wittier moments: "The eggs are smashed, and the chicken tenders are in the cooler."

****

Very early on the Monday morning, before the 'survivors' photograph was taken, the American elements of the party were picked up by Black Chevvy SUVs in convoy and taken to Mildenhall, from whence they reached home in time for the president to take up the reins of office at the morning press briefing in the oval office. Lucas, Leah, Raphael. Esther, and Patti made their way back to Brussels, via the Eurostar. Charles followed them back to Brussels later that week.

For the next week, for the security forces, everything seemed to mark time. It would be the following Monday, when the official visit by the president, to the United Kingdom and then Europe began, that they would next be called into action.

For Leah and Patti it was back to work, and rehearsals, as usual. The Ommegang was only ten days away and everyone was becoming very excited. The horse riders met and walked the route of the procession. The Gilles went to their assembly point at Zavel. Lee watched the Gilles, yet again.

On the Monday before the Ommegang, Air Force 1 flew into Heathrow and Martha and Edward Howland began their state visit.

That same morning the bombs at The Montcalm Royal London House were disarmed and removed and all the known members of the Rubinsky gang in the UK were taken into custody.

Jenny Taylor headed for Brussels on the Wednesday of the week of the Ommegang; she was accompanied by Jerry Gregory and his wife, Marianne. It was the first time that Marianne had tagged along on something that was going to be essentially a working holiday for Jerry, but it was thought likely to be helpful to have her along as cover. It enabled Jerry to give a more realistic impression of being a tourist and, with the location of the bombs at the key places in Brussels, including the Grand Place, already worked out, the visit of Jenny and Jerry was thought to be less important than it might otherwise have been. They checked into their hotel in the early afternoon.

There was still something nagging at the back of the minds of both Jerry and Jenny. To them it all seemed too easy, and they had still not quite worked out where Lee Corland fitted into the picture. It worried them both that Lee had been in Leavenworth, clearly had significant small arms and munitions experience, and yet had not been seen to involve himself in any of the bomb planting or general surveillance of the bomb locations in Brussels. And why was he so interested in the Ommegang, and Patti Howland?

Jenny, Jerry, and Marianne went along together to watch the last bit of the building of the stand.

"There are six of the Rubinsky gang here," said Jenny. "And I saw at least twelve of them in that bar. So, what are the others up to?"

The members of the gang in the Grand Place appeared to be busy just replacing a few of the loose cobbles right under the VIP stand. They had put one of those screens round the area; it was difficult to see exactly what they were doing. Jenny watched for a while and then noticed that they took away a fair amount of dirt and debris.

"When we were at St Joseph's one day, they were fixing the cobbles in Front Court," said Jenny. "They had a little sand and cement in a bucket. They dug up the cobbles, they cemented them back with a small sort of grouting trowel. I don't remember them coming away with large amounts of debris."

Jerry was immediately on the phone to Charles.

"Pretty sure we just saw Rubinsky's lot place a bomb under the VIP stand," said Jerry.

"Thanks, Jerry," said Charles. "We'll check it out as soon as the workmen have gone."

"We think they buried it under the cobbles," said Jerry. "The stones would scatter and take out dozens of people. We think it's quite a big bomb because they took away a lot of debris."

When Jerry came off the phone, Jenny repeated her question: "What are the others up to?"

"Let's go and see," said Jerry. "You know where their base is, and we could put a watch on it, and follow any of the others that go out. We still have a couple of days before the Ommegang starts and before the Howlands get here."

"I'm not going alone," said Jenny. "It scared the crap out of me last time."

"I don't think you should come, darling," said Jerry to his wife. "Might be dangerous and that's not what we signed up for."

"I agree," said Marianne. "I'll get my cousin to come and keep me company at the hotel while you two go and play secret agents." There was only a small hint of sarcasm in her voice.

The detectives and Marianne were staying at the Marriott Hotel near the Grand Place, the same hotel that Jenny had stayed at on her previous visit. The three of them had supper in the rather pleasant restaurant. They were joined by Marianne's cousin and the two ladies went off to the bar.

Jenny and Jerry headed off to the Molenbeek district. They were both armed, and they were both wearing body armour. They told Charles where they were going, and why. Charles had provided them with the address of the Rubinsky gang's apartment, and they promised to keep him informed if they found out anything at all.

"I want to get photographs of every one of the people in that gang," said Jenny.

"Good idea," said Jerry; then he added. "Doesn't Charles already have the photographs?"

They rang Charles and he, rather sheepishly, had to admit that he had not managed to obtain photographs of all the occupants of the flat. The only photographs he had were the ones that Jenny had given him from her last visit to Brussels.

"Jesus, it's a miracle that the president stays alive," said Jerry.

Jenny and Jerry got into position early, somewhere where they could see everyone leaving the building but were, themselves, concealed. They each set up a camera and focussed on the doorway. Twelve people, including Michu, Laslo, Lee Corland, and Zsofia, all went out together for a drink. They went to the bar where Jenny had managed to frighten herself previously.

"We could do with hearing their conversation in there," said Jerry. "Neither of us speaks the language but I wish we could get a recording."

"I can't go in," said Jenny. "The way I left last time, they might just recognise me and then the best I can hope for is a gun fight which I win."

"I can," said Jerry. "If I can get hold of a bugging device, I can get it in there and leave it under a table or something. My French is pretty well perfect, even my accent is pure Parisian, thanks to Marianne."

Jerry called Charles.

"We have all the photographs you could want but we need a listening device, a bug. How quickly can you get one to us?"

Charles and Jerry arranged a pickup well out of sight of the Bar and within thirty minutes Jerry had what he wanted. His fluency in French was going to be very helpful.

He dirtied his face a little, scruffed up his clothes and made himself look more like a workman than a policeman. It helped that Marianne often bought him French clothes back from one of her trips to "Maman." Jenny was amazed that within ten minutes Jerry did not look out of place in the neighbourhood.

"Bloody Special Branch can pay for the replacements," said Jerry as he caught his trouser leg on a nail and developed a suitable rip in it and also slightly ripped the pocket and lining of his jacket.

Jenny watched from a safe distance as Jerry entered the bar.

The twelve who had left the flat together were sitting at three tables towards the back of the room, with their backs to the wall and clear views of the main entrance and the additional entrance that led in from the courtyard at the back of the building where the lavatories were situated.

Jerry ordered a 'Jupiter', Belgium's most popular beer, it was just another thing that made him inconspicuous. He sat at a table comfortably to the side of the building. One where he could see both entrances. He was careful not to be seen to be watching the terrorists.

The bug he had been given was a very sophisticated device in that it could be pointed in the direction of the conversation you wished to hear and did not have to be directly next to the speaker. Jerry's position to the side and slightly in front of the three tables occupied by the gang meant that his microphone was picking up every element of the conversations. Apart from the occasional contribution from Lee Corland, in mid-west American, everything else was in bad French or some version of an eastern European language which Jerry could not begin to understand. The bugging device was faithfully recording everything.

After two more 'Jupiter' beers Jerry, as Jenny had on the visit earlier, noticed that the gang were getting more than a little drunk and definitely very boisterous. He, as Jenny had previously, decided that retreat was a good option. A small, rather jolly elderly man got up from the next table and wobbled his way towards the door. Jerry stood up and followed him, caught the man's arm just as he started to stumble and, in perfect French, and in a very friendly way, offered to help him find his way home. Laslo looked up and said, in much less good French, that it was a very kind gesture; he wished them both goodnight. Jerry beat a grateful, but not too hasty, retreat.

Jenny left her hiding place with the two cameras carefully stowed in her bag. She had already transmitted the pictures to her own laptop, to Jerry's laptop, and to Charles.

Jenny joined Jerry and they escorted the older man back to his flat a couple of blocks away.

"Did you get anything?" asked Jenny.

"I got the whole conversation for the whole time I was in there but apart from the odd bit of American and bad French it meant nothing to me."

"Well, I bet the CIA and the US Secret Service have people who speak every language there is," said Jenny.

"Yep," said Jerry. "Let's get it to them. Bloody hell, this Belgian beer's strong, I think I'm a bit pissed."

It would not be true to say that Jenny helped Jerry back to the hotel, but he was tired, and he was glad to allow Jenny to navigate. A quick telephone call to Charles and the courier was waiting at the hotel when they got back there. Shortly after that the recording was in the hands of the CIA analysts.

Both Jenny and Jerry were handed envelopes by the receptionist when they went to request morning wake up calls and get themselves cups of coffee from the machine next to the reception area. The envelopes contained hard copies of the photographs they had sent to Charles, with the names of the known terrorists written on the back. Everyone, apart from Lee Corland, was part of the Rubinsky gang. For completeness Charles had also included photographs of Irina and

Ludovic. Jerry took his envelope up to his room, threw it on the desk, and crashed out on the bed.

Jerry slept well that night. The caffeine in the coffee was not going to overcome the effects of the three beers and the long day. When he woke in the morning it was quite late and he decided to use room service to bring him up a breakfast. Marianne had already gone down to the restaurant where she had met Jenny and they had shared a breakfast table. When Marianne came back up to the room Jerry was still tucking into croissants and drinking yet another cup of coffee. He had laid the mug shots out on the desk in the room.

Marianne looked at them.

"That woman's quite pretty," she said, looking at Zsofia's picture.

"Who are they?"

Jerry explained and Marianne looked carefully at each one. She made some sort of comment about each of them and, when she came to Lee Corland, she simply said that he looked like an American.

"It's the haircut, the perfect teeth, and the Kansas City Chiefs T-shirt. No one but an American would wear a Kansas City Chiefs T-shirt."

"You're right," said Jerry. "He's a nasty piece of work who's broken his parole and fled here from the States."

"Can't they send him back?" asked Marianne.

"They think it isn't worth it, yet. They're just keeping an eye on him."

Jenny meanwhile had left the hotel and gone for a walk to clear her mind. There were so many thoughts buzzing around in her head. Why were there five other gang members and Corland here when only six of them were working on the Grand Place project. Was there something that she, Jerry and Charles were missing? It was now Thursday. The Ommegang started tomorrow, the president was coming today, for meetings tomorrow, and the Saturday evening performance. If something else was going on, then they had only three days to find out. She decided that she was going to haunt Lee Corland. And she wanted to know what, if anything, Jerry had managed to get on that tape.

Jenny was lost in thought when her phone rang. It was Charles.

"They have a complete transcript of that conversation," said Charles. "I called Jerry and he said he would come over and look at it later this morning. He suggested you might come over now. He reckons you would be at least as good as he at spotting anything significant."

"I could do that," said Jenny. "Where are you?"

"I'm at the flat that Patti and Leah share in Etterbeek. The address is 16, Rue des Erables. We'll put the coffee on."

Jenny arrived to find Leah, Charles, Esther, Raphael, Patti, and Lucas, all sitting in the generously proportioned living room drinking café au lait and tucking into a huge pile of pastries. Judging from the state of undress, and the untidy hair, they were not long out of bed. That included Charles. The fold up double sofa bed in the living room still had ruffled sheets sticking out under the seat cushions. Jenny could not help noticing that the double beds in the two large bedrooms were also still unmade. She smiled inwardly. *'Making up for lost time,'* she thought.

They chatted for a while. Jenny, who had also managed to see "Chicago," congratulated Lucas on the amazing lighting and sound, then filled all of them in on the state of play with Ludovic, Irina and the other gang members who were under interrogation back in the UK. She also updated them on the position in Brussels. She said that the intelligence services knew where the bombs were at the European Parliament Building, and where the members of the gangs hung out. She added that they had already discovered a bomb in the Grand Place and it, like the other bombs, would be dealt with before the president got there.

Patti let Jenny know that the Ndlovu parents and siblings were joining the presidential party at the Ommegang and that the plan at the moment was for everyone to meet first at Richard's in Petite Rue des Bouchers so that Patti could serve them a genuinely Belgian moules frites. Jenny made a mental note to check that out too. It seemed highly likely that the gang, who clearly knew about Patti, would have explored the possibility of attacking the president there, even if there was a more remote chance of her visiting Patti there than at somewhere a little more salubrious. Rue des Petite Bouchers is near enough to the Grand Place that it made sense for them all to eat there on their way to the Ommegang. Charles had got there first.

"I can almost hear your wheels turning," laughed Charles. "Don't worry. We checked it out already, and we will check again before the event; but we don't think they are particularly interested in doing anything there. They want a public statement, and we think the Ommegang is where it's meant to happen."

"Can we see the transcript?" asked Jenny.

It took her quite a while to read the transcript through. She played the tape alongside the transcript in order to link the different voices to the translated words. The analysts had managed to piece together the three separate strands of conversation going on at the separate tables and there were almost two hours of conversation at each table. Much of the conversation was obviously fairly inconsequential. Zsofia, the only female voice, and Lee were clearly an item and were conversing in English. Most of it was the sort of conversation that two lovers might have in a bar after a long day, and before going home to sleep together. One group, six voices, was talking about the work in the Grand Place and how the preparations for Saturday were now complete. Jenny and Charles both knew that the reference to Saturday, rather than to Thursday the start of the Ommegang, was highly significant. The third group, four voices, seemed to be talking about a fireworks display. The gist of that conversation was that if the sparklers and thunder flashes didn't go off then the whizz bangs would have to step in.

For some reason, Jenny suddenly realised what that conversation was all about, and her blood started to run cold. She remembered her great-grandfather, a veteran of World War One, singing a song about whizz bangs and she remembered him saying that the whizz bangs were terrifying because you heard the whine of the flight before the bang. They referred to shells from the light artillery or mortar shells from the German trenches.

"Charles," she said, "I think the bastards are setting up to use mortars as well as the bombs in the Grand Place."

There was a stunned silence. All seven of them realised the implications. The mortar could be situated almost anywhere within a radius of eight kilometres.

"Bastards, bastards, bastards," said Charles. "We have to either find the mortars before they deploy them or, if they have deployed them already, we need to find out where they are. No more pussy footing around. We need to round up the gang, defuse the bombs in the Grand Place, and risk the Rubinsky gang coming up with plan C."

There was a frantic hour and a half which involved members of the Belgian police, the American Secret Service and the Belgian Army in surrounding the two flats in Molenbeek, Lee Corland's and the Rubinsky gang base. On a single command sent by radio to all units, signal jamming was begun in the area of the Grand Place and the two flats were raided simultaneously. And that should have been the end of plans A, the bombs, and B, the mortars; but it wasn't. The mortars had been long deployed.

Lee and Zsofia had gone to Mass, Zsofia was very devout, and then had breakfast at a café and stayed out to enjoy the sunshine. They went back towards the flat only to see all the security activity going on. They diverted towards the gang's base but noticed immediately that this area was also crawling with police and soldiers.

"I think the operation is blown," said Lee. "I wonder how many of the boys they caught?"

Zsofia called Michu on his mobile.

"Hello," he answered in their own language. "What do you want?"

"Where are you? The police are crawling all over Lee's flat and our place? Are you all OK?"

Michu sounded very surprised. They spoke in their own language.

"I called you last night and told you what we were doing. Still, I expect you were shagging Lee and haven't checked your messages."

"Don't be so vulgar," said Zsofia. "I haven't checked my messages. We went to Mass and then had breakfast. So, what was that message?"

"I was telling you to stay with Lee until further notice. We all left the flat early this morning and we aren't going back. I spoke to Viktor last night to tell him all the explosives were in place, the explosives and the mortars, and he told us to get out and disappear until Saturday when we could go to the mortars and use them."

"Why did he do that?" asked Zsofia.

"He said he was worried that the CIA might have more intel on us than we thought," Said Michu. "He said that they had managed to stop the bombs in London and Cambridge, and that they almost certainly had Irina and Ludovic in custody. He thought Ludo' and Irina might crack and give away our positions, so he told us to get out as soon as possible. There was no need to stay where we were, we could just converge on the Grand Place and the mortar base on Saturday and meanwhile we should disappear."

"Has everyone got enough money?" asked Zsofia.

"Plenty," said Michu. "We all have our phones, and we're all going to different hotels. In pairs. I've told everyone to stay in and watch movies and use room service until H-hour. Make sure and check your phone a bit more often, even if you are screwing Lee. Get yourself a hotel. Stay there until I tell you."

"Just stop being so offensive, you dumb bastard," said Zsofia. "Won't they miss the gang working on the scaffolding?"

"Job finished yesterday evening," said Michu. "We're all on vacation, and we all have tickets for the Saturday Ommegang." Michu laughed. "Like we are going to go? I think not."

"I hate you," said Zsofia, in her own language. "You're a graceless vulgar thug." And Zsofia hung up.

Zsofia translated everything that Michu had said, except the vulgar bits.

"So, all the guys are still around, nobody's been caught yet?" asked Lee.

"That's how it seems," said Zsofia.

They smiled at each other and then they went to Brussels Central and Lee took a rucksack out of one of the automated lockers. It contained spare sets of papers, a handgun, and a lot of money. They went shopping and bought a suitcase each, plenty of clothes, and some toiletries, then they diverted to book into a hotel for a week. Inevitably they booked into the Marriott.

The state visit to the United Kingdom had been followed by visits to Paris and Berlin, all without incident. The president met every European Head of State, and on the Thursday arrived in Strasbourg for a meeting of the European Council. From there she went to Brussels and stayed at the embassy. Friday was to be a day of meetings, and it would be Saturday before she could meet up with her family and enjoy watching her daughter in the grand pageant that was the Ommegang.

Chapter 21

Both sides took stock of the situation following the unsuccessful raids. For the Rubinsky gang it was a case of biding their time until the Saturday afternoon. They had no reason to believe anything other than that it was Irina and Ludovic who had given away their locations. They had no reason to believe that the security forces knew the location of the bombs in Brussels, and they were equally confident that the mortars were safe in their location. But they went to check just in case. Everything seemed to be as it should be.

The police and the security services searched the two flats thoroughly. In the Rubinsky flat they found nothing of value. There were no fingerprints, the flat had been wiped clean, there was no clothing, no food, no IT equipment; the only thing they did find was a case of English Gunpowder Beer.

"They're taking the piss," said Jerry when he heard about it.

There was more to find in Lee's flat. All his clothes were still there, as were Zsofia's discarded underwear from the day before, all their toiletries, a laptop, phone chargers and the general accoutrements of living. These items were sent immediately for analysis, and the laptop, which was not password protected, was very carefully examined. It yielded nothing of interest.

The only odd thing was that they found a lot of fruit there, especially oranges.

"I would have thought that Lee was more a 'steak and fries' man," said Charles, as he tucked into a large Jaffa orange from the kitchen.

Charles had been overruled about removing the bomb in the Grand Place. Instead, under cover of darkness, they had removed the detonators and replaced them a convenient distance away from the explosives. There was still no urgency and, with the gang now having gone into hiding, there was no need to spook them further. It was Jenny who suggested that the gang might still not know about the extent of the information the security forces possessed. It was Jenny who suggested that they might now know about Irina and Ludovic and that they might be assuming that it was through Irina and Ludovic that the police had known where to raid. It was Jenny who suggested surveillance cameras and facial recognition be used around the bomb locations.

"We might just pick up a member of the gang and be able to follow them," she said.

That still left the question of where the mortars might be but the only way that problem was going to be solved was if they could find members of the gang and follow them to the hide away. The evidence from the interrogation in the United Kingdom was that neither Irina nor Ludovic knew anything about mortars. Their only involvement had been to bring some of the explosives over from the store in the UK.

The rest of Thursday passed by and the Ommegang had its first public performance. Martha Howland called Patti after the pageant and asked about it.

"It was so exciting, Mum," said Patti. "The horses behaved beautifully, and the lighting of the festival was magnificent. I loved the music, the Gilles bands, the bright costumes, the fireworks, the whole pageantry thing. It goes back hundreds of years before modern America even got started. You'll love it, mum. I can't wait to show off our horse-riding skills. And I get to show you where I worked all year. And you'll love moules frites. Better than New England Clam Chowder any day!"

They chatted for about half an hour and then Patti went off to meet the boys who had arrived earlier that day, with Sara and Graham, to spend an extra day in the city before the president got there. Lucas, Charles and Esther had entertained the Howland siblings and their partners all afternoon and, after the Ommegang, Leah, Patti, and Raphael, joined them. Sandrine, Therese and Sandrine's brother, Allain, also joined the group and they all went to the chateau to spend the night there with Therese's family.

Over dinner at the chateau, Allain was full of excitement. It was the first time he had had a major role in the Ommegang, as a sort of section leader for the dance. He had enjoyed the whole thing, but he was a little upset that he had not been able to use a brand-new mask which he had ordered from the shop in Binche where Jean-Luc Pourbaix manufactured the masks from the traditional materials in the old-fashioned way.

"This mask of mine is getting a bit tacky now. A few bits of the surface could do with a repaint and the colours are fading quite a lot. It was my dad's. Jean-Luc is getting old you know. I was supposed to go over to Binche on Wednesday morning and collect another mask. I was going to collect two more spares that we had ordered, and Jean-Luc confirmed that they were ready, but his workshop burned down on Tuesday night, and it was all lost. The workshop was apparently a write-off."

"What bad luck," said Patti, giving him a consolation hug.

"Yes," said Allain. "I'm easily the tallest of the Gilles and I have the worst mask. They're making me stand at the back. There was one spare new mask but in the end I decided to stick to Papa's mask. Tradition is important."

"We had a few bits of costume missing," said Leah.

"And someone might have nicked a bit of the armour," said Therese. "There were a few bits missing anyway. I wouldn't be surprised if they were planning to sell the items to a museum or a collector."

Allain took his own mask out of his backpack and each of them tried the mask on. There was a lot of photographing with mobile phones, and a lot of posting on Facebook and Snapchat and Tik Tok and every other form of social media they could think of. By the time it was done the mask, with all its cracks and faded colours, was firmly imprinted in everyone's mind.

The next day, accompanied by Lucas and Esther, all the visitors who were not involved in the Ommegang had a day of sightseeing. The whole party met up briefly for lunch, which was held, inevitably, in Richard's. That evening they visitors went to the Ommegang as an extra treat and to show support for Patti and the others. The Ommegang was well received.

Patti and Leah, comfortable on their horses, found it easy to pick out Allain from among the crowd of Gilles. He was almost six inches taller than those around him, and his mask was, sad to say, a little the worse for wear. Despite his great height, his throwing of oranges to the crowd was distinctly lacking in coordination, and distance. They were much too polite to tell him so.

After the show, and after grooming and seeing to the horses, all the youngsters again stayed at the chateau and, again, there was a lot of conversation until well into the early hours of the next morning.

Saturday was the day designated for the visit of the president to the Ommegang. The morning was taken up with sightseeing, accompanied by several Secret Service guys, who stuck out like a sore thumb but, that was part of the idea. There were also film cameras and news reel reporters everywhere. At around lunch time the Howlands returned to the American embassy and then sneaked out by a back entrance and joined Leah and Patti at the flat in Rue des Erables. The flat where Leah and Patti had lived for the best part of the year was host to a very interesting lunch party. The Secret Service couple who lived in the flat below were joined by some new arrivals. The level of security went up several notches.

Chapter 22

Earlier that day, while the Howlands were still playing tourist, Thembani Ndlovu and Horatio Madiba had arrived at the flat in Rue des Erables. Lucas was astounded. Not having heard from his father for over six months, as members of the opposition hid from the secret police, he had been deeply concerned: although Charles had regularly told him that the reports from Marine Lusinga suggested that Themba was still active and well. A short reunion followed, and an introduction to Horatio, and then President Howland, her advisors, and the delegation from the Coalition Party, for that is what the combined moderates of the two parties were now calling themselves, adjourned to the flat below for some hard-line discussion on political and possibly economic support from the United States. It was made very clear to the two African leaders that no military aid could be given but that recognition of a democratically elected government would come quickly from the USA, if the result of a free and fair election returned them to power. Patti Howland and her team did not want to know how the new party would protect itself from the ruling party dominated armed forces. In fairness, Thembani and Horatio were not going to reveal their plans anyway.

After the talks everyone returned to the top floor flat and this time, they did eat lunch. Baguettes, cheese, fruit, cold meats, and several other elements of charcuterie; there was also one of Patti's favourite dishes, *remoulade celeriac*.

The British detectives, Marianne, and Maman spent the early morning shopping at a large out of town supermarket. Jerry and Marianne bought two cases of decent French wine, a case of champagne, two bottles of scotch, and two of gin. It would last them until Marianne's next visit, which would probably be in a couple of months' time. They all went back to the hotel for a late breakfast and then Jerry, and Jenny Taylor, went for one more walk to the Grand Place and wandered around for a while before finding a café nearby and having a quiet cup of coffee together. Maman and Marianne went to lunch.

"I don't know how we are going to find those bloody mortars," said Jerry.

"We don't have a clue, do we?" said Jenny. Then she thought a bit more.

"Was there any other slightly dodgy ordnance that those guys had access to?"

Jerry went to pick up his phone to call Charles and realised he had left it at the hotel.

He borrowed Jenny's and called Charles.

"Charley boy, we have to find those bloody mortars. Was there anything else?"

"My dear Jerry," said Charles, "the manifest we found, the bloody idiots left an invoice in one of the drawers, showed that there was enough to equip an infantry platoon."

"Like what?" asked Jerry, putting his phone on speaker. "Like bloody what?"

"Mortars, grenades, assault rifles, lots of ammo; oh, and a rocket propelled grenade launcher."

"How much?"

"4 mortars and about twenty bombs, twelve assault rifles, some pineapple grenades, two RPG rockets."

"Oh shit. You've been sitting on that?"

"Not sitting on it. I tried to call you, but you weren't answering your phone. We've started doing something about it."

"Like what?" said Jerry, embarrassed by his lack of foresight in leaving his phone at the hotel.

"Every building in the Grand Place has been shut down since first thing this morning. Every room is being searched; all the roof tops are being searched. Once we've cleared the buildings nobody can be allowed back without searching. And nobody can be allowed into the square without a permit. An RPG could be used from any window overlooking the Grand Place. Any building with line of sight of the grandstand needed vetting, and we're doing it."

Charles paused for breath.

"That should take care of the line-of-sight weapons," said Jerry. "I wish I'd known what you were doing but I guess it doesn't make any difference. I didn't actually have a heart attack when you started telling me about the ordnance. You're doing the right things anyway."

"But, Charley, the mortars are something else. We would need to search every building within a five, possibly even a nine-kilometre radius. If they're going for mortars, and we don't find them, we may just have to call it all off."

"I don't think we're going to find the mortars; but we have to assume that the people planning to use them aren't yet in position, and we've got to assume that they're known to us. Do we have face recognition software we can use on any of the roads in the city? Will the Brussels police give us access to all the feeds within a nine-mile radius. Have we the computing power to monitor enough of them to pick up any of these thugs?"

Charles thought about it, put Jerry on hold, and made a telephone call to the security section in the embassy, and to Langley, they came back with a positive response. Charles went back to Jerry and told him the news, then he ended the call and got ready to talk to the local police.

"I don't feel a whole lot better about this," said Jenny, as they walked back to the hotel. "Do you?"

"No," said Jerry, "but I'm going to pretend I do until the very last minute. At least we have tickets for the Ommegang tonight. Charles got me an extra one for Marianne, which reminds me. I haven't told her yet. It was all a bit last minute and Charley boy only gave them to me this morning. I tried to get one for Maman but they are a bit like gold dust."

"Hadn't you better go and tell her?" asked Jenny. "You haven't got your phone so you can't call."

"I guess so," said Jerry. "Otherwise she and Maman will probably book something else. I'll see if one of Maman's relatives can come over and keep her company."

For the first time in quite a while Jerry caught a whiff of a Gitane and was sorely tempted. He was more stressed than he had been in years. *How long is it since I gave up? When did Maman stop sending me*—Jerry snapped out of it, settled the bill, and he and Jenny walked back towards the Marriott.

When they entered the lobby, they were immediately accosted by the concierge.

"I 'ave been waiting for you monsieur, mademoiselle," said the concierge. "I 'ave an urgent message for you. You must call your wife *immédiatement*."

A slight look of panic spread over Jerry's face. What could be wrong, what had happened to Marianne or Maman; he bet it was Maman; all those years of smoking Gitanes and Gauloises.

"You can use the telephone at the desk, monsieur."

Jerry rang the room. Marianne answered immediately.

"Oh, *mon Dieu*," she said. "You went out without your bloody phone."

"I know, stupid of me. Is Maman all right, are you all right?"

"Just listen," said Marianne. "You know that pretty girl who's with the gang, the one you showed me the picture of with Sergeant Taylor?"

"Yeh, Zsofia Varinska," said Jerry.

"*Merde*, shut up and listen," said Marianne rather crossly.

"I saw her an hour ago in the corridor on the top floor when I went to the executive lounge after lunch for a coffee. I'm sure it was her. She's even prettier in person than her picture was."

I wonder, thought Jerry, *I wonder.*

"Jenny, didn't you say you saw a some of Rubinsky's people here when you came on that previous visit?"

"Yes, I did. Michu, Zsofia and maybe three or four others."

"Think back. Was there anything strange about them? Did they have anything with them?"

"Not that I recall."

"I didn't think of this before, but should we show the pictures to the concierge and the other hotel staff?"

"Too right we should," said Jenny.

"You want to sign up as a detective?" said Jerry to his wife. "Can you fish out those photographs please. They're on the dressing table in that big white envelope. Can you get down here to reception as quickly as you can? Please can you bring my phone?"

Then Jerry said what both he and Jenny were thinking: "I wonder if the mortars are here?"

Jenny suddenly looked very interested.

"Come to think of it the air conditioning was out of action when I came last time," she said. "The hotel manager said the workmen were coming to fix it on the morning I left. I remember the concierge saying that it had only been serviced a week or two before and the hotel was certainly not going to pay for the repairs."

Marianne was in the lobby in a matter of less than three minutes. The lifts at this hotel were incredibly efficient. She handed over the envelope. DI Gregory and Sergeant Taylor took the envelope and went up to the concierge's desk.

"Monsieur DuBois, were you on duty the evening of the 11th of June? Please can you tell us who was on duty that day. The receptionists too please. We've some photographs of people who may have been here that evening, and we would like to see if anyone can recognise them. It could be very important."

"Non, monsieur; I was not on duty that evening but let me look in the staff schedules and I will get back to you."

Ten minutes later the detectives had their list. They were in luck, the team that had been on duty on 11th June was here again on 1st July. The staff worked regular shifts each week.

The concierge, Pierre DuBois, arranged for the detectives to go and sit in a small office in the business centre on the second floor and, one by one the staff members came in, looked at the photographs, and then left. The only two that the lobby staff and porters recognised were Ludovic and Irina, who had registered under the name of Kransky.

"*Merde*," said Jerry.

"Shit," said Jenny.

Pierre DuBois came in with the last member of the reception team. A very young woman who turned out to be his daughter. The two detectives told him that the reception staff and porters had recognised only Irina and Ludovic. DuBois shook his head sympathetically.

"Francine," said Monsieur DuBois, "will you go and get these two guests a cup of coffee from the restaurant please? I believe they may need it."

Then he changed his mind.

"Francine, you should perhaps go back to the desk. A touring party is arriving very soon, and you will be very busy checking them in. I will get the coffees." And M DuBois left the two detectives, with a strangely enigmatic smile spreading across his face.

"What was he grinning about?" asked Jenny very crossly.

Jerry just shrugged his shoulders. They sat in silence licking their wounds.

Ten minutes later DuBois was back with four of the restaurant staff and a grin the size of the Grand Canyon.

"*Monsieur Gregoire*," he said. "I am sorry I was so stupid. Of course, the people who are the front of house staff saw only the two who checked in, but it is likely that the others you are interested in simply came for a meal or a drink. Mimi here was the head bar person, and Jules was the head waiter that evening. Bernadette and Robert were also serving in the restaurant. Perhaps they can help you?"

Jerry took a good sip of his coffee, opened the envelope again, he had put the photographs away after the disappointment of the previous viewing session, and he spread the photographs on the table.

No sooner had he put them down than all four of the hotel staff cried out, almost simultaneously: "I saw them."

Michu and Zsofia had been spotted dining with Irina and Ludovic and having a drink beforehand. That was nothing useful, for Jenny already knew about it. One of the waiters, Jules, also recognised Lee Corland.

"That man, he is staying here," said Jules, "I took him up some dinner with room service. I saw a very pretty woman in his room. I believe it was that one who had been here on the evening you asked us about." And Jules pointed at Zsofia.

There was a stunned silence.

"Those two are staying here?" asked Jerry.

M DuBois came over and looked at the pictures. His face went very pale.

"*Monsieur Gregoire,*" said DuBois, "I do not know what mischief these people are involved in but that one, and that one, are staying here." DuBois pointed at Lee and Zsofia. Then he dropped the bombshell. He picked up five of the photographs, one at a time.

"I have seen these five too. I was not on duty the night you asked about, but I was here very early the next morning because the workmen were coming to fix the air con. Although I cannot be certain, I think these five," he put down the pictures of Michu and four of the others, "I think these five were the workmen who came to repair the air conditioning."

Jerry had not moved that fast in years. He almost fractured a finger speed dialling Charles.

"Charles," said Jerry, "I think I know where those bloody mortars are. Can you get a team over to the Grand Place Marriott in about two seconds. We need the bomb squad, in case things are booby-trapped, and we need a SWAT team. We have Corland and Zsofia here as guests, and the concierge recognises five of the gang as having been here to repair the air conditioning about three weeks ago. I think that only Corland and Zsofia are here at the moment, and I would expect more of the gang to arrive nearer the time of the parade, so please can we keep it discrete."

There were some expletives at the other end of the phone and a lot of orders were barked out very quickly, then Charles turned back to the conversation with Jerry.

"We'll be there in ten," he said.

Chapter 23

Lee Corland had left the hotel after breakfast. He and Zsofia had ordered a continental breakfast to be delivered to the room. Lee met Michu at the Rue de Tabora inside St Nicholas Church. Michu was waiting in one of the pews, lighting a candle, and pretending to pray. He had been taken into Lee's confidence about plan D shortly after they had received the twin items of news that Ndlovu would be joining the presidential party at the Ommegang, and the bombs in Cambridge and London had been defused.

"Have you got them?" asked Michu.

"Yes," said Lee. "Have you?"

"Yes," said Michu.

"Then let's go and have brunch and keep out of sight. There'll be plenty of time for us to dress for dinner this evening." He grinned.

They headed out to the Sportcity at Woluwe-Saint-Pierre. They had swimming costumes and towels in their back packs, along with their clothes and equipment for the evening. Keeping out of the centre for now was important. Keeping off the streets and not attracting attention, equally so. Swimming for an hour or two, having lunch and then making their move. That was the plan. They needed to be back in Zavel by about 6pm. Before that they needed to be invisible.

It had never been intended that Lee and Zsofia would fire the mortars, just that they would escape with the mortar team after the successful bombing of the Grand Place.

Fifteen minutes after the SWAT teams and the backups arrived 'room service' knocked on Zsofia's door. She looked through the spy hole, saw someone with a big bunch of flowers, got hold of her gun with the silencer, draped a towel over her arm and opened the door. She fired at point blank range and the flowers and the policeman holding them fell to the ground. It was to no avail; three more policemen were on her before she could fire another shot. Zsofia was in custody and could take no further part in the assassination attempts.

The policeman that she had shot was glad to have been wearing body armour. Bruised, but still alive, he sat in the bar drinking an enormous cognac bought for him by Charles.

Knowing where to look, where the workmen had been, made life relatively easy for the search team and they soon had a number of mortars and mortar bombs in their possession. There were a couple of pineapple grenade booby-traps, simple string pull of the firing pin when items were moved, or doors opened. These were easily dealt with by the experienced anti-terrorist squad. They were fairly confident that they had now removed another major threat from the presidential visit to the Ommegang.

Not surprisingly the forces of law-and-order sat in the bar, drank large cognacs with their recovering companion, and felt very pleased with themselves. One by one, as the remaining gang members came into the hotel to take up their positions for the mortar attack, they were picked off and taken away to be questioned.

The questioning was not civilised. It was brutal and determined. It yielded nothing that the British, American, and Belgian law enforcement agencies did not already know.

"The only things we haven't got," said Jerry, "are a few of the gang members and that bloody Lee Corland. It worries me that they are still out there. I would have expected them all to be here for the big event."

Lee Corland had no intention of returning to the hotel until the mortar bomb attack had been completed and, even then, he was going to make for the secondary rendezvous at Brussels Central Station and join up there with Zsofia and the others. Michu also was going to travel with Lee and Zsofia. It did not worry any of them that they had not heard from each other for a while. It had been agreed that they would maintain telephone silence until the rendezvous at Brussels Central.

Lee and Michu finished their swim, their loitering in Woluwe-Saint-Pierre, and a half decent tea, caught the train to Zalim, changed into their clothes for the evening and moved towards the place where the Gilles would start their walk towards the Grand Place itself. They retrieved some items that Lee had previously hidden near the Gilles assembly point. There were false passports and some money, among other items.

Despite congratulating themselves on their good fortune the forces of good decided that it was far too dangerous to carry on without a briefing meeting. Jerry contacted Charles and a rendezvous was arranged at the US Embassy. The American Security Staff, the head of security for the Brussels district, the security team for the Ommegang, the two British police officers, the Africans, all the youngsters, Martha and Edward Howland, and Lucas's mother, brothers and sister, were all present.

Jarry explained where they were.

"These guys had at least three plans to get you. Madam President. We neutralised bombs in Cambridge and at a hotel in London where they falsely believed you would be staying. We have neutralised a bomb under the staging for the stands in which you will be sitting this evening. Finally, we managed, I must admit more through good fortune than ultraclever policing and intelligence, to neutralise an attempt to attack the Grand Place with mortars."

There was a general murmur of approval around the room.

"We have taken into custody several members of the Rubinsky gang, including the party that were planning to fire the mortars. Our surveillance cameras picked them out one by one as they came to the hotel to take up their positions for the evening. But a man called Lee Corland, and the local leader of the terrorist gang, Michu Meszaros, are still at large. Lee Corland is especially dangerous. He is a former special forces guy, a dangerous white supremacist who broke parole shortly after his release from Leavenworth. He was sentenced for war crimes. Corland and Meszaros are still out there. We wouldn't be so worried except for the fact that we discovered a lot of arms and ammunition when we raided the gang base in Molenbeek, and there was an inventory. We think we have accounted for all the ordnance except a couple of assault rifles, some rocket propelled grenade launchers and several pineapple hand grenades."

There was a lot of muttering, and consternation on the faces of all those in the room.

"Those weapons would require the terrorists to get pretty close, wouldn't they?" asked Thembani.

"Yessir," said Charles. "Damn close. They would have to either ambush one or more of you on the way to the Grand Place or be in the Grand Place itself to make an attack. We think they want to get both you, Madam President, and you, Dr Ndlovu. They probably want to take out as many of your family as they can, at the same time. That means we're putting our money on their trying to enter the Grand Place and making some sort of attempt there. Everyone entering the Grand Place is going to be put through a metal detector. Brussels Radio has put out a warning to get there early and everyone who bought tickets online has received a similar message. It should be OK."

"What about the RPGs?" asked Patti.

"They have to be line of sight, and we've checked every roof top and window or door with line of sight on the Grand Place. We've searched every room overlooking the Grand Place. I think we can rule those out as a possible attack weapon, unless, somehow, they get into the Place itself. We'll have marksmen on the roof tops, and we think we could shoot anyone we see trying to launch an RPG."

There were a few more questions but nothing else much to say. Pictures of Michu Meszaros and Lee Corland were shown to everyone, a specially reinforced vehicle was offered by the embassy to Horatio and Thembani, an offer which was gratefully accepted.

The meeting broke up.

Back at the flat in Etterbeek, Patti Howland was getting ready. She could not put her finger on what it was that made her so uneasy, but despite the briefing by Jerry, Patti was on high alert.

"You know, Leah, from what Jerry was telling me they were a bit lucky about finding the mortar bombs. Fair enough they got the bombs in Cambridge, London, and here, by good sensible police work, but I can't help thinking there is something they've overlooked. I can't see a smart terrorist like Meszaros simply trying to walk into the Grand Place with a machine gun."

"Nah," said Leah. "You're just uptight cos your mum and dad and Lukey and everyone you love is in that bloody square. I bet there's nothing to worry about."

Nevertheless, Patti did worry.

"Could you face wearing a bullet proof vest?" she asked Leah.

And the two girls did head off to their rendezvous with the horses, wearing bullet proofs.

Chapter 24

That same afternoon, an amazing reunion took place in a café very near to the Atomium. Thembani Ndlovu's great-uncle had indeed managed to contact Mathula, and the arrangement had been made for Mathula to meet Thembani and Horatio in Brussels.

"Themba," said Mathula. "I've missed you, my brother."

Thembani looked at this giant of a man standing tall in front of him. He had a presence, an aura of strength and command.

"Will you lead our army?" asked Madiba.

"If you will lead our country in unity," said Mathula.

Then Mathula introduced twenty or so of his fellow warriors, many still in remnants of their service uniforms, either French Foreign Legion or French Air Force. They were impressive, powerful, strong, and handsome. Free movement within the EU for these warriors, many now French nationals, had made the trip to Brussels easy for them. There was an eagerness in their manner.

One of them, Remembrance Moyo, looked around the assembled company and then turned to Thembani and Horatio.

"We'll follow Mathula," he said. The others nodded.

"We'll follow Mathula, but you must swear to us that you'll work to preserve democracy and try to copy your namesake," he looked at Horatio Madiba, "the great Madiba, Mr Mandela, with truth and reconciliation."

"You have our word," said Horatio. Thembani nodded his acquiescence.

"We go back home a week tomorrow. Before that we have more meetings with European leaders. The elections are not long now. What will you do?"

Mathula spoke for the soldiers, "We'll get ready. We have troops to train, tanks, and planes, to steal. Don't worry big brother, our country will have its army back. There are others of us who will join us in the homeland."

There was a lot of detailed planning. The elections were now only a few weeks away and it was looking more and more likely that the opposition party would win a majority and re-form with its allies as the Coalition Party. Mathula explained carefully to the two politicians, for they were now politicians, both of them, how he and this picked handful of leaders would capture the airplanes, tanks, and communication systems of the government.

"I've been back home since Uncle contacted me. All our forces are on standby, and we've managed to arm them a little better than we had feared. There are machine guns, assault rifles and other items, courtesy of the Americans. Marine Lusinga has been amazing in helping us. I believe you know her quite well Horatio."

Horatio nodded.

"She was the one who put the idea of coalition with your brother into my head."

"Will she have a place in government?" asked Mathula.

"I think so," said Thembani. "We could do with a good foreign secretary. Or an ambassador to the United States."

"I hate to cut this loving reunion between you two brothers short, but we need to get to the Grand Place for the Ommegang. Mathula, we have a spare ticket for you. You'll meet the president of the United States."

"I have tickets for all these men," said Mathula. "It will not just be the Americans and the Europeans who will be guarding you."

And with that, the party headed off towards their hotel.

The Ommegang itself begins as a show quite late in the evening, at around 8.45pm. In a late change to the plans, the original intention had been for the Howlands to take dinner at Richard's, the presidential party had an official reception followed by an informal dinner at the American embassy in the Boulevard du Régent. This was arranged to allow several of the European Leaders to meet Thembani Ndlovu and Horatio Madiba in secret and was also a prelude to the further official diplomatic meetings between Martha Howland and several of these important European allies, scheduled for the next two days.

One of the armoured vehicles from the embassy drove Martha Howland and her husband to the centre of Brussels and they walked on foot through the metal detectors and the security checks into the Grand Place. Over the next half an hour the stand gradually filled and, by 8pm the stands were full. The Africans in the VIP party arrived in the borrowed Chevy Suburban SUV; Mathula's colleagues arrived on foot and went through the security checks, just like everyone else.

Several European political leaders also arrived, including the Belgian, French and German prime ministers. The VIP stand was packed.

The security presence was much more evident than usual. Every four or five metres on the roof tops there were marksmen, similarly there were armed guards lining the Grand Place. They were all anxiously scanning the crowd, looking for Lee and Michu. It was almost impossible that either of them could get unobserved into the Grand Place to watch the Ommegang.

The mounted part of the parade was all drawn up at the rendezvous point and the Gilles were also milling around at their start point. Still obsessed with Les Gilles, Lee Corland was at the Gilles start point; Michu was with him. They were dressed as Gilles, they were ready to walk with the procession towards the Grand Place itself. They both had a big basket of oranges to throw, like the Gilles, to the crowds.

Right on time, the procession began. Lee and Michu went along with it. The Gilles were throwing their oranges and sweets to the crowd and dancing their rhythmic dance, with which, by now Patti and Leah were very familiar. Michu and Lee seemed to be saving their rather large Jaffa oranges for the Grand Place. Lee did not really understand when one of the Gilles said something to him about being mean with the goodies. He just shrugged his shoulders. There was no point in grinning, the grin would be hidden behind Lee's mask.

Again, precisely on time, the procession entered the square and the horses drew up in front of the presidential party, opposite the central stand in the Grand Place. Patti was on higher alert than ever. Some of the tension transmitted itself to her mount. Normally very well behaved, the mare was restless. It took all Patti's skill to maintain control.

Behind the mounted nobles and dignitaries, Les Gilles came pouring in, and started their mad dances and their throwing of the oranges. The pace of the drums stepped up and so did the pace of the dancers. Edward Howland caught one of the oranges and handed it to his wife. Several other VIPs caught oranges too.

The eyes of the security forces remained rivetted on the crowd, scanning constantly for any clue that a gun or a grenade might suddenly be brought to bear on President Howland or any of the other leaders. The eyes of the crowd were rivetted on the splendour of the pageant.

Then the fireworks began, exploding into the night sky and filling the square with even more sound.

It was then that Patti saw it. It was almost as if a mirror had caught the sun and flashed into her eyes. Not one mirror, but two. Two of the Gilles, two very tall men standing towards the edge of the Grand Place, bringing up the rear of the troupe of Gilles. Two men over two metres tall. She had only ever seen one man that tall among the Gilles on the previous night. That man was Allain. She recognised Allain, he was throwing his oranges as badly as always and his mask was a dull mess. The other exceptionally tall man she had not seen before. He had a brand-new mask, shining in the lights of the spectacle. Close to him was another tall man, not as tall as Allain and this stranger, but much taller than most of the Gilles.

And Patti remembered what Allain had said about ordering new masks, and how the workshop of poor Jean-Luc Pourbaix had burnt down. The two tall Gilles were not dancing, not in the rhythm of the true believers; their masks were shiny and new. They did not know the steps. Allain moved forward, they stayed where they were. Processing was not why they were there. The masks of Jean-Luc Pourbaix had not perished in the fire, they were here hiding the faces of Lee Corland and Michu Meszaros.

As she watched, Patti saw the two Gilles sorting through their oranges. Every now and again they threw an orange onto the floor, selecting only some of the largest ones to retain in the baskets. They separated from the main group, and, as the Gilles and their bands moved forward, they were left further and further behind, waiting near to the edge of the stand in which the presidential party was seated. Patti knew, she had worked it out. The slightly shorter one was fiddling with something metallic on one of the oranges, it was all the confirmation she needed.

Patti drew the Smith and Wesson she had concealed in her clothing, and she shot the man dead. Her gun was silenced; all that people would have seen was one of the Gilles sitting down suddenly as his legs collapsed from under him. The grenade he was about to arm fell from his hand and rolled under the staging, the pin still in place. Patti shot the second man about a second later. He too slid to the floor, still clutching the grenade that he had been about to throw. Their passing was unnoticed by the crowd who were intent upon the pageantry, the fireworks, and the flying sweets and oranges. The security forces too had their eyes higher than street level, looking intently at the crowd for any disturbances.

Patti put her gun away, nobody had seen it except Leah, and a little boy, who thought it was part of the performance. Leah looked at Patti, who shook her head.

There was a conspiracy of silence. The Ommegang continued to its completion and, afterwards the crowds dispersed. Most people left towards the back of the Grand Place; the horses went off to their stables. Patti, Leah and the other young riders returned by more conventional transport to the American embassy, where the president and Edward Howland were staying.

Patti and Leah picked up the cases of some of the fireworks: "For souvenirs," said Patti, rubbing them all over her hands. Leah knew exactly what Patti was doing.

It was only when the crowds had dispersed, and there were two very tall Gilles still sitting there in their full costumes, at the foot of the apron of the staging, that the police became aware that something untoward had happened. Until that point, they were congratulating themselves on the successful completion of their mission to protect the VIPs.

As they approached the bodies, the blood-stained clothing showed that these were not natural deaths. A very superficial observation of the bullet holes in the tunics confirmed that both men had been shot. They were surrounded by oranges, one had a grenade in his hand, another grenade was found near the second body; and in the baskets lying near their bodies were very large oranges, each of which contained a pineapple hand grenade. Removal of the masks revealed the features, engraved on the memory of every security person in Brussels, of Lee Corland and Michu Meszaros. Within seconds there was a cordon round the area and the investigation into the deaths was begun.

On his way back to the embassy Charles received a telephone call from Jerry, who was still there with the Brussels police, to tell him that Meszaros and Corland had been shot dead.

"Trying to escape?" asked Charles.

"No," said Jerry. "They were in the Grand Place dressed as Gilles. Each of them was carrying a dozen grenades hidden inside Jaffa oranges."

"Jesus," said Charles. "What happened?"

"Someone saw what was about to happen and plugged the bastards dead. One shot each, right through the heart. If they hadn't done it, there would have been a lot of dead national political leaders."

"Nobody saw anything, nobody heard anything, nobody said anything?"

"Must have been when the fireworks were going like mad, and those bloody noisy drums. I reckon someone had a silencer on a handgun. It must have been a professional," said Jerry.

Charles had other ideas.

Back at the embassy, Charles asked Leah, Patti, Therese, Allain, Raphael and Lucas to join him in the office of the cultural attaché. In this particular instance the cultural attaché was a cover role for the chief of intelligence. Charles and the other CIA officers used the office as a base when they were in Brussels.

Charles looked hard at the group of youngsters in front of him. There were other members of the security team in the room, including the chief of the Brussels homicide and terrorist police squads.

"Which one of you shot them?" he asked.

Six innocent faces looked back at him. Patti said nothing.

"Shot whom?" said Therese; she was practising her perfect English.

"The two terrorists disguised as Gilles who were about to throw hand grenades at the president and all the heads of government."

When you are a theatre 'techie', and Lucas, Leah and Patti were all involved in theatre, you do learn how to act. If you had distilled a bucket of innocence and poured it over the heads of all three of them, they could not have been more convincing. The shock and horror on the faces of all six could not have appeared more real. For Lucas, Therese, Allain and Raphael, the shock and horror was genuine; for Patti and Leah...

"Mon Dieu," said Raphael, "I thought we were done with death in the Serengeti."

"Well, you haven't," said Charles. "Which one of you shot them?"

There was quite a long silence and Charles stared intently at Patti, but she just smiled and shook her head in a slightly puzzled way.

"It wasn't me," she said. "I was having too much trouble controlling my horse to have been able to shoot anyone accurately. But I'm very grateful to whoever did it because Lukey and I both still have a mother and father. Who were they? Who were they working for?"

"Do you mind taking one of those swab tests that show whether you have fired a gun recently?"

Charles was ignoring Patti's question for the moment.

"No problem, Charles," said Patti, "but we all picked up firework cases as souvenirs. Will that invalidate the tests?" She smiled.

Inside his head, Charles said the 'F' word several times, loudly. He knew that smile. Charles knew. He knew who had done it. He knew he would never be able to prove it. He knew he did not want to be able to prove it. He started to think how he could help to prevent anyone else knowing what he knew. The first thing he needed to do was to find, without anyone else knowing, a Smith and Wesson M&P Shield 9mm, fitted with a silencer. Then he would have to exchange it for one that somebody in the room had almost certainly fired just that evening. Then the one that had been fired probably would be safest at the bottom of the river Seine.

Charles went back to the square and joined Jerry and Jenny with the local police at the crime scene. It was very scary to think how close to success plan D had come. One orange, that had dropped to the ground with Lee, was found to contain a pineapple grenade with the pin halfway out. It was handled very gingerly until the pin was safely back in place. One second more and the grenade would have been primed. The resulting explosion would have killed a lot of people. Not only that but the baskets of oranges that each of the two dead men had with them contained the missing pineapple grenades from the inventory that had been seized at the Rubinsky gang's apartment.

"Clever bastards," said Jerry. "They would have got away with it if someone hadn't shot them. The locals suspected arson with the burning of poor old Pourbaix's workshop, but they couldn't think of a motive. Now we know. It was to hide the theft of the masks and make sure we didn't think to vet the Gilles and the horse riders."

"Plan D involving the Ommegang, we were bloody lucky again," said Charles.

"And bloody stupid," said Jerry. "We knew the gang had infiltrated the work force for the building of the staging. Why didn't we think it through. Infiltrating the performance was an obvious thing."

"I guess we were relying on the groups of performers to know each other. But those masks! And who was counting the Gilles as they came into the Grand Place. Nobody. And why would they?"

Of course, the crime scene was investigated fully. Angles of entry of the bullets, weapon calibre, possible directions, and elevations from which the shots were fired; you name it, they did it. The conclusion was drawn that the bullets were fired from a handgun, a 9mm, probably fitted with a silencer. The bullets were found and kept for forensic matching if the weapon were ever found in anyone's possession.

The coroner suggested that the shots were fired from less than three metres or so above the ground, no higher than the eighth row of seats in the stand, or (as

Charles thought quietly to himself) the saddle of a horse. It could not be determined from which direction the shots had been fired because they did not know which way the men were facing when they were hit. Only the elevation was certain.

They combed and combed the CCTV footage of the event, but the angles of the cameras did not allow them to see the two dead men at any point close to the time that they must have died. Nothing in the coverage of the crowd showed anything suspicious. Cameras focussed on the performance were basically aimed right at the centre stage and, for quite a lot of the footage, some of the performers on horseback were concealed from the cameras by the staging to the side of the square. Only the central section was continuously in view. Patti had not known that when she drew and fired, but she was lucky. Two metres further to the left and her actions would have been recorded for posterity.

To begin with there were lots of unanswered questions, such as how anyone got a weapon into the Grand Place when every single person entering the area was put through a metal detector. Then the police, just like the security forces, realised that not everyone entering the square had been through the metal detector. Those on horseback would have set off the detectors every time. The metal involved in stirrups, bridles, horseshoes, and bits would have certainly set the alarm bells ringing. They, and the Gilles, did not even go through the security process for entry.

Charles was not the only one who had worked it out. A couple of days later, after all the solid police work and the post mortem reports had given the police something to work on, the Inspecteur Principal in charge of the case had also concluded that the combination of opportunity, not being vetted on the way into the Grand Place, and angle of entry of the bullets, from the level of someone on horseback, suggested one of the riders had murdered the two men. Inspecteur Principal Louis LaPlace voiced his suspicions to Charles.

"Do either of your English girls have a gun?" he asked Charles.

"Of course not," said Charles. "They do not have a permit."

"Do you think we might search their appartement?" asked LaPlace.

"Why not?" said Charles. "You do know that Leah Shapiro is English, but Patti Jones is American?"

"No difference for me, monsieur, they both speak perfect French and quite good Flemish. Shall we go now?"

Charles was very glad that he had gone to the apartment and removed the weapon and thrown it into the middle of the Seine. He had not yet replaced the gun; that would be done after this visit to the flat. For the moment the risk to Patti was minimal, she could do without a weapon, at least until she got back to England. It would be better for Patti if she remained Patti Jones, did not have to claim diplomatic immunity as the daughter of the president, and could return to St Joseph's to finish her degree.

Charles had the replacement gun in his overcoat pocket, and a new silencer to go with it. Just in case Jerry decided that *he* wanted to investigate further, it might be as well to have covered that base too. Jerry would expect to find a gun in Patti's possession; Inspecteur Principal LaPlace certainly did not.

Epilogue

The Ommegang being over, and the end of the year abroad fast approaching, the youngsters went back to their bases. Leah and Esther went back to Oxford; Lucas, and Patti back to Cambridge; Therese back to Sandrine; and Raphael back to Paris.

In July, in Africa, the incumbent president had died a natural death from the prostate cancer that had troubled him in his last years. The election had been brought forward as a result. By the following September, there was a new president and a new prime minister. True to their promise, these two had organised an inclusive government. Mathula's plan to prevent a coup reversing the democratic decision had worked, and he had been made the head of the armed forces. Almost all the serving members of those forces had remained in their posts under General Mathula Ndlovu. The troops had sworn loyalty to the new regime.

The sense of purpose and hope that Thembani and Horatio brought to proceedings promised a new dawn for all the inhabitants. Thembani, which translated as "bringer of hope," joined Madiba, "father of the nation," in a government of reconciliation. Nomusa was made a special adviser to the Minister of Agriculture.

Martha Howland was back on track for a second term as president. Patti had a new sister-in-law, Sara, and a new brother-in-law, Graham.

The destruction of the Rubinsky gang had given the Africans, and Stanislowsky, breathing space to spread their ideas of democratic reform. True Rubinsky was still at large, but the foot soldiers were all dealt with.

Everything in the garden might just have been thought to be coming up roses.

Patti Jones was back in residence at St Joseph's, her identity still undiscovered by most. Lucas was also back for his final year. Charles came to visit, probably on his way to see Leah in Oxford. Very quietly, and with nobody else present, he handed Patti her new gun.

Sitting in the early October sunshine at one of the outside tables at Savino's, Patti, Lucas and Charles were joined by Jerry Gregory, Jenny, Taylor and Adrian Armstrong. Antonio came out of the coffee shop with carrot cake and coffee for all. He put them on the table, welcomed back the youngsters and left them to it.

Jerry looked at Patti. "I expect you to plead the fifth amendment, but it was you, wasn't it?"

"Superintendent Gregory," Patti smiled, "yes." Charles caught his breath. She paused a moment. Made a gun with the fingers of her right hand. Pointed it at Jerry Gregory and said: "I plead guilty. I did arrange for Antonio to bring us coffee and cake, and I paid him already."